Critical acclaim for

A Blessed Event

"Jean Reynolds Page can spin one heck of a tale. . . . A narrative that grows more and more compelling as Page unearths secrets, reveals character, and lays—and layers—the groundwork for an ending that is moving, believable, and earned."
—*The Boston Globe*

"Tight plotting, sympathetic characters, and intriguing moral issues will make this book a good choice for reading groups."
—*Booklist*

"An assured and poignant first novel."   —*The Seattle Times*

"Out of a tortured tangle of friendship and betrayal comes this fast-moving, timely tale. . . . Jean Reynolds Page knows how to hold the reader riveted while her story races on to its surprising conclusion."
—LEE SMITH, author of *The Last Girls*

"Jean Reynolds Page makes an extraordinary debut with *A Blessed Event*, a wonderful, riveting novel that explores human relationships from every angle. There is betrayal and there is redemption; in between there are complex situations and wonderful details of the life of a mother, daughter, lover, friend—most of all, a friend. I couldn't put it down."
—JILL McCORKLE, author of *Creatures of Habit*

"The author displays true genius as she allows her characters to move forward, away from past secrets and half-truths best forgotten, to a conclusion both realistic and hopeful."
—*Romantic Times*

Also by Jean Reynolds Page

A BLESSED EVENT

Accidental Happiness

Accidental Happiness

A NOVEL

JEAN REYNOLDS PAGE

BALLANTINE BOOKS ◫ NEW YORK

2006 Ballantine Books Trade Paperback Edition

Copyright © 2005 by Jean Reynolds Page
Reading group guide copyright © 2006 by Random House, Inc.

Published in the United States by Ballantine Books, an imprint of The Random House Publishing Group, a division of Random House, Inc., New York.

BALLANTINE and colophon are registered trademarks of Random House, Inc.
READER'S CIRCLE and colophon are trademarks of Random House, Inc.

Originally published in hardcover in the United States by Ballantine Books, an imprint of The Random House Publishing Group, a division of Random House, Inc., in 2005.

Page, Jean Reynolds.
    Accidental happiness / Jean Reynolds Page
       p.   cm.
    ISBN 0-345-46218-1 (trade pbk.)
       1. Shooters of firearms—Fiction.   2. Female friendship—Fiction.   3. Accident victims—Fiction.   4. Gunshot wounds—Fiction.   5. Widows—Fiction.   I. Title.

    PS3616.A33755A63 2005
    813'.6—dc22

                                                                2004062000

Printed in the United States of America

www.thereaderscircle.com

9 8 7 6 5 4 3 2

Text design by Joseph Rutt

This book is dedicated to

RICHARD LEIGHTON PAGE,

FRANKLIN REYNOLDS PAGE,

GILLIAN GRACE PAGE,

and EDWARD BATTEN PAGE

with hope for the future,

and to the memory of

HUBERT ALDERMAN REYNOLDS

and

GRACE REYNOLDS MASSENGILL

with gratitude for the past

Acknowledgments

The dedication of this book says part of it, but not all. My family, Rick, Franklin, Gillian, and Edward, deserve so much more than simple gratitude for the patience and enthusiasm they've had over the last year. Thanks everybody. I love you.

Many thanks to Susan Ginsburg for holding my hand (no small feat from across the country) through every phase of this book. When an agent can also be a trusted friend, it's nothing short of a blessing.

Colleen Murphy and Victoria Skurnick have continued to cheer me on with advice and encouragement. Life is too short to thank you both enough.

Thanks (and congratulations!) to my editor at Ballantine, Charlotte Herscher, and abiding gratitude to Dana Edwin Isaacson, also at Ballantine, for stepping in to edit when Charlotte stepped out to give birth. Dana, you made it better and you made it fun. Thanks also to Arielle Zibrak for helping to fill the void (and for calming me down) on many occasions, and to Signe Pike for all her hard work.

Boatloads of gratitude to Roger Page and all the folks at Island Books on Mercer Island, WA, for hosting a great reception and so much more. Roger, you've offered wise counsel during a hectic year and I thank you. Also thanks to the people at SMU Continuing Studies, especially Barbara Wedgwood, for the wonderful party in Dallas.

For the excellent advice and valued friendship (not to mention eye-blurring hours of reading), love and appreciation go to my writers group in Texas: Ian Pierce and Jeanne Skartsiaris, who doubled as therapists over the phone; Mary Turner and Lou Tasciotti, who have also been there from the start; Kathy Yank, relative newcomer (to me, at least), but oh so appreciated; and Chris Smith—that sabbatical can only last so long, buddy . . .

Joyce Ross and Lynn Saunders (sister and cousin-who-is-like-a-sister)—thanks for getting me through those rough days in March when I had to become an author (and for so much more, of course). (And thanks to Neil and Mike for letting me "borrow" you both for a whole week!)

Mary (Turner, that is) gets another round of thanks for her expert advice on matters of mental health. The same goes for Steve Juergens, M.D. Thanks for reading so carefully. Appreciation also to Linda Malcolm at Indigo Books on Johns Island, SC, for Charleston-area information (the parts I got right, at least). And to Andy Ziskind for putting me in a good light in the author photo. And, of course, to Hilda Lee for showing me a bigger world all those years ago.

It has to be said that this year had the highest highs and the lowest lows, with the publication of my first book that followed just months after the passing of my mother. Through it all, good and bad, there was family.

I have so much love and appreciation for all of you. Rick and the kids, of course. Joyce and Lynn (again). We propped each other up, didn't we guys? My mother's sisters, Lois McQueen (the closest thing to "Mom" now), Frances Thompson, and Edna Lee Smiley, and Mom's wonderful husband, H. V. Massengill. My brother Ralph Reynolds and my uncle Bob Reynolds, and all the spouses and kids of the above that make up this amazing gathering of souls. Also H. V.'s family, especially Lynne and Gene Griffith, who showed Mom boundless love and care. Thank you. This book deals with finding a way back from grief, and this year we've been there—together.

Ellis Page, Tim Page, and Betsy Page Sigman and their families gave me additional shoulders to lean on. So many thanks.

And finally, to all the folks in Troy, NC, especially the people at the Montgomery County Public Library and the *Montgomery Herald,* thank you for proving, once and for all, that Thomas Wolfe was mistaken.

Accidental
Happiness

Prologue

Gina

On the night I shot Angel, everything in my life changed—again. Up until that evening, two terrible events had altered the shape of my world: the drowning of my younger sister, when we were both kids; and the death of my husband, several months past, but still recent enough to seem like yesterday. In an instant the sadness of these losses became married in their unlikely, surreal occurrences.

Someone once told me that groupings of objects should be displayed in threes. Three provides both tension and balance among items of varying size and heft.

The accident of my sister made me an only child; the accident of my husband made me a widow. Part of me will always believe that Angel was the third, the one that left me with hope.

1

Reese

"Is the sailboat a good place to sleep?" Angel asked, eyes on the blue-hulled yacht in its marina slip. She leaned tight against Reese, hands pulling lightly on the gauzy material of her mother's skirt. Reese knew she was too young to worry so much. She needed a normal life.

"Sure it is. Remember? Inside the sailboat," Reese said, her voice suggesting whispered confidences, "there are long seats with cushions. We can stretch out, feel the motion of the water rocking the whole boat, but just a little bit. Like this." She moved Angel slightly back and forth, a soothing, lullaby cadence. "You'll sleep like a puppy. I promise."

Angel nodded. Smiled.

"That's my girl," Reese said, pulling slightly away so Angel would pay attention. "I need for you to stay here," she told her daughter.

They were on the outside of the dock's security gate. The lights that lit up the marina at night were muted, but, even so, shone brighter than she'd expected. Still, she didn't see anyone around. If they were quiet, everything would be okay. Angel looked small—too small to be almost eight years old; too small for what Reese was asking of her.

"Where're you going?" the girl asked.

"I'm wading through the water to get to the dock on the other side." She tried again to remember the security pad code. She'd seen Ben punch in the numbers, but that had been months ago, and who knew she'd be returning in the middle of the night like this? "Once I get around, I'll open the door for you. That way, you don't have to get wet."

Reese looked out over the inlet, over a calm so complete, the water looked slick, frozen. But it was summer and muggy. South Carolina in August. Still air kept the day's heat intact. But if she opened all the windows on the boat, she and Angel could sleep comfortably, safely, for the night. They could rest before she got in touch with Ben.

"Are you sure that's it?" Angel pointed to the sailboat, a large, midnight blue hull sitting in one of the middle slips. "It's the right color, but it looks smaller than I remember." Most of the boats were white, making Benjamin's easier to spot.

"That's it," Reese answered. "*River Rose*. It's thirty-five or thirty-six feet. But it looks smaller from over here." She felt the flutter of nerves, tense energy that built up in her stomach. But she loved the unknown seconds before the risk.

"Is he there?" The small voice sounded hopeful.

"No, baby, we talked about this." Reese tried to sound patient. "I'm sure Ben's at home."

"Didn't you call him?" Angel looked uncertain. She needed a kind of reassurance that Reese couldn't offer.

"His cell phone's not working. I'll call him tomorrow, okay?"

She wondered how much of her plan she could still salvage. Maybe enough to give the two of them a shot at an honest-to-God normal life. At the very least, it would leave Angel with that option. That was the important part. If things got worse, she didn't want to bring Angel down with her. She'd hoped it wouldn't come to this, crawling back to Benjamin for help. But after what they'd just run away from in Boone, she had no choice.

"Can't you call him now?" Angel stared through the chain-metal gate, eyes large, mouth set with a slight tremble.

"Come here, sweetie. It'll be okay."

Angel came closer, leaned in against her again. Reese knelt down and held her daughter; felt the slightness of her frame. She was strong and healthy, but sometimes seemed so fragile.

"The water looks dark," Angel said. "Are you sure you won't get hurt?"

"I'll be fine." Reese bent to kiss the girl's head, felt earrings dangle lightly against her cheek. "I'm going to be around the gate and on the dock over there before you blink twice. Then we'll have a place to stay for the night. Okay?"

"Okay." Angel still seemed to lack confidence in the plan.

Reese stood up, took a deep breath. She wished she had time for a cigarette. Angel made the signal—a balled fist tapped onto a flat palm. The girl had made it up for luck, and Reese knew that the superstition gave her daughter boldness in their adventures. Reese returned the gesture, then turned and walked down the length of shoreline until she reached the edge of the gate.

A dinghy sat beached on the mud bank, and she had the notion of taking it to the dock, letting Angel inside the door as planned, and then returning the boat to the bank. But that would take too long, make her far too visible to the security station. Instead, she stepped from the brittle grass into the soft tidal mud. She kept on her flip-flops to keep from cutting her feet. Shells, some still housing living creatures, no doubt, crunched under her weight. She felt bad crushing them, but let go of the thought and moved deeper into the water, hoping to avoid anything that might want to sting or bite.

As the surface came waist deep, her clothes slowed her progress. A skirt had been a bad choice for this operation. Shorts would have made more sense; but then again, she hadn't had much time to prepare. Her clustered bangle bracelets had a tinny sound. They unnerved her, and she put her arm in the water to silence them. She moved carefully to keep from making noise, splashing. She reached up to brush a hair from the corner of her mouth and tasted the moist brine of the inlet on her fingers.

The salty glaze settled against the skin of her arms. "This feels good," she mumbled aloud to no one. She hadn't swam in saltwater in so long. The feel of it evoked memories of childhood, of hot summers—memories of Benjamin, some of them very good. But she hadn't regretted her decision to leave. Not then. They'd had good years, she and Angel. But now it was time to make a change.

Angel stood quiet, motionless at the gate, an outline of a girl. Reese pulled herself up. Drenched, she landed, sitting, on the dock, then waved at Angel, put her finger to her lips for Angel to stay silent. Even though her daughter was only a shadow, backlit by the marina lights, she saw the child wave back. Reese could imagine Angel smiling, relieved that her mother had kept her word, after all. Just as she'd promised, she'd made it safely to the other side.

2

Gina

Benjamin came up behind me, slid his arms around my waist. Heat from the late sun warmed the skin under my sweatshirt, rejected the chill of October. We stood in the open air. Around us, pumpkins of all sizes pebbled the field with orange, with bins of butternut squash and sweet potatoes off to the side. The farmer who owned the land presided over his yield. He was large and, it seemed to me, bored with produce. People wandered, trying to choose, and he watched, sitting on a stool beside a table that held nothing but a metal box filled with dollar bills.

Benjamin's presence circled me like a cloak. His fingers moved just underneath the low waist of my jeans, traveled the surface of my belly, insistent, kneading soft muscle, tender skin. It left me shy. An older couple averted their eyes from us, but the farmer watched without apology, his ample monotony in need of diversion.

Benjamin's boldness made me weak. My mind's eye could see his hand moving over my body. He didn't speak, but I wanted him to. I wanted to hear the hoarse register that would tell me we were leaving, going, perhaps, no farther than the car. But he said nothing. Then, as if something had jostled me out of my dream, I became aware. There was no breath on my neck, no comfort from his arms. I woke up to the hot August night and felt the loss new again. I wasn't sure which was worse: the stray emotions that made their way in from time to time, laying me low all over again; or the rest of the time, when I felt that my brain had been neutered, all capacity to feel removed.

I'd been a widow for three months, though it seemed less because the season had yet to change. With nothing marking the time, it could have been a week or even a day before. I sat up, breathed only in spite of myself. The pumpkins were gone, were never there, in fact. I had fashioned a memory from air and longing.

I was hot—damp and unfamiliar in my bed. But I wasn't in a bed exactly. It took me a moment to recognize the small quarters, the salt air smell. My boat. Benjamin's boat. That was where I lived, where I'd run to when I couldn't stay in our house anymore. I'd sold our house, hoping to find some peace. Even so, I rarely slept. Not since the funeral, anyway. When I did, the wakings were always full of confusion.

"Come on, Georgie." The dog settled down beside me. The boat rested easy in its slip.

The scenes that occurred when I slept weren't exactly like dreams. I saw them as *visitations,* but not of a ghostly sort. Until recently I had barely acknowledged God. I certainly didn't buy into spirits, sinister or benevolent. But I'd had these images over the years, little wordless narratives involving Elise, my little sister. She died when I was twelve and she was eight. Sometimes in my visions she was at the pool where she drowned, sometimes at unfamiliar places. But always she was eager, her eyes begging me to see her, to watch.

With Elise, as I got older, she remained young and we drifted apart in my mind; my ability to manufacture her in my head seemed to weaken. Although, so often decisions in my life relied on her memory. I wondered what would happen with Benjamin. As an old woman, would I let him go; or would I continue to see him as I slept? A man eventually young enough to be a grandson.

The air off the water stood still, heavy as the tide, a terrible time for the onboard air-conditioning unit to be out. I considered walking the short path to Lane's house. Instead, I abandoned the V-berth for the main cabin, where it was cooler, turned the small fan full on my face.

Stretched out in what amounted to my living room with hatches open to the air, the night became bearable. I tried to drift off, but by three-thirty in the morning sleep had yet to come again; one of the restless nights when Ben was everywhere and nowhere. Hours and decades became twins of time, especially at night. Who the hell becomes a widow at thirty-three?

I'd tried to work my way back to life. Ben's mother said that I expected to feel normal too fast, that I needed to allow myself time to grieve; but indulgent grieving only took me deeper into the loss. So when I had a choice, I settled for a state that was more than dead, but less than alive. A zombie existence.

In my scarce efforts at recovery, I'd tried the disparate avenues of studied spirituality and casual sex. Both very new for me. Although they seemed to be at opposite ends of the spectrum, the two shared certain qualities of exhilaration, but neither helped for too long. I suspected the problems existed in me more than in the methods.

"What do you think, Georgie?" The dog kept a vigil at my side.

Even in the near-dark cabin, I could see the envelope, white and still sealed, sitting on the desk. Opening the check meant I went one step closer to accepting the money as a kind of apology for Ben's death. It had come in the mail just the morning before. Maybe that had inspired my nocturnal thoughts of Benjamin, alive again.

The lawyers who helped me after the accident regarded the settlement as a victory, a triumph before we even saw the inside of a courtroom. A similar case with the same lumber company had hit the newspapers in a big way just months before. The story had gone national, and the exposure made them eager to settle with me before the publicity of a trial. I'd gotten the same deal as the earlier case, but with none of the work.

Looking through the shadows at the pale envelope, I felt everything that was missing, and nothing that had been gained. A leg or a lung would have been no more vital than Benjamin. How could a bigger bank account make any difference? I'd left the envelope intact so far, trying to decide what to do. The sale of the house would keep me going for a good while. And Ben had good insurance through his job at the marketing firm. He used to tell me I was lucky he'd decided to be a commercial artist instead of a starving one. He was wrong. Benefits or no, I didn't feel lucky at all.

So I hadn't dealt with the envelope yet, didn't even remember the exact amount I'd been awarded. Maybe I'd never open it. On the other hand, depositing it and the others that were to follow over the course of eighteen months would make me rich, at least by my standards—a sight that Benjamin, of all people, would have enjoyed.

I imagined sleep; hoped seeing it in my mind would make it come. Nothing came but more pictures, genuine memories of Ben, alive and living in our house, absent the unwelcome discussions that surfaced regularly during our last weeks together. Ben, talking again about having children, long after I thought the subject had been put to rest. For the most part, I avoided the thoughts of those talks. When I focused on our time together, it was only the seamless days of partnership, of love.

I hadn't done it in a while, had a night of the memory reels. The memories were of long before he was gone, before the sadness drove me to a smaller life on the boat. I wanted them and dreaded them in equal measure.

Georgie shifted, sat upright.

The dog's ears perked up, her posture tensed. Even with the windows open, I couldn't hear anything unusual outside.

"What is it, girl?"

Over the last two months, the miniature schnauzer had become my alarm system, my closest companion. Lane had given her to me, the dog already full-grown, when the owner, an older friend of Lane's, had to give her up. Georgie had bonded with me right away. Or maybe it was more the other way around.

I shifted the fan to low, listened. The floating dock gave slightly, an occurrence magnified by the lifeless night. Georgie stood up, kept herself between me and the companionway.

"It's okay," I whispered, putting my hand down on the animal's head.

I sat up, heard footsteps, and waited to see where they might be headed. Three-thirty was too late for Derek to be working security rounds, too soon for sport fishermen wanting to get an early start.

Maybe Derek was making a late-night visit to my boat. I closed my eyes, almost hoped that was the case. I listened for his absentminded humming, could see his dark hair, angular features. A mistake in judgment on my part—borne out of a lonely moment just the week before—had left him eager, gently insistent. But he was six or seven years younger, nearly a kid still—I put him just a few years out of college—and I was a widow. I figured anything I felt too embarrassed about to tell Lane defined a bad idea. I'd been putting him off on a daily basis since our single close encounter.

The footsteps kept an irregular cadence. Hurried and slow, coming toward the dock where my boat sat in the slip. It wouldn't be Derek, not showing up in the middle of the night. That wasn't his style.

Someone outside coughed. Who would be out there? Reaching in the drawer, I felt the pistol, reassured somehow that it was there.

"You need something to protect yourself," Lane had told me when she gave me the gun.

I'd laughed, tried to give it back.

"People target live-aboards. You're essentially sleeping in an open room. Put it in the drawer. It'll be there if you need it."

Soft steps sounded on the wooden part of the dock nearby. Probably *was* just someone arriving early, ungodly early, to go out fishing, but I couldn't quite buy it. I kept my eyes on the porthole. Heart pounding, I lifted the gun out of the drawer, felt around quietly for the bullets.

"Hush, baby . . ." I whispered to Georgie. Her small sounds were escalating.

I waited, barely let myself breathe, then moved closer to the starboard porthole, strained to see outside. The light from the moon had shifted out, over the water, offered little help. I thought again of Derek, tried to fashion a scenario that would bring him out. A dockline that had come loose, needed securing. From his caretaker's apartment above the Ship's Store, he could see most of the marina from his window, would notice if something like that happened. But the night rested windless and still, nothing to cause a stir among the boats. Even working at it, I had a hard time making sense out of that theory.

Georgie growled again, low and uncertain. She knew her job, wasn't given to false alarms. I sat back down, held the pistol loose on my lap, reached my other hand down to touch the dog. Vibrations of the growl traveled through the muscles of her neck. She tensed, shifted away from me.

Then I felt the footsteps, the delicate shimmy of the dock as someone stepped nearby. I saw a flash of shadows, close outside the porthole. Someone, maybe more than one person, had come onto my dock. The pulse points in my neck quickened and I found it hard to take in air.

"It's okay, it's okay . . ." I caught myself mumbling to the dog again. But it wasn't okay and I knew it.

The instant the boat gave way, Georgie launched into a frenzy. The boat rocked as the intruder boarded, the dog lunging at the companionway. With loaded springs for legs, she tried and failed to scale the ladder, fell back hard at my feet.

I don't recall pointing the gun, but the sound of it repeated over and over in my head. *Staccato.* The absurd musical reference occurred to me at the moment of the explosive pop, both small and deafening. Seconds froze and my pulse raced. I'd fired it, through the canvas-covered companionway of the boat. I hadn't meant to. *Shit!* The gun hot, screams came from somewhere. Screams from just outside. Only the canvas drop fell between me and whoever was out there. My ears numb from the loud noise, I barely heard the cries outside. A woman's keening wails sounded faint, distant. But they were there, on my boat. Someone was on my boat!

Georgie barked continuously—a high, terrified register—and my body shook, violent, trembling, as if illness controlled me. The gun clattered on the floor. I could still feel the vibration of the single shot in my empty hand.

These things must have happened all at once, no more than an instant; but my memory recalls it in long stretches of time.

As I pulled back the canvas to go into the cockpit, I saw her. A fictional character come to life. Kneeling, with blood everywhere.

"Reese! Jesus! Is that you?" My voice reached a high unnatural pitch, drowned out by her screams as she bent forward, her head down.

I don't know how I recognized her, my husband's ex-wife. Pictures, some videos, that's all I'd seen of her in my years with Benjamin. But then, even so, she'd made an impression.

I scrambled up toward her, then fell, hard, as my bare foot hit something slimy, slick on the deck. My foot was red, covered with blood, and I sat there unmoving, stunned and unable to act.

"Oh, God!" she wailed.

Time slowed as I stared at her, at the red smears running up her bare arm. Reese Melrose. Her name presented itself, unbidden as I watched her—wondering in detached horror where the bullet had hit her, what I should do. In spite of the blood, she looked okay, unhurt if that was possible. She knelt over, rocked back and forth, and at first I didn't even see the girl. Then my eyes registered the child, nearly covered by the cloth of the woman's long skirt.

"Jesus Christ!" I lunged forward, put my hands out in an offering of help, but with no clear purpose in mind. "What do you need?"

"Do something. Help her, for God's sake!" Reese Melrose screamed. Her voice rang low and raw as she cradled the child, a small creature, too little to have so much blood. The sight of the girl stopped me. A kid about the size of my sister when I last saw her. Memory paralyzed me somehow as old horrors stirred again.

"Don't just stand there!" The pleading wail brought me around, but my efforts had no order. What *could* I do? My mind ran through what had happened. How it had happened. How could I fix it? Indecision became another kind of paralysis.

"Help us!!" Reese Melrose screamed again. "What the fuck are you standing there for? Somebody call for help!"

I turned, nearly fell, frantic to get my cell phone from the cabin below, but then saw Lane, who had shown up on the dock like a vision. She wore pajamas with no housecoat, her gray-blond hair in short disarray.

"I'm calling," she said, more to me than the wailing woman and child.

"When did you get here?" I asked, watching her dial her cell phone.

She didn't answer me. I don't think she even heard me; but I looked around, saw people standing on the balconies of the marina condos along the shore. A handful of people, no one I recognized, made their way over from the other docks. Everyone, it seemed, had come out for the commotion.

"We have an emergency," Lane was saying into the phone, her voice loud, urgent. "At 1720 Creekside Road. At the marina. C dock. A little girl is bleeding. A gunshot, I think."

Lane paused, listening. "Is she breathing?" She leaned over, asked Reese Melrose.

"Yes," she answered, breathless. "Yes, she's breathing. They're little, though, short breaths."

Reese was crying, sobbing as she spoke. Then after the words, her sounds fell again to loud, arcing moans. It was the sound of fear. My mother had made that sound as she stood over Elise. I'd made it when they told me about Ben. I knelt to touch Reese, put my arm around her, then pulled back, knew at once it wasn't my place. In one way or another I'd allowed it to happen, all of it—Elise, Benjamin, and now another one. The single shot rang in my ears. So I sat near her, but still apart. We both shivered as if chilled, but the air pressed in around us, thick and warm.

"What do we do until they get here?" Lane asked the person on the phone, then turned to us. "Don't move her, they say." She paused, listened. "Make sure her head is supported and that nothing is obstructing her airway. Check her mouth for vomit or blood. Anything that would hamper her breathing."

Reese had gone quiet, looked to Lane for instruction, and did as she was told. She felt around in the child's mouth. The girl gagged as the fingers poked around.

"That's good," I said to no one; muttering, feeling like an idiot.

The water in the inlet was glassy calm. I saw Derek coming down from the security station, a tall figure in jeans and no shirt. He had towels in his hand and I figured he'd been down before and had run back up to get them.

"Where's she hit?" I asked, urgent now. And when Reese looked up, her face mirroring my panic, I continued in calmer tones. "Where's she bleeding?"

"Here . . . here . . . here . . ." she told me. The mantra came in short bursts. Her hand held a piece of cloth, pressed it against the girl's shoulder, high on the right, away from the heart, not near her head.

"Okay, okay," I said, mostly to myself, then I struggled to remember high school biology, the diagrams of the body and the major arteries. *Dear God, don't let it be bad.*

My muscles went weak and everything fell silent. The calls had been made. Waiting was all we had left. Reese looked at me and we regarded each other with uneasy glances. I looked at her closely, realized she wore only a camisole. The white cloth in her hand was a blouse.

Derek leaned over from the dock and handed me the towels. His sense of purpose made him older, more capable than I'd ever imagined him to be, and I felt a wash of gratitude. Reese took the towels from me, pressed them against the child's shoulder. The girl made sounds, small whines cut through and through by sobs that sounded like hiccups. That, more than anything, brought the crisis into bright focus. A child had been shot. I had done this to a little girl.

"Everything will be okay," I offered, not knowing if that was true at all. The skin of my cheeks had gone flush and numb. Through and through my very center, pervasive dread rode the low buzz of fear.

Reese was crying, sweating, covered with the child's blood. But it was more than that. She looked wet all over, clothes soaked through.

"What happened? Why are you here?" I asked, careful to keep my voice a question, not an indictment. In the odd calm of waiting, the inquiry seemed irrelevant, so before she answered, I moved ahead. "Reese? You are Reese, aren't you?"

"Yes," she said in barely a whisper, thick with sobs. "We came back to find Benjamin. Where's Ben?"

Why here? Even if he *was* still alive, he wouldn't be on the boat. "He's . . ." I began, didn't know how to answer. I felt an absurd fear that she'd come to reclaim him, felt it almost as if it could happen.

But it couldn't happen. She would never see him again, any more than I would. The thought reached me and I waited for sorrow to drive me hard, back into bent grief, but it didn't. Blunt fear, it seemed, overrode all other emotions. At most, a small blessing.

"He's not here, Reese," I managed finally. "I tried to reach you . . ." The loss of Benjamin, so very raw, mixed with the sight of the bleeding girl. "It's been several months . . ."

Police sirens followed by an EMT van took the moment from me and I felt grateful. The urgent rush to care for the child would give me time to fashion words for Reese Melrose. Time to prepare for the answers she would give to my questions. First among them, *why* was she here? The second, *who* was this child?

"Where is she?" One of the paramedics barked out the question as a team of three or four came through the security gate, then down the dock.

My boat rocked wildly as they stepped aboard the blood-smeared deck, further violating the surface with black-soled boots. I stepped out onto the dock to give them room to work. Derek and Lane stood on either side of me, stayed close as if standing guard. I glanced at Derek, realized again how solid he seemed to me all of a sudden. A different person in a crisis. I felt a slight ease, just having him there.

Reese moved back against the stern railing and gave over the care of the girl. Her eyes found mine and I felt a necessary alliance. Of a world full of people, only the two of us could answer questions that would set our lives back in order.

Then under the light of the paramedics I saw the little girl clearly for the first time, the dark mass of blood covering her shoulder. My fault. All my fault. But what the hell were they doing on my boat? I lived there, for God's sake. What had they expected I would do, frightened in the middle of the night by strangers?

As they worked, a policeman approached me. He moved slowly, evoking deliberate calm.

"I need to talk with you about what happened," he said. I listened for anything accusing in his tone, but heard nothing but the statement, plain and simple.

As the EMTs continued their job, I told Officer Hanlon everything I could recall, which wasn't much. He made notes, said that would be enough for the moment.

"We'll get the mother's statement . . . Is she the mother?"

"I guess . . ." Was she? Could Reese Melrose really have a child that old?

"Well," he said, closing his notebook, "we'll sort it all out. I don't think it will get complicated unless she plans to press charges of any sort." He nodded toward Reese. "And even so . . ." He put up his hands as if to say, *She came onto your boat.* For anyone upholding the law near the coast, unlawful boarding of a vessel meant serious business.

But I wasn't worried about charges, anyway. I couldn't think of anything except how small the girl looked, how much blood there was everywhere.

The men lifted the child onto the stretcher, secured every part of her to the cot. Reese bent over them, frantic with questions. One of the EMTs stood up, spoke with her softly, and Reese stopped, stepped off the boat, and came to where I stood.

"She's stable," Reese said. "They've got the bleeding under control. They're taking her to the hospital now, and he says it'll be better if I follow them, give myself a chance to calm down." She was talking to me, but still watching the men maneuver the stretcher off the boat. "Do you think you could drive me?" She turned to me, nearly pleading. The fear in her voice pulled at me, devastated me with her simple request. "I'm not sure I should get behind a wheel," she finished. The admission carried such defeat.

"Sure," I told her. She looked one nerve shy of hysterical. "Let me get my keys." My boat had finally emptied, save Georgie, who had resumed her barking. I stepped back on board to get my stuff, and realized I still wore pajamas. My blouse from the day before lay on the floor along with my pocketbook, so I grabbed the whole pile, pulled the shirt on over my sleep camisole.

When I came out, I saw Reese in the distance following the men with the girl. I followed too, my flip-flops slapping loudly against the heels of my feet. People still watched from the condo balconies overlooking the inlet, everyone staring in the direction of my dock.

"That blue one," they would say tomorrow and the day after, all the while pointing to my boat. "That blue yacht there," they would explain to those who had missed it. "That's where that little girl got shot." My legs felt weak and I wanted to cry. I wanted to cry because I'd panicked, shot a small child, and because I wished Ben was around to help me sort this out.

The urgency, the ambulance . . . It all brought back the day I found out Benjamin was gone, and three months' worth of healing went null and void. I wasn't healed. I'd made no progress. I felt damaged beyond repair. I looked at the men carrying the girl and I wished I could be the one lying on the stretcher, not a small child who couldn't possibly be at fault for anything.

"Where is it?" Reese Melrose was screaming the question at me as I approached the parking lot. She stood, waited for me to catch up. "Hurry! Which one is your car?"

"Over there." I pointed. "The old brown Volvo."

She sprinted toward my car, her wet skirt clinging limp around her legs. As I ran, I glanced over at the marina, the gathering of masts sprouting like bamboo from the inlet. All around the boats, the still water looked too calm for the crisis at hand.

In the absurd quiet of the idling car, the two of us waited for the ambulance to leave. Benjamin's two wives, bound by events I couldn't begin to comprehend.

Why is she here? The question came to me again and, with it, another irrational flash of jealousy skimmed my conscious mind. I pushed the feeling down again, deemed it ridiculous—but the irony remained.

"Do you want air-conditioning?" I asked.

She shook her head no, glared at me as if I was crazy to be concerned with something so ordinary.

I pushed the button that rolled down the windows, allowed myself the small pleasure of sea smells and balmy air as I prayed silent, repetitious phrases in my head. At the marina, I saw Lane walking with Derek. She carried Georgie in her arms, and I felt guilty for not having thought to ask her to look out for the dog.

"Do you have a cigarette?" Reese asked.

"No." I shook my head, and she let it go at that.

The only comforts I found, at least in those moments of waiting, were born out of the crisis itself. Emergency lights, police and ambulance, cast colors over the water, and the loveliness seemed somehow a response. Pulsing yellows, blues, and reds stained the white moonlight across the inlet, skipped fast over the calm waters of a windless night.

The hospital was twenty-five minutes away in traffic, less in the dark hours of the morning. We drove in wild excess of the posted limits, moving fast through the shelter of trees that lined the two-lane high-way. Low-hanging willows reached near, but the unyielding body of ancient oaks worried me more. A whisper of error meant disaster on the narrow road. Even with my best efforts, the flashing lights grew distant on the road ahead.

"Do you know where the hospital is?" Reese leaned forward, as if headlong momentum could propel us, shorten their lead.

"I know it better than I want to," I said, then regretted saying it. I didn't want to talk about Benjamin, not yet. But she just nodded, didn't ask why.

"I'm getting blood on your car." She held her arms up to keep from touching anything. Thin bracelets, a dozen or so, jangled on her wrist. She reminded me of some entertainer. Deeply theatrical. Artfully genuine.

"It's okay," I said. We existed inside a warped world where the etiquette of bloodstained leather provided distraction, if nothing else. "Don't worry about it. There's an old blanket in the backseat you can put around yourself. You're wet and you look cold. I'll clean up the car later."

"Thanks," she said, reaching back to find the comforter. She wrapped herself in it. "I'm just worried about Angel." Her voice stayed far away. "She's really little."

"It's good, what the EMTs said about her vital signs." I watched the road ahead.

"They said that she was stable," she corrected me. "A lot can happen. She lost a lot of blood."

"She's going to be okay." I took the liberty of keeping the glass half full. But then again, it wasn't my kid. "She'll be fine."

The disrepair of familiar shacks and churches along the way gave them the look of abandonment. Absent the usual complement of people milling about, the communities became shoddy and exposed. I felt a kindred soul with the empty yards, dark windows. Before the moment that I fired the gun, the weeks had come and gone. I hadn't realized how numb I'd become. Not a bad place considering the alternatives. But the night's events had slammed me back into the worst of my reality, and then some.

"How did this happen?" Reese asked. Her voice was suddenly hard, as if she'd just identified me as the source of her misery.

"What do you mean?

"Tonight. Jesus, were you just sitting there with a pistol? What the hell were you doing?"

My gut was to go on the defensive.

"What was *I* doing? I live on that boat. People don't just *drop* by for a visit at three o'clock in the morning."

"You didn't look. You just fired the goddamn thing before you even saw us." The edge in her voice stopped me. "And why the hell are you living there? Have you two split up?"

I thought I registered a note of hope in her voice. I didn't answer, couldn't have if I'd tried.

"Never mind," she said. "It doesn't matter right now." She talked more to herself than to me. Her voice had changed again, fell to low and bitter tones, but was no longer angry. I could barely keep up with my own emotions, but hers were all over the place. I regrouped my thoughts, tried to sort out what I could tell her, how I could explain.

"What were you doing with that pistol?" she mumbled again before I could fashion an answer. "Were you waiting for us?"

In the thin light of the night, I searched her expression for sarcasm, for anger; but didn't find any. She was asking the question, as if it could possibly be true. She looked worn-out, scared.

"How could I have been waiting for you? Why the hell would I have fired the gun if I'd known it was you?"

She shrugged, her paranoia apparently having run its course.

"I couldn't sleep," I went on. "I have trouble sometimes. I heard you and I thought . . . I don't know. When you stepped on the boat, I just reacted. I don't remember pulling the trigger. I wish I could take it back. I didn't mean to hurt anyone, especially not a child. God, you have to believe that much."

She turned her head, looked out the car window, and I didn't press. Everything felt too raw. I glanced at her again, couldn't get over actually seeing her, having her in my car—after all the years of wondering what she was really like. In her gypsy getup—wild, curly hair falling around her face—she looked exotic, the precise opposite of my straight hair, ponytail look. My clothes ran toward the casual coastal, entirely ordinary variety. I owned a few skirts, but I wasn't at all sure where they were. How could Ben have chosen such different women to love?

After a few miles and an eternity of silence, she spoke again.

"I know you didn't mean to hurt Angel," she said, her voice

softer. "I just don't know what to do. I'm here and she's there with God knows what happening all around her."

"We'll be there in five minutes," I told her. "They're probably arriving with her now. We aren't that far behind them. Just hang on."

She'd settled back, gave over at least some level of trust to my navigational skills. She stared out her window again, didn't say anything more, and I realized how much I was dreading the conversation we would have about Benjamin. She would ask again and I would have to say it. *He's dead.*

I went for days, still, forcing those words out of my thoughts, denying them by omission. I had friends whose husbands were in the military. Those guys shipped out, stayed away longer than Benjamin had been gone, a lot longer sometimes. He could just be *away*. The fantasy seemed more plausible than the truth. That he had died. How could he have woken up beside me one morning and died that afternoon?

"It's getting light over there," Reese said absently. "See the way the sky changes color?"

She was making noise so she didn't have to think. I knew the drill all too well. Making your mind busy, wanting to travel back to yesterday's dawn, before anything happened. On some days, occasional mornings, it was still possible in the gauzy prewaking moments of the day to *not* know that Ben was gone, if only for seconds at a time. Even allowing for the crushing reality that followed, I craved the naive awakenings, took each one as a gift. A brief moment of life as I'd remembered it, handed back to me.

"I'm going to be sick." She interrupted my thoughts.

We were near the hospital, on the back street that went around to the Emergency entrance.

"Let me pull over." I was veering toward the curb as I spoke and before I'd even stopped the car she had the door open, was leaning out.

Blood and vomit. I'd have to burn the car when everything was said and done. I turned away from her, hoping to offer privacy, but the sounds of her retching were heartbreaking. I handed her a roll of paper towels from the backseat. She took them without saying anything.

"Can I do anything?" I asked, still looking away.

She didn't answer, so I turned to face her. It seemed that she had missed soiling herself and the car after all. Small wonders. I saw in her face that she had moved already from sickness to sorrow; was hunched over, the comforter still around her. She sat half out of the door, crying. When she straightened, she lifted the edge of her skirt, still wet for reasons I had yet to sort out, and rubbed the drenched material down the length of her face, her throat.

Even unkempt from distress, and God knows what else, she was beautiful—and I hated seeing it. I'd always known—from pictures, from the way Benjamin talked about her—but seeing it was a blow. I don't know why. It was irrelevant, what she looked like. Benjamin would never have the chance to want her back. A stupid collection of thoughts. With everything going on, could I really be feeling jealous?

"I'm scared to go in there," she said. "What if it's gone bad? What if she's—"

"Let's just park in the Emergency lot. I'll go in with you," I said. "I'll even go in first, if you want. I can find out how she is and come right back."

It felt good to be the strong one.

"I should go," she said, looking miserable, not moving. "But Angel . . . God, if anything happened to her . . . Will you stay with me?"

"Sure. Nothing's going to happen," I said, working to sound confident. "Come on. Everything's going to be fine."

It was all a bluff. I knew all too well that things didn't always turn out fine; but I kept up the ruse, as much for my sake as for hers.

She nodded, even managed a weak smile, as I drove to the lot around the corner and parked as close to the entrance as I could without risking a tow.

"Her name is Angel?" I asked, a belated recollection of what she'd said.

"Angelina," she said. "I call her Angel."

I nodded. Thought of telling her that the name was pretty, but realized the compliment would sound trivial under the circumstances.

We walked through the parking lot toward the bright lights of the Emergency Room. As we got to the entrance I took a breath, but didn't reach for the door. My hand was shaking, my whole arm, really. Rogue muscles defied my efforts at control. Panic moved through me, but then calmed when I took a deep breath; went away as quickly as it had come.

"Are you okay?" she asked.

"Yeah, I'm fine." I opened the door. Simple.

"If there's a shrink on call, let's get him on board," she said without looking over at me. "I think we could both use a session or two—along with a pack of Marlboro Lights." I sensed she wasn't kidding about the cigarettes. She turned her head, offered a weak smile, and the effort seemed noble somehow.

The reception area was across the room. A Plexiglas window separated the office staff from the hoi polloi outside.

"I'll go check at the desk," I told her. "You grab anybody who looks official if they come this way." Then I left her there to find out what I could. I hoped to God the news was good.

Beside the reception area, a hall led toward where the action occurred. There was a woman ahead of me telling them about her infected toe, and as I waited, I looked down the hall for any sign of Angel and her entourage. Fluorescent lights reflected off the pale green walls. Busy people moved around without stopping to regard one another.

After a minute or so of waiting, the toe injury woman looked as if she was just getting started. Down the hall I saw a nurse, an older woman, standing off by herself, looking at a chart. A couple of people had gotten in line behind me, so it would be taking a chance, but I decided to go talk to the nurse anyway.

"Excuse me," I said as I got close enough to grab her attention. "I'm trying to find out about a little girl who's just been brought in."

"The gunshot?" the woman asked.

I didn't answer. It sounded too horrible. *The gunshot.* Gunshot victims, especially kids, were always drive-by shootings or drug deal cross fire. The idea that I had shot a child branded me somehow. I wondered if the woman noticed, if she knew it was my fault.

"Ma'am?" she prompted me. "What child are you looking for?"

"Yes," I answered. "The girl who was shot. How is she?"

"Are you the mother?"

"No. I'm . . ." What was I? "I'm a . . . I'm with her mother. I followed the ambulance and drove her here."

"Where is she? The mother. Is she here?" the nurse asked.

She looked particularly capable, but I was losing her. In the background the intercom crackled as someone paged a doctor on the overhead. *Jesus, don't they all have cell phones by now?*

"She's over there," I told her. I looked across the room but didn't see Reese anywhere. "She's in here somewhere. I drove her here. She's really upset." It sounded odd, my choice of words. *Upset.* Upset is what you are when a kid sprains an ankle. What are you when your kid has been shot?

"She's freaking out." Eloquent. "She got sick a little bit ago, so I told her I'd find out what I could."

Too much information always sounded like a lie, but I was beginning to get pissed off, so I didn't care.

"How is the girl? Can her mother get in to see her? I need to let her mother know." I spoke with force, conviction.

"I'm sorry," she said, without sounding sorry at all. "We have new regulations regarding patient information. Unless you're the guardian—"

"Please," I said. "I don't need a full report. Just tell me if she's okay." I glanced around again, wondering where Reese had gone. "It shouldn't be this complicated."

"Tell the mother," she spoke very deliberately, but with an underlying kindness, "that the doctor will need to discuss all matters of in-patient admission with her. And we need to find out about insurance. The girl likely won't be discharged until tomorrow, at least."

"I'll be covering any charges," I told her.

Discharge. Nurse code. The kid was okay.

"I'll make a note of that and you can talk with them at the desk," she told me.

"Thank you," I said. We exchanged conspiratorial nods.

"Oh," she said as I turned to go back out. "What is the girl's full name? I need to get her chart filled out."

Angelica? Angelina? I couldn't remember. "She goes by Angel," I said.

"Last name?" It was a reasonable question.

"I don't know." I felt uneasy. That was a whole other conversation I had to have with her mother. "I really don't know."

"And you're a relative?" She looked skeptical.

I thought for a second.

"By marriage," I said finally, realizing that it was almost the truth.

Then before she could ask anything more, I headed back across the room to find Reese and give her the news.

3

∞

Reese

It was hot outside the E.R. waiting area, but Reese was shivering. Inside, she had begun to feel her legs go weak, the nausea rising again. Prickly trembling in her hands followed and she figured she better find a place to sit down before she risked passing out. It had happened before. Since the waiting room looked full, she stepped outside where she'd seen some benches.

Where the hell was Gina? Reese strained to see as someone opened the doors. She had been in line at the window, and then she was gone. She sat back down, willed herself to take a deep breath.

"I've got to get up," she mumbled to herself. "Go back and find her. I can't be this fucking weak with my daughter inside there."

Where the hell was Benjamin? Why had his wife been on the boat—with a gun? He'd said once that she was high-strung, this new wife. But a gun? Still, the woman hadn't been expecting her to show up. Lord knows why she was sleeping on the boat. She registered the old hope that something had happened with the two of them. Maybe the issue of having kids had escalated. She told herself to stop it. She couldn't help but feel a little jealous. She had expected Gina to be smart, pretty. Ben had said as much. But Gina Melrose was more of these things than Reese had imagined. It got under her skin.

The bottom line was, she needed to find Benjamin. She had to explain everything to him. But that was all for later. First, she had to know that Angel would be all right. She hoped to God the paramedics had been right. That it wasn't nearly as serious as it looked.

"Reese?" Gina stood at the door, holding it open. "Jesus, what are you doing out here? Somebody told me they saw you leave."

"I felt weak, needed to sit down." Reese's heart raced. She felt vaguely nauseated again. "How is she?" Her pulse throbbed in her throat, in her arms.

"She's fine. I'm sure she is," Gina told her. "They won't tell me anything else specific. But they need to go over her information with you now. Fill out her chart. Routine stuff."

"Are you sure?" Reese stood up, fought to keep control of her limbs, her breathing.

Gina nodded. "I'm sure. The nurse said they'd need to go over follow-up with you for when she's discharged. Do you need to take something? Your color's not good."

"I'm fine," Reese insisted. She felt a sudden euphoria. The kind that floods in, filling large spaces that worry has abandoned. "Did you see her?"

"No," Gina said. "The trauma Nazis wouldn't let me anywhere near her. I barely got a nurse to talk to me."

Reese felt strong all at once, and strangely calm. She should have gone to ask herself. She shouldn't have involved Benjamin's wife. The woman had shot her daughter, for God's sake. But she was involved already, and she wasn't crazy. Gina had held herself together when she was falling apart.

"Come on," Gina said. "I'll find the nurse and she'll get you to Angel."

Reese followed Gina into the hospital and down a hall that had been painted a ghoulish green. "Why do they think this color will help anyone feel better?"

"Gives you pretty good incentive to get the hell out, huh?"

Gina was blunt, just a hint of a dark side; and she had an elegance, even in her unkempt middle-of-the-night state. Everything about her made her Ben's match. His equal. Gina *was* what she had wanted to be the whole time she'd lived with Ben. Reese wanted to punish her for it somehow. She wanted to lay blame for Angel's shooting, but she couldn't muster the anger for it.

"Thank you for running interference," Reese told her. "I'm better now."

Gina nodded, and the two of them walked together, looking for the elusive nurse. They must have seemed a mismatched set, the two of them. Reese glanced down at her own damp patchwork skirt, then over at Gina's polo shirt and pajama shorts.

"They asked me her name," Gina said. Her voice had a casual tone, but Reese felt the current underneath the words. "I told them her first name. I said I didn't know her last."

Reese didn't want to explain any of that. Not yet. Not without

Benjamin. But she wouldn't lie either. Even at her worst, she'd never dealt in open lies, not about important things.

"Melrose," Reese said, looking over at Gina as she said the last name. "The same as mine."

Gina nodded, and Reese saw something in her eyes, something profoundly sad.

"I've just never changed my name," Reese said, trying to soften the information. "I'm still Melrose. That's Angel's name too."

Reese watched Gina's face, didn't see anything she could decipher.

"The police are sitting in the waiting area," Gina said. "They want to talk to both of us. I told them before that you were a relative of my husband. We're going to have to explain it all, but I'd like to keep as many of the details out of the paper as possible."

Reese didn't know how to respond, whether to be offended or relieved at the woman's discretion.

"I write for a number of local publications," Gina explained when Reese didn't say anything. "I don't want a lot of gossip to get around to the people I work with. I like to keep to myself as much as I can."

"I understand," Reese said. "We'll spin it any way you want to."

Gina just nodded. Reese thought she was dreaming if she really believed this could stay out of the local gossip. Charleston wasn't that big a place. Besides, Ben would want to weigh in on it too. She needed to talk with him. But for the moment she'd do her part.

"And Reese?" Gina stopped walking. Reese turned to look at her, saw that she was almost in tears. "What about Angel's father?"

Gina kept her eyes steady, and Reese tried to think of something to say, but some questions were too large to answer on the fly. She didn't have time for studied explanations.

"Gina," she said. "We'll talk about it. About everything. But I've got to get to Angel now."

As if on cue, the nurse appeared down the hall.

"That's her," Gina said, gesturing toward the woman. "We'll talk later." She almost seemed relieved. "I'll finish with the police and then I'll stay here. I want to know what they say."

Reese started down the hall, then stopped, turned back around.

"While I'm doing this," Reese said. "I know this is awkward, but I need to talk with Benjamin. Will you please try to reach him?"

"Reese—"

"Gina, I've got to get in there. Please, just understand. He'll want to know I'm here."

As she walked away, Reese glanced back at Gina, intending to convey a look of apology, of gratitude, something. But all intentions became irrelevant when she saw the tears streaming down the younger woman's face. The sight almost stopped her, almost made her go back. But she had to get to Angel. Her daughter was waiting. That's all that mattered.

4

Gina

I woke up, registered bright sun through the thin curtains of my boat. A small breeze came through, but even so, the air inside the boat had to be 90 degrees. I tried to recall why I was sleeping in the middle of the day, then remembered. The little girl. The gun. Reese Melrose in the hospital corridor asking me to call Benjamin.

I wanted to go back to sleep, but the hazy moment had passed and I'd come fully awake.

Georgie was curled on her rug at the head of the berth.

"Hey," I said. "I bet you need to go out."

Her ears perked up. She'd heard the word *out* and there was no turning back. I pulled on my shorts and my shoes and headed outside.

"Wait up!" Lane called over from her yard. She came up beside me as I walked along the dock. "I'll go with you."

At sixty-three, Lane had been alone for two years. I recalled meeting Harlan, her husband, once or twice around the docks, before he died. He'd been a lawyer, a quiet, deliberate man. To me, Lane was just the woman who lived in the house by the marina before I moved in. In two months' time she had become my family. No, she'd become better than my family. My own mother tended to be useless in close proximity, whereas Lane always knew what to do and how to do it.

"I came over before, but I didn't want to wake you. You had a long night, darlin'."

She wore jeans with the ease of a teenager. Her short, wash-and-go hair was still damp from the shower.

"You're not kidding, a long night. Did you hear? The little girl, Angel, she's gonna be okay. They were moving her into a room when I left."

"I saw her," Lane said. "This morning."

"You did?" I glanced at my watch. It was just past noon.

"I figured the mother, Reese, would need a change of clothes, so I called the hospital and asked her what I could fish out of her car for her. A toothbrush and cigarettes ranked high on her list."

"I'll bet. That's nice of you," I said, tugging Georgie away from a fire hydrant. We began walking again, instinctively left the area around the docks, moved toward the road that wound around the marsh. "Did Reese get any sleep? They were going to pull a cot in for her, which is a good thing, since I don't think she had anyplace to go."

"Yeah, she said she rested for a few hours." Then she paused. I stopped by the edge of the marsh while Georgie explored a crab shell.

"Who is she, exactly?" Lane asked. "Was she really married to Ben?"

I had sketched in some of the details for Lane in the frenzy of the previous night, or early morning, depending on how you looked at it.

"Yeah. Her name is Reese Melrose," I said.

Lane cut a glance my way. "Still?" she asked.

"Apparently so. They were married for six years, had been together since college. She skipped out on him without much explanation, then sent him divorce papers from an island somewhere. I don't know how she made it happen, but it was legal and he was free to marry me by the time I met him, which was all I cared about. I know they talked once in a while. He sent her money sometimes."

"What's she doing back here?" Lane looked sideways at me again.

"I don't know, but I guess I'll find out. She doesn't know about Benjamin because she asked for him, wanted me to tell him she's here."

"Oh, Jesus," Lane mumbled under her breath.

I began walking again with Georgie in the lead. She raised her leg over a rock like a boy dog.

"You pathetic, confused animal," I said, shaking my head.

"She's liberated." Lane reached down to scratch the dog's ears. "I do remember you telling me he was married before, but I didn't think much about it at the time. What about the girl?"

"I don't have a clue. I didn't know she had a kid. Benjamin certainly didn't know. Reese asked me if we'd split up. She figures something is up since I'm living on the boat. Jesus, Lane. I thought I was done having to tell people."

I sucked in air, tried to keep the tears from coming, but it was too late.

"Aw, sweetie," Lane said, her hand on my arm.

"I'm okay." Marsh air, thick with salt, felt heavy on my skin. Low tide heightened the pungent smell of the shore. "I just thought the surprises were over, that's all. I'll be okay."

After the funeral, I realized that living in the house, *our house,* was making me a wreck. That's when I moved onto the boat, thought I was making progress. Standing by the side of the road, holding a dog leash I couldn't even see through my tears, I figured I still had a ways to go.

"Just breathe," Lane said. "Let it pass." She didn't try to touch me, didn't say everything would be all right.

Georgie was tugging to go faster, so I willed myself back together, felt like Humpty Dumpty, patched up with all the cracks still showing.

"Anyway," I said. "I didn't tell her, and I didn't get anything figured out last night about why she's here. Everything was all about Angel and doctors. I told her I'd come by today and we'd talk. They're letting the girl out this afternoon, I think."

"Any theories at all about why she just showed up like that?" Lane asked.

I shook my head. "Not really. Money, maybe. I don't know. It'd be pretty ironic if she came to get Benjamin back, huh?" I said it without thinking, just blurted it out, and the air seemed to stop around us, an unnatural silence. I glanced over at Lane, and the laughter took us both by surprise. Dark, cathartic humor that brought me sudden, momentary peace. "Oh, God," I said, wiping my eyes with the back of my hand. "Everything's so screwed up."

"Well," she said, her long legs matching my stride as we moved forward. "After Harlan died, I tried to do everything the same way, only without him. It was too hard, too sad. I've felt better since I stopped trying, started making things up as I go along."

"So what's the moral of that story?" I asked.

"Hell if I know, " she said.

I laughed. God bless her, she could make me laugh.

The road curved back, ran through the marsh, built up with a solid path along each side. Egrets glanced up from feeding, but didn't bother to move. Georgie strained at her leash to reach them, her scope well short of success.

"I guess," she added, as if she'd considered my question anew, "I'm telling you to do what feels right. This has to be one from your gut."

"I don't know, Lane. Last night brought so many urgent feelings back to the surface." I needed to put the words into open air. Try them out. "I've tried so hard to make life normal again, and I'd come up with this sterile sadness. But I was functioning, at least. Now . . . I don't know, I feel scared, but I don't know exactly what I'm afraid of. I've run through all the things that might be freaking me out—other than the girl's injury, which is enough, I guess. It seems like more than that but I can't pin it down. I have this fear that Reese could claim something, some part of my life."

"Honey, you've got to stop analyzing this thing as if you can make any sense at all. It's like Ben's accident. A bizarre event. But that's all."

I wanted to make her understand the fears, but they didn't have a form or a name on which I could draw to make her see.

"There are all these feelings and I don't know what to do with them. She can't, can she?"

"Can't what, hon?" Lane looked a little frightened.

"She can't take Ben away, can she?" It was a crazy question. One that I could answer for myself. "He's gone. I know that. What could she do to me now?"

"She could never have done anything. You know that." Lane treated me like a sane person, whether I acted like one or not.

The strangest part of it, I didn't even say to Lane. She *would* think I'd gone nuts. But on some level, even though it was an unspeakable night, it felt good to feel *something* again. Even fear, anger. With emotions directed at *anything*, other than Ben's death, his absence. I felt almost human for the first time in months.

"In some way, Lane, last night seemed like something I was waiting for, anticipating . . ." Then I stopped, remembered what Reese had said to me. "She even asked me why I had the gun, if I was waiting for them. Maybe I was."

"Gina, I gave you that gun. You weren't waiting for anyone, and you know it."

"Not for them exactly," I pushed forward with my thoughts. I needed to try them out. "But for something . . . for something to begin."

"You didn't hurt anybody on purpose," Lane said. She put her hand on my arm. She was missing the point. But then, so was I. I didn't know any more about what I meant than she did.

"Just let it go," she said.

"I know, I'm overanalyzing," I said finally. "That's all."

"It's called grief, Gina. You're allowed to feel bad. You lost your husband. And on top of that, all this has thrown you for another wild spin." Her eyes were straight on mine. "But hon, you have to understand that it's not rational, this feeling that you anticipated that fiasco last night. They came onto *your* boat. You didn't go looking for anybody. These feelings, they're just aftershocks."

"How do you know that?"

She didn't hesitate, not for a second. "Your husband is dead, Gina. The worst has come and gone. That's the only decent thing to come out of all the hurt. Ben can't die again, and you've paid your dues on that one. Same for me."

"What about Angel?" I asked. "The bullet grazed her shoulder, but it could have been a lot worse. And now I have to look at her, see her with the bandages and the shoulder she can't move . . . It just doesn't stop."

"The child is fine," she said, stopping to make her point. "Things happen in life, Gina. And they're not cosmic, they're not related. They just *are*. And what I'm trying to say is, nothing can be worse than what you've already weathered. And look at you, you're still putting on your shoes every day, making breakfast, walking the dog . . . That's all you can ask of yourself right now."

It was an odd brand of comfort, but I let it settle on me—the idea that just getting up in the morning carried the ring of success over failure.

One of the egrets moved, startled me by going airborne in a swift, unexpected rising. I watched it stream low over the sea grass and felt a turn in time, an occurrence short of remarkable, but in the general direction of good. In all my gut feelings about the night before, that was one thing I'd yet to determine. If Lane was wrong, if it did fit into some cosmic plan, some purpose of the soul, was it leaning toward a better end of the spectrum, toward getting me back to myself somehow?

Faint hope lingered as I watched the bird grow smaller in flight.

I turned to face the path that led back to the marina. I wanted to tell Lane, but the words would have fallen short. So without saying anything more, we walked the flat stretch of road that would lead us home.

"So is Benjamin out of town?"

Reese's accent recalled old movies, languid belles, contrasted with her bohemian dress. I looked down at my tan Capri pants, realized I didn't own anything with even a blush of color.

We sat in a restaurant, a bistro to be exact, in the old section of Charleston. It was still early afternoon, and I'd picked her up from the hospital parking lot half an hour before, had a devil of a time getting her to leave Angel, but I didn't want to have the discussion with the child in earshot. And even though all the reports were good, it made me uncomfortable to look at the bandages.

But Reese didn't appear any worse for the wear. She'd showered at the hospital, changed into an outfit that Lane had brought. With the exception of being clean and dry, it looked nearly identical to the one she'd had on the night before.

"Gina?" She spoke up again, and I realized I'd spaced out into my own thoughts without answering her questions about Ben. I wanted to tell her anything but the truth. "Where is Benjamin, Gina?"

"I'm sorry," I said. "I'm a little off." She waited. My escape routes had been exhausted, but I still didn't have the words, much less the heart, to tell her. "I've got to talk to you," I said finally. "There's a lot of stuff I have to tell you. Just let me go to the bathroom and I'll fill you in on everything."

I stood up, glanced around for the ladies' room. Inside, salmon-colored walls gave my skin a brighter tone. At a glance, I almost looked healthy. I splashed water on my face, tepid, midsummer tap water that failed to refresh. Then I rubbed on a little rouge, a little lip gloss, made my way back out to the table.

"The waiter came by," Reese said, "so I ordered the bisque for both of us, along with iced tea. Hope you don't mind."

"That sounds good," I said, admiring her ability to recover from the night's ordeal. She seemed like a different woman from the one I'd seen the night before, absent the paralysis of fear.

"And you said you wanted trout for an entrée, right?"

I nodded. I hardly remembered mentioning the menu, but trout sounded fine.

"Okay," I said, then stopped to get a full breath. "You asked about Benjamin."

"He's not around," she said. "I've figured out that much out for myself. Are you two on the outs?" She tossed off the remark. I thought she looked pleased at the possibility, but I could have been seeing what I expected, nothing more.

"No. It's not that." I felt the blood going through my temples; a kind of panic fluttered in my chest. But it had been a while since I'd had to say it, to actually tell someone who didn't know.

"He had an accident," I managed. "Three months ago."

I watched her face change. The structure of her cheeks, her jaw, seemed to wither somehow as my meaning settled in.

"He's gone, Reese. He died in a car accident."

Her eyes, large and intent on me, registered the pain, and for just a second, a flash of something else. Panic? She bit her bottom lip, shook her head slightly as tears came into her eyes.

"We looked for you," I said, my words gathering speed to keep my own emotions at arm's length. "The lawyers and I contacted all the addresses we could find, but you'd moved on. We didn't know how to find you, and . . ."

And what? There was nothing else to say, really. Her expression was terrible, the edges of her mouth pulled down, like the pure sadness of a child. She still cared, beyond what I'd imagined. I wondered why she'd ever left him. If she hadn't, I don't see how Benjamin would have ended up with me. I had the odd notion to thank her, but it didn't seem like a sane thing to do.

"What happened?" Her voice had gone passive, almost trancelike. "What kind of accident?"

The words formed in my head, but they were hard, nearly impossible, to say. I suddenly wanted her to go away. I wanted to have a different story to tell. I was so tired of the one life had handed me. But the images wouldn't leave me. The lumber, the truck, Benjamin's car. I allowed the words to come, even though I knew tears would follow.

"A truck carrying logs was on an overpass when the binding that held a section of the timber snapped. The logs broke free," I explained.

I didn't tell her where I'd been, couldn't reveal my part in it.

Running out of gas, begging him to leave his meeting and bail me
out. *Gina, just call AAA.* I'd told him AAA would take too long, I had
an interview to get to. *Please, Ben. I know it's a pain, but I'll owe you one.*
No one said I was to blame, but still, the thought rubbed in me, left
me raw and blistered.

"Are you okay?" Reese was saying. I'd clearly lost myself again.

"I'm fine," I told her. "It's just hard to think about it without . . ."
Muscles tightened in my throat, stopped any words that might have
followed.

"So," she said, her voice shaking. "Is there more?" I wasn't sure
what she meant.

As she spoke, she stared past me, as if a video of Benjamin's
demise played on the wall of the restaurant and I only added com-
mentary. The waiter brought our tea, apologized for the small amount
that sloshed onto the white tablecloth near my hand.

"A log," I said after he walked away, "it came down end first into
Benjamin's windshield just as his car started underneath . . ." My
words embellished what seemed obvious to me, but she listened anyway.

I could see the overpass, logs falling like pickup sticks. Benjamin
would have heard it before it hit. They said it was too fast, gave me
the sanitized, widow's version of the report, but I didn't believe them.
Benjamin was bold but careful, and alive to everything around him.
He would have seen them falling. This bothered me the most. That
he might have had a moment of awareness, of terror. And as it happened, I was less than a mile away. Waiting. Irritated at his delay.

"It fell on Benjamin's car. He was crushed, never aware of what
happened. They said he most likely never felt anything." The widow's
version for her too. Was an ex-wife still a widow?

The air-conditioned room pressed cold against my damp cheeks.
I wanted my emotions in check. I didn't even know this woman. But
then, I looked at her. Tears fell free down her face. She'd had him
longer than I did. A lot longer. Six years married, longer than that together. The thought of it brought anger, brief and irrational, to the
surface of my thoughts.

"He's really dead?" The high pitch, the garbled quality of her
voice, sounded familiar. It sounded like mine.

I saw myself dialing his cell phone, irritated that he was taking so
long. I heard it ringing and ringing in the car beside his lifeless body,
until his voice mail said, "Hello, this is Benjamin . . ."

"It happened fast," I said again, words thick in my throat. "He probably didn't feel anything." Those were the only words that had comforted me. I offered them to her with vague hope, surprised that I wanted to spare her pain. Then I moved through the explanation, parroting the words of the policeman who found me the day Benjamin died. "The one log landed directly on the car, crushed it in an instant." A soft-top convertible. They said it would have been the same, regardless of the top, that the logs would have crushed anything but an army tank. "It was a really freak accident." My face was wet, my voice weak. I felt exhausted.

"Were you with him?" A wounded quality existed inside of her question. The answer implied a lonely death for Benjamin. Ben didn't like to be alone.

"I was down the street," I told her. "In my car. I wasn't there."

She nodded, looked out toward the window, as if taking her eyes from me could negate what I'd said. I took in long pulls of air, pushed the images out of my mind. Away from the car. Away from the crushing sound. I'd trained myself to do this. Very Zen, my strange friend Avis told me once. *Just breathe.* I had natural Zen instincts, she told me. This from a woman named after a rental car.

As I was forcing calm into my muscles, into my thoughts, Reese took me by surprise, switched sides, and came over to the chair closest to mine. She leaned in toward me. Her presence warm, she smelled like Coppertone.

"I'm sorry," she said, as if she had secured the faulty log bindings herself. "He was too fine a person to die. It should have been anybody but him. He was . . ." She couldn't seem to finish. "It should have been someone less . . . I don't know." She finally let it go at that.

Even as her tears went unchecked, she reached up, brushed my face with her fingers, smoothed my tears with her open hand. It was an odd, inappropriate gesture from someone who was, essentially, a stranger to me. Worse than a stranger, a rival, of sorts. But something made it all right.

"I'm sorry about some of the things I said last night," she said. "Angel and I just needed to stay someplace until I could talk to Ben. I never thought you'd be there. What happened, it was an accident. Bad luck for everybody. Just like what happened to Benjamin."

When she said his name, the quality of her voice changed. She *had* loved him, on some level she still did. We had that much in common. The last person to offer the same connection had been his mother. But ultimately, her extended visit after the funeral had been too hard on both of us.

"This is so awful," Reese mumbled, pulling wet strands of hair from her cheek.

The waiter stood by the table holding our soup. He seemed confused, in a quandary over where to put the bowls.

"I'm over here," Reese said, standing up, going back to her seat.

"Is everything okay?" he asked. He was thin, almost handsome, but not quite. His face offered genuine concern.

"We're fine," I told him. As Reese reached across the table to lay a hand on mine, I reminded myself that she was Benjamin's ex-wife. That finding comfort in her lingering love for my husband was nuts. The waiter glanced down at our connected hands, offered a slight smile as if he finally understood our display. I wanted to laugh, but the effort seemed too great.

"This really blows." Reese's rough tone, the exclamation itself, took me off guard. It sounded cathartic, and I laughed, without warning. The sound of my own laughter embarrassed me.

She looked at me, straight at my eyes. So few people made eye contact with me when I told them about Benjamin. But she did. The acknowledgment made me bold.

"You're right. It sucks," I said, giving up on propriety. Giving in, somehow. "All of it. It's goddamn awful." Through the distorted vision of tears, I saw the edges of a smile at her mouth too, though her eyes spoke only of grief. It seemed a profound kindness, somehow— that effort on her part, as if she might show me the way back, away from the edge.

"Fucking logs," she said, voice breaking in pain. The extreme inflection landed like a punch line. She squeezed my hand and I gave in to the terrible humor, rich and relentless. One thing I'd learned in my short stint of widowhood—comfort was a quirky animal, offered freely, but rarely felt on the receiving end. Anything that helped was a blessing.

"I was so worried about Angel," she said, "and then so relieved. It never occurred to me that anything could have happened to Ben."

There was nothing else for me to say. Glassware clinked as the table next to ours was cleared. The summer hires yelled back and forth to each other, moving in and out of the kitchen, and a car horn honked on the street outside. The sounds came to me, familiar but misplaced. We found ourselves again in the normal world, straightened up, and moved toward calm again. The people at the next table, two men on a business lunch, I guessed, regarded us without looking directly.

"Oh, Jesus, just look at us," Reese said. A final coda on our outburst.

I wiped my cheek with an open hand, smeared the damp tears across my face. I felt spent, but relieved just the same. Something had changed, but I couldn't say what. I wiped my eyes with my napkin, then put it on my lap and took note of my bisque.

"I'm not hungry," she said, but lifted the spoon to her lips all the same.

I nodded. There were dozens of questions to ask her. One in particular. But I had played all of my emotions for the time being, needed to regroup, to prepare for the answers she would give. Later, at some point, I realized the waiter had brought our meals. I couldn't say when. Reese and I, we made slight efforts at our entrées, but finally gave up, sipped our tea instead.

"Benjamin was happy with you," she said, unprompted, breaking a long silence. "I could hear it every time I talked with him. He always talked about you."

"Thank you," I managed, feeling the thinness of the response weighed against her odd compliment.

She leaned back, lit a cigarette. I waited for them to come and tell her to put it out, but no one bothered. We'd outlasted the lunch crowd. I pushed my plate away, finished without really tasting anything at all. As I waited for the waiter to bring me the check, I realized that contrary to all expectations, the strangeness of the day had fallen away. For the second time in a single afternoon, I seemed to catch a passing glance at the person I used to be. Even more, maybe it was the person I wanted to be.

5

⚮

Reese

"I'll be back to pick you two up around four," Gina said as Reese got out of her car. "Isn't that what they told you?"

"Four or four-thirty," Reese said. "I'm surprised they're letting her leave so soon, but I guess they know what they're doing. Why don't you make it five? That will give me time to talk with the doctor again."

Reese wanted to go through everything with them one more time, how to change her daughter's bandages, how much painkiller to give her. For the first time since she'd found out Angel was okay, she was frightened. What if she screwed up? But she wouldn't show fear. Angel had to be confident that everything was okay. Besides, Reese knew she had gotten very good at masking her bad feelings, both physical and emotional.

"Five," Gina said, her elbow leaning out of the car window. "I'll be here."

"Thanks, Gina, and . . . I don't know what to say about Benjamin. I'm really sorry you've been through all this." Reese struggled with the condolence. There were no Hallmark greetings for an ex-wife expressing sympathies to the widow. Maybe there should be. More and more, everyone was somebody's ex-wife, ex-husband.

"There's not much to say," Gina offered. "Do you need for me to pick up anything for you? Toothpaste? Shampoo?"

Reese felt relieved. This woman didn't want to delve any deeper into emotions than they had already gone. Their moment of bonding had passed and Reese still felt overexposed.

"No, thanks. We're good."

Gina had offered to let her and Angel stay on the boat. It didn't seem like the best idea in the world, but there weren't a lot of options out there. She had sixty-seven dollars in her wallet and a gift certificate for a meal at Shoney's.

Reese stood outside the door to the hospital, watched as Gina drove out of the parking lot, heading back toward the marina. Then she pulled out her second cigarette in less than two hours from the pack Gina's neighbor had brought to the hospital. She allowed herself no more than five a day—a decision borne of economics rather than concern for her health. If finances didn't improve soon, she'd have to consider quitting, but the way she saw it, with all the problems she faced, she and Angel might both be better off if she kicked off in her fifties from lung cancer.

Still, she never smoked around Angel. Not to hide anything. Reese took care to always stay honest with her daughter. She just didn't want the child breathing in smoke, plain and simple.

"Terrible the way they treat us, huh?" A skinny, middle-age man in his pajamas stood on the other side of the concrete cylinder that served as an ashtray. "Sending us outside in the heat like we got something catching."

Reese regarded the man. The hard set of his mouth suggested a life of disappointment, or perhaps simply discontent.

"My daughter's a patient in there," she said, keeping her distance. "I don't want her around this kind of air, so I really don't mind being outside."

The man shrugged, made a short, snorting sound, and walked to the other side of the entryway. Reese turned away from him, let her thoughts go again to Benjamin—and to Angel. Telling Angel would be hard. She had laid her plans carefully when she first told Ben about Angel. She'd screwed everything up when she panicked that last time they saw him. But this . . . She couldn't have done anything to change what happened to Benjamin.

"Could I bum one of those?" An old woman, ancient really, stood in front of her. The woman's back curved over in a perfect C shape—but at least she was on two feet. "My daughter took my last pack away and these damn nurses have no sympathy at all." Reese looked at the woman; she liked her.

"Sure," she said, reluctant still, but offered a cigarette out of her pack nonetheless. She'd cut down to four today. Not so bad.

"Thanks." The woman produced a lighter from her pocket, shuffled away toward a bench at the edge of the circular entrance drive.

Maybe Benjamin's patterns would have changed if she'd done things differently. His driving habits, usual routes. Maybe it wouldn't have happened if . . . Reese ground out her cigarette, refused to let her mind go that way. It happened. That's all. Benjamin wasn't alive anymore, as impossible as it seemed.

She made her way through the heat and stagnant smoke, went back inside, and tried to navigate back to the elevators hidden inside a maze of halls. Why were hospitals so complicated?

"Hold that, please," a doctor called as she pushed the button for Angel's floor.

She put her hand out, waited for him to get in. Good-looking guy. No ring. But her heart wasn't in it. She couldn't get her mind off Benjamin. Thirty-five years old, and suddenly he's dead. How could that be true? She imagined his car, crushed and ruined, the skin of the convertible top shredded through by the timber.

"Here," the doctor said, startling her. She turned her head to see him looking at her. He had a cup of coffee in one hand, held out a cafeteria napkin for her to take from the other. She felt the tears on her cheek and was suddenly angry with him for being there, but she took the napkin, mumbled a halfhearted thank-you.

When the door opened, she walked out without looking back.

Aside from the emotions, the overwhelming sadness of it, she had to deal with how to move forward. Gina seemed to be an obvious part of the solution, as odd as that was. Reese had let her hopes rise and fall, then rise again, looking toward another ending, one that didn't involve Ben's second wife. After meeting Gina, she saw that it would have never happened that way. But that hardly mattered anymore. Of all the scenarios she played out in her mind, she never envisioned that Ben would be the one missing in the picture.

"Hey, there." The nurse smiled at her as she came off the third-floor elevator. "We've got a little girl who's ready to get out of here."

"How is she?"

"She's good," the nurse answered. "Her energy comes and goes with the pills, but overall, she's bounced back like a champ. Kids are amazing."

Angel sat cross-legged on the bed. Her curly brown hair fell around her face as she looked down at the mound of Tootsie Rolls piled in front of her.

"Where'd you get those?"

"An old lady two doors down the hall got a basket of stuff. She gave me the bag of Tootsie Rolls that was in it 'cause she said they pull her dentures out."

"Sounds like you did her a favor."

Angel's arm was in a sling. Her eyes had a slightly loopy look, probably from the painkillers, but she looked awake, happy with her stash of candy. They said she'd have a scar that would get smaller and smaller with time. She would have to do exercises to get her arm strength back after keeping it in a sling for the wound to heal. Overall, they were lucky. Might as well choose the bright side. It could have been a lot worse.

"You have lunch with that lady who shot me?" Angel asked. The question alone sounded like a recipe for therapy, but Angel's tone made it as normal as toast.

"Gina," Reese said. "She was married to Benjamin." Reese stopped when she heard herself use the past tense, glanced at Angel to see if she noticed. She hadn't. "She feels really bad about hurting you. We've talked about this. It was an accident. You understand that, don't you?"

"I know." Angel sounded unconcerned.

"We scared her when we stepped on her boat. She thought we were people who might hurt her. She understands who we are now. I think you'll like her."

"I know, Mom. You told me all that this morning. Besides, Ben said I'd like her too." Angel opened a piece of candy and put it in her mouth. She'd gotten pretty good at handling the wrappers with one hand. Through a mouthful of candy she muttered, "She doesn't look like her picture."

Reese tried to remember if she'd shown Angel any pictures. Or had it been Benjamin?

"She's pretty, isn't she?" Reese said, all the while thinking ahead. She had to get around to the truth, the news about Ben.

"I guess so. When's Ben coming?"

Reese ordered the words in her head, the phrasing. But nothing made saying it seem simple.

"What's wrong?" Even Angel could tell that she was stalling.

Reese sat on the edge of the bed, picked up a piece of candy, took it out of the wrapper, but just held it. She suddenly felt she might not be able to swallow if it was in her mouth.

"Honey," she began. "I just had a long talk with Gina. We're going back to the boat with her this afternoon. But Benjamin's not there."

"Where is he? At his house?"

Reese listened to the sounds out in the hall, listened for something that would take the moment from her. But nothing did.

"Benjamin had an accident. Gina just told me about it. He's, well . . . baby, he died. About three months ago. He's not here anymore."

She didn't know what to expect from her daughter. She sat, waited, braced for tears, questions, whatever would come.

"Where did he go?"

The question sounded so fragile. It stopped Reese. Angel knew about death. It was an odd thing to ask. Maybe the pills made it hard for her to understand.

"I don't know, Angel," she said. "I guess he's in heaven."

"So God's looking after him, then." Angel's voice sounded faraway.

"What?"

"That's what happens, right?" Angel picked up a loose candy wrapper, moved it around with her fingers. "They change into spirits and God takes care of them."

"Yeah, sweetie," Reese managed. "He's doing fine. God's looking after Benjamin for us."

Reese had never been one for church services, but from Angel's lips, she was almost convinced that it could be true. She couldn't imagine where her daughter would have heard about God and spirits. It went against Reese's nature to confirm something she had no idea might be right. But it seemed important to Angel. Important that it at least be possible.

"I wish he didn't die," Angel said, her face beginning to show the sadness that had to come. The tremor of her lower lip caused Reese's maternal urges to flail about.

"It's okay to cry, Angel. Even if he's with God, it makes me sad that he's not here. I cried when I heard about it."

"You're crying again," Angel said, her own eyes bright with tears.

"You're right." Reese put her arms around her daughter, careful to avoid pressing on the child's bandaged shoulder. The living, breathing child offered proof that miracles existed along with all the pain.

None of it was playing out the way she had hoped as she and Angel had driven into town the night before. And she realized that she'd have to explain to Angel again about how she couldn't talk about Benjamin in front of Gina. Not yet, anyway.

But those concerns could wait. For the time being, she would hold her little girl and let herself feel the sadness that was only beginning to take shape in her conscious thought. At the very least, she had the right to feel sad. Seems that she'd been letting go of Benjamin over and over again for as long as she could remember now. But that wouldn't happen anymore. He was finally gone for good. This time, he'd been the one to do the leaving.

6

Gina

With Georgie as crew, I motored out of the slip and headed past rows of docks, toward the Edisto River. One of my few outings since Benjamin died. Moving to the boat, I thought I'd be out all the time. I imagined the healing wind, bringing me back to life again. But that hadn't happened. I generally kept my distance from the river, stayed in the marina where life felt neutral.

"Takin' her out?" Derek called from the haul-out dock. His dark wavy hair fell long around his face. He wore knee-length shorts that hung low on his hips and no shirt. The sight of his bare skin recalled that ill-conceived afternoon on the boat. I felt my cheeks go warm. But something had changed. His strong presence the night before had made me see him in a different light.

"Just a short one," I yelled back. "Need to clear my brain after last night."

"I hear that." He shook his head, acknowledging the rough events of the early morning hours. The well-defined lines of his nose and chin lent his face a maturity that balanced out his youth. "That was pretty wild stuff goin' on. How's the kid doing?"

"She's okay," I called out, then gave an exaggerated nod in case I was getting out of voice range. He smiled again, then stood up.

"Hey!" he yelled, as if something had just hit him. "Can I hitch a ride to Ray's Marine?"

I gave him a thumbs-up, maneuvered toward the end of the nearest dock. As I drew up near, I looped a line around one of the cleats and waited for him to run over and board. Ray's was on the way out of the inlet. I'd just drop him off, but he was on his own getting back.

Derek had only worked at the marina for about six months, starting midwinter, before spring season got busy. But he'd grown up on the coast, near Savannah, he told me; felt more comfortable on water than on land.

He must have met Benjamin at some point, but Ben and I hadn't taken the boat out much in the colder months. By the time spring came in full-blown, Benjamin was gone.

"Thanks," Derek said, grinning as he stepped on board. Georgie growled as he came on deck, but settled when he rubbed her ears. "I need to bring a Bayliner over for haul-out."

"Isn't Ray's the competition?"

He shrugged. "I guess. But there are too many damn boats on the water this time of year. John, the guy who runs the shop over there, called and asked if I could get to it. We're all backed up with more business than we can handle."

I freed the line, steered out toward the middle of the channel.

"I thought you just worked security at night," I said. "You put in time at the marina too?"

"Just since I finished up my graduate courses. I've had more time this summer."

I remembered then. He was working at the marina while he built up his clip file. Wanted to work for a magazine. He'd stopped by the boat to ask me how I broke into freelancing with major publications. That's how our afternoon had gotten started before. I felt myself go shy. What the hell was wrong with me? I tried to think of something to say, but he beat me to the next line.

"So, how have you been?" he asked. "I mean, other than last night."

"About the same," I said, whatever that meant. *Good job, Gina. You're dazzling him with your wit.* Why did I care anyway? I didn't want a repeat of what had happened before. "I'm working through a lot of things. I'm not nuts, honestly."

"I don't think you're crazy at all," he said. Maybe I'd fooled him, or maybe he just wanted to get laid again.

Alone together on the boat, it was hard to ignore the fact that we'd had sex just the week before. I wanted to think I'd been drinking at the time, but I was stone sober and desperate to feel halfway alive again; game for anything that didn't feel *widowlike*. It hadn't been my first encounter of that kind since Ben's death. But it was the first one with someone who lived in my own backyard.

"Listen, Derek . . ." I decided I had to tackle it head-on. "What happened before . . . I'm at a weird place right now. I'm sorry . . . I didn't mean to let it go that far."

"Don't apologize," he said, his eyes green and impossibly kind.

"Last week . . . I mean, I've watched you ever since you moved in. I've wanted to ask you out, but I didn't know if it was too soon; how you'd feel about it. I was working up the nerve when things just . . . happened. I know it's ass backwards, but I'd like to go on a real old-fashioned date. It takes a lot of courage to move on after what you've been through."

Courage. That was me. Braveheart with breasts. I didn't know what to say. A motor cruiser passed us, heading out to open water at an impatient clip. The sound of the boat's substantial engine precluded any response I might have made. After it had moved on ahead, I decided changing the subject would be my best option.

"So what was your graduate work again?" *Ask something you know. Try to avoid surprises.*

He leaned back against the lifeline, putting a comfortable space between us.

"Contemporary lit," he said. He pretended not to notice the abrupt transition of topics. "I wish that I could have gotten journalism, but I decided to stay around here and it wasn't offered as a graduate program. The closest degree that I could get without moving somewhere else was in the English department. I've gotten a few assignments here and there with smaller publications."

"That's what matters, anyway," I said. "Getting some articles to show around. Starting wages at newspapers and magazines are the same no matter what degree you get—barely enough to feed a cat."

"Yeah, well, that's why I went for the big bucks—working two jobs at a marina." He was grinning.

I could see Ray's as we rounded a turn where the channel opened up into the Edisto River; was surprised to find that I felt disappointed.

"Your stop, sir."

I maneuvered alongside the gas pumps. Derek moved up and off my boat in a fluid series of steps.

"Listen, maybe I'll come by later this week," he said, before I could head back out. "Is that okay?"

I nodded, unable to come up with a decent response. Finally, I managed, "Derek, I can't say where my head is right now."

"It's okay," he said. "We'll have a beer. Hang out for a while. I don't expect . . ." He stopped. "You know." The color in his tanned cheeks took on a deeper color.

"I know," I said, feeling my own face grow warm.

He offered a gentle push to get the boat off the dock, then turned and went inside the marina offices. Still, I could almost feel him watching me as I pulled away.

Around the bend, at the mouth of the channel, I saw a dolphin arching off the starboard bow, a baby following just behind. They were going toward an old shrimp boat just up the way, long wrecked and nearly submerged. A gathering of small fish lived among the algae growing on the ruins of the old boat. Benjamin told me about that. We anchored once near the wreck, split a bottle of wine, and watched the dolphins and the otters come and go.

I slowed the motor to watch them. The mother and baby were moving just under the surface.

"There you are," I said out loud. At best, I was getting eccentric; at worst, crazy.

"Georgie, look." I lifted up the dog to see if she would notice the dolphins. She didn't. Instead, she squirmed to get down and resume sunning herself on the cockpit floor. It was the only home she'd known with me.

I thought about the house I'd sold, the rooms that Ben and I took for granted as we lived our normal life. If I'd stayed, could I have reinvented them and made them my own? I wondered if I'd done the right thing, moving. I'd made the decision a month after the funeral. The place was too sad, so full of Ben's stuff. Only after he was gone did I realize how few things actually belonged to me. *Us* was mostly *him*, it seemed.

Even after the move, I hadn't let go. Far from it. I'd kept everything in storage. On a good week, I went to the storage place once or twice, just to sit there for a few minutes and feel Ben's presence. On a bad week I went every day. Lately, I'd had more good weeks. But whether I went there or not, knowing his things were in reach, that they existed somewhere, served as an emergency kit. I kept it there, safe and locked, but ready for that moment when I just had to smell him again, feel him somehow. His suits, pullovers, weekend sweaters. Jackets that carried his scent, maybe even a stray hair on the collar.

It's funny that I needed to move out of the house where there were constant reminders, but I also needed his things to be waiting for me. Maybe the difference was the control I felt with the storage unit. It allowed me to choose when to have those feelings. Nothing to take me by surprise.

After *River Rose* cleared the inlet, I let out the head sail to make a show of sailing, but all I really wanted was fresh air and some space. The luffing as it unfurled into the wind sounded large, menacing. Georgie took a stance in the cockpit, barked loudly against the noise. I felt a surge, fell off the wind, and let the sail fill. The clean rush took the boat forward, and for a second my mind cleared of everything, felt momentarily at rest.

I turned off the motor and took in the silence. Torn clouds moving fast with the air offered occasional sun, both fierce and fleeting— and glorious. The world opened and I realized how confining the marina had become. And it would soon get worse. In a couple of hours I would pick up Reese and Angel. After that, what happened was anybody's guess. But for an hour, maybe more if I pushed it, I could forget about Reese and Angel. I could even forget about myself.

I looked at my GPS, then checked the tides to make sure I stayed clear of the shoals. Benjamin knew the river by heart, and it occurred to me that maybe I avoided sailing because on the water, like in our home, he was so clearly absent. We'd met on a boat, crewing at a local regatta.

My worst fears lay in unanticipated memory—like the ice-cream shop in Charleston just a week before. I'd left the place in tears, no ice cream, nothing but a confused manager calling after me, asking what was wrong. The young man behind the counter had no recollection of me, but he would have remembered Benjamin.

"What's your pleasure?" That was all the kid had said, just trying to be cute. The same kid, spouting the same line he'd used six months before when Ben and I had gone in.

Benjamin shot back, "I don't know. Maybe a double devil with a halo, and make it insane."

"Where the hell did you hear that?" The kid was grinning.

"I saw your T-shirt," Benjamin said, and shook his hand.

Some club at State, I gathered, where ice cream had worked its way into the vernacular. At any rate, we were the only ones in the place, so the kid challenged Benjamin to make it himself, and I sat down for the duration because my husband never backed down. The delighted clerk gave him a hat and a paper apron, and Benjamin made both of us a fudge ripple ice cream and brownie concoction with pistachios and whipped cream. Then he added some kind of flavored syrup that had me nauseated for the rest of the night.

He was entirely himself that day—his mood high, his life easy.

That was during the holidays. Sometime, not long, before he began focusing on having a child again. Bringing it up as if it was a new discussion we should have. The Ben at the ice-cream shop was the person I most wanted to see again.

The guy wouldn't take money from us, so Benjamin said he'd work it off. He'd stayed on serving customers with the kid for another half hour, the two of them cutting up like eighth graders. I finally told him to either go with me or take a taxi home. He left wearing the hat, the apron on under his winter coat. The kid was still grinning as we walked out the door.

Benjamin was like that. People knew him as a friend in five minutes' time. Loved him in ten. I loved him a lot longer, but it wasn't enough.

I'd sailed too far, lost myself in thinking, and completely missed early signs of a squall coming in from behind. I started the motor again, but by the time I turned the boat around and furled the sail back in, the storm was on top of me.

"Damn." I set the boat on autopilot, took Georgie below, and got my foul-weather jacket. Then I stepped back out into the fray, closed up the cabin hatch, and hunkered down to weather the stinging rain as it played out against the current on the slow ride home.

Except for the sling, Angel looked like any kid climbing around on a boat. I had tried to talk with her, but she seemed indifferent. At least she wasn't scared of me. She could still use the hand on her hurt arm, but the doctors wanted to keep the shoulder stable, immobile. She'd already gotten adept at maneuvering her fingers for tasks without shifting the rest of her arm.

"Keep hold of the lifelines, please," Reese called up to her from where we sat in the cockpit as the girl explored the deck. It was after five o'clock, but the August sun stayed high, had come out as bright as morning after the squall. Reese leaned back. Long curls of hair fell toward her face, so she fished beaded combs from her purse and secured the wild strands. My hair, too straight for combs, suffered a plain elastic band.

"I couldn't believe all the blood last night. Looked like buckets, didn't it? I couldn't tell how bad her shoulder was." Reese was telling me about Angel's injury; her tone had a manic quality, a notch up from her usual drama. *Buckets of blood.* She might have been talking about a horror movie, or a news story she read. She seemed to hold nothing sacred. "But after they cleaned it up, it was much more of a grazing wound than anything else, they said."

She relayed Angel's ordeal with an enthusiastic narration, as if such terrible things came and went in their lives all the time. I felt dull next to all of her emotional colors. She seemed to have forgotten that I had been there, at the hospital, when she got the update on her daughter.

"We need to watch out for infection, but other than that, she shouldn't have any trouble. She'll need some physical therapy to get her shoulder muscles up to speed again once it heals."

She wasn't kidding about the blood. I'd done the best I could with my cockpit, but even as I glanced around, I could see streaks of red that I'd missed when I'd gone to work with sponges and towels after getting home.

"I know it's been a bitch for you too," Reese said. "Did the police give you a hard time?"

"No." I shook my head. "They talked to me at the hospital, said they'd file a report, but since both of us agreed it was an accident, there won't be any more to it. The gun is registered, so that's not a problem."

"And we were intruders," she added, saying what we both knew but I wouldn't have voiced.

We sat high on the Stern Perches. Reese's heel tapped with nervous energy as she nursed a margarita from the batch I'd made below. I drank with more enthusiasm. The melting ice diluted the bite of the lime.

"I don't blame you for any of this," Reese said.

Generous of her, I thought, but didn't say. I did blame her, the intrusion into my life. But didn't say that either. She seemed sincere enough, but I didn't trust it. There were shadows trailing all of her words, meanings and intentions that were obvious but not clear. After our lunch-time bonding, my suspicious nature had taken hold again.

"Yeah, well you couldn't have known I was here either." I tried to be charitable. "It was just bad luck."

Just one big lovefest. I didn't mention that people, even former wives, had no right sneaking around on private property in the first place. We'd come to a decent place with each other. No need to get defensive.

"Why are you living here anyway?" she asked. "Do you still have the house?"

If her motives ran beyond curiosity, she didn't show it.

"I sold it. It was too hard being there without him."

I wondered if she had designs on money or property. Ben's will had been standard, no frills. A young man's document that seemed little more than a formality to us at the time.

I looked over at Reese. The pause in conversation, the loose tequila mood, made the moment ripe for inquiry. Trouble was, I didn't know where to start.

"Listen, you up for some questions?" I asked.

"Shoot." She sipped from her glass, kept a cautious look about her.

"Why *were* you two coming on the boat, Reese?" I decided to begin with the simplest one for her to answer.

She sighed, looked as if she needed a minute to think. She touched the edge of her glass with the tip of her tongue, closed her eyes, seemed to savor the salt crystals, elevating them somehow with her response. Then she looked over at Angel, rubbed her fingers together in anxious repetition, which I took to mean she could use a cigarette. I wondered if she'd even heard me; but when she spoke, something about her seemed defeated, as if everything had become pointless.

"We drove into town late," she said. "It's the high season and I didn't think our chances of finding a room that we could afford were so great to begin with. And, to be honest . . ." She turned her eyes to me. "Money's a little scarce at the moment. I knew the boat was here, figured the padlock combination was probably the same one Ben used for the whole time I knew him . . . Gina, I just thought it'd be a safe place for us to sleep for the night, that's all."

A safe place. I looked for irony in her expression, but only saw fatigue. She couldn't have slept much the night before. I felt bad pressing forward, but I'd waited long enough.

"That doesn't answer any of my real questions. Why are you back in town? What did you bring Angel here for?"

I saw Lane coming down the path to the dock. As she neared us she must have sensed a serious conversation because she gave us a brief greeting, then moved toward Angel, who was sitting on the bow. Seagulls flew low overhead as Angel tossed pieces of crackers high in the air.

"Any luck?" I heard Lane call out.

"The big one's pretty good at it," Angel told her without taking her eyes off the birds. As she stood, chin tilted up with her brown curls moving in the breeze, Angel looked like a miniature version of Reese—identical curls, only darker hair. The resemblance startled me for some reason.

"Reese?" I forced myself back to our conversation, didn't want to lose the small momentum we'd had. "Why are you here?"

"It doesn't matter anymore," she said. She watched Angel still, lines of concern slight in her brow. "I needed Benjamin's help on some things. Financial questions, decisions that have to do with Angel. Planning for her. I'm a good mother, but terrible with really practical things. But he's gone now, so it doesn't matter why I came. I have to figure things out on my own."

It was the second time she'd mentioned finances. I wondered if I'd been right, if that's what she'd been working toward all along. Had this all been an elaborate play for cash?

"Do you need money?" A cautious question, noncommittal.

She smiled. An expression that looked amused, parental some-how.

"You live on a boat, Gina, and last time I looked into it, commercial artists don't leave huge estates. It doesn't take a whole lot to figure out that Benjamin hadn't planned on dying. I appreciate your concern, but I don't imagine you're in any position to be our savior."

Something gave way in me. Who the hell did she think she was?

"I didn't make any offers to bail you out," I said, my voice even, my hands calm. It felt good to maintain my own emotions for a change, to own feelings again rather than avoiding a grief that seemed so far beyond me. I thought again of the unopened envelope down below in the cabin. I wondered if she *had* heard about the money; if she was working some scam. "I just asked why you came looking for my husband with a seven-year-old child in tow. I didn't suggest I'd bankroll you or be your *savior.*"

"Point taken," she said, her tone remaining calm. "I didn't mean to offend you." Not an apology. Not even close. Her eyes stayed level on mine.

"You didn't offend me," I said. "You just didn't answer me."

"Gina, you're not the person I came to see."

A motorboat went by, the engine drowning out our voices. I was glad. My empowered moment had passed. I hated the direction our words had taken. Insults mixed with vague explanations. I'd gone from wanting answers to sparring for points.

"I'm not trying to grill you," I said, forcing a softer tone. "Imagine you were me, Reese. What would you be thinking?"

"I'm sorry," she said, with an apology that finally sounded genuine. "I know you have questions. I have more than I had two days ago. The problem is, there aren't any answers."

"But there are *some* obvious answers." I glanced over at Angel. "She came from somewhere."

The sun passed behind a cloud, and the momentary shade brought a kind of relief. It occurred to me again that Reese's arrival had brought another kind of relief. At least since Reese landed, literally, on my boat, I hadn't thought about how hard it was to get up, to move through the day.

"Start with the simple parts," I said, trying to make my voice more gentle, less accusing. "I just want to understand."

She sat up, shifted and rolled her neck around like she was getting ready to exercise, then took a sip of her drink. Her skirt fell around the edges of the seat, moved with the slight air around us.

"Angel needs different things now. She's not a baby anymore. She should have a stable school, friends, a real place to live. I don't know where to start with most of that stuff. We've had a fairly free-floating existence all her life. Different jobs for me, different places. A lot of kindness, frankly, from strangers."

She looked and sounded like a Tennessee Williams character. I wondered if she even got her own reference.

"But the older she gets, the more complicated things become. I moved her twice last year when she was in first grade, trying to find a good situation for her. But the places I can afford to live don't usually come with good schools. Plus, she needs eye exams and booster shots, maybe braces in a few years. We've been lucky, so far, but this hospital stay only shows me what bad shape we're in with health benefits . . ."

"I'm covering the hospital, Reese."

"They told me," she said. I couldn't read into how she felt about that. "Thank you. But that doesn't change the fact that a lot of things could happen. And I haven't thought very far ahead. Even about things I knew would come. I've been pretty stupid, actually."

She was talking about more than Angel, about more than school
and work benefits. I knew it, but I couldn't read beyond the riddle of
her words.

"What about Angel?" I asked, scared to articulate the question
any further. Did I really want to know the answer?

"What about her?" Reese looked across to the marsh. She had to
sense what was coming. I heard a solid shift in her tone. Our moments of bonding, it seemed, had passed.

"She's what, seven? Eight? You know what I'm asking," I pressed.

"Her father." Reese turned back toward me, her expression as
flat as her words.

I nodded, barely managed to breathe.

"I don't know for sure," she said, then looked away again, as if
that was all the explanation she needed to offer.

"What do you mean, *you don't know?*"

My arms, my shoulders, felt weak. My drink shook slightly in my
hand. I put the glass to my lips, felt the coarse salt as I drained all that
was left. The internal hum of the alcohol steadied me, allowed me to
focus on the moment.

"I don't know who her father is," she said again, looked me in the
eye. Bold. Unashamed of all the statement implied.

"Well, is Benjamin one of the candidates?"

"Gina—" she began. But at that moment, Lane called out to us. I
think we both felt more than a little relief.

"Angel tells me she's hungry," Lane said. She sat with the girl
on the bow. They looked like any typical grandmother and granddaughter. "I suggest Ollie's. My treat."

A stay of execution. Reese's expression mirrored mine.

"Great!" she said. She glanced back over at me. "We'll talk more
after dinner. I'll try to explain everything then."

I nodded, ready for a break myself.

Georgie sensed the rhythm of the group change, knew we were
going somewhere. She sat up, eager for an invite.

"Lane," I asked, "can I leave Georgie at your house? The guy
from the boatyard is coming to look at the air conditioner while
we're gone. She'll go nuts if I leave her here."

"Sure, want me to walk her over?"

"That'd be great," I said, happy to be dealing with logistics again.
"I'll get the car and pick you up over there."

*   *   *

The fish house sat less than half a mile down the road, practically a walk from the marina, though with mosquitoes in high season, it made more sense to take my car. Even with considerable effort on my part, bloodstains from the night before soiled the cracks in the leather passenger seat. Seemed my ordeal with Angel and Reese had left a mark on all the different areas of my life.

On the ride over, Reese's face was bright again. As Angel smiled back at her, I realized how good Benjamin's ex-wife was at deception. With her daughter, it ran toward a good cause; stability within the crazy life she'd made for the girl. But it still bothered me. What ran behind the changing faces she offered? Even with the uncertainty of her motives, I felt for her. Maybe that had been Ben's mistake too.

I parked at the far end of the lot. "I think you'll like Ollie's," I said to Angel. I'd barely spoken to the child before, felt awkward even trying. I found it impossible not to stare at the sling that held her arm, the large hump of the bandage on her shoulder. She looked like a homebound veteran of war. "They have really good fish and french fries."

"I only want a hamburger," she said, her expression going flat as she turned to me. She didn't even attempt the cute persona I'd seen her employ with Lane. Either she had my number or I had hers. I couldn't tell which, but something about her defiance struck a chord with me, gave her points on my, admittedly unreliable, measure of character.

"Angel?" Reese gave a slight shake of her head in the direction of her daughter. "Watch your manners, okay?"

Angel nodded, but didn't say anything more to me.

We all piled out and headed for the door.

Lane and Angel sat side by side. Reese joined us after stopping for a quick smoke outside. Lane and the child had bonded right away, but the girl remained wary of me, kept her distance. Kids, like horses, sense fear, and I was terrified. Of her, of what she could mean. But there was something more, and it didn't take a shrink to sort it out. I thought of Elise. Even when I was a kid, I had little understanding of children.

"I'll have a hamburger," Angel said as she looked at the menu.

"Baked potato or fries?" the waitress asked.

"Nothing else. Just a hamburger," Angel told her. At least she was true to her word.

Looking at Angel, reality blurred with memory and I felt the shadows closing in. A child that age, that size . . . But a different creature from Elise; a different species, almost. Even in my brief interaction with Angel, I knew that. Unlike Elise, with her insecurities and her endless needs, Angel seemed stubborn and guarded. The two only resembled each other in slight build and dark coloring, but even that much . . . I couldn't let myself stay in the comparisons. It was too hard.

Lane didn't know about my younger sister, couldn't have known the source of my discomfort, but she saved me nonetheless. She launched into the role of surrogate grandmother without flinching. She and Harlan had two sons, one married for five or six years with no kids to show for it, and one unattached and gay. She'd been ripe for years to spoil a kid.

"My birthday's next week," Angel announced after we'd ordered our drinks. "Can we come back here that day if we're still around?" She glanced at her mother, and some kind of code passed between them, it seemed.

"We'll see." Reese remained noncommittal.

"How old will you be?" I asked. I tried to make the question sound casual, but it came out an octave too high.

"Eight," she said.

It would have been close, the timing, but possible. I needed to force that issue next with Reese. She clearly wasn't going to offer much in the way of unprompted information.

"Congratulations!" I said with too much enthusiasm. Lane shot me a look that I was sure meant *calm down*. Reese's scattershot energy was rubbing off on me.

Plates rattled as waitresses brought food to the table next to us and voices rose and fell among the rowdy summer crowd. But there was no mistaking the odd silence at our table. All of us, with the exception of Angel, knew what lay implicit in the child's age.

"Remember the clown we went to see last year for your birthday?" Reese said to Angel, filling the awkward pause.

The two of them launched into descriptions of some friend of Reese's who worked as a professional clown. As they talked, I looked at Angel, her expressions, her skin color. Nothing gave any hint of her place in Benjamin's genetic line. The more I stared at her, the less she even looked like Reese's daughter to me, a changeling substituted for the child I watched earlier standing on my boat. *You're losing your mind, Gina.*

"Lane said we could have a picnic," Angel said, "on a deserted island like Gilligan! Maybe we could do *that* for my birthday—if we're still here, that is." Again, the necessary disclaimer laid against all plans. She was a smart kid. A bit of a brat for my taste, but I had to admire her bold approach to her new situation.

"There's an island just across the way," Lane explained. "You can only get to it by boat. If you're here for your birthday, that's great, but we can do it any day, really. We'll anchor, take my boat to the beach, and have the place to ourselves." Lane had an old Boston Whaler tied up at her dock. The flat bottom could go right up on the sand.

Angel grinned, then looked at Reese. She was searching for something . . . instruction, maybe?

Reese gave a slight shake of her head, barely any movement at all, but Angel seemed to understand.

"Maybe your dog can come with us," Angel said, addressing me. What was it with those two? The looks. The signals.

"Georgie would like that," I told her.

It was true. She and Georgie had taken a liking to each other. Georgie rarely made a misstep when it came to character. Her instincts ran sharper than mine. I hoped for my sake that the dog's batting average held when it came to the girl. If she *was* Benjamin's only child, I at least wanted to like her, whether I got on well with her mother or not.

"Why didn't Georgie come to dinner with us?" she asked.

"Restaurants aren't crazy about dogs," I said.

I wondered if the AC guy had made it to the boat. I had high hopes of sleeping cool again, and the last thing I needed was a houseguest or two on a stifling hot boat.

"Do you know how to make a doll cake?" Angel turned to Lane, the subject of the dog replaced in an instant. "I saw one once where the doll's skirt was the cake. Do you know how to do that?"

The words held a reverence. She sounded hopeful, but frightened of the hope itself. It was the first time she'd looked like a complete kid to me, and I wondered what her life had been like, with Reese. The two were devoted to each other, that was clear, but something about their interaction seemed to mix up the roles of parent and child. Lane's presence offered no ambiguity, and Angel allowed her kid persona to shine when she talked with the older woman.

"I've made a cake or two in my time," Lane said. "I bet I could figure it out. Chocolate or vanilla icing?" she asked.

"Pink." Angel's smile changed her face.

"Pink's not a flavor," Lane said, smiling. "Strawberry maybe?"

Angel smiled, nodded.

I had an odd feeling. I wanted to warn Lane, to tell her not to get so attached, but the concern seemed unfounded when weighed against rational thought. Maybe I simply didn't want Lane's loyalties divided. My gut sensed a competition in the works and I had already fallen behind.

"Lane said she can teach me to sail too," Angel added, looking at her mother. "She's got a little boat, called a . . ." She glanced over at Lane.

"A Sunfish," Lane filled in.

"Well that's a lot of plans. We'll have to see," Reese said. "Sounds like fun, though."

It is fun. Lots of fucking fun. I suddenly felt like the last one picked for kickball. Seemed the party would continue whether I showed up or not.

"I could lend a hand in the sailing department," I said. Angel turned to look at me; her face showed no response at all. Reese made a small noise, something between a cough and a grunt.

"Thank you," Angel said, after the prompt from her mother. "That would be fun too."

The waiter brought hush puppies, fresh from the vat, hot grease staining the paper that lined the basket.

"Where're we sleeping tonight?" Angel asked her mother.

"Let's talk about that," Reese said as she took a hush puppy, then bounced it from hand to hand to cool. She turned to Angel. "Careful with these, honey. Wait a minute to pick one up." She turned back to me, said in an offhand tone, "I know you said we could stay at your place for the night, but that's going to be pretty tight."

"There's plenty of room," I said, the lie heavy in my throat. "The biggest headache will be the one bathroom." The tension between us remained. She'd barely acknowledged me since she sat down.

"Well," Reese told me, "we could find a room somewhere. Something that doesn't cost too much." It was a fairly transparent protest, designed to give me an out if I really wanted to be an asshole.

Angel looked out the window. A salt creek ran behind the restaurant, and she stared at two seagulls vying to land on the same post. I got the feeling she'd heard this routine with her mother before, felt vaguely embarrassed by it. But maybe I was projecting too much. Maybe she just wanted to look at birds.

"I've got an idea," Lane said. "Why don't you two stay with me? Or at least one of you. I've got an extra room, plus a pull-out in the den. That might give you some time to figure out what you plan to do."

"That's nice of you," Reese said. "Maybe if Angel stayed with you, Gina and I could have a chance to talk."

"That's what we'll do then," Lane said, looking delighted with the outcome.

I helped myself to a hush puppy, suddenly registering a biting hunger that I'd been too preoccupied to notice before.

"So, did you two travel far to get here, you and Angel?" Lane asked, trying to make her question light and conversational.

Reese had dodged the where-did-you-come-from question several times already. They'd lived "outside of Baltimore," visited friends in Georgia, stayed a season on the Outer Banks . . . The list went on and on. Relentless, Lane had continued to ask, rephrasing it each time just enough to make it new.

"Lately, we've been traveling in the western part of North Carolina," Reese said. "We haven't stayed in any one place for too long. We were living near Boone, in the mountains, just before we came here. I've got a friend who runs a restaurant there, and I was able to pick up some work."

Closer to an answer, but still vague. Reese's life didn't make any sense. I knew she and Ben had married during college. She'd graduated from State the year before he finished. Worked as a sales rep for a local radio station from that time until she left him. But the bits and pieces she'd offered about her life over the course of the afternoon didn't offer any consistency, no big picture of what her life with Angel had been like.

"Mom?" Angel sat beside Lane near the window, had to speak across the table to get her mother's attention. "Can I have a gumball? There's a big gumball machine by the front door." The request seemed perfunctory, her face suggesting that she'd given up before she even spoke.

Reese put her elbows on the table, leaned in toward Angel, then sat up again and began fishing in the bottom of her purse for a quarter. Angel's face changed as her mother began to look for coins. "You may go *get* it now," she said, her hand rooting inside the macramé bag, "but I don't want you to chew it yet. Our food is coming any minute."

Reese's hand was still feeling around in her bag.

"Here, I've got one," Lane said, handing Angel a coin.

Reese nodded at her daughter. "What do you say?"

"Thank you." She beamed at Lane, then went off, momentarily delighted.

We all watched her go, marveled at the happiness of unanticipated permission.

"Wouldn't you like to be seven again?" Lane asked, her eyes following the girl. "Even for a few minutes?"

The sound of a blender rose and fell in arcing spurts from behind the bar.

"Not me." Reese's words came out solid, the edges sharp and dangerous. "I wouldn't go through childhood again for love or money."

It was a dead-end remark. No response could naturally follow, so we let it go, looked around for the waiter who could bring us our salads, maybe another round of beers. I watched Angel struggle to work the gumball machine with her left hand. A bit awkward, but she was managing. Still, guilt fell over me again.

"Excuse me for a second," Reese said, suddenly standing up. I figured she was going to literally give Angel a hand, but she headed toward the back of the restaurant instead.

Lane watched her go, shrugged her shoulders as if to say, *Who knows?*

After a short time, Angel came back with the gum tight in her fist. When she put it on the table in front of her, the inside of her hand was blue. Lane stuck the corner of her napkin in ice water and rubbed the child's sticky palm.

"Where's Mom?" Angel asked.

I took a stab at answering. "She went to the bathroom, I think." Better to go with something concrete. The bathroom. Angel nodded, but continued to look around. Sometime after that the salads arrived, but still no Reese.

"I guess we should go ahead and start," Lane said, gesturing toward the plates in front of us.

Angel picked up her fork, tried to look blasé, but a current of something—concern, maybe even fear—flashed in her eyes, then was gone.

"You think I should go check on her?" Lane asked me, keeping her voice light.

"I'm sure she'll be back any second," I said. "Let's finish our salads. She wouldn't want us to hold up the entrées."

With Angel at the table, questions passed between Lane and me with only glances, no words to alarm the little girl. But we both wondered what Reese was up to. With a child present in the equation, the stakes became high, much more than the curiosity the situation would normally have warranted. After what seemed to be hours, but had in fact been about twenty minutes, Angel's face changed entirely.

"Mom!" she called out, her eyes fixed across the room. The waiter was clearing salad plates, but Reese's sat untouched at her place.

Lane and I turned to see, and sure enough, there was Reese. Late sun through a side window caught her jewelry. Carrying a tray in her hands, she passed a group of men who sat drinking at the bar, and her skirt brushed the bare legs exposed below their shorts. The men followed her with their eyes as she moved across the room.

"Where'd you go?" Angel stood up as her mother came closer to the table. The tray held tall glasses that overflowed slightly around the edges with something—a concoction, dark pink and frozen. Strawberry daiquiris was my guess. Four of them sat cold and sweating on the tray.

"My treat," Reese said, still standing over us, as if in triumph. She smelled of cigarettes, and I guessed that while waiting for the drinks, she'd bummed a cigarette from one of the guys at the bar.

"Reese, " Lane said, "you shouldn't have done that. Those are expensive—"

"It's okay," Reese interrupted her. "I get the employees' discount—in advance. I just got a job."

"A job?" I replayed the sentence in my head. "Here?" I asked. For an instant everything stopped. "You're going to work here?" The day had been a rush of Reese and Angel, but when she spoke, the moment froze into a photograph.

"Yeah. I start next week," she announced.

She had a job? Planned to stay? What kind of person was she? What kind of mother drags a child hundreds of miles and makes a life decision on a whim? Still, after less than a day with Reese, nothing about her seemed out of bounds. Lane looked over at me, mouth slightly open, eyes wide. I was sure my expression mirrored hers.

"So?" Reese stood with the tray, waiting, clearly expecting a more enthusiastic response. I forced myself to sit up straight, to smile.

"That's great," I said, unable to animate my tone beyond the phonetics of the sentiment. Could I possibly deal with having Reese in town indefinitely? It was too late, in any case.

"Congratulations," Lane managed, with a little more expression.

"So we'll be here on my birthday?" Angel asked.

"You bet," Reese answered, smiling, putting a glass down in front of each of us, even her young daughter. "The green straw means it's virgin," she said when Lane's eyebrows went up.

She put the last one at her own place and sat down, then lifted hers toward the middle of the table. Angel held hers out, followed by Lane, then me. The glasses clinked together, held high, pink as party balloons. Whipped cream topped the festive drinks, and in the center of each mound of white sat a different colored gumball.

"Cheers," Reese said.

"Cheers," we answered with varying degrees of enthusiasm; but Angel remained unconflicted, her voice calling loudest of all.

7

Reese

Reese noted the cold sensation that ran down her arm. She thought about what she'd done, hoped to God it was the right thing. She rode in the backseat with Angel on the short drive back to the marina. Lane sat in the front with Gina. Angel stretched out with her head in Reese's lap, her bandaged shoulder the only sign of what had gone so wrong the night before. Reese pulled her fingers through Angel's hair, the soft curls yielding at her touch. Angel snuggled as if settling down for a journey, rather than the short ride home. Then again, everything was part journey to a child. Only adults began to see life in terms of destinations.

"Mom?" Angel asked. "Are we going to live on a boat here too, like Gina?"

"I don't think so, baby. I have to find us a place to stay, though."

Reese had dreaded arriving in Charleston. Even as she sorted through the details of how she might work things out with Ben, she understood how torn she would feel when it was done, when she was actually sharing her daughter with him. Months before, when she brought Angel to meet Ben, she'd had hopes of another outcome, one that would give Angel the family she deserved. But Ben had made it clear what the terms would be.

She'd been stupid to take Angel away, to panic like that. Ben wouldn't have turned against her. He wouldn't have tried to keep Angel from her, no matter what her problems were; no matter how intent he was on staying with Gina. Gina's feelings about children had left her with the slightest thread of hope; hope that Ben would have to choose between the girl and his wife.

But that was before. With him gone, everything had changed, and she now had to rely on the woman she'd wanted to replace. Her options had become slim. And as Angel asked about the future,

Reese realized how muddled everything had become. How hard it would be to find a solution without him.

"Well, we don't have to worry about where you're sleeping tonight," Lane said. "We'll have a great time at my place, Angel, and your mom and Gina can spread out and have a slumber party of their own."

"Right." Angel smiled, but glanced up at Reese for final confirmation.

"That sounds like a great idea," Reese said. A night with Gina didn't have the makings of a party, not with the conversations they had in store, but she could feel her daughter relax—the muscles in her neck, in her good shoulder, eased against Reese's thigh—and that put a better light on everything else. She saw how much Angel liked Lane, trusted her. Reese trusted her too, and she hoped it was mutual. She needed all the goodwill she could muster.

"We're here," Gina said as she turned into the lot of the marina. "I don't know about you guys, but I'm exhausted. Where's your car, Reese?" she asked. "Don't you need to get stuff out of it?"

"The Plymouth there." She pointed to the maroon car. Her South Carolina license plate read DOG-MAA. In a lot full of fancy sport vehicles, even Gina's Volvo looked out of place. Reese's old boxy sedan looked prehistoric.

"South Carolina plates," Gina said. "That was fast."

Reese smiled. Gina was fishing. But nothing would be biting today.

"Like I said, we've moved so much. I haven't gotten around to changing them. Good thing, huh?"

"Pretty lucky," Gina said. "Okay, I'll let these two off at Lane's, then I'll meet you at the boat."

"Go ahead and park," Lane said. "Angel and I can walk to the house. We might even stop and get an ice cream at the Ship's Store."

Lane had a natural way with Angel. But what about Gina? Could she be trusted? Benjamin had loved her, relied on her. Hell, he married her, which had surprised Reese from the beginning. That was almost enough. But not quite. Reese sensed something off-center about her. She had all that baggage from her childhood, but hell, who didn't? The real problem came from the notion that she didn't seem to care much for Angel.

A breeze stirred the air. Halyards on the sailboats responded, clinked against the aluminum masts like wind chimes, dozens of them at once.

"I could use a shower," Reese said, feeling the salt air thick on her skin. "Should I bathe on the boat or go up to the marina showers?"

"Either way," Gina told her. "The water pressure's a little better up at the guest showers. It just depends how lazy I am on any given day."

"I'll go to the marina, then. I need to throw in a load of clothes at the laundry up there anyway." After the catharsis of their luncheon, Reese had felt things go cold with Gina. She wanted to minimize girlfriend time as much as possible.

"I've got quarters on the boat if you need some," Gina offered.

"I've got plenty."

Marina living reminded Reese of apartment life. Temporary. Angel would need more soon. Maybe she needed more already. Reese watched her little girl walking away with Lane. They were making plans for Angel's birthday picnic.

"I'll check on you in a few minutes," Reese called out. Angel gave her a slight wave, unconcerned about her mother's plans.

"What am I going to do?" Reese mumbled to herself, watching the two of them walk away.

As she leaned into the trunk to find what she needed for the night, she saw Gina glance over. Reese realized she'd spoken out loud. Gina continued locking up the car, didn't say anything. Reese tried to read the other woman's expression, but came up blank.

"The security code on my dock is 1282," Gina offered after a moment. "It's easier to walk to the boat from here than swim." Gina was smiling. It took Reese a second to get the joke. She wondered how much bite lay behind it.

"Don't worry about me. Just keep your pistols in the drawer, cowgirl," Reese volleyed. She felt a smile settling in at the corners of her mouth. Maybe, just maybe, she and Benjamin's widow would find some middle ground.

"See you at the boat," Gina called out as she headed toward the docks. The marina lights exposed her, made her look vulnerable, lovely somehow, amid the surrounding shadows that hung over the marsh and the water. Reese felt secondhand next to Ben's widow.

She did a last survey of the trunk of her car, examined the contents of her life to date. She'd taken out only what she and Angel needed. She saw the manila folder tucked in at the side of the trunk. The two things inside would get her through this nightmare. She wouldn't need them just yet, but knowing they were there gave her piece of mind.

She picked out a change of clothes for both of them, tooth-brushes and shampoo. No need to clutter the small living space on the boat with any more than that. Besides, the more she took out, the more she would risk revealing herself. Lane had been through her things earlier, when she brought clothes to the hospital, but it wasn't likely that she'd gone rifling through the folder with all her papers.

Lane came the closest to Reese's idea of a confidante, but there wasn't enough trust there yet. Not enough history. She'd have to wait before she let anyone else into the complicated world she shared with her daughter. The time wasn't right. Not yet. She put the few items she'd gathered inside the smallest of her duffels, locked up the car, and headed toward the docks.

8

∞

Gina

I wasn't in the mood to take Georgie for a walk, so I made her pee on the grass near the Ship's Store and then settled back, still restless, on the boat for the night.

"We'll go for a long walk tomorrow," I told the dog. "I promise." She didn't look convinced.

I poured myself a cognac, set out to put sheets on the quarter-berth cushions for Reese. "DOG-MAA." That was just flaky enough for her.

On the one hand, the thought of Reese living in the same town seemed like something I'd dreamed. One of those weird, passing fears that vents itself at night, then meets relief the next morning. But then I remembered the strange comfort of sharing my story with someone else who knew Ben. Someone who felt a loss similar to mine. I wondered what relationship would eventually evolve between us.

"Hey." I heard Lane call from outside before she stepped onto my boat. It seemed everybody had gotten a little skittish about boarding my vessel without decent warning.

"What's up?" I asked. "Where's Angel?"

"Reese brought her things over and is getting her tucked in before going to take a shower. Angel's asking for a stuffed alligator. Did she leave it here before we went to dinner?"

"I don't know," I told her, pulling an extra pillow from under the portside berth and stuffing it into a pillowcase. "I don't remember an alligator. Sorry."

Lane stood there, leaning against the corner that was my kitchen, looked as if she wanted to say something.

"What?" I asked.

"I don't know." Lane shook her head, the light strands of ash-blond gray shifting color as she moved. "It's not really my place to say, but . . ."

"Come on. Something's on your mind," I said. "Just say whatever it is."

"You're not real keen on Angel, are you?" she asked, moving out of my way as I bent to spread a light blanket on the makeshift bed.

I finished with the blanket, sat down at the front of the quarter berth. Her direct stab at the topic took me off guard. "I don't know if you've noticed, but we've got a few issues here."

"I know. But I think it's more than that." She was relentless.

"More?" I did my best to sound indignant. "More than unexplained paternity questions?"

"You wouldn't blame the kid for that. You're making an effort with Reese, for God's sakes. There's something else going on."

I bought time with my cognac, took a sip, saw my distorted reflection, liquid features in the amber surface inside the glass.

"You're right." I didn't look up at her. "But I don't want to talk about it now."

"Fair enough," she said. "But for Angel's sake, if you could try to get to know her . . ."

My instinct ran to the defensive stance. "She's not exactly fuzzy and sweet when it comes to me either."

"I'll talk to her. She'll take a lot of cues from you, though. Just try."

I nodded. It was all I could manage.

"There's something else," she said. This time she was the one hedging her words. "What do you think is going on with those two?"

"Damned if I know," I said, setting my drink on the navigation table. Lane sat opposite me. "I asked Reese about Angel, about her father."

"And?"

"She said she doesn't know."

"She doesn't know?" Lane's face took a rare cynical turn.

"Yeah, I don't know if I believe it or not either, but that's what she told me."

"Did you ask her how she happened to *not know*?"

"Not yet, but I'd say playing bedroom hopscotch would be one way to cause a little confusion." I sounded judgmental, hated myself the second the sentence came out of my mouth. I'd had a few moments in strange beds myself since Benjamin died. Pain will lead you to various avenues of self-medication if you let it, and no telling what pain Reese had been through.

"I don't know what the story is." I ended the subject. "You said there was something else?"

"Yeah. I need to get back to Angel, but I just wanted to tell you about something unusual she said."

"Who?" I asked.

"Angel. Just now."

I picked up my glass, noticed I was fidgeting, tried to will myself into calm.

"I was telling her," Lane went on, "that for her birthday, we'd take my boat to the island for the picnic. You know, I talked about it at the restaurant too. Anyway, I was brushing her hair and she was getting a little sleepy, I think. This was before Reese came in."

"Yeah? What did she say?"

"I talked about the island, made it into kind of a bedtime story."

"And?"

"And she asked me if it was the same island with the salty pond in the middle."

I felt gooseflesh up my arm. My heartbeat ran high, toward the middle of my throat. "How did she know?" I took a sip of my drink, felt shaky as I lowered it from my mouth. The cognac burned warm into my chest.

"I asked her when she had seen the pond."

I waited, still barely able to breathe.

"Her lids were closing. I thought she was asleep already, but then she kind of opened her eyes a little and said that she'd gone once. 'On the blue boat,' she said. 'Gina's boat?' I asked her, and she opened her eyes wider, more awake. She wouldn't answer. Reese walked in about that time and Angel got really agitated, looked upset. I think she realized she'd said something she wasn't supposed to."

"She said she went on my boat to the island?"

I felt invaded somehow. Looking around the cabin of what had become my home, I sensed a violation.

"That's what she said, but she could have been really confused. She's not even eight years old yet. She could have been playing make-believe, telling a story. Especially if her mom's talked about the island."

"But the salt pond," I said.

"The pond too," Lane said, standing up to go. "Reese said she grew up around here, so she would have been out there before. I don't know. I didn't want to bring it up until we were alone. You can ask her about it tonight."

"Maybe they've even come out here before," I said, more to myself than to Lane. "Slept on the boat like they were trying to do the other night. God, maybe Reese was just crazy enough to take it out to the island. I don't know."

I thought of Angel, toes deep in the sandy mud bank of the pond. When Benjamin and I would go there, I felt as if the place belonged to us. No one else was ever there. For brief moments the two of us owned the pond. Everything. The marsh, birds, little fish . . . I had to stop. It brought too much of him back, thinking of the place. And I resented the hell out of Angel's image inside that memory.

"Like I said, you should bring it up with Reese. See if you can get a straight answer out of her."

"Yeah, well, I can put that one in line behind all the other questions I've got for her."

"I better get back over there," Lane said, starting up through the companionway. Before she got to the top, she stopped, turned back to me. "Like I said, try not to blame Angel for any of this. I know it's hard not to, but whatever Reese has done, she's just been along for the ride."

Lane could read me too well. I felt both comforted and disturbed by how close inside my brain she could get sometimes.

"You're right," I said as she headed out into the cockpit. "I'll do my best." It came out vague, noncommittal. But it was all I had to offer.

I finished one cognac, had the impulse to pour another one, and decided to let it ride for the night. I was drinking too much lately, even before Reese's blunt arrival. I needed something else to anesthetize myself. Mindless sex hadn't exactly done the trick. Booze didn't seem to be much better. My last hope was the religion thing. Maybe that was the ticket. Ben's mother had dragged me to Mt. Sinai, a little church near her vacation cottage on Sullivan's Island. To my surprise, I'd gone back on my own after she left, and not just to visit the grave. Something about it, the place, the people; the songs, the words . . . All of it together felt like lotion on sunburn. I hadn't been there in a week or two, but I thought it might be time to try it again.

It took so much effort to reinvent my world without Ben, and these new problems—they didn't help at all. Only after Benjamin was gone did I realize how much I'd counted on him to decide who I was. Together, we'd been a step ahead of the world. Without him, I'd fallen so far behind.

"What's taking Reese so long?" I said out loud to myself. Georgie looked up. Her eyes looked clear, nearly human, and I half expected her to answer me.

Half dozing and listening for Reese's return, I thought of the last time Benjamin had taken me to the island, one morning a month or so before he died. A day more like fall than spring. The winds were high, with more bite than usual, and the sun had come out strong.

"Let's take the boat out," he said without any preface. His tone was light, free of the serious overtones, the ragged edges that had begun to dominate our conversations. "We can anchor and grill out, take the whole day."

It was a Thursday, and I had a piece for *Coastal Living* due before the beginning of the week. We'd had yet another discussion the night before about having a child, but he showed no lingering signs of baggage over the argument.

"I've got to work," I told him, already mentally recalculating my schedule.

He had just come out of the shower, and I was sitting down to work at the computer, still in my plaid bathrobe.

"Yeah, me too," he grinned. "That's the best part."

He wore nothing but a white towel, low around his waist.

"That's why we say, what the hell, and take off. I can play catch-up tomorrow. So can you. Look at it out there! It won't be like that after today. We've got rain the rest of the week. And Genes?"

"Yeah?"

"I want to have a good time. I know I've been hard to be with lately. This whole thing about children. It's been wearing on us. I want to forget everything but us for a change. We deserve it."

Branches moved outside the window. Fast air rattled the new leaves, as strong sun brought out the details of the day.

"Come on. Just look. That's what you're writing about, isn't it?

How fucking gorgeous it is here. How *this* is the kind of place where you take off on an impulse and go sailing."

Distant across the marsh, I could just make out the ocean, tiny white caps marking the surface.

"It's rough out there, Ben." I was already saving my article, preparing to shut it down. I was sunk the minute he had the idea. "I hate it when you do this to me."

"Do what?"

He walked to his dresser, dropped the towel, and rooted in the drawer for some boxers. His lean frame was a kinetic wonder. Every movement he made suggested a force against time and space, and nothing he did ever seemed passive.

"You're a bad influence," I said, getting up and putting my arms up around his neck. I locked my fingers as if to steady his motion. For small moments I could hold him still. "If I'm late and they cancel the article, it's your fault," I told him. Drops of water from his hair fell light on my hands.

"You're too damn talented for that," he said. I felt his breath on my hair, his hands slipping inside my robe. "They need you, and so do I. The difference is, they can wait." His voice registered low as he said this, and I imagined he had more on the agenda at anchor than just grilling dinner.

"Okay. Get dressed." I pulled away gently. "If you can put some ice in the cooler, I'll change clothes and pull together the food."

He watched me walk away from him, stared without a hint of apology as I dressed, then went to get the ice.

As I rummaged through the fridge to gather what might be a meal, I thought of his eyes on me. Wondered, not for the first time, why he loved me. I knew my strengths. I was pretty, I was smart. But I wasn't extraordinary, not in my own assessment, at least. I wondered if I would always feel a light step behind him. He gave so much, but asked for even more.

"Ready, Genes?" he called out from the garage.

"Coming!" I shouted back. And for a brief second before the feeling passed, I'd felt as if I might cry.

Reese brought back ice-cream sandwiches from the Ship's Store. Her hair, brown but a shade darker than mine, was still drenched from the shower. It hung loose and curly, left wet stains on the shoulders of her T-shirt. Even in ordinary clothes she looked foreign to me.

"The kid working at the store gave me these when I went in to buy toothpaste on my way back." She bent over slightly to put her toiletries away and I saw a small tattoo, a tiny blue flower, at the small of her back. It almost looked like a bruise.

"Oh, Charlie. He's a flirt," I said. "He's some relation to Derek, the security guy who's been working nights for about six months now." I tried to make my reference to Derek sound casual. "Best I can tell, our friend Charlie's looking at a world of hurt when he gets caught sleeping with somebody's wife."

"Well," Reese said, "you're nobody's wife. Why don't you go for it? They're both cute as can be."

I thought of Derek, with me in the very space where I stood talking to Reese. I looked away from her as the hot rush took over my cheeks.

"Jesus, Gina. I'm sorry," she said. I tried to recall exactly what she'd done. "I wasn't thinking. That was such a fucking stupid thing to say. I honestly didn't mean it like that."

She thought I was offended by the wife remark. The *widow card* was often a get-out-of-jail-free ticket. I almost wanted to laugh, she looked so horrified.

"It's okay," I told her. "I don't care. I'm tired of people editing everything they say around me. And you're right about Derek and Charlie. They're adorable. And they're among the few people who don't treat me like I died too."

"That's because they're babies. Mortality's still a nasty rumor at their age."

It was okay, sometimes, to have Reese around. As bizarre as it seemed, there were odd moments when she felt like family.

"You mind picking up where we left off? You know, talking about Angel and . . . and Benjamin." I said it fast, as soon as it occurred to me, to keep from losing the nerve. Like diving into cold water.

"I don't have much more to tell you," she said. "I'll try to answer whatever I can."

She put down her brush, then stopped for a second to steady herself on the edge of the counter, as if she'd lost her balance. But the night was calm, no motion from the waves.

"You okay?" I asked.

"I'm fine," she said. "Being on a boat takes a little getting used to."

"Do you sail?" I asked, careful to keep my tone light. "Did Ben ever teach you?"

"Wouldn't try it by myself on a bet," she answered. Settling down opposite me, she began to take the wrapper off her ice-cream sandwich. "He dragged me out a lot when I first knew him, in a smaller boat he had when we were in college. I just barely put up with it by the time we were married, even after he bought this thing." She stopped. *Married.* Neither of us was married anymore, and I couldn't think of anything to fill the awkward void, so I stared down at my drink.

"Anyway," she said finally. "You had some questions. Ask away."

I did ask, point-blank again. About Benjamin. About Angel. By the time she got a couple of sentences into her story, I decided that second cognac sounded like a good idea after all. Her breakup with Benjamin, the length of time it took for it to "take," became the central factor in the saga. He had told me she left him, as if that was the end of it. She told me so much more.

"The first time I left, he found me in Myrtle Beach," she said. "He tracked down my credit cards. It took him two weeks. He deserved a better explanation than I gave him at the time. I felt bad about that part. But I didn't plan on how much it would hurt him. He always seemed . . . I don't know . . ."

"Beyond vulnerability." I finished her thought.

"Yeah," she said. "I mean, I knew he loved me. Don't get me wrong. He wasn't cold. Just the opposite. But he was so fucking confident—about everything. You know?"

"You're preaching to the choir," I told her, surprised at how good it felt to hear someone else's insecurities when it came to my husband.

"If this is wrong for me to be saying . . ." She kept her eyes level with mine. She never looked away, never apologized for her story. "Just tell me to stop. You asked, so . . ."

"I want to know." I left it at that.

Seems Benjamin had convinced her to come home that time. The time after that, he found her in Charlotte, and the time after that outside of D.C.—living with someone else.

"You just kept using your credit cards?" Either she was stupid, which I doubted, or she wanted to be found.

"In Charlotte, yeah. By D.C., I'd pulled together some cash, but then I ran into friends. Somebody told him. But it didn't matter; I knew he'd show up again. I was beginning to realize I needed to push some new buttons if I was going to make him understand."

"Understand what?"

She let the question sit stagnant between us.

"Why didn't you just refuse to go home with him?" I tried again.

She raised one eyebrow. "You lived with him, Gina. You loved him. How many times *didn't* he get his way when his mind was made up?"

"Once," I told her, leaving it at that. "But I still don't understand. If you loved him, why . . . ?"

"That's the part you don't ask me about." Her voice changed, hardened. She wasn't kidding. "That's my story. It's not one I want to tell. Not now."

"Okay," I said, feeling reprimanded somehow.

"Anyway, D.C. is where it gets confusing, I mean about who Angel's father is. Benjamin found me again—staying with James, a guy I knew from State," she said. "I thought he'd just leave when he saw everything. But he didn't. James left instead. Benjamin acted calm, as if I'd, I don't know . . . misbehaved. He talked me into going back home with him. It was a kind of panic that set in, when I realized he wouldn't give up. It was kind of scary, Gina. How determined he was."

I thought of him, of our brewing conflict over children that had never been resolved.

"But you did go back?" I pushed everything else out of my mind. "Part of you must have wanted to."

"I loved him. No matter what all this sounds like. But I had my reasons for going. He had to . . . *control* everything. I . . . I really don't want to talk about it."

I almost understood. Not *how* she chose to leave, but why. Ben could be overwhelming. He didn't mean to be so dominant, but sometimes his energy seemed to consume everything in proximity to him.

"I'm sorry," I said. "But I'm trying hard to understand all this, Reese. It doesn't make a whole lot of sense. But I'll lay off. How did you finally get him to accept it—that it was over?"

She finished her ice cream, threw the wrapper in the trash.

"I went too far." She stopped, left it at that.

Georgie nudged in the trash after the wrapper and I pulled her away.

"Come on, Reese," I said finally, irritated with the dramatic pauses. "Just tell me what the hell happened. It can't be any worse than . . ."

She looked over at me, her eyes straight on mine. I saw that she wasn't pulling an act. The pain in her expression made me stop.

"I went out when he was working late one night," she said. "I went to a local bar."

"And?" I could barely get air in my lungs.

"I left with someone, some tourist in town with a bunch of buddies. Young guys, like Derek and Charlie." She looked so tired, the words held no momentum. "I almost invited a couple of the buddies, just for good measure, but then I figured not even I was that hateful."

"So this guy?" I wasn't sure I wanted to know. "Benjamin found out?"

She nodded; her eyes looked beyond me.

"I brought the guy home with me. I told him my husband was out of town, that he could stay the night. Benjamin found us in bed, in our bed, when he came home from work."

"Didn't you know . . ." My mind still tried to make it a mistake, a miscalculation on her part. But it was no accident that Benjamin found them. The truth was, it made perfect sense.

"Benjamin looked . . . he looked like I'd never seen him look before. Destroyed. I destroyed him that night." Her voice was breaking. I didn't look at her, didn't want to start crying over her fucking mistakes. He was my husband too.

"I felt so terrible." Her words ran close together, almost slurred, as if they were too hard, too much effort to say. "It's what I'd intended to do. He knew it was on purpose. He wasn't loud, or angry. His face was so flat, had no expression at all."

I couldn't imagine Ben like that. Stunned and defeated. He had more life in his eyebrows than most people have in their entire body. When she described how he'd reacted, only one image came to my mind. Benjamin laid out in his casket. It was the first time I'd ever seen him still. Maybe that was the second time in his life that he'd died.

"He said he should have taken me at my word when I left the first time, or the second, the third . . ." She went on with her story. "He hadn't believed it was how I really felt."

"How did you feel?" I asked.

She bowed her head slightly, then raised her eyes to meet mine, but didn't answer. I knew better than to push for more. I wanted to hold Benjamin, comfort him. The impotence of the moment overwhelmed me.

"What happened after that?" I forced myself to stay with the facts, to keep moving forward.

"He helped me pack my stuff, gave me some money, and told me to call if I was in trouble, if I needed anything. Than he kissed me good-bye."

I saw them. In the driveway of their house, the same house I'd sold two months before. I saw him kiss her, then stand in the empty yard after she was gone.

"And you were pregnant?" I asked.

"I found out a couple of weeks later," she said. She leaned her head back against the cushion, tucked her legs up underneath her on the seat. The confession had drained her.

"How could you have done that?" I barely managed a whisper.

"Don't judge me." She didn't look at me. Her tone stayed solid, not defensive. She didn't need my approval. "You don't know me or my reasons."

I rubbed Georgie's head, gave her the comfort that I wanted to offer Ben, but never would. Benjamin had never hinted at the story she told me, had never said a single negative thing about her. He simply called her a "wild child" and left it at that.

"Ben would have wanted to know," I said. "About the baby." I needed to speak for him, but against all reason, I felt sorry for her. "There were tests you could have done. And even if there was just a chance she was his, he would have—"

"That's why I didn't tell him." She spoke, but her eyes were closed. She said the words as if they explained everything.

"That's not good enough. You can't think that's right."

"I'm not trying to make a case with you." She looked up. "I'm just trying to answer your goddamn questions. You asked for the truth. This is the closest thing I have to the truth." She was unapologetic, her composure unnerving. "By the time I had Angel, no one was in the picture, not even Benjamin."

"You talked to Benjamin half a dozen times, at least, after I knew him. You'd call, out of the blue, to just 'talk.' How could you do that? How could you talk with him and not tell him?"

She pulled her legs around to the floor and sat up, put her heels down with a percussive emphasis, then stretched her arms, as if the tension had become too great in her muscles, her limbs.

"I had a life with Angel," she said finally. For the first time, she began to sound irritated, as if explaining something simple to a stubborn child. "It wasn't a conventional life, but we were happy. You know what Benjamin would have done. If you don't see it, you're blind, because I sure as hell knew."

Benjamin would have taken action. He would have taken Angel.

"A custody fight," I said.

She nodded, never took her eyes away from me. "And he would have succeeded. I'm not stupid. I know how people see my life. My choices. And there were other things too. There's no way they would have let me keep her."

The rest of it, we didn't say. That, like it or not, if Reese had acted differently, Angel would have been in my home; would have been my stepdaughter. Even as I thought it, I knew the real truth that lay behind everything. *I wouldn't have married him if he'd had a young daughter.* The thought was too hard to keep in my head, made me feel weak, queasy.

"I couldn't lose her," Reese went on. "I couldn't allow her to lose me. So I kept it simple. I didn't tell him. I didn't tell any of them. For all practical reasons, it didn't matter who her father really was. Angel was my child, and no one else's."

I couldn't argue anymore. It wasn't my argument to make anyway, and it ran up on hypocritical ground regardless of where I stood with it. I let it go. I had to let it go.

"And you came back now because you changed your mind?" It wasn't really a question. More of an accusation. Any camaraderie we'd ever shared had faded and I wanted to lay blame. More than anything, I wanted to finish the conversation, to go to sleep.

"It doesn't matter now why I came back." She stopped at that, made no attempt to go into it again.

The air conditioner sounded its steady hum. I was grateful for the comfort, but felt disconnected somehow from life outside, isolated in a bubble of time with my dead husband's ex-wife. Like extreme, couple's therapy, people locked in a room until they resolve their issues.

"Reese, I'm part of this, if only by circumstance." I made one last effort. "You've eventually got to tell me what you wanted from Ben . . ."

"He's gone." The harsh tone said more than her words. "Those are the only circumstances that matter. What I need is some sleep." She stood up, but there was nowhere to go really. I could have pushed deeper into it, but I felt as tired as she sounded, and my heart wasn't in it anyway.

"We have to talk about this sometime. About why you're here. What you want." I felt only relief at bringing the conversation to a close. "But you're right, we're both tired tonight."

"I'm here with you tonight because you offered me a bed. Beyond that, it's not your problem. *We're* not your problem."

But I sensed she was wrong. Whether I liked it or not, my days would be tangled with Reese and Angel.

"I made up the quarter berth for you," I said. "There's a light under there if you want to read."

She sat, unmoving. "I won't keep my eyes open that long," she said. A weak smile was all she could offer.

I put all the glasses in the sink, decided to let them sit until morning. As I headed toward the V-berth for the night, one question still lingered. A curiosity more than anything. "Does Angel look like any of them?" I asked. "I can't really see Benjamin in her, but—"

"No," she interrupted me, shook her head. "Only me." She stood up, gathered her purse to head back to her quarters. Before she went in, she turned slightly toward me. "But, for my own peace of mind, I always thought of her as Benjamin's. I hope you don't mind me saying that."

My emotions were too jumbled to sort out how I felt; so I just shrugged, didn't respond.

Later, much later, as I was trying, and failing, to sleep, I found myself angry with her. I hadn't felt the full complement of anger while she was saying all of it, telling me how she treated Benjamin; but afterward, I found it there, and I was surprised the feelings took so long to surface. How could she have done all those things? Nothing could have justified it, none of her mysterious reasons. But something kept me from full-blown hate, some quality in her that I couldn't define. Some quality in her evoked patience, sympathy. Ben had felt it. He had never come to hate her, I was sure of that, even after all she did.

In the night, I dreamed of our house, the house all three of us had shared at one time or another. It was evening and I looked on from outside, deep in the yard, and I saw a girl on the front step. I was half aware that the scene was a dream, knew on some level that my bed and my life were far removed. But the house, the girl—Angel, I guessed—seemed so close to me.

I stepped forward in my yard. Lights came bright from the windows. The girl turned toward me and, when she did, I woke up, eyes wide, my heart beating fast as my head pressed back against the pillow. Elise, not Angel, had been the child in the dream, the girl standing on the stoop of my house. Fully awake, I felt my own weight, where seconds before I'd had none. Thin dampness rode up my neck and across my scalp.

Lying in bed, the image in the dream stayed with me. I could see Elise, her expression pleading, her face clear as she turned toward where I stood in the yard.

As I calmed, I allowed myself to embrace the vision, could picture it all clearly. My little sister, young still, as always, asking for what I couldn't give. The house where I'd lived with my husband framed her small body. A glow had burned bright in the windows behind her, but I couldn't discern the source. I couldn't tell if the lights were from lamps, offering some level of welcome; or if they were something stronger, something dangerous. A fire burning out of control.

Reese was still in her berth, had been all morning. I slept poorly and woke up early, so I envied her rest. I poured myself another cup of coffee, careful not to clink the cup too loudly.

"Hey, Georgie. Want some food?" I scooped from a Tupperware bowl inside the sliding door cabinet behind the stove. Georgie's food took up more space than mine in my limited kitchen storage. Then again, she ate at home more than I did.

"Here you go," I said, putting her bowl on the floor.

I'd been up since seven, made coffee, walked the dog. I had no plans for the day, realized I was waiting, looking to my houseguest for inspiration. She seemed to do the one thing I'd been unable to do since Benjamin died. Make something happen. I'd lived out my days in a dream state. Reese had been the wake-up call of all time.

I picked up my cell phone—the only phone I'd had since I moved onto the boat—decided it was time to check in with the world. In the three days since Reese and Angel had shown up, I hadn't turned my cell phone on. After the shooting, it had begun to ring and ring. The papers had my number from the freelance files, and reporters took advantage of the access to bug the hell out of me for information and quotes. So I turned it off. The police would show up at the dock if they needed me for any more questions. They were persistent little buggers, if nothing else. The reporters could go to hell.

I hadn't even checked my voice mail in all that time. That kind of neglect would have seen me starving if I was counting on a real income from writing. But I had money. Money from the house, money from Ben's policies—and I had a check that could buy me the world, with more to come in the months ahead. But all that money couldn't buy me real answers with Reese; it couldn't bring Ben back. Wealthy or not, no one could call me fortunate.

Out of more than a dozen messages on my voice mail, most were from reporters, one was from the pastor at Mt. Sinai, one was from Ben's mother, and three were from the features editor at the local paper. At first I thought even he was pressing me for quotes on the shooting, but in fact he called about an article I'd promised him for the *Sunday Living* section. He was asking if, after everything that had happened, he could still count on a story from me about the culture of food inside the rural Southern church. Homecoming Sunday had been set at Mt. Sinai, but I couldn't remember the exact date. I'd planned to build the story around that event. Geez, I'd forgotten about the article, hoped I hadn't missed it altogether. I looked up the number for the church and dialed.

Ben and I had never been big on religion, but part of me wished we'd shared the place together. I wondered if Maxine had ever taken him there. I thought of the sanctuary. The candle smells, the oiled pews held distant familiarity, although the service was different in every way from the liturgical lullabies I'd suffered at my parents' church in Virginia.

"Hello." I recognized Martha Mincey's voice. "Mt. Sinai."

"Hi, Martha," I said. "It's Gina Melrose."

"Oh, Gina." The words, a near whisper. "How are you, hon?" Pity? Concern? Probably a little of both. She'd read the paper. Everybody had read the paper.

"I'm fine. I really am. The girl has her arm in a sling, but everything's going to be okay."

Martha was in her fifties and divorced. Plump and eager, her natural instincts were that of a mother always ready to make the world right.

"It sounded so awful, what you went through. Preacher Hanes left you a message and we held a prayer vigil for you the day after it happened."

"I appreciate that, Martha," I said, forcing enthusiasm into the words. Truth was, the *prayer vigil* thing freaked me out a little bit. "Like I said, everything turned out okay. The little girl is fine. I'm fine."

"Oh, I'm so glad." She *was* glad. That remained the amazing part. The whole church was like that. They could make themselves *care* about people they hardly knew.

"Listen, Martha." I moved on quickly to the topic at hand. "I need to find out something. Have I missed Homecoming?"

"No, sweetie. It's this weekend."

"That's great. That'll be perfect," I said. "Remember that story I told you about? The one the paper wanted on food and churches?"

"I do remember, now that you mention it." She sounded like Martha again, perky and ready to help.

"Well, my editor needs the story from me next week. Did the preacher say it was okay?"

"Oh sure, hon. The more people who know about our little congregation here, the better. Just come on Sunday and bring that photographer you mentioned and we'll do the rest."

"Thanks, Martha."

I hung up the phone, heard a clamor outside in the cockpit that rattled the boat. Georgie growled, but didn't bother mounting a full-scale bark. I made note again of the bullet-sized hole in the companionway canvas. A constant reminder of how life had gone askew. After a second, Angel pulled back the canvas and stuck her head in. Her face appeared but her body remained hidden by the blue cloth, giving the appearance of a floating, disembodied Oz.

"Lane's making eggs and country ham," she announced. "She says y'all come on over for breakfast."

"What're you doing?" Reese cracked open the door that separated her sleeping quarters from the main cabin. She leaned around to look at Angel, eyes blinking against the sun that came streaming into the cabin.

"Breakfast," Angel said again. "At Lane's house. Eggs, ham, grits . . . All the stuff you like."

Then Angel disappeared. I heard her turn on her heel, sneakers squeaking against the fiberglass deck.

"Eggs," Reese said, making her way back into the main cabin. "Now that's what I had in mind after a bout of late-night drinking."

"Are you hung over?" I asked.

"Aren't you? You had me two-to-one on the cognac."

I shrugged it off, shook my head; tried to remember how many times I refilled my glass.

"Where's the bathroom again?" she asked.

"The boat's not that big, Reese. The head's over near my berth."

"The *head*, right." She pointed herself in the right direction. "Benjamin used to make me use that nautical language crap. I hated it then too."

Lane's story about Angel and her trip to the island rang in my thoughts. Reese hadn't been the one to take the girl to the island. She'd said the night before that she didn't sail, didn't even like it. In truth, the woman could barely make it from one end of the cabin to the other without losing her balance. Maybe Lane was right, Angel had known about the place somehow, decided to play make-believe. I should have just asked her about it, but there were too many issues on the table as it was. As hard as it was to accept, Ben had probably taken Reese to the island too. Angel could have heard stories from her mother.

"Where's my towel?" Reese asked, finally locating it deep in her berth.

She shuffled off toward the front of the cabin, disappeared inside the coffin-sized bathroom that rivaled the facilities on a commercial airplane. I was still hearing the bump-and-swear routine of Reese's morning washup as I left to go across the lawn to Lane's.

9

∞

Reese

Camping on Benjamin's old boat with his wife wasn't going to last. Reese sat back on the toilet so that she could manage to open the door and get out of the bathroom—no, the fucking *head,* she corrected herself. Space on the boat was tight to begin with, and when you crammed in all of the questions Gina had, there was no room left to breathe. She had to make a new plan. How the hell could she make this come out all right without Benjamin?

She looked around for her sandals and, when she lost patience with the search, found a pair of Gina's flip-flops and headed out for Lane's house.

She left the dog on the boat, and the air-conditioning on, which she hoped was okay. If not, Gina could drag her ass back and put everything in order the way she wanted it.

"Come on in," Lane said.

The outside of Lane's house looked like a dwelling out of a children's book. Flower beds and a slate stone walkway leading to a porch with a mango-colored glider and matching chairs. The dwarves from Snow White couldn't have managed a more charming existence. Though small by house standards, it was a mansion compared to the boat—and the neatness alone made it seem palatial. The nicest part was that it looked like a home. A mat at the front door, a real lamp on the table in the corner.

"How long have you lived here?" Reese asked as she settled on the couch with a cup of coffee. Gina stood at the counter in the kitchen, looking busy. Angel was nowhere to be seen.

"Harlan and I owned it for years. We'd come out on weekends. He kept a boat a little smaller than Gina's, but I sold that. After he died, my son and his wife moved into our house in Sumter and I moved out here. We'd always planned to retire here anyway."

"It's nice," Reese said. Nice summed up the entire feel of the place. Something about it made tears come to her eyes. She couldn't imagine what brought on such a reaction. It certainly wasn't from recollecting any prior domestic experiences of her own. After her mother left, her father barely managed anything resembling a home. He worked, went to endless church meetings, and came home when he had nowhere else to go. The idea that he was a deacon, a church elder, meant far more to him than the notion that he was a father.

"You want some juice, hon, or you can join Gina with a Bloody Mary?" Lane called over to her after joining Gina in the kitchen.

"I'm fine with coffee for now," she said, sitting down on the couch. "Can I help with anything?"

"Just stay put," Lane said. "We're almost ready to eat."

The small dinette table took up one corner of the kitchen. It looked like something in a cheery family-style restaurant, a bright red top with matching diner chairs around four sides. Lane had arranged a country breakfast. Food was laid out along a yellow-patterned runner, with place settings on either side. Plates of biscuits, grits, potatoes, and ham ran the length of the table. Everything but the eggs, and Lane moved to the stove to finish those.

"How do you like your eggs?" Lane asked.

"Cooked." The notion of eggs suddenly seemed like heaven to Reese in spite of her tender stomach. "I like them any way they're served."

The coffee tasted fresh. Reese felt overwhelmed at being cared for, pampered. It occurred to her that Angel had no notion of this kind of life. Until now, anyway. No wonder the child adored Lane. Compared to their vagabond existence, this had to be a kid's dream. As if to illustrate her thoughts, Angel came into the room from the back of the house.

"Doesn't this look great?" she said, eyes eager, watching Reese.

Reese felt compelled to respond with appropriate enthusiasm. This was important to Angel, and Reese understood the urgency to embrace Lane, to let Angel know it was okay to love her. Otherwise, the girl might feel that her mother was jealous. Was she? Reese wondered. The last time—the only time—she'd begun to seriously share Angel's affections, she'd taken the girl and run away. For Angel's sake, for Benjamin's sake, she regretted that now.

"It looks fantastic!" she said, with enough exaggeration in her tone to make herself wince. No one else seemed to notice. Angel didn't notice, and she usually tuned in to every false note her mother played.

"It's ready," Lane announced, and Reese steered Angel toward the kitchen table, where Gina already sat with the Bloody Mary in her hand.

"Hair of the dog?" Reese asked.

"I'm not the one feeling hung over," Gina answered. She wasn't smiling.

The glare between them, a virtual standoff, was interrupted by Lane's arrival at the table with an oversized pan. Reese knew she had to make more of an effort with Gina, but they got to each other, and it was hard to get past the knee-jerk responses.

"This is hot," Lane said, holding the heavy skillet a safe distance from her body. She waited as everyone settled into their seats. "Don't let me brush against you while I'm doing this." She leaned over, portioned the steaming eggs onto each plate.

Gina sat closest to the window, across the table from the child. She didn't seem to know what to do with Angel, kept her distance, kept quiet. Reese knew she should have expected as much after the little bit Ben told her about Gina's views on children. Then, once you took into account the way she and Angel had arrived . . . But Reese wanted it to be different. She wanted everything to fall into place. Suddenly, more than ever, all her questions about Gina were critical to the situation, and she didn't know any of the answers.

"I didn't realize I was so hungry," Gina said, digging into her eggs. "My appetite's been spotty for months now. This tastes really good."

Angel helped herself to more grits. Her bum arm didn't slow down her efforts in the least.

"I'm glad," Lane said. "We all deserve a break from the last few days. That's what I think anyway."

The mood eased as the food disappeared. The air in the house stayed warm, even with the AC on high. Too many bodies with the addition of a hot stove made the space toasty. Despite all that, everything felt right, Reese realized. She reasoned it to be brief; but still, allowed for some small measure of hope for the first time since her arrival.

Even Gina seemed more relaxed. She cupped her hands around

a mug of coffee, indulged in an easy smile, an occurrence that Reese had deemed rare. It seemed to be either laughter or tears with Ben's strange wife—like Billy Joel said, sadness or euphoria—and little in between.

"I'm doing a story on food in churches," Gina was telling Lane.

"What do you mean?" Lane asked. "Food pantries, like for the homeless?"

"No, not that." Gina sipped her coffee. "For the lifestyle section. The culture of food in rural churches, the covered-dish supper kind of thing. The role food plays in pulling religious communities together. I'm going over to the Homecoming at Mt. Sinai this weekend. Want to come?"

Her question seemed to be directed at the table in general, and Reese piped in just in case.

"Don't look at me," she said. "I haven't been to church since my crazy father made me march down the aisle in front of some TV preacher so I could be 'healed' when I was fourteen."

The room went silent, even Angel looked stunned, and Reese found herself at the blunt end of the conversation—again.

"What was wrong with you?" Gina asked finally.

"Best I could tell, he thought an interest in boys was a disease." She tried to sound light. "I suppose it all fell under the general umbrella of 'the sickness of sin.' I really don't know what he was thinking."

She managed to laugh as she talked about it, but regretted bringing it up. Why had she? The televised revival. The dynamic preacher with his big paws flat against her head. How his robe smelled like detergent and cigarettes. She left out the part about how oddly compelling he was. How he'd evoked strange tugs of mind and muscle that drew her in, but at the same time made her want to run from the place, find some air. And she did run before the night was out. It seemed she'd been running ever since.

"You should have seen it," she said, forcing a casual tone. A simple anecdote. Why had she begun this story? It was too late to go back, so she went on with it. "The people who go to those things are bizarre."

She used funny voices as she described the "healing" chants, the followers laid out like beached whales all along the altar. But she didn't tell them everything that had happened. She didn't tell them

that, in spite of her revulsion and her fear, she had felt something—
something strange and outside herself. Instead, she acted as if she'd
been amused all along by the preacher's gibberish words.

She especially didn't tell them about the rest of it. The most
frightening parts that she had never told anyone. Or about the following Monday at school, the day after the show aired, when she was
just about the only one not amused by everything that happened.
She didn't share with them how on that day, she'd been the only one
not laughing.

Gina maintained a weak smile, but Lane looked troubled. "God,
how awful!" she said.

You don't know the half of it, Reese thought.

Angel just stared, eyes wide, with no expression defining her
face. Reese realized she had broken her own rule. She'd opened up,
if only a little, let down her guard when she hadn't intended to.
Maybe that surprised Angel more than the story itself. She'd have to
be more careful.

"So anyway," Reese finished. "Count me out of your research for
this assignment. I don't do churches." Then she added. "Mt. Sinai.
Isn't that the little church you pass on the way to Ben's old family cottage on Sullivan's Island?"

She took a biscuit, tried to look unbothered by the turn the conversation had taken toward religion. Not her best topic.

"That's the one," Gina told her. "Ben's buried out there, and
that's where we had the funeral. Since we didn't have a church of our
own, and I wanted him to be close by, Maxine said she'd like to have
him there, near the cottage."

"Is she still hanging on to that place?" The small house was on the
water. Reese remembered going there a few times with Ben. In particular, one unpleasant weekend with Maxine, Ben's mother, in tow.

"Yeah," Gina said, picking up another piece of bacon. "She rents
it out in season. The realty company manages the maintenance, so
it's not much trouble for her. Besides, as an investment, it's better
than the market right now. Land value is on the upswing. She's able
to rent it through the summer. Sometimes into the fall."

"Do you ever go out there?" Reese asked.

"I haven't been there in a while," Gina said. "We had Thanks-
giving there the first year Ben and I were married, went back a few
times after that, but . . ." She stopped.

Reese wondered what memories the cottage evoked for Gina. She thought of all Gina's memories with Ben, wondered if they were as cluttered and conflicted as her own. She doubted it. Funny, until she met Ben's new wife, she'd somehow seen him frozen in time, the same person she'd left standing in the yard the night she left. Even knowing about Gina, Ben's life beyond her leaving had never truly existed for her until the last couple of days. Less than forty-eight hours had brought so many things into bright relief.

"Anyway," Gina said, after no one jumped in to change the topic. "I think she keeps it for sentimental reasons more than anything else. They went there a lot when Ben was little. So, about Homecoming. Anybody want to tag along with me? How 'bout you, Lane?"

"I would," Lane said, pouring herself another cup of coffee. "But I'm on Altar Guild this Sunday, so I have to show up at my own church or there'll be no proper communion."

Lane stood up and began clearing plates. Reese was disappointed the meal had to end.

"I'll go." Angel spoke for the first time since Reese's holy-roller confessional.

"I'm sorry?" Gina was clearly at a loss.

"I want to go to church with you." Angel seemed clear on her intention to tag along.

Reese wondered what she should do. Should she say no? The last thing she wanted was for Angel to get spooked by some speaking-in-tongues crowd the way she was as a kid. On the other hand, Gina hadn't warmed up that much to Angel. An outing together might soften things up a little between them, which wouldn't be a bad thing.

"I think that would be a lovely thing for the two of you to do together." Lane spoke before Reese had a chance.

Reese weighed the situation again in her mind, allowed herself to trust the older woman's instincts when it came to Angel. *And* her instincts when it came to Gina, for that matter.

"It's fine with me, I guess," Reese said.

Gina looked cornered. She could have put a stop to it, but it would have been awkward, almost insulting. It seemed to Reese that the decision had been made.

"Okay," Gina said finally, looking anything but okay. "But it probably won't be the most interesting outing for a child. I mean, I'm going to be nosing around, getting quotes for the story. I won't be a lot of company for you."

"That's all right," Angel said, her voice sure and easy. "I'll stay out of your way."

The way she said it, the adult tone she took, made Reese smile. Angel had a way of taking adults back to square one.

"Well, I've got to make sure I've got a photographer lined up before I do anything else," Gina said, standing up. "You need help cleaning up?"

"Go," Reese told her, before Lane could answer. "Get your Sunday come-to-meetin' shindig all lined up. Angel and I will pitch in on kitchen duty. Right, kid?"

Angel nodded, but she seemed subdued, worlds different from the child who had announced the meal only an hour before. Reese felt the panic begin to rise. Fear could paralyze her if she let it. That wouldn't do Angel any good at all. But life was changing fast, and Angel had noticed. The world they had come from, the only world Angel had known, wouldn't be intact for much longer.

Gina mumbled her thanks to Lane and made her way out.

"Come on, sweetie," Reese said, standing. Her leg was numb from sitting at the cramped table. She stretched it out, tried to shake off her unease. She couldn't let her guard down until she knew what to do. She reached for the empty bacon platter, hoped to God her hands would cooperate. "Let's pitch in here, okay?"

"Okay." Angel began to gather the dishes. She took it as an earnest task, her brow creased with good intentions. The sight of her daughter trying so hard was enough to break Reese's heart.

10

∞

Gina

I sent Angel inside the church. She wanted to hear the songs. Jake, the photographer, had been late meeting us at the marina, so the service was well under way when we got to Mt. Sinai. I stayed outside to help decide the shots he would need, but Angel wanted to go in. I'd agreed to take the child for Lane's sake, little more; but if I'd imagined the outing to be a sharing experience for the two of us, I would have been disappointed. Best I could tell, she just wanted to go to church.

I looked up at the small bluff where the graveyard sat. The temperature had dipped to under 90 degrees, making the day almost pleasant outside. From the distance, I couldn't make out the new ground of Ben's grave any longer. Grass had grown over it, and I hadn't gotten around to choosing a headstone for him. I hadn't been back in a couple of weeks.

Just after the funeral, I'd come every day, but the ritual, the one-sided conversations with Benjamin, started to wear on me. The cemetery stood above the small brick church, as if the dead were charged with steady watch over all they left behind.

"Ground's more solid up there for the bodies." The woman's voice startled me.

I turned to see a plump matron in a green shirtwaist dress. The starched cotton collar at her neck stood up admirably to the midday humidity. I thought I knew all of the women at Mt. Sinai, at least by face if not by name. The entire membership barely reached two hundred, and that included the nursing home shut-ins who remained on the roster. But I hadn't seen this woman before.

"Solid ground?" I wasn't sure what the proper response would be to such a statement.

"For the bodies," she repeated. "That's why the cemetery is up high, so far away from the church." As she talked, she spread a large cloth over one of several picnic tables behind the building. It was the last one to be covered, the white cloths lending an altarlike quality to the plank-and-nail constructions.

"The ground is soft down here this close to the water level," she explained. "We go to higher ground for the cemetery."

"What do you mean?" I wasn't sure I wanted to know.

"This close to the water, the ground stays saturated; tides shift it here and there. That's why the church is raised."

There were shrubs and a fence to disguise it, but I'd noticed before that the foundation of the church consisted of raised blocks.

"We want to make sure those caskets stay where we put 'em." She smiled, as if the mischievous dead bodies might misbehave given the slightest opportunity. I imagined Benjamin and all of his new, otherworldly companions, making a swim for the shore as the water rose.

"I'm Rena," the woman said, having completed her task. She extended her hand to me.

"I'm Gina," I said. "We rhyme." She didn't get my humor, so I thought it best not to mention my imaginings about my newly buried husband. "I've only been coming a couple of months, but I don't think I've met you."

"No," she said, getting busy with the organization of plastic utensils on the table closest to the church building. "I've been staying with my daughter this summer. She had a baby in June. I'm just back this Sunday. Very nice to meet you . . . Gina, was it? How come you aren't inside, dear?"

"I'm here on business today," I said, watching her lay out silver serving spoons for people to put with their dishes as they'd set them down. "I freelance for the Charleston paper and I'm doing a story on food and churches."

"Well," she said in a newly affected tone, "you came to the right place."

The music inside the church gathered volume as the voices picked up on the final hymn. Outside with us, Myra, a thin woman in a blue suit, stood at a smaller square table off to the side. She held a rhythmic course, scooping ice from a cooler and pouring it into plastic cups. The crunch of the ice provided a percussive quality to the lumbering hymn.

Two other women—Martha, who worked in the office, and Jane,

a younger girl—were putting salt shakers and various condiments at the ends of each table.

"So you all don't get to hear the sermon on Homecoming?" I asked Rena as she unfolded metal chairs in a row off to the side.

"We slipped out during the offertory." She smiled, as if the clandestine exit had thrilled her. "So we caught most of the service. He outdid himself today, I'll tell you."

I considered asking if she skipped out on her offering as well, but decided that my humor might once again escape her.

"I would help you," I told her instead. It felt awkward, watching her work. "But Jake's taking pictures of the setup and I don't want to be in them."

"Oh, we're used to this, hon," she said, still opening chairs. "It doesn't take any time at all. Are we going to be in the paper?"

"He takes a lot of shots, so it's hard to say." She looked disappointed enough for me to add, "But there's a good chance you will be."

The photographer, an older guy who'd taken pictures for the paper almost longer than I'd been alive, moved at odd angles around the women. He looked over at me, gestured for me to offer up any ideas. I shrugged and shook my head. Later I'd ask him to get a long shot of the trail and the cemetery overhead.

Minutes after the service, the efficiency with which food came out of the cars and onto the tables amazed me. Coolers full of deviled eggs, cheese straws, Jell-O molds, pork roasts, oyster casserole, and fried chicken . . . not to mention all manner of local berries baked into pies and cakes that looked like bakery displays. The tremendous spread finally got the best of Jake, and he put his camera aside and filled up a plate. I was right behind him.

I glanced around for Angel, saw her sitting off to the side, balancing a plate on her knees while she searched for a level spot to set her iced tea. I watched her struggle to accomplish this with her bum arm interfering at every turn. As I started toward her to help, two ladies came her way and immediately adopted her, so I decided to concentrate on getting notes for my story.

"My mother got that recipe from the governor's housekeeper in 1932," Miss Ronnie Meeks, an older lady in the parish, explained as I juggled my own paper plate on my knees while trying to jot down notes on a pad. Even with *two* working arms, I found it difficult.

The flower attached to Miss Ronnie's Sunday hat hung by barely a thread, so the flower itself bopped around with her animated gesturing.

"It was the governor's favorite," she told me.

The recipe involved was the oyster casserole, and, having just taken a bite, I decided that the governorship had its perks.

"My mother was hired to hang drapes at the governor's residence, and she smelled the casserole cooking one day. She offered to pay the old housekeeper if she would raid the cook's recipe box for the ingredients. That old woman said no, but Mama happened to mention that my daddy made homemade spirits in his spare time. The housekeeper was happy to trade the recipe for a bottle of moonshine. My mother drove back that afternoon and made the trade. The housekeeper declared homemade liquor was the only thing that cleared up her chronic chest congestion."

Moonshine . . . congestion . . . governor's house . . . drapes . . . I hoped my scrawl would make sense to me when I got home. I suddenly wanted to talk to Ben, the way we always had. I wanted to tell him the anecdotes, see the quirky center of the day filtered through his eyes. Our experiences became whole, three-dimensional, when we shared them with each other. The last three months had been a flat screen to me.

I slipped in another bite of food, a variety of fried okra with seasoned cornmeal that did wonders with my least favorite vegetable. The low buzz of insects and conversation ran like a current through the thick salt air. It felt soothing and right. Church people—most of them no more than acquaintances, some downright strangers—seemed to anchor the world in a way that left me safe. If I'd had time, I would have planned on several gatherings at different churches before writing the article. Especially since my life was shy of home-cooked meals since moving onto the boat. But a short deadline put an end that that idea, so I had to be satisfied with the one afternoon.

I watched Jake at work again. He moved through the crowd, squatted low, bent back—all in the service of good photographs that would bring out the best in the story. After a particularly acrobatic series of shots, especially for a man his age, he headed over my way.

"I got a picture of the preacher surrounded by a half-dozen women all shoving food onto his plate, then standing there to watch him eat it. He looked damned uncomfortable." Jake stood behind my chair, leaned over to share his thoughts with me in low tones, but not low enough.

"It's the funniest thing," Miss Ronnie chimed in. "His wife won't pay him a bit of mind, but not a woman between the ages of twenty-five and fifty in this church will leave him be." Then she added, " 'Course I'd be over there myself if I was ten years younger."

She was right. Andrew Hanes had a lot of admirers, but Diane, his wife, seemed to either not notice or not care.

"Just look at 'em over there," Miss Ronnie said, inclining her head toward the preacher and his female entourage.

Jake shook his head, gave up on discretion. "I've taken pictures of rock stars that don't get that much attention."

For my money, I didn't think the preacher had any extraordinary attributes. He was a few years older than I was, not particularly tall, though he did appear compact, like muscle and bone all came together tightly for an efficient result. His hair was short, very short, a few millimeters shy of a crew cut.

"I don't know his wife very well," I said to Ronnie. "Or him for that matter. What's their story?"

Over two months' time, I couldn't say I'd ever had this much conversation with anyone at the church. I came and went, just listening to Preacher Andrew's sermons, which were quite good for a country congregation, then leaving quickly with only polite exchanges to mark my attendance. As Miss Ronnie was answering my question about the preacher and his wife, I jotted down a note to myself about food and socialization, how eating together brings out easy, intimate talk among people. After a moment she stopped, my note-taking apparently making her nervous.

"Don't you write this down," she interjected in midexplanation of Andrew's former military career.

"No, I'm making a note about something else that just occurred to me. I'm not writing anything down about the state of the preacher's marriage. I wouldn't do that. Sorry."

"Well, as I was saying," Ronnie launched back in, obviously satisfied that I would keep the pastor's dirty laundry out of the Sunday paper. "She may have signed on to be a military wife, but I don't think she counted on this turn of events."

Jolly and talkative, Ronnie offered a perfect chorus to the drama of Saint Andrew and his groupies, a narrative that had shifted, abruptly, to the dessert table.

"Besides, I think Diane Hanes has other things on her mind, other concerns."

"Like what?" I had gotten way off the topic of food, but I couldn't bring myself to change the subject.

"I don't know. She seems out of her element sometimes. Maybe she misses the life she came from. Like I said, he was military before. There's a certain amount of excitement that goes with that. Moving around, travel . . . I think it suited her. This church lady business . . . I don't know." The older woman paused, taking an impressive bite of ham biscuit midsentence. I waited for her to chew and swallow, and had plenty of time to feel guilty for being so curious in the first place. "The other thing is," she continued when she could speak again, "I think children are an issue. But I'm not sure what the problem is, exactly."

Something ran through me. She'd hit a little too close to home, and I hoped she wouldn't linger on the subject; but between the biscuit and the thrill of an interested person on the receiving end of her conversation, I don't think she noticed my unease.

"And," she went on, "it's got to be a little hard on her here. I feel right bad for the woman. 'Cause truth be told, nobody much likes her."

She stood up.

"Just listen to me talk," she said. "Now, like I told you, don't you go printing any of that old-lady gossip." She chuckled at her own indiscretion as she headed off toward the dessert spread that had just been vacated by the preacher and his loyal flock.

"What do you think, Jake?" I asked.

"About what?"

"About all this." I looked around. The lines were thinning at the tables, but there seemed to be the same amount of food. "And how come there's still so much food?" I asked before he came up with an answer to my first question.

"Loaves and fishes," he said. An enigmatic response from a less-than-poetic guy.

"Listen, before you go," I changed the subject. "Would you get some pictures of the cemetery up there? From down here looking up is fine. In fact, far away is better since I'll be talking about why it's so removed from the church."

"Higher ground," he said as he headed off to take the shot. "Keeps the bodies from moving around."

It seemed I'd found a second source to confirm information gleaned while breaking bread with Miss Ronnie.

Most of the parishioners had begun to gather their leftovers. I'd managed to get more than enough material for my story. I'd also consumed just enough fried chicken and peach cobbler to make me queasy.

Jake packed up to go, assuring me that he could find his way back to town.

"Have you seen Angel?" I asked him as he put the last of his equipment back in his car.

"Well, earlier, a bunch of mother hens were feeding her within an inch of her life," he said, closing the door to the backseat of his car. "Wait a minute. I saw her after that, heading up the path to the graveyard, I think. That wasn't long ago, just when I was finishing my shots."

"Well, I better find her," I said, glancing up toward the cemetery.

I'd already sent her to the Emergency Room. Reese wouldn't take it too well if, on top of everything, I lost her.

Angel wandered around the headstones. I watched her from midway up the path. She stepped lightly, occasionally reaching out to touch a stone with her fingertips—a soft gesture that seemed to suggest some fondness for the soul resting beneath the marker. But she didn't know any of them. I didn't know any of them—except one.

From a distance she could have been any young girl; but through my own distortion, I thought again of my sister, Elise. The image from my dream took an immediate presence in my thoughts, and I pushed against the feelings of panic that followed. She wasn't Elise. With her self-possession, her calm resolve, she was everything that my needy younger sister had never been.

"Hi," I said when I was still a distance away. I didn't want to scare her, make her imagine some voice from the beyond.

"Hey," she said, barely looking up at me. She didn't frighten easily. Her accent echoed the lush tones of her mother's Southern singsong.

She appeared entirely at ease among the dead. Strange, for a child. Then again, most everything about Angel seemed strange. Her demeanor around me had moved from downright cold to a mild disdain. All in all, an improvement. I didn't care to be Aunty Gina, but I'd just as soon not be Cruella de Ville either.

"See anything interesting?" My tone carried effort, condescension; but I had no internal guidepost when it came to children. Honesty would have rendered my interaction fearful, and very nearly mean. I wanted to do better than that, even if it rang false to both of us. "Any good epitaphs?"

I realized that she probably didn't know that word, but before I could speak, she looked up at me with clear eyes. "Where is he?" she asked.

"Who?" I bought a moment of time, if not composure, with the question; but I didn't really need to ask.

She seemed to study her response. I wondered why she would want to know, why she took such care in the asking.

"Your husband," she said. "You said before at breakfast that he was buried here."

I looked at her, hoped to see some betrayal of motive. But she was seven years old. What deeper concern could there have been?

"Over here," I told her, walking toward the spot. As a new grave, Benjamin's plot had been tended with special care to get the covering to take. The grass was literally greener on top of his patch of land. I could have found a joke in that somewhere if I hadn't felt so miserable. "I don't have a headstone yet. I've still got to decide on the engraving."

Again, she just nodded, walked over, and stood by the grave.

I came up beside her, stood there mute, unable to choose words that made sense. The rising pressure in my chest, something I'd come to define as physical grief, began its familiar swell. I wanted Benjamin with me. I wanted with a fierce internal drive that felt like a scream. But no sound came. Fighting tears, I looked over at Angel, hoping to find inspiration for diversion, for small talk. Instead, I found her crying. Large, quiet tears with only small catches in her breath to mark their existence. She looked broken.

"Angel." I said her name out loud and it sounded to my ears like a word I had invented.

She turned and saw my face, my tears. The corners of her mouth pulled down in the terrible show of misery that children cannot disguise. With instincts that had escaped my notice for thirty-three years, I reached to touch her, pull her toward me, and to my amazement, she let me. She felt soft, altogether different from the prickly associations I'd come to have with her. She was just a little girl.

She pulled up the hem of her T-shirt, wiped her whole face, then stepped away from me, looked up as if she expected something. I had no idea what to offer.

As I stared at her, the questions came full in my head. In the rush of our shared misery, it hadn't occurred to me to ask why she felt such emotion for a man she'd never known. I thought of her comment to Lane about the salt pond. Even as these thoughts were forming, I knew at least part of the answer.

"When did you meet Benjamin?" I asked. I kept my voice gentle, without accusation. She'd be skittish. It was a secret Reese had bound her to keep; betrayal would not come easily.

She looked at me, didn't speak. But at least she had none of the defiance that had marked our infrequent interactions. I reasoned that she wanted to tell me.

"It's okay, Angel. I understand why it was a secret. But it's okay now. Tell me about your time with Benjamin." She sat down, cross-legged, on the grass just next to the grave, her eyes down.

The elevation of the graveyard allowed for a small breeze off the water through the trees. Strands of Angel's curls, dark like her mother's, blew around her face, left her in constant battle with her good hand to free herself from the nuisance.

"Here," I said, taking the elastic out of my hair and pulling her hair back into a ponytail. Only afterward did it strike me as odd that I would offer such a gesture—or that she would accept.

"Thank you," she said.

She scratched at a small rock, her fingernails digging at a stone half buried in the ground. I sat beside her, my Sunday pants sacrificed to the South Carolina soil.

"He was funny, wasn't he?" I asked.

"Who?"

"Benjamin." I tried to convey an air of camaraderie, shared knowledge. "What did y'all do? Go to the salt pond?" My heart was flying in my chest, but I kept a surface calm. It took most of what I had inside me to do it.

"He said you like puzzles." Her voice stayed at whisper level, and

I leaned forward enough to hear her. I forced myself to stay quiet, to wait. "The puzzles on the computer where the numbers get out of order and you have to put them back," she said. "He had a computer he carried in his car with the puzzle on it. He could do them real fast, but he said you were faster."

My satchel with my notebook and tape recorder lay on the ground beside me. I reached in and found my Palm Pilot, turned it on and tapped the icon for the number game, then handed it to her. She stared at the screen, and I saw shades of a smile play at the corners of her mouth.

"This one is different from his. How do you do it on here?" she asked.

"With this." I leaned over, touched the spaces with the stylus to show her how to move the numbers, then gave it to her to try.

She worked as if it mattered, as if something real depended on the outcome, on how quickly she completed the task. I saw her mistakes, wanted to help her, but I sat back, thought of Benjamin. For someone who stayed in constant motion, Ben had reserves of patience that contradicted everything else about him. I could see him with her, could almost accept that it had happened. But then I would see him coming home to me. His silence implied more than I wanted to believe. What had Reese been doing while he taught Angel puzzles, while they explored the pond?

"I did it," Angel said. The hesitation in her voice had disappeared. She handed it to me, her face open and glad, but with images of the three of them in my head, my generosity grew thin.

"That was fast," I said, trying, but my words came out void of the enthusiasm they suggested.

I watched her expression, saw the confusion at my reversal, and wanted to offer more. I wanted to be a better person than I was; but it hurt too much. Benjamin had lied to me.

She handed me the organizer, and I saw the numbers laid out in perfect order. She tried to stand, but found balance awkward with her shoulder sling, so I held my hand to steady her. Her small arm steeled against my efforts and she stepped away from me as soon as she had firm ground under her feet. I admired her instinct for self-preservation. And I thought again of Elise, wondered how I'd ever compared the two of them.

"We should get back to the marina," I said, but she had already gone ahead of me.

We worked our way down the path, leaving Benjamin silent behind us. As before, he was unable to tell me the truth about Angel. The truth about Reese.

Through the stained glass of the chapel, I saw a figure moving, alone near the altar. Most likely the preacher. I thought of his wife, unhappy and withdrawing from him—if Miss Ronnie's assessment held any weight. As Angel got in my car for the long ride home, I realized that feeling lonely had little in common with being alone.

Conscience got the best of me on the drive home. I'd changed the rules after getting her to open up with me. She was a kid, just a little girl. I had to keep telling myself that because I wanted to make her into someone manipulative. Someone to blame.

"Listen, there's a stand that's on our way. It sells homemade ice cream," I said. "You have enough room left after lunch to get a cone?"

I'd seen documentaries of wild animals, lured to benevolent capture by scientists wielding fresh chunks of meat. Angel, I sensed, had been hunting for herself during much of her existence, with varying degrees of success. At the mention of ice cream, she turned to me, looked suspicious. I put my attention on the road ahead, gave her time to decide.

"What kinds do they have?" she asked finally.

"They change the flavors every week. My favorite, when they have it, is pink bubble gum. They actually put pieces of gum in the ice cream."

I glanced over at her again. Her small smile took me by surprise, brought me close to a sappy, Hallmark variety of emotion. I took a breath, blinked, and hoped she hadn't noticed. I had a hunch that any overt display could scare her off.

"How 'bout it?"

"Okay." One small word, but it seemed like so much more. She looked out the window again, but the air in the car had changed. I felt myself relax as I kept an eye out for the roadside stand.

We finished our cones, standing in the sandy lot by the car. The heat melted them faster than we could eat, and we ended up sticky and laughing. She looked happy, and I felt it too, watching her, thinking that I'd somehow allowed it to happen.

Back on the road, my cell phone rang. It cut through the relaxed silence between Angel and me with alarming volume. When I pushed the button and said hello, Lane's greeting served as a calming antidote to the obnoxious ring tone.

"Listen, Reese just left," she said. "They called her here from Ollie's wondering if she could come in tonight. Somebody got sick and left an open shift."

For a minute I wondered if I'd have Angel for the day. In spite of our softer moments, I didn't want an extended *Sesame Street* session on my boat.

"Well, if she's working, what's Angel going to do?"

"Bring her over here," Lane said, with no apparent resentment. "I'm going to look after her."

"Lane, you're not a day care center," I protested. "You can't start doing this."

"Can she hear you?" Lane asked in a reflexive whisper, and I realized that, of course, Angel would know what I was saying.

"Yeah, you're right," I said, wondering why everyone else seemed to be born with parental instincts. "We can talk later. I'll be there in about twenty minutes."

After I hung up, I waited for Angel to ask what was going on, but she didn't. She asked fewer questions than any child I'd ever seen. All the ground we'd covered seemed lost, moot.

"You're mom's had to go into work at the restaurant," I said. "You're going to Lane's house."

"Okay." She turned her head to look at the flat expanse of tidal marsh outside her window.

If it bothered her, she didn't show it. But then, I got the sense she kept a lot of feelings to herself. I wanted to say more, to sound cheerful or comforting. But any effort would emphasize my knee-jerk response to Lane's babysitting and further highlight Angel's ragtag, gypsy status.

By the time we got back to the marina, I'd convinced myself that Angel was okay, that she hadn't caught the gist of what I'd said to Lane. But as she was getting out of the car, she took the elastic band out of her hair, laid it on the console between our seats.

"Thank you for taking me," she said with perfect articulation. Her starched-and-pressed manners told me more than I wanted to know.

11

∞

Reese

Reese stood at the bar, balanced a tray of drinks with her right hand. The weakness through her arm caused her to reach up with her other hand and steady the tray. She'd be okay, she just had to concentrate. Her choice of work didn't suit her recent problems, but there didn't seem to be too many other options. Waitress jobs were always available, and she knew how to bring in tips with just a little banter and a frequent smile.

"Thanks for coming in on short notice," Randy, the manager, said as he came up beside her. "And you don't have to dress fancy, darlin'," he said. "Most of the girls just wear shorts and T-shirts in the summer. It gets hot comin' in and out of the kitchen."

She glanced down at her peasant blouse and muslin skirt, thinking she'd have to go shopping for regular shorts.

"But thanks again for comin' in." He shifted the position of his belt, a habit Reese had noticed in him. "One hand shy on a Sunday night in high season is a real problem."

"That's okay." She smiled back at him. "I need the work."

"I like to hear that." The sound of a crash in the kitchen interrupted his good humor. "Oh, hell!" He shook his head as he left her to her drinks.

The bartender set the last of her drink order on the tray and she started for the table of six women, celebrating someone's birthday. "If they want me to sing, they're out of luck," she mumbled to herself. Women tipped other women badly. The rule almost always held. But this group looked a little older; maybe they would be more generous.

"Long Island iced tea?" she asked as she arrived at the table.

"That's me." A red-haired woman raised her hand. She looked to be about fifty. She seemed fit, good color and a strong voice; but beside her chair rested a walking cane. To most people that would have seemed baffling, but not to Reese. She thought of her episodes, the bad ones that required a cane. She'd even gone briefly into a wheelchair once, but that had been a long time ago. Still, the possibility remained.

"Daiquiri," she said, putting the pink beverage at the place of a stout black woman in an expensive blouse.

The rest were piña coladas, the prime drink selection of coastal vacations. As she lowered the tray to serve the concoctions, her arm began to give way and she grabbed the edge with her other hand. But another hand steadied the tray from the opposite side. The woman with the cane. She glanced up at Reese; her kind expression seemed to read everything that Reese normally kept to herself. Maybe the slight falter in her step had given the woman a heads-up, or maybe she had simply been the closest to the tray. Either way, Reese felt a wash of gratitude.

"Thank you," she said.

"No problem," the woman answered.

Reese headed to the kitchen to check on their appetizers, wondering if she could possibly make it through the shift without a mishap.

12

∞

Gina

The Mercury Marquis in the parking lot of the marina was unmistakable. I pulled in and parked beside the large sedan. Maxine Melrose. I was glad that Angel had stayed another night with Lane. The last thing that I wanted was to have to introduce Angel to Benjamin's mother. I especially didn't want to explain about the girl's obvious injuries. If Maxine had heard about the accident, she would have called immediately. With any luck, the shooting hadn't gone beyond the local news. The Columbia papers wouldn't have picked up such a minor story.

As I got through the security gate, it occurred to me that, while Maxine had come looking for me, she'd likely found someone else entirely when she got to my boat. A surprise wake-up call for Reese, no doubt.

The marina Internet was down, so I'd gotten up early to turn in my article at the paper, then stopped by for groceries, or what passed for a full load of groceries in my doll-sized kitchen. I'd left Reese asleep in the quarter berth. She'd come in late. I'd been in my cabin, still working on the assignment, when I felt the familiar shift as she boarded the boat. By the time I opened my door to at least say hello, she had closed herself off in her room. Just as well. I didn't want to risk the possibility of opening up a discussion with her—not when I had a deadline looming the next day.

Judging from her late slumber the morning before, I figured I'd wake her up when I got home. Looked like I figured wrong.

"I wonder what's up with you, Maxine," I mumbled as I shifted the groceries to my other arm. Regardless of the complications, the thought of seeing my mother-in-law lifted my mood. We'd taken to each other the first time we met, and she'd come to feel more like a mother to me than my biological version. Between her and Lane, I had an abundance of maternal care.

Maxine's arrival didn't surprise me. Following her weeklong stay after the funeral, she had taken to just showing up on occasion. Always unexpected. Always nearing a breakdown. I worried that she was like that constantly. Then told myself that perhaps when insanity began to set in, she jumped in her car and headed for the coast to find me. At least I hoped so. I'd certainly ended up on her doorstep before.

"Nothing good can come of this, Reese." Maxine's voice coming from the cabin of my boat sounded unyielding, as if rendered by a superior. It reminded me of my tone with Angel.

"Come on, Maxie," Reese said, employing a nickname I'd never heard before. "You've got to admit there's something real tidy about it. Two wives, one boat."

At least there was nothing to suggest they'd come to blows.

I stood on the dock for a minute. Not so much to eavesdrop as to prepare myself for entering the fray.

"I have to say," Maxine countered, "that the years have not improved you, Reese. You're as childish as the day I last saw you."

Benjamin had told me that the two of them never got along, even before Reese did her disappearing act. *Acts.* I corrected myself, adjusting for Reese's recent revelations. I had figured as much when I first met Maxine. After fifteen minutes of conversation on my first visit to her house, she'd leaned back against her kitchen sink and smiled. "Thank God, you're normal!" she said.

I felt like the *good child.* The one relied upon to make the family proud.

"If that's a compliment," I'd told her, "you're going to have to take another shot at it."

"Honey," she countered, wiping down the counter as she spoke, "after that last one, normal is the highest praise I can offer. She was a flat-out nut."

Maxine loved me from the very beginning. After Benjamin was gone, she almost loved me to death. During her stay at the house, the idea was that sharing our grief would lighten the load for both of us. We barely made it a week before we both agreed that distance had its merits.

"Just tell me why you called me and I'll go back home," Maxine said. "Gina's a big girl and she can have any guests she pleases. Including you."

Reese called her? *Why the hell would she do that?*

"Hey, Maxine." I tried to sound casual as I stepped onto the boat.

"Gina!" Maxine turned to me. "It's wonderful to see your face, sweetheart."

Reese rolled her eyes. Something was different about her, but my focus shifted quickly back to Maxine.

A good four inches shorter than I was, Maxine had to reach up like a child to give me a hug. She looked younger than the last time I'd seen her. Slimmer too. She'd maintained her original hair color of deep reddish brown, but the cut was shorter, more contemporary. Either she'd pulled her life back together or found a top-notch plastic surgeon. Either way, I was delighted to see her looking so much better.

"Do you want something to drink?" I asked. I'd had larger gatherings on my boat before, but the cabin suddenly seemed as crowded as it had ever been.

"No, thank you, sweetie," she said, turning back to Reese. "I'd just like to find out what this one has to say, so I can go on back."

I looked at Reese. She mouthed Angel's name to me, tilted her head in the direction of Lane's cottage.

"What's wrong with you?" Maxine caught my awkward communication with Reese.

"Nothing," I said. "I'm sorry I interrupted."

"No interruption, sweetheart," Maxine said. "You've liberated me. I have to head back."

"Maxine. Wait." Reese's voice had lost its taunting quality. "I'll be right back. Don't leave." Her sincere plea stopped Maxine's progress toward the door.

Angel. She wanted to spring Angel on Maxine. I couldn't imagine why. Maybe I'd misjudged Reese all around. Maybe she was out to get cash or simply throw the child in Maxine's face. I wanted to intervene, to warn my mother-in-law. But I looked at Reese and, somehow, I couldn't rely on those theories. There was something else, something she had in mind.

"Wait here just a minute," Reese told us. She left the cabin, headed over toward Lane's on the other side of the Ship's Store.

Maxine shook her head. "That woman! What's she doing here?"

"It's a really long story," I said.

The air felt lighter without the tension between the two women.

"You look wonderful," I told her. She did. She looked . . . new.

"I've tried so hard," she said. "This damn thing has almost killed me, but I'm determined to get through it intact. "How 'bout you, honey? I called to check on you a day or two ago, but I just got your voice mail."

I felt bad that I hadn't called her back.

"I'm fine," I said. "It's been a weird few days, but everything's okay now."

She didn't ask me to explain. I guess she figured *weird* days were the norm when your husband's ex-wife arrives for a visit.

"Gina?" she began, but didn't go on.

"What?" I asked.

She looked sly, more like her old self than I'd seen in months, even before the accident.

"I'm seeing someone," she said. "A CPA in town. His wife died two years ago and . . ." She stopped for a second as if she'd run out of words. "We just found each other, Gina. He's a wonderful man." She smiled, looked happy.

"That's great, Maxine!" I reached over and gave her a hug.

Even Benjamin's mother was doing better than I was. The rogue thought surfaced in the middle of my genuine pleasure for Maxine, and I was mad at myself for giving it clear passage in my brain. Something subliminal should squash anything that selfish. Still, I couldn't help but wonder how everyone could deal with Benjamin's death except me.

"I'm really glad," I managed. And I was. She'd been through a lot in her life; at the very least she deserved to be loved.

She and Benjamin's dad had divorced when Ben was fifteen. I'd seen Henry, his dad, a half-dozen times in our three years of marriage, the last time at the funeral. He came with his second wife, Alicia. Seeing the two of them together made the day even harder for Maxine. She'd dated off and on over the years, but never anything exciting. The spark I saw as we waited for Reese to come back brought out colors I'd never seen in her.

"He's a rascal, Gina," she told me. "But in a really good way. We have so much fun. We've been going out about a month."

"A month? We've talked three or four times in the last few weeks."

"I know," she said. "But I didn't want to say anything until . . . until I knew it was going to stick."

"I'm happy for you, Maxine."

She sat down, crossed her legs, and let out a long breath, and I settled down opposite her. I could see one corner of Lane's house through the portside window. I wrestled with whether to warn her. To say something—anything.

"How are you holding up?" she asked. "You don't look so good."

"Stop with the compliments," I said, smiling.

"You know what I mean. Is it just everything, or has *she* done something?"

"I'm fine," I said. "I was working on deadline late last night. I'm a little tired, that's all." I wanted to avoid thinking about Benjamin, all my confusion over Angel. I certainly didn't want to let on about anything to Maxine.

"Well, that woman gets under my skin." Maxine didn't push with the questions.

"I know," I said. "But try to go with it. Really try, Maxine. I'm telling you the honest truth. She's not always as bad as you think. But it's going to get worse here in a minute, and you've got to keep it together."

"What's going on?" she asked.

I didn't have to answer. I felt the shift of weight as Reese and Angel stepped onto the boat. I heard the child's shoes hit the deck with a heavy slap, winced as she jumped from the seat to the floor. In spite of the fact that I had no personal stake in any of it, I wanted it to go well. I felt nervous, surprised that I even cared.

Maxine sat up straight when she heard the steps on the boat, as if she needed to stay sharp, at the ready. When Reese stepped through the companionway, I sensed that her demeanor had changed. Even her face looked different.

Angel was obscured, followed in her mother's wake; Reese's hand stayed behind her back, holding the child's good arm, offering a gentle pull.

"Come on, honey," she said to Angel.

A panicky feeling rose in my chest and I changed seats, sat beside Maxine, though the gesture was instinctive and of little practical value. Angel wasn't going to attack anybody. If anything, Reese had the most to lose. She was putting it all on the line, and for reasons that I couldn't imagine.

"Maxine, this is Angelina," Reese said. "Angel."

Then, she was there. Angel stood at the bottom of the stairs inside the cabin. Her hair was combed, held back with a barrette, not something I'd seen in my few days with the little girl. Her face held a pink flush as if it had been wiped clean with a warm cloth. It smacked of Lane's involvement, but taking a serious look at Reese, I had to wonder. For the first time since our unfortunate introduction, she wore conventional clothes, slim navy pants and a white blouse that I realized she'd rummaged from my limited closet. That's what was different about her.

She could have been a senator's wife, dressed for a luncheon. Part of me wanted to explain to Maxine how hard she was trying; the moment hung there forever before Maxine responded.

"Hello, Angel," she said. "I'm Mrs. Melrose." It was a cold, formal response, unlike the woman who had cried with me, even thrown things across a room, in the days that followed Benjamin's funeral. Either she didn't understand what the moment held, or she knew, and rejected it anyway. I couldn't tell.

"What happened to her arm?" Maxine directed the question at Reese. A simple question, but the tone suggested that Angel was little more than a broken vase or, at best, an injured pet. I waited, prepared to explain why I had a gun and why the hell I'd fired it anywhere near a child.

"She had an accident." Reese was retreating, offering no more than she was given. "But she's going to be fine."

Angel's expression didn't change. Unlike most kids, eager to pop in with their own inflated versions of any event, she accepted her mother's answer. I got the feeling she'd learned early on to go with the flow of Reese's narratives.

"That's good," Maxine said. She looked over at me. The flat line of her emotions centered in her eyes.

Reese kept a hand on Angel at all times, touching her hair, rubbing her back. A lost connection, it seemed, could lead Angel into harm's way.

I wanted to shake Maxine, bring her fully awake. Even if she wanted to dismiss Reese, how could she act as if the girl was some object? Then again, I hadn't exactly been kind to her over the last couple of days. I thought of Angel at the grave, crying over Ben, smiling at her unexpected success with the puzzle. Then I'd turned on her, gone stone cold. Lane was right; whatever mistakes the adults in her life made, the kid wasn't to blame. It occurred to me that maybe that was why I'd gotten a pass when my sister died. *I* had been a kid, only a couple of years older than Angel. I wanted to comfort her, suddenly, but one look told me she'd put up her own protective barriers. She was used to it—taking the heat by association for Reese. The girl's eyes stayed level on Maxine, refusing to look away.

"Angel's having a birthday soon," I chirped. The tone of my remark landed in the room as a glaring off-key note amid the taut exchanges, but I decided to press on. "We're going to have a picnic party for her."

"How old will you be, Angel?" Maxine asked. I thought I heard a slight softening in her voice, but I couldn't be sure.

"Eight," Angel told her.

The climate in the room changed; the sound of the air conditioner seemed to grow louder. Sitting close to Maxine, I heard her breathe. The air caught in her throat, skipping rather than flowing into her lungs, but her face maintained composure. Then she looked at Reese, her forehead wrinkled as if a question would follow, but she didn't speak. I wasn't sure she could. Instead, I heard Lane coming onto the boat; she gave a small knock, then lifted the canvas that covered the companionway.

"I don't want to interrupt," she said. "But I did want to see Maxine before she took off somewhere."

Lane squatted in the entryway above us, and Maxine, looking relieved to have the diversion, got up and greeted her with a hug. Maxine was pure Junior League next to Lane's Sierra Club, but they had always gotten along, *enjoyed* each other, as Maxine put it. As different as they were, they both possessed an edge, an irreverence that most women of their generation lacked—although Lane's existed in more subtle zones.

"How are you?" Maxine asked Lane.

"Busy," Lane said, smiling. "I'd forgotten how exciting it is to have a child around."

I couldn't tell if the remark represented some attempt on Lane's part to lobby for acceptance of Angel, or if it was a polite, throwaway observation. Either way, the issue of Angel had to be dealt with somehow. Whatever Reese's motive for arranging the awkward encounter, I wanted her to get to the point so that I could reclaim my home to some small degree.

"I won't distract you from your introductions here," Lane said, following my thoughts with perfect timing. "I just wanted to say hello."

Maxine turned to sit back down, but the small wake of a passing boat rocked the cabin and she grabbed the edge of the navigation table to steady herself.

"Damn!" she muttered it under her breath, but we all heard it. Things weren't going well. She sat down, looked irritated at best. Angel cut her eyes over to Maxine as if to size her up. I couldn't tell if the girl was intimidated or simply confused about why her mother was dressed in funny clothes, acting perfectly proper for a change.

"Could I go with Lane?" Angel spoke up before Lane stepped off the boat. Reese didn't even try to mask her frustration, but she nodded her consent anyway.

"Go on," she said, forcing a smile.

Angel climbed back into the cockpit, and Lane took the child's good hand.

"Maybe I should go too," I said. "Let you two talk."

"If you don't mind," Reese said a little too urgently, "I'd like for you to stay." I couldn't help but wonder what alien entity had taken hold of the woman's likeness. "I'll get to the point now," she added.

"Well, thank God," Maxine responded. "I thought there might be an entire Mother Ginger cast of characters paraded through here before we got to the meat of things."

"Maxine, please stop," I heard myself say. Enough was enough. Maxine was acting the bully and my instinct to protect the underdog kicked in. "This is difficult for everyone. Reese wouldn't be putting herself through this if she didn't have a reason. I know this is hard, but let's do the best we can."

Maxine sat back down, let out a long sigh. It was as much of a concession as she was willing to offer.

I began eyeing a bottle of merlot on the counter just behind where Reese stood. We could all stand to take it down a notch, but it was still early afternoon. I didn't think I'd have any takers if I offered.

"Angel and I need a place to live," Reese said without any preface. She sat opposite us. Her expression suggested that the words themselves held a bitter taste. "I've called you here for help. For a favor."

Maxine inclined her head slightly to one side. She waited, but when Reese didn't continue, she managed to ask, "You want to live with me?" She sounded too astonished to even ridicule the idea.

"No, no." Reese shook her head. She looked so tired. "I was hoping to rent your beach house. I can't afford what you would normally get, but it's coming up on off-season and I thought—"

"Is she Benjamin's child?" Maxine blurted it out, interrupting whatever well-thought-out speech Reese had composed. My mother-in-law had full tears in her eyes as she spoke. "Is she his? Is that what this is about?" This last came out with such effort that I felt myself crying too. Reese looked stunned, unable to respond.

"Reese?" I said, hoping to elicit some response.

She looked at me. Her breathing had quickened, and I realized again how much had gone into this request, how much pride she had to hold at bay. I waited, wondered if she would lie.

"I don't know," she said. She kept her eyes direct, never looked away from Maxine.

The muscles in my neck and my arms relaxed. I was relieved at the honesty if nothing else; but Maxine's face changed, held the beginnings of disdain.

"I know that statement alone confirms everything that you think of me," Reese continued. "And the God's honest truth is, I don't care what you think. I won't make apologies or offer explanations beyond saying that it was a confusing time when my marriage to Benjamin ended. When I found out I was pregnant, so much had happened already—"

"And now you want my house." Maxine cut her short.

"I want to rent it." Reese kept stone features, masklike in their evenness.

"It's already rented through the end of this month. Besides, I can't just hand it out to you because some child you parade in here may or may not be my grandchild." Maxine's voice was breaking.

Grandchild. The word brought Benjamin so near. If Angel *was* his, that would bind everyone in the room, as well as the man I loved, together by blood. Everyone except me. For the first time I realized how much I *didn't* want Angel to belong to Benjamin. It was a selfish, terrible recognition on my part, and the guilt alone, I believe, spurred me to petition further on Reese's behalf.

"Maxine, take a couple of minutes to breathe before you go on with this."

I fought to think beyond that. Reese looked defeated, ready to give up. The effort had been too much already, it seemed, and she'd gained no ground that I could see. She looked unsteady on her feet; pale, as if she might pass out.

"Sit down, Reese."

She didn't argue. She sat opposite Maxine, reached to take the water I offered her, but her fingers wouldn't move into a solid grip. I watched her try to clasp the glass. She looked at me, helpless, before she lowered her hand.

"That's okay," she said. "I'm just a little shaky. I may have a stomach bug."

I put the glass down, sat beside her. "Are you okay?" She nodded, offered a weak smile.

"This is ridiculous," Maxine said. She seemed at a loss for how to go forward.

"What are your biggest problems with this?" I asked Maxine. I still sat at Reese's side, hoped this wouldn't put Maxine on the defensive. I asked it as an earnest question, hoping to get the idea in play again.

"What am I *not* worried about, Gina? And why are you defending this woman? She damaged Benjamin in ways you can't imagine—and that was *before* she left him."

"Please stop, Maxine," I said again. Why did I feel the need to argue for Reese? I should want her to leave, to take the child with her. But for reasons that were beyond me, I needed for Maxine to say yes. My feelings remained jumbled, so I simply flew by gut instinct. "I know this is all overwhelming, but let's try to look at it as clearly as we can."

If Reese had thought it out more, she might have arranged a lunch with Maxine, somewhere neutral. In town, maybe. She would have worked up to the subject of Angel, laid the groundwork for the idea before she confronted the older woman with a flesh-and-bones child. But she hadn't.

"There is not an ounce of love lost between me and Reese," Maxine began, "and that house, along with the property it sits on, are just about all that I got out of my marriage to Benjamin's father—except a wonderful son, and now, even my son is gone." She'd given up on fighting her tears, they spilled quietly down her cheeks, but her words held composure. "There are emotional issues I won't go into . . . all the things I had planned the house would be for us when you and Benjamin had children."

Reese glanced over at me, and my cheeks went warm. Had Ben told her? What else had he shared with his ex-wife?

"I looked forward to grandchildren in that house, Reese," Maxine continued, not noticing the exchange between me and her former daughter-in-law. "But not like this, and certainly not involving you. I'm not trying to be horrible, but you understand all too well my reasons for that." Her voice went hard when she addressed Reese directly.

"I understand, Maxine," Reese said calmly. "I know what a shock this is. You have to know that, with all that's gone between us, I would never have come to you if I had any other options. You held far more against me than Benjamin ever did."

"He never knew enough to hold all of this against you," Maxine countered, her words back to venom.

I saw Angel again at the cemetery, eyes full of tears. I faced the reality that he *had* known. Could Angel's revelations have any other explanation? I could barely bring myself to imagine how he might have felt about Angel. But even as the questions formed in my head, I knew the answers. Daughter or not, Ben would have adored the child. But if he'd spent time with her, why didn't he tell me?

"I'm asking this for my daughter," Reese continued, ignoring everything but the question at hand. "I need to get her in a good school. I'm going to be working, but I won't make enough to afford the kind of neighborhood I want for her. Your cottage would solve that problem. I'm asking you. I'll pay you what I can and I'll make other arrangements as soon as I'm able to sort them out. But school starts soon, and I need to get things settled for her. Just tell me yes or no."

Maxine sat unmoving, then finally spoke. "There are a lot of things to consider. This isn't like asking to borrow my car. There's rental income, the proper upkeep of the place. You haven't proven to be what anyone would call trustworthy, Reese. This situation does nothing to change that fact. All the emotional issues aside, if something were to happen to the house—"

"The lawyers who helped with the estate." I acted again on reflex, barely thinking the words before they were spoken. "They could set up an agreement. Something binding to protect you, Maxine."

"But she can't—" Maxine began.

"I'll guarantee money for any damages," I said. I had no time to think, to analyze why I wanted to do this. But I needed to. I knew that

I had to be involved. If nothing else, it brought me into the equation, in some crazy way. "Maxine, we can make it work."

"Gina, this isn't your problem to solve. This woman . . ."

I felt the tide pushing us backward.

"You're right, Maxine. She hurt Benjamin. But I know how he talked about her, cared how she was. He would have helped if she was in trouble."

Reese stood back, an object of discussion with no valid voice in her own defense. This had come down to my mother-in-law and me. That fact alone gave me some sense of leverage, of strength. Maybe that's why I wanted to help. Some weird power trip on my part.

"And the girl, Maxine," I finished, with the biggest part of Reese's case. "She may *not* be Benjamin's child. But there's a good chance she is. She might be your granddaughter."

Maxine dropped her head, rubbed her temples with her fingers as if to physically manipulate the thoughts jumbled in her head. Her long-standing dislike for Reese played against the possibility of a grandchild. I didn't envy her.

"It won't be free until the beginning of September," she said finally. She spoke in a near monotone. "I'll need the usual deposit. I'll work out a cut-rate off-season deal with the realty company." She looked up at Reese. "You'll deal with the realty company with any problems. We'll have no need to talk about anything."

"What about Angel?" Reese asked. "Do you want to see her again?"

Maxine sat unmoving. Her eyes were closed. When she opened them, there were tears again.

"For now," she said, "I'd rather not. I don't think I can."

Reese nodded. "I'll go over to Lane's, let you two visit." Then, as she was climbing up into the cockpit, she turned back to Maxine. "Thank you," she said. Then, before she moved out of sight, she mouthed the same to me. Before Maxine could choose to respond or not, Reese left the two of us there, and, oddly enough, the room seemed nearly empty without her.

13

∞

Reese

Reese stood on the dock, steadied herself on a wooden post. She wasn't sure if it was shaky nerves or something worse, although she suspected the latter. Confining clothes didn't help. She needed to find a willing pharmacist. All she knew for sure was that she didn't feel right. Things had been a little better since she left Boone. All the adrenaline, most likely. But her luck seemed to be failing. She decided to walk around before she went in to check on Angel. Moving around, finding distraction, sometimes made things better.

A storm pressed in from the south. The sun, still hot on the marina, would soon be overtaken by the moving wall of gray.

"Hey there." Charlie, the young guy from the Ship's Store, spoke as she walked by. He knelt on the dock near the shore, wearing board shorts and no shirt. His dirty blond hair, shorter in back with longer bangs in front, fell over his eyes as he pulled up a boxy, metal cage— a crab pot—filled with a half-dozen clanking, defiant crustaceans.

"They look meaner than fleas," Reese said, staring at the wagging claws.

"Pinch the shit out of you, that's for sure," he said, keeping to his task. Wearing a heavy leather glove, he lifted the fierce creatures into a plastic bucket. He stood taller than Reese, but still managed a taut presence. When he was done, he tied several chicken necks to the inside of the trap, closed the door, and wiped his hands on a towel.

"Smells terrible," she told him.

"That's the chicken," he said as he stood up, squinted at the high afternoon sun. "The older the meat, the more crabs go for it."

"You eat these yourself?" she asked. "That's a lot of crab."

She stood behind him, watched the muscles of his back tighten as he picked up the trap, lowered the contraption back into the water.

"No, ma'am," he said, turning toward her, balancing on one knee, "I don't even like crab all that much. But I take the little bastards home. Steam 'em, then ice them. After that, I set up shop with a cooler out by the side of River Road. They go quick during tourist season, no matter what you charge."

"You can skip the 'ma'am' next time. I'm not that much older than you."

"Sorry," he grinned. "Just a habit."

"No problem."

Reese knelt down to look inside the bucket. The crabs, all about the size of a man's hand, went at one another with fierce intent. She'd gone crabbing as a girl. Her young uncles, her mother's baby brothers, had taken her whenever they went out in their boat through the shallow marsh creeks. The two were identical twins, looked like mirrored images as they checked their pots, traded jokes and stories while they worked. As she got older, she realized they simply felt sorry for her, wanted to make up for her mother's lousy disappearing act when she was still so little.

"Reese?" Charlie was saying. His smooth features looked puzzled, questioning, and she realized she'd missed something he'd said.

"I'm sorry," Reese said. "What was that?"

"Well for starters, do you mind me calling you Reese?" he asked. "When somebody's not a 'ma'am,' I usually call them by a first name."

"Reese is fine."

He smiled, eyes level with hers. The smell of the salty shore eased the tight urgency in her temples. Growing up, her memories outside, mostly alone and near the water, had been better ones than any of the others. Even the musty smell of dark mud and damp sea grass brought pleasing associations.

"Well," Charlie went on, "I was trying to say that we ought to get together sometime."

She looked at him, too surprised to speak. She'd gone out with younger guys before, but they never initiated it. This guy had a pretty solid opinion of himself.

"Nothing fancy." He filled in the silence. "Just beer and seafood, maybe. I know Derek's been working to get your sister to go out. Maybe the four of us could get together."

"My what?" Sisters. She and Gina. That's what he thought. It made more sense than the truth, she supposed. Though she assumed Derek would have told him otherwise.

"We're not sisters," she said finally. "But that's a long story," she added when he looked as if he might ask. "Let me think about it. It might be fun to go out. You know I've got a few years on you, right? How old are you?"

"Twenty-seven," he said.

Older than she thought, and just shy of a ten-year spread. She could live with that.

"I'm game," she told him. "As for Gina, I don't know. After every-thing she's been through, I don't know if she's thinking much about men right now."

Charlie got an amused look on his face. He raised his eyebrows and smiled like a kid who'd found the Christmas closet full in mid-December.

"I think that ship sailed with her and Derek on it a week or two ago," he said. "Not to talk out of turn, but Derek's got it pretty bad for her, and she keeps going hot and cold."

"Really?" Reese thought of Gina. She was hard to read, but any-thing was possible.

"Maybe you could talk to her—about going out, I mean." He wasn't giving up. "Like I said, we don't have to make it a big deal. Just do something fun."

He had an open way about him. Any one of his features, when isolated, ranked less than perfect. His mouth was too wide, his eyes just a hair small. But together his face looked adorable.

"I'll mention it," she told him.

He nodded. They'd run out of logical topics, and still kneel-ing on the dock, Reese felt a numb sensation settling into her an-kles.

"I better go," she said. "I'll see you later up at the store. Are you working tonight?"

"I go in at five." He stood up, lifting his bucket by the handle. The scratch and clatter of the crabs inside resumed with his move-ment.

"Well, if you're working nights," she teased, "it'll be hard to find time for a date."

"I'm switching shifts with Randall the rest of the week, working the morning slot instead," he said as he walked. "Just think about it," he called out, not turning to look at her again.

She offered a slight nod in response all the same. He was cute all right. But cute had gotten her in trouble before. She walked along the dock in the opposite direction with no clear idea where she wanted to go. Still, the thought of Charlie's interest cheered her.

Something else worked on the periphery of her thoughts too, something that lifted her spirits in spite of her growing concerns. She ran through the events of the last days when she hit on what it was. She was out, walking by herself, and she wasn't worried about Angel. Lane was looking out for the child and she was safe—absolutely safe—with the older woman. The liberation of leaving her daughter with someone she trusted made her feel nearly happy. She'd become so accustomed to worry, the absence of nagging concern seemed a miracle.

It wasn't that she hadn't trusted Janet, her friend in the mountains. After the . . . episode, Reese had landed in the hospital for the better part of a week. She'd had to leave Angel with someone. Janet had done her best, but her own life wasn't safe. That boyfriend of hers. Janet had told Reese all about him and his shady buddies, had warned her to stay clear of them. Turns out they were into something bad. Drugs, she figured, though Janet never said for sure. She hadn't put it together until Angel's call. Reese didn't hold it against Janet. As a mother, she knew she should have had sharper instincts, should have known better. And, in the end, Angel was fine. Reese still wondered if Janet fared so well.

But Reese would never forgive herself for what Angel had gone through. She'd never forgive herself for not letting Ben do it his way when she had the chance. Everything would be different if . . . She had to let it go. None of that mattered now. She would play the hand she'd been dealt. But the whole thing with Janet's boyfriend had been a wake-up call. All kinds of problems could come crashing down on them if she didn't get things planned out right. She'd thought nothing could be worse than if Ben decided to take Angel away completely. Well, then she *saw* what worse could mean and went running back to Ben—too late.

She couldn't get stuck in the past. More urgent problems demanded action. The small trembling sensations dogged her. Then sometimes she had the opposite, stretches of time when the fingers on her right hand went completely numb. The elevated feeling, even that could be part of it, part of what she sensed coming on. Sometimes, her moods went haywire. That's when she needed the pills.

She needed to find a pharmacist who would bend the rules a bit, help her out. Problem was, she didn't have the money to make that happen. She didn't even have the money to pay the people she already owed. Jesus, what a mess!

Over in the parking lot, she saw Gina standing with Maxine beside that tank Maxine drove. She looked over at the sailboat, knew Gina's purse would be on the counter where she'd dropped it when she came in. The women looked deep into their discussion, probably about her. For unexplained reasons, Gina had been on her side, had convinced Maxine to let her use the cottage. It made what she was considering just that much harder to justify. But she couldn't hesitate. Besides, she'd done worse to people who had treated her better. Benjamin, for starters.

She doubled back and headed for the boat. After she got the credit card from Gina's wallet, she would drive into town and figure the rest out on the way. Whatever she did, she'd have to do it fast. Time was running out on several fronts, and the one who stood to lose the most was Angel.

14

Gina

I stalled Maxine's departure as long as I could. Her presence meant I didn't have to think about what Angel had told me at the grave. And for the life of me, I couldn't figure out what compelled me to jump in and save the day for Reese. My head and my gut were working on two different levels. Reacting alternately to both, my actions contradicted themselves from one minute to the next. Maybe I'd finally slipped to the other side of sanity. It would almost be a blessing to realize I was crazy and be done with it.

I looked around for Reese, felt relieved when I couldn't find her. I needed to confront her about Angel's time with Benjamin. But I dreaded it; dreaded it the way I'd dreaded the visitation and the funeral, the burial and going home alone. All of the spare moments that led to the truth about Ben's death. This could hold another truth about Ben, one I didn't want to hear.

"Hey, Georgie," I called to the dog. She'd been pouting in the V-berth since Maxine left. She loved Maxine. "Want to go for a ride?" I had to begin facing my questions. Maybe some digging on my own—*before* confronting Reese—would make things easier.

The dog stood up. I didn't have to ask twice to rouse her. I wished that my own funks were so easily cured. As we headed for the car, I considered where I was going. It was a frequent destination, but never with any specific task at hand. Before, I'd always gone there for comfort. This time I was going for answers.

The storage facility stretched out on a flat piece of land behind the Piggly Wiggly grocery store. I'd splurged on the space, paid extra for climate control. It seemed odd at the time that I had to put Benjamin in the ground, leave him to the elements, while all of his stuff remained heated and air-conditioned in human comfort. But the large storage cubicle had become my sanctuary, even more than his grave.

I wondered if that would change with this latest news; if Ben had really known about Angel. Ben and Angel. What was I supposed to do with that?

"Hey, Gina." Bob, who ran the place, was moving a supply of broken-down mover's boxes into the office. A large man, about my age, his cheeks were blister red from the heat and the effort. I pulled into an open spot near the office door, saw Bob struggling with the boxes.

"Want a hand?" I asked, opening the car door. Georgie jumped out and ran off ahead of me. "Georgie! Stop!"

"No, go ahead, I'm good," he said, holding the door with his foot while he slid the boxes inside.

I took off after the dog. She knew the exact row of warehouse buildings our unit was in, waited for me at the outside door. All that told me was that I'd been at the place far too often.

I entered the cool building, turned the light timer on, and headed down the hall after the dog. I took off the combination lock, but for the first time hesitated before raising the garage-type door that protected the belongings. Knowing what I intended to do, it seemed as if I was trespassing, sneaking through Benjamin's drawers and betraying his privacy.

Inside, everything seemed intact, just as it had been when I left the time before. If it had been ransacked, left in disarray, it would have fit my emotions better. As it was, I simply stood there, lost, wondering where to start.

"You okay?" Bob's voice surprised me. He stayed in the hall, his size imposing as he stood, framed by the cubicle opening.

"Yeah, I'm sorry." I wondered why he had followed me. "I'm just kind of a mess these days."

He held out something in his hand. "You left your car running. I shut it off, figured you'd want these." He gave a shy smile as he held out my car keys. He looked embarrassed for me.

"Thanks." I took the keys, remembered my mad dash after Georgie.

"No problem." He turned to go.

"Bob?"

"Yes, ma'am." He turned back toward me.

"You're married, right?"

He nodded. "Nine years. Why?"

"Do you tell your wife everything?"

He was beginning to look uncomfortable.

"I mean," I tried to elaborate, "do you think a good marriage has everything out in the open?"

"Pretty much," he said. His face relaxed. He was a genuinely nice man. "I mean, I try to tell her everything. But sometimes, I flat out forget. Not everything that's important to her seems important to me."

"What about something that's hard to tell her, but you know it's important?"

"I'd definitely try and tell her anything like that." I could tell he was a little bit worried about where the conversation might go. I didn't imagine he was the type to analyze his relationships.

"Do you put it off—you know—wait longer than you should before you bring it up?"

I noticed that he stepped back, put physical distance between the two of us. I didn't blame him.

"I don't know," he said finally. "Seems like if there's something going on, she halfway knows it. But when I try to work my way around to it, she makes it into something else, or gets me arguing before I really get to the point. Some things, I don't think she wants to hear. Like I said, I don't know. We always work through things—eventually."

"Thanks." I nodded, tried to smile. I felt grateful for his candor, but he'd pointed out the one thing he had with his wife that I didn't have with Ben. Time. I would never have the opportunity to hear the explanation for this directly from him, no matter how long I waited.

As he left, I heard Bob's soft sneaker footsteps on the concrete floor moving toward the door. Georgie had found a rolled-up wool rug and settled at the end closest to the space's entrance.

"You watch out for me, Georgie."

With no more excuses to delay me, I fished out the boxes I needed, the ones that held his knickknacks and others that had his files. In all the times I'd visited the space, I hadn't thought about those. I'd only opened the ones with his clothes, his sweaters and coats. The wools and down-filled jackets turned out to be the most loyal fabrics, the ones that refused to give up his smell. Key rings and cuff links offered visual triggers, but nothing that bypassed conscious memory, mainlining straight to the grief.

So they had remained sealed since the day when Maxine and I sat with a bottle of bourbon between us, putting items by the handfuls into U-Haul book-sized boxes. I'd pulled out a bottle of wine to start off the project, but Maxine shook her head.

"One thing I learned when Henry divorced me," she'd said. "The men have it right when it comes to drinking. If their day's gone to hell in a hand basket, it's whiskey or bourbon. None of this chardonnay nonsense." We were both looped by the time we got to the second box. I had little recollection of what went in.

Packing tape secured the box lids. I felt in my pocket for the small Swiss Army knife that Ben had given me one year on Valentine's Day. It was tiny and pink. He'd called it my Camping Barbie knife. Every small moment in my life, it seemed, held a dozen references to him. As I built more of my life without him, I knew that would change, but in the meantime I simply had to step through each memory. I cut the tape along the lid of a box, the slit running rough and uneven, the result of a hand that wouldn't stop shaking.

A half-dozen boxes gaped open, their contents loose on the concrete floor. I'd gone out to reset the timer for the light outside twice and still I hadn't found anything that would answer questions about Reese and Angel. I wasn't even sure what I thought I might find. I only knew that finding nothing would be preferable somehow.

Every time I started in on a pile from a new box, I could feel my pulse get faster, then settle as I sorted through all of the expected items. Ticket stubs, loose keys, and matchbooks from restaurants we'd gone to. Ben had been such an open book. How could he have kept Angel from me? I began to hope that my concern had no basis. As long as I found nothing, there was a chance that Angel was playing make-believe, that Reese had told her enough about Benjamin, enough about Charleston, to create a fantasy father with an imagined relationship.

Even the puzzle, the bits and pieces about me, could have come from Reese. She'd talked to him every once in a while. I knew that. I'd always known that, and it had never bothered me. Crazy, unpredictable Reese came with the territory when I fell for Ben, and she'd never been intrusive. I'd never even met her before all of this.

By the time I got to the third or fourth box, I had calmed down. One small box had different markings than the others, and I realized it was from his office desk at the agency. He'd worked as a graphic artist at a marketing firm. In addition to his drafting table, he'd had a desk with a computer. He could work up a proposal by hand or a computer mock-up; either way his ideas stood out, formed in line with his personality, strong and sure, never second-guessing his instincts. It was easy to let him make decisions; he did it so well.

I opened the box, turned it over to spill the pens and floppy discs on the floor. Georgie had moved beside me. Stretched out, the length of her back pressed against my leg, she felt good, warm, and I realized the AC in the windowless warehouse had made me cold.

I sorted through the hodge-podge of office supplies. The only item of interest was a small rectangular box. The surface was leather. As I picked it up, I saw the gold engraving of the jeweler's name on the black leather surface. I could just see the shop. It was on a little street in Charleston, the window bright and dazzling with sapphires, rubies, and diamonds. I wasn't even big on jewelry, just a few nice pieces. But I'd always stop and look. Ben called it a grown-up candy store.

"What do you like best?" he'd ask.

"Who wants to know? You're a starving artist, remember? I'd need a rich boyfriend on the side to get anything from this place."

"Hey," he'd say, his fingers threaded through mine as we stood at the window. "I'm a *commercial* artist—halfway to selling out completely. Besides, if I ever have a windfall and want to do something stupid, I at least want to buy the right damn thing."

So I'd tell him, fancy to simple, all the things in the window I liked.

I didn't want to look in the box. It was almost too much. I'd come looking for Benjamin's secret life, but I hadn't counted on a secret that was for me. Our anniversary had come and gone in June, just two weeks after he died. I marked the day by returning the binoculars I'd bought for him. Then, not wanting to go back to our house, I had gone to the boat, where I drank as much red wine as I could before passing out. It was the best sleep I'd had since the funeral. That was the day I decided to move out of our house.

I stared at the box. It wasn't wrapped, but had a fancy gold ribbon tied around it. It had never occurred to me that he'd bought a present for me before the accident.

"Oh, Ben," I said out loud. Georgie raised her head, then settled down again on the rug. "Okay." I took in a deep breath, needed something of an internal pep talk to get me through the opening of the box. "It's not that big a deal. Just a present." But it was a big deal. It was Benjamin, a *new* thought from him, a show of his sweetness, revealed after I no longer had those things to count on.

I touched the ribbon, had the impulse to leave it be and let his intentions remain unspoiled, take the effort as my gift. But he hadn't bought the present for it to stay inside the box. He'd bought it to be worn. I tugged at the gold bow and it loosened, fell away. My fingers felt almost too weak to grasp the lid, but I focused, tugged slightly at one edge, and lifted. The hinges made a creaking noise, protested the disturbance. Inside, a gold necklace, attached near the clasp, fell in loose array on a white satin inlay. A small pendant of pale green hung at the bottom of the chain.

I imagined the store, the glass display. I tried to recall if I'd ever seen the necklace before. The chain looked impossibly delicate, and, as I examined it, small. *Had I ever mentioned the necklace? Had he pointed it out, asked me?* I fixed on it, hoping for some memory to come clear. But there was no memory. He'd picked it out cold. That was okay, wonderful even. I dropped the hope of some last connection of our two minds and tried to lose myself in the surprise. But something bothered me. Something too simple to miss.

With the tips of my fingers I detached the chain from the satin, lifted the necklace in the pale storage room light. The lovely, square-cut stone was set in a slight gold pendant. As I brought the necklace to my neck, prepared to put it on, everything in me began shaking. The shivering seized me, traveled to my gut, and I thought I might be sick. As tears arrived, the moment of clarity I'd hoped for arrived full on and it was nearly as terrible as the very moment I'd laid Benjamin in the ground. The chain was too small for me; the stone, the setting, too delicate to belong on a grown woman.

All at once I could hear her, sitting at the table in the restaurant. *My birthday's next week.*

I looked at the necklace. A child's pale, green birthstone. Peridot. August. The present wasn't in anticipation of our anniversary, or even anyone's birthday for that matter; it was a present that spoke of a father's affection for a small girl he'd accepted as his daughter. The necklace was for Angel.

I gave up on any attempt at controlling the wave of pain that came over me; sat on the hard floor surrounded by all that was left of my life with Benjamin. And as the timer for the lights clicked down to nothing and the world around me went dark, I heard my own sobs echoing in the empty hall outside my space. I heard, but couldn't stop, because for the first time since the day I'd met my husband, I felt betrayed. *What else had I missed in our marriage? Had he been better at lying than I ever imagined?* Those doubts took Ben from me in a way that death could not. Georgie pressed close beside me, her warmth the only kind thing left in the world.

I don't know how long I sat there. Someone came into another part of the warehouse. The bright light that suddenly returned as they turned on the timer startled me. Then I heard the echoed rumble as they opened their unit. I wondered what they came to bring or to take away. And as my thoughts jumped around, avoiding the random sadness and confusion of the necklace, I saw a wardrobe box, the tape already cut open. It held Ben's wool sport coats, the ones he wore to work in the winter.

I stood and opened the box all the way, fingered through the jackets, one by one, hoping to feel the immediacy of him the way I always did. The smells remained, the familiar feel of the fabric. But he no longer came to me. It was as if he'd left. For the first time since I'd been coming to the space, I felt completely alone. On one shoulder of his favorite blue blazer, two delicate strands of hair lingered, and I touched them with the tips of my fingers, could barely feel them. I thought of Angel's hair, recently discarded on my car console with the borrowed elastic band. Nearly the same color. But there was only one way to tell if the hairs shared the same mysterious genetic concoction that would make Angel and Ben belong to each other in all the ways that nature offered. I took the strands from Ben's coat, then secured them under the plastic that held my driver's license.

On the way home there was a laboratory where I could stop. I'd done a story once on siblings who found each other after thirty years through a DNA match. A couple of technicians at the lab had answered my questions. One of them had asked me out for a drink. I'd declined, playing the "I'm married" card even though it would have been another excuse if I hadn't had that one. But he'd been a nice guy and I figured he'd remember me. I could take in the two samples of hair, Ben's and Angel's, and then there would be an answer. At least to one of the questions that plagued me.

My hands were shaking as I lowered the door to the storage space. Did I want to find out? Did it really matter? An answer wouldn't change the idea that Ben and Angel spent time together. I wouldn't answer my questions about Reese. What he may or may not have begun to feel for her again. But finding some measure of truth in the messy mix of questions was somehow important to me. If I could discount Angel at least through science, then maybe I could take back some part of Ben again for myself. If the flip side of the coin came up, knowing would count for something.

Maybe in the days or weeks (I couldn't remember) that it took to get the results, I could convince myself that some kind of answer would be enough to make a difference; perhaps enough to let me put it to rest. But driving away from Ben's things, the automatic gates closing behind me, I felt less and less sure that I could reclaim any good from the memories I had of Ben. The question was, could I cut out that part of my life, the same way I'd tried to cut out my failures with Elise, and still be whole enough to go on?

15

Reese

Reese went through the door at the glass storefront. The strip mall looked plain and familiar. The kind of place that paid little attention to who came and went. She'd traveled through at least half the country in the eight years since she'd left Ben, and the one thing she could count on was how much the generic outskirts of any good-sized town looked just like the one she'd left before.

For her own tastes, she preferred the small, beating heart of Charleston: a last holdout of horse-and-buggy clopping streets, and the market where black women sat surrounded by displays of baskets that their mothers and aunts and grandmothers had taught them how to weave.

But for the moment she needed an ugly strip mall. She needed a pay-by-the-minute computer that would connect her to a pharmacist who would ask no questions. She had a prescription pad with the DEA number of a doctor in Boone, North Carolina. She'd slipped it out of the manila folder in the trunk, leaving her other papers inside. And thanks to Gina, she had a valid credit card. With any luck, through the magic of FedEx, she would have the solution to her most pressing need in her possession by the next day. That would get her through the short term. Long term? That remained a work in progress. At some point she'd need real help, the kind of help she almost got in Boone before she got Angel's hysterical call.

A large pharmacy sat at the end of the strip. It would be more immediate, and it was tempting to try. But someone might turn her in. She'd been all over the news with the shooting. Passing off an illegal prescription would land her in jail, and they'd take Angel away for sure. She could wait a couple of days if she had to. It was safer to go online. The delivery would be a bit tricky. She couldn't have it sent to the boat. Then she thought of Charlie. He'd be in the Ship's Store the next morning, taking over the day guy's shift. That would work. Maybe she'd even agree to that date with him after all.

16

∞

Gina

A storm had threatened, but passed on by. The sky looked clear again. I drove to the laboratory, broke any number of rules by walking in with my wallet and the elastic band in one hand and Georgie tucked under the other arm.

"You can't bring animals inside," the receptionist told me.

"I'm sorry. It's too hot to leave her in the car. I wanted to drop off these samples and see if they are a match to be blood related. I know Jonathan."

At the mention of the tech's name she softened. "What's your name?" she asked.

"Gina Melrose. From the newspaper story a while back."

She called back and confirmed my favorable status with the talent. Told me to fill out the paperwork in the car and drop it back with her.

"And hurry, if you can," she added. "I get off work in fifteen minutes and I need to lock up."

It took me twenty minutes to finish up, but she waited, and I drove away wondering if I could possibly handle finding out that Angel was really Ben's daughter. I could put the answer to that on hold for the time being. I hadn't opted for an additional charge for rush results. It would be a couple of weeks, at best. They would mail the information to me when the tests were complete.

A surprise waited on the boat when I finally got back. Derek. He sat relaxed at the helm, two unopened Heinekens sweating on the seat off to the side. Tanned skin played against his dark hair, gave him the look of an island race, something exotic, to be visited—vacationed upon, then *vacated,* in lieu of home. I felt glad to see him.

"Hey," Derek said as I came alongside on the dock. His smile brought out all the angles in his features. I realized how familiar they had become to me.

"I hope you don't mind that I waited here," he said. "I meant to come by yesterday, but I got caught up in things and—"

"It's okay," I said, stepping onto my boat. He shifted to give me a clear path into the cockpit.

What the hell? Temporary. Permanent. What did all that mean anyway? After my discovery of the necklace among Benjamin's things, the entire notion of home had become ridiculous. It was a temporary world. Derek fit right in.

"What's up?" I asked him, struggling to seem normal after my ordeal at the storage place.

"Why don't you tell me?" His tone changed. He looked at my face, at my eyes, and his expression took me off guard. It registered genuine concern. "What's wrong?" he tried again.

I could feel the raw balloonlike quality of my cheeks and skin, and knew, without the benefit of a mirror, that my bout of crying had left me looking like a circus refugee.

"What do you mean?" I stalled.

"You look like hell."

"You know just what to say." I tried to joke, but it came out flat. "Now, excuse me while I down a bottle of Drano."

"Seriously," he said, undeterred. "Sit down. What happened?"

I sat near him on the Stern Perch, up and away from him. I felt exposed, on display, but I was afraid to get too close to him, afraid of dissolving again into the mess I'd been before. From my higher vantage point I could see the sun setting low over the marsh. It had been the longest day since the funeral.

"I found something," I told him, too exhausted to lie. "Something in Benjamin's things." I stopped. This was where I should have left it, but I didn't want to stop. Ben didn't deserve discretion. For the first time, I acknowledged what lay beyond the hurt feelings, the betrayal. Real anger.

"He'd bought a necklace," I went on, feeling bolder with each word. "A present for somebody else."

"Jesus," Derek said, a low muttering—genuine and unguarded. "How do you know that?"

"I don't want to get into it," I told him, realizing that in the small world of the marina, somebody would figure things out—who Reese was, who Angel was—and my business would be everywhere. "I just know, that's all."

He looked off, toward the marshes. The sun's fierce slant put his profile in relief, and within the shadow that fell across his features, he was ageless, no resemblance to the near-boy I'd fashioned him to be when we first met. He looked strangely like Ben—a younger version, of course, but unmistakable. I realized for the first time how similar they were. In features, in size and coloring. Was that why I'd given in so easily to Derek in the first place?

"Listen," he said, breaking the silence with conspicuous resolve, "I didn't know Ben any more than to speak to him on the docks. But he didn't strike me as the kind of person who'd cheat on you. I know he'd kid around a lot, but even when he was joking with women, he didn't send out stuff like that."

"You watched him that closely?"

"I watch people all the time," he said, again looking off, away from me, as if embarrassed by his admission. "Remember? I plan to make a living at it the way you do. Write for newspapers or magazines. I've learned to watch everything, made it a habit to remember what I see. And best I could tell, whenever I saw Ben around, he wasn't into anything but you."

His gaze remained on the distant marsh, but the way he said it, his voice getting lower with the last phrase, it sounded like a secret he was telling me. Something just between the two of us.

"I don't want to talk about it anymore." I really didn't. And I especially didn't want to tell him about the DNA tests. Doing it without telling Reese would sound like an invasion of privacy, no matter what kind of spin I tried to put on it.

"I mean it, Gina. I just can't see it happening."

I tried to shake off the feelings that stirred as I watched him. I wasn't sure just what I'd responded to—him, or the things he said. Maybe they were of one piece.

"It's complicated, Derek."

Derek thought I was talking about Ben having an affair. That was unthinkable. But then, so was his relationship with Angel.

Derek turned his face toward me, a gesture I hoped would break the spell. But I'd seen him new somehow. I'd seen him as more than a boy, and it scared me a little to think I could actually feel something good again. I moved down to sit beside him, put my hand on his arm. His warm skin felt damp from the heat of the day.

"But I meant it. I don't want to think about Ben anymore. Not right now."

When I heard myself say Benjamin's name, the feelings I'd had while I was sitting in the storage room shot through me without warning. I leaned into Derek, and he put his arm around me, pulled me closer. Instinctively, I rubbed my face, my mouth, against the skin of his neck. He was *real*. He was salty and warm, and kind. And he'd never lied to me.

"Why don't we go below?" I whispered. "I don't want to be such a mess out here." I thought of Reese, couldn't remember if I knew where she'd gone. She could come back at any time, find me with Derek.

What the hell did I care? My husband was dead, and for all I knew, it was worse than just a child's necklace. Maybe Derek was wrong. Maybe Ben had been paying attention to Reese too. It seemed impossible that Ben would screw around, but, then again, I'd never have thought he would lie about Angel either. It was the first time the real possibility of infidelity had formed fully in my head, but pieces of it had been there since the day Reese showed up. Why had she come back? To see Ben. The three of them, a happy family.

Once in the cabin, Derek was kissing me, running his lips down my cheek, my collarbone. I felt his breath, warmer than the air, on my skin, and I bent my head slightly to find his mouth. His open hands, fingers spread wide, traveled just under the hem of my T-shirt, up my sides. The feelings overtook my thoughts of Ben, and relief came with the momentary absence of pain. It had happened before when I was with him, but never more acutely. Never more welcomed.

I opened my eyes, aware of a shift in his posture, a shift in the air itself, almost. Lane stood at the cabin door, looking lost. In her hands she held a Tupperware container full of something; but the three of us had been rendered mute. We stayed frozen in our respective poses. The irony was that Derek's position left him with his hands slightly under my clothing, his fingers light against my lower ribs. I pulled away from him with as easy a motion as I could manage. No need to look panicked.

"Hey," I said with a ridiculous cheer.

"I fed Reese and Angel some pasta for an early supper," Lane said by way of explanation—as if she needed a reason to drop by my boat early on a Monday evening. "You were gone so long, I thought I'd bring you dinner and check on you."

"Come on in," I said, motioning for her to join us in the cabin. Derek and I maintained a few inches of daylight between us, but I could feel him. Phantom hands lingered on my skin.

"I'll leave this for you," she said, bending down to hand me the plastic container. "Whenever you're ready to eat. There's enough for both of you."

"Lane . . ." I began as she turned to walk away. Derek had yet to make a sound.

"Gina." She looked at me. Smiled. "I'm glad you're heading back toward normal life again. I was a little surprised, that's all. But I shouldn't have been. I'll talk with you tomorrow, okay?"

I felt myself breathe again, could do little more than nod in response.

"Reese is asleep at my house," she offered, as an afterthought. "She wasn't feeling well when she came in, so I told her to lie down. Oh, that reminds me, I should probably get her stuff and take it to my place. I imagine she's there for the night."

The implication brought new heat to my cheeks, and I hoped the abuse of my face, from August sun and recent crying, masked the color of my embarrassment. I reached in the quarter berth and got Reese's duffel. All of her stuff seemed to be inside, but I didn't want to take too much time to search around. Every minute became more awkward than the one before.

"Okay," I said, handing the duffel up to Lane. She was gone before I had to say more.

"That was weird," I said.

Derek grinned, looked every bit himself again. "I guess we're *out*."

An awkward silence settled and I wondered if we could make our way back to where we'd been, or even if we should try to get there. I wanted more than anything to overwhelm the images of the necklace, the images of Ben with Angel, or worse, Ben with Reese. But being with Derek, I realized for the first time, should be its own destination, not a diversionary stop.

"Derek," I said. "We shouldn't, I don't know . . ."

"I know." He stepped back. "Listen, Gina. I'm as into you as I can possibly be—"

"It's okay." I cut him off. I didn't want to hear the apology that followed a rejection. He was backing off, and I wanted to spare both of us the explanations.

"No, listen to me." He pressed on, put his hand on my arm for emphasis. "After what you've been through today . . . Gina, I don't want to be the guy you screw around with because you're pissed off at your husband . . . I mean, your former husband . . ."

There was no easy way around the word *dead*.

"I know what you mean, Derek." I wanted to pull back, to protect the small amount of strength I had left to call on.

"No, you don't." His voice went firm. "I *want* to be with you. You don't know how much, really. I wouldn't have waited here half the afternoon if I didn't. But I don't want this to happen just because of how you're feeling about someone else. It's not . . ." He stopped, stared at me, shook his head as if the words had taken flight, leaving him stranded.

"I'm sorry," I said. "My feelings are all over the place." I reached over, laid my hand on his arm, and I felt him give slightly. I put my fingers lightly on his neck. His pulse moved fast under his skin. Maybe he wasn't looking for a way out. God, maybe he *did* feel as conflicted as I'd been feeling. "But as far as thinking that I'm just reacting . . . Derek, there's more to us than that."

"I know." He voice was low, slightly hoarse. He leaned toward me. "I knew that before you did."

He was right. He had known. I was just figuring it out, and I had nearly dismissed him. Because he was young, I thought he couldn't be serious about what we were doing, but I was wrong.

"I'm older than you are." I stated the obvious. "As long as we're getting it all out there."

"So was the last woman I dated seriously."

Reference to the old girlfriend. A bad sign. "Is that why you broke up?"

He shook his head "She decided she liked girls."

"That'll do it." I stopped, didn't know what else to say. "Listen. How about I put this in the fridge and we go get some barbecue?" I held up Lane's Tupperware. "Or we can get burgers, fish, whatever you want. I just want to go somewhere."

"Whoa!" he said. "You mean actually go on a date?" He was smiling, back in his comfort zone.

"It could work. Give me a second to brush through my hair."

"Sounds good. I need to pick up my keys at the marina and I'll be ready to go. I'll take you to a place where they serve alligator."

It was something Ben would have suggested. The notion stopped me and I almost bailed on our plans. Instead, I forced my mind to move on, went below to see if I could resurrect my splotchy face for a decent night out.

It sounded like Reese had gone down for the count anyway, and mercifully, *not* under my roof. Tomorrow would be soon enough to find out the truth about the complicated existence my husband had kept from me. The questions alone seemed unbearable, let alone the answers. A night out with Derek, a good microbrew and an alligator appetizer, should be distracting enough to avoid thinking on either one for too long a stretch.

17

∞

Reese

"What time is it?" Reese asked no one in particular. She was only half awake, but realized that she was in a bed. A nice bed. The sheets smelled like fabric softener and something else. Lavender.

"I can't tell time on clocks without numbers," Angel answered, sitting in the bed beside her. She had her pj's on. "I got up and Lane made breakfast for me. Then I decided to get back in bed until you wanted to get up."

Reese sat up, looked at the bedside clock: 9:20. She'd gone back to Lane's after getting called in to finish a shift at Ollie's. Lane had fed her pasta, but she'd been tired. Too tired to even sit at the table and talk like any normal person. Lane had told her to lie down, and the bed had looked so good. She'd slept all night in her clothes. Damn it to hell. She was a mess and it was getting worse.

"I gotta get up, baby doll," she told Angel. "I've got something to pick up at the Ship's Store before ten."

"Can I go?"

Reese looked at her daughter, thought of how she'd been taking Angel for granted the last few days. And the poor kid was injured, at that.

"Get your clothes on," she told the girl. "Do it fast. I'm going to wash my face, brush my teeth, and then we have to go."

Angel smiled, ran to a drawer, and began sorting with her good hand through the scarce choices for clothes to put on. As Reese stood up to go to the bathroom, she glanced inside the drawer and saw that Angel's clothes sat stacked inside, all of them folded and clean.

"Did Lane tell you that you could put your stuff there?"

"Yeah," Angel said, still selecting and not even looking up as she answered. "She took everything out of it for me and said that even when we move into that other house, I can keep this drawer as mine for when I sleep over."

"And she washed your clothes?" Reese asked.

"Uh-huh." Angel stood up, pink shorts and a white shirt in her hand. "They smell good." She held them up for Reese to smell.

"Lavender," Reese said. "Like the sheets. She must put something in the dryer."

She thought again of how she'd let herself get out of touch with Angel. Relying on Lane's obvious affection for the child, Reese had given in to Lane as a safety net, allowed herself a brief reprieve from responsibility. Not entirely, of course. She'd made sure to follow the doctor's instructions and change Angel's bandage each day. She kept the antibiotic salve around the wound just as the nurse had shown her. But had Lane been giving Angel the pills if her arm hurt? She must have; she'd been on top of everything else. One look at Angel's clean and pressed clothes in the drawer told her that much.

But regardless of who the child had in her life, Angel stayed tight as glue to her. It was natural, but it worried Reese. She wondered if Angel would be able to adjust to all the changes that had to come.

"Go find your hair clips," Reese said, mainly to give the child another task. Angel hated being at loose ends. "Have Lane brush through your hair and put them in if she isn't busy."

"She's taking a shower," Angel said. "I hear the water. She has a tooth appointment this morning. But I can do my hair by myself."

After Angel left, Reese stretched out her arms, her fingers. Tried to get the blood flowing. With any luck, some of it would make it to her brain and she'd be able to think straight. She hoped her package had gotten to the Ship's Store. She'd paid extra for an overnight delivery and they'd promised it would be there before ten.

Reese went into the bathroom. Clean towels hung on the bar beside the shower, and it was all she could do to resist stepping into the cool spray, washing her hair, her neck, her entire body. A shower like Lane's could cleanse you of so much, she thought.

"Ready!" Angel came into the bathroom before she'd even begun. She washed her face hurriedly, rinsed her mouth with toothpaste, and found her pocketbook. She still had Gina's credit card to return. So many things to remember.

"Let's go, honey," she said to Angel, but the child was already halfway out the door.

She could hear the shower running in the other bathroom near Lane's room.

"Do you need anything from the Ship's Store?" she called in from the door.

"No, thanks!" Lane called back.

She moved fast to catch up with Angel, and it occurred to her that it had become harder and harder to keep up. Maybe that would change, but maybe it wouldn't. She had to make her decisions sooner than she'd hoped.

"Come on!" Angel yelled from the door to the store.

"Hold on," she called back.

Hold on. Hold on, Reese, she thought. But everything seemed to be slipping out of her grasp.

As she went into the store, she saw two welcomed sights. The FedEx box on the counter behind the cash register, and Charlie, smiling at her in a way that made her feel younger after all.

18

Gina

$\mathcal{D}$erek's studio apartment above the marina had the look and feel of a permanent living space, not at all the storage-room-with-a-cot existence that I'd imagined. Copies of *Atlantic Monthly* and the *Oxford American* lay wrinkled and read on a maple coffee table that sat in front of a sage green futon. A wrought-iron bed sat in one corner, and across the room, in the kitchen, a grind-and-brew coffee-maker shared counter space with a bread machine. Nice prints, a jazz festival and a black-and-white sailing shot, hung on the walls. Not bad for a guy just out of graduate school, working as a night security guard.

In the full light of morning I could see the entire apartment from the bed. Beside me, Derek slept on his back, in the position of an animal that rests secure from danger. His arm splayed out above his head, legs sprawled. It either meant that he trusted me or that he was simply used to sleeping alone.

We'd ended up at his place after dinner. Not right away. He'd taken me home first. I'd followed him around on his security rounds. Georgie tagged along and it passed for the evening walk she'd missed. Then we'd gone back to my boat for a beer. By two A.M. it became clear that we were stalling our good-bye.

"I need to get back up to my place," he said. "I can see the front gate from there, and I get up to check out the marina several times a night. It's easy work, but they *do* pay me to do it."

"I don't want anything to happen with us tonight," I told him as we were discussing our options. "I took things with you really casually before, but now . . ."

"I think a lot's happened already." He seemed amazed, and he was right. The kind of night we'd had was the last thing I'd expected from such a terrible day. "I'm guessing that you're talking about sex, and I suppose I agree. There seems to be more at stake than there used to be." Then he added, "Unless you change your mind. Then all bets are off." He smiled. The off-kilter features of his face, all the angles of his nose and chin, looked impossibly beautiful to me.

"Yeah," I offered. "I'm sure." *Jesus, Gina.* A uniquely inarticulate response from someone whose stock-in-trade involved words.

"Listen, don't take this wrong, but I'd like to wake up with you," he said. We sat in the main salon of my boat. Light movement of the night air caused the water to lap gently against the hull. "We might as well see the night through. I mean, at this point, waking up is only a few hours away."

"Right," I teased. "Just a slumber party. I heard about that course in college."

"Which one?" A smile played at the edges of his mouth.

"The one that teaches guys how to tell a date anything to keep the options in play."

"I never actually got into that course. It was booked up solid every semester."

The boat shifted with a small, steady movement of the water. I thought of night sails I'd taken with Ben, occasionally dropping anchor long after dark had set in. The breeze made the boat seem restless, eager to go, and the memory took on a quality of longing. Maybe Derek would be game to just take off, set sail. But then I remembered that he was working. His time between eleven P.M. and daylight belonged to the marina.

"Seriously," he said. "How about coming up to my place?"

I shot him a sideways glance.

"I'm not trying to pull anything. That's God's honest truth," he said, his face earnest. "I just don't want to leave you now. Gina, you've been through a lot today. Don't shut me out of it." Then he added, "I know all of this has something to do with Reese."

"What do you mean?"

"All this business about Benjamin, and the necklace. Listen, Gina. I know that she was his ex-wife. I didn't say anything—not to anybody—because I know you haven't made a point of introducing her that way, but—"

"Who told you?" I couldn't imagine Lane talking with him about it, and the police report and the newspaper had been generous enough to identify her as a relative. One of the perks of living in a small place was that people actually showed compassion from time to time.

"An old guy who works on boats at the yard here. He knew Benjamin from way back," he explained. "He'd seen her before."

"Yeah, well, it's not a big secret," I said. "It's just something I'd rather not explain over and over if I don't have to."

"I know. But I figured she's the person you were talking about with the necklace and—"

"It wasn't for her," I interrupted him. "Ben bought it for Angel. Her daughter."

Derek's face took on a skeptical expression. "That doesn't seem like such a big deal. I don't mean to trivialize it, but I don't think that's any reason to be as upset as you were."

I listened to the halyards again, wondered why I was opening up about everything to someone I'd considered an overgrown boy just hours before. But my picture of Derek was changing. I was changing.

"Angel might be Ben's daughter." I sounded tired, even to myself. "He didn't know. I mean, for a long time, he didn't know. But he'd found out about it somehow. Recently, I think. Reese must have decided to tell him for some reason. He'd spent time with Angel and he kept it from me. And where Angel goes, Reese goes, so I don't know what the story is. He never told me about any of it. And the necklace . . . The necklace is clearly a child's, and it's Angel's birthstone."

"Jesus . . ." Derek sat with his mouth partly open, shook his head.

"Like I said, I don't know exactly how Reese plays into all this." I looked over at him. In the small confines of my cabin, he seemed larger. Capable, perhaps, of holding some of the weight I'd been carrying. "It's possible he was sleeping with her again. I can't believe he would do that—not the Ben I knew—but why would he lie to me about Angel?"

Derek didn't try to respond, not with words. He simply leaned in and held me. It came as unexpected comfort at an hour when sleep should have been necessary but would have been hard to come by. It occurred to me that staying with him might lend me enough peace to actually get some rest, and suddenly it felt like the most reasonable decision in the world. I pulled away from him, sat up, and took in a full breath to try to avoid a new round of tears.

"Let me get my toothbrush," I told him. "I'll go back to your place with you."

Moments later I was putting the splashboards on the cabin door. I decided to leave the lock off in case Reese came back before I did. Georgie looked confused as I peeked in and said good night. Derek and I walked the short path and took the outside stairs up to his apartment. At two A.M., no one but a prowling tomcat made note of our presence.

Derek had stayed true to his offer, expected nothing more than slight conversation followed by blessed sleep. The latter was more than I could have hoped for. In the brighter light of morning as he still slept, it occurred to me that I'd done something for entirely the right reasons for a change. By the time he had opened his eyes, I was rooting around his kitchen looking for cinnamon to add to the pancake batter that I'd mixed in preparation for a home-cooked breakfast. And trying not to feel guilty about making the dog wait for her first walk of the day.

"What are you looking for?" he asked, standing up and arching backward in a morning stretch. He wore boxers, blue with Japanese cartoon characters on them. My earlier assessment of him as a grown man began to wane.

"Cinnamon," I told him. "You can't make pancakes without cinnamon."

"Who says?" he asked.

"My great-aunt Lett. She was a lousy aunt, but a great cook."

"Well, I don't have cinnamon," he said, coming into the kitchen. He stuck his finger in the batter and licked it.

"There are raw eggs in there," I said.

"I'll take my chances." He hugged me. Even in one short night, his sleep smell had become familiar to me, something akin to candles and pie on the comfort scale. When he started to pull back, I leaned in a little harder and he held me longer. He held me until I let go.

Still wearing my clothes from the previous day, I took the indoor stairs down to the Ship's Store to look for cinnamon. The emotional roller coaster I was on had only topped the first hill. I sensed there were a fair number of highs and lows to go before the ride settled. And the scariest part was, there was no real way off until it stopped.

*   *   *

"Where did you come from?" Charlie stood at the hardware shelf, straightening up cans and bottles of deck cleaner and spider spray.

"I stayed up at Derek's place last night," I said. Charlie's broad grin held a dozen or so remarks that he blessedly kept to himself. But there was no need to be secretive. This one wasn't going to be in the bag for long anyway. "I thought Randall worked days in here."

"We're switching today," he said. "Didn't Reese talk to you?" The bells on the front door announced customers coming in. A couple of kids making a beeline for the ice-cream freezer. I looked at my watch. It was nearly eleven o'clock.

"I haven't seen her yet," I told him. The mention of Reese's name left a stain on my thoughts. The morning had been better than it had any right to be. I didn't want to let it go. "Do you have any cinnamon?"

"Yeah, two aisles over," he said. "Listen, she was going to talk to you about the four of us going out tonight. I thought you'd be the hard sell, but . . ." He glanced over toward the back stairs to Derek's apartment. "I'm guessin' now that maybe you won't." His exaggerated Southern inflection implied even more than his words. He raised his eyebrows and smiled.

"So you want to go out with Reese?" The thought of a double date with Ben's ex seemed too bizarre.

"Yeah, she'll talk to you," he said, back working with his shelves. "She was in here a little bit ago. She picked up your package for you."

"What package?"

"Some FedEx that came this morning. She said she'd give it to you. I guess she didn't know you were upstairs." He grinned again, shook his head. "So how about tonight? You guys up for it?"

"I don't know," I said, wondering what package would have come. "I'll have Derek talk to you about it."

"All right," he said as I made my way back to the stairs. "Think about it. We could all have a blast."

I nearly fled back up to Derek's place, and it wasn't until I got to the door that I realized I had taken off without even paying for the small container of ground cinnamon I was holding.

"Hell, he knows where to find me," I mumbled to myself as I went back inside.

Before I could begin to sort out my conversation with Charlie, Derek added another twist to my morning.

"Your cell phone rang," he said. "I'm sorry. It's like mine and I just picked it up out of habit and answered."

"Who was it?"

"Some woman. Maxine? She said to call her back."

"Shit." My mother-in-law would have been on the bottom of the disclosure list when it came to my night with Derek. What the hell. The coaster was heading back down and I had to hang on for the drop.

"Who was she?" he winced as he asked.

"Ben's mom."

"Shit." He echoed my sentiments.

We set about making pancakes together without any more talking.

"Hi, Maxine," I said after hearing my mother-in-law's cheerful hello. "Derek said you called."

I'd gotten back on the boat. Reese had come and gone and there was no package to be found.

"Hey, darlin'," Maxine said. God bless her, she didn't sound weird about the Derek thing. Maxine was about the best person I knew. "I've got a few things to talk to you about."

"Okay, what's up?"

"Well, the first is that my realtor over on Sullivan's Island called. The Bensons, who always finish out the season with us, cancelled. They have a family illness. She didn't say, but Herb's had problems with his heart, so I'm thinking that's probably it. Anyway, that frees up the house right away."

"Do you need any money up front?" I asked. "I'm going to cover things until she gets a paycheck."

"Don't worry about it. It can wait until things settle out with her job. I'm not charging her much anyway, mainly enough to cover utilities. The realtor I work with was horrified." She didn't try to explain herself, but I knew she was pretty soft inside that hard shell. "So go ahead and tell what's-her-name that she can move in."

What's-her-name was beginning to dominate every conversation I had.

"I'll tell her when I see her," I said, settling down with a Diet Coke. "I've heard rumors of Reese sightings all morning, but I haven't talked to her today."

"Aren't you the lucky one?" she said. "Listen, Gina. Tell me what's going on."

"Narrow that question down a little and I'll do my best."

"Well, for starters," she said, her voice getting lower, more serious, "my neighbor brought me the Charleston paper from last week. Why didn't you tell me?"

I should have known Maxine would see the paper, should have told her about the shooting when I was standing in front of her. It wasn't the kind of thing to talk about on a cell phone.

"I'm sorry, Maxine." A weak start, but what else? Why the hell hadn't I told her? "I was embarrassed, I guess, and I didn't want to get into it. Angel was fine and there didn't seem to be any point . . . Then Reese skirted around it . . . Honestly, I wasn't trying to keep it from you. I just didn't feel like telling it again."

"Is that why you stood up for her about the cottage? Out of guilt?"

I took a sip of my drink, let myself feel the cool liquid travel the length of my chest. Why had I stood up for Reese?

"Could be, I don't know. I don't understand half of what I've done in the last couple of days, Maxine. I'm acting on gut impulses and not much more, and there's been another turn of events that I'm sorting through. But with Reese . . . part of me actually feels bad for her. Regardless of all her screwed-up decisions, I think she wants the best thing for Angel. And we can't completely dismiss the idea that Ben might be her father."

"But?" she said.

"But what?" I asked. She was relentless.

"But something else is going on. You sound as nervous as a bird." Her instincts made me feel like a child who had misbehaved. She read me too well. "Is it the man who answered the phone? Because if it is—"

"No, Maxine. I didn't keep anything from you on that. This thing with Derek—whatever it is—has just taken a turn in the last day. I wasn't hiding that from you."

"Good." She sounded like a mother, like the mother I'd always wanted my mother to be. "Because *I* know what you've been through over Ben. I've seen it, and it's worried me to death. You weren't making normal progress, Gina. This is not a bad thing, your time with this man—whatever it is. Let yourself be happy if you can."

Dammit, I was crying again. This time it was different. She was unbearably kind, and she loved me. She loved me the way I thought Ben had loved me. Could I have been wrong about that?

"So," she said, her tone changing back to business. "What is this *turn of events* in the last day or so?"

"I don't know what to tell you. There are some things going on with Reese and Angel. I need to find out exactly what I'm dealing with. I just don't want you to think I'm keeping things from you. I promise, as soon as I sort out what's going on—what's *gone* on—I'll tell you everything."

"I won't pry, Gina. But I'm your biggest fan. Don't think you can't come to me—about *anything*."

"I know."

"And Gina?" Her voice was almost too low for me to hear, as if we were conspiring on something, "You need to be careful with Reese. Don't get sucked into her stories, her . . . I don't know . . . her needs. She's like arts funding—no matter how many donations are made, there's never enough to turn a profit. Reese *will never* turn a profit, Gina. She'll always be playing catch-up."

I laughed. Maxine saw things from the oddest angles.

"And are you *sure* you want me to let her live in the cottage?" she added. "I'm doing this mostly because you asked me."

"Maxine," I said, "I know you're concerned about the house, but—"

"Oh, please." She laughed. "I was just being difficult. She could burn the thing down and I've got it insured for every penny. You have to be covered with God-knows-who renting it all summer. It's just that when she asked . . . Well, that woman rubs me every way except the right one. But it seemed to be important to you that I let her do this. And you're right . . . there are issues about the child we have to consider. Do you still want Reese to move into the house? That's what I'm asking. Yes or no? If I don't give it to her, she might just go away. That could be the best thing for everybody."

"Maxine," I said, "it's your decision, but yes, I still want you to help her out. I don't know what part of my instincts to go with when it comes to Reese. I know Ben helped her out, sent her money, from time to time, when she needed it. But part of me doesn't trust her to be honest about what she ate for breakfast, much less about Angel, and Ben." I stopped. I'd almost said too much. "But I don't want her to take off anywhere until I get some answers."

I took another sip of drink, wondered how I would find those answers when I was dealing with the flakiest woman with a pulse. "On the other hand," I went on, mumbling half to myself, "I want her off my fucking boat." When I realized I'd said it out loud, my cheeks ran hot. "I'm sorry, Maxine. I shouldn't have—"

"It's okay, dear," she interrupted, with the exaggerated annunciation of her best club lady voice. "I want her off your *fucking* boat too."

I'd barely taken a shower when the phone rang again. Naked, except for the towel, I went looking for where I'd put it down. I wondered if Maxine had forgotten something. I found the cell phone on the kitchen counter.

"Hello?"

"Gina?" It was my mother. Like always, her tone was polite, impersonal enough to be somebody raising money for the local wetlands conservatory.

"Hi, Mom. How are you?"

"I'm good. How are you, sweetheart?" she said. Her cadence fell on even beats. A Stepford Wife at cocktail hour. I could see her. Going about her day in her manicured neighborhood, with her manicured fingers. "I just hadn't talked with you in nearly a week and I thought I'd check in, make sure you're okay."

It's what mothers do. She always did what mothers were supposed to do. But it was like the set of a play: all false fronts. Behind it, the raw guts of the backstage area remained functional and bare. It had been that way for years, even before my sister jumped in that pool. Maybe that was why Elise jumped in the deep end before she'd gotten good at swimming. Maybe that was why she'd always gone to any lengths to get five minutes of attention.

"I'm fine," I told her. "How's Dad?"

"He's in Richmond this week for the regional meetings. He'll be back on Wednesday."

"Why didn't you go with him?" I'd always thought she might travel with him once I went away to school. Instead, they seemed to have less in common than when I was home.

"I've got my book club here tomorrow morning. Which reminds me, I need to run out and get a new coffeemaker. The old one won't keep a pot hot for five minutes."

Coffeemakers. A delightful new recipe for baked sole. Some friend of mine from high school she'd just seen at the dry cleaners. These topics held the meat of our conversations. Weren't mothers and daughters supposed to have more than that? I thought of Maxine, how I could say just about anything and, most of the time, she could guess what I wasn't saying. Lane too, for that matter.

"Mom?" I had to take a chance. Too much had happened, and I was sick of playing tea party every time we talked. "Can I ask you something?"

"Sure, honey. What is it?"

"Do you think that Elise felt like she had enough love?" My heart was going fast. It was the most personal question I'd ever asked my mother. "I mean, she always needed so much from us. She asked for so much. Do you think we gave her enough?" In a sense, it came out of nowhere; in other ways, it seemed as if it had been there all along, just waiting to be asked.

"What in the world are you talking about, Gina?" She sounded panicked. *Good. Let's crawl out of the comfort zone, Mom.*

"I just want to know what you think." I tried to sound calm, something less than crazy. "Since Ben died, I've been thinking about a lot of things. Elise . . . well, sometimes I felt like—"

"I think you've got too much time on your hands," she interrupted. She'd gone from panicked to irritated. Panic might have jostled her out of her suburban stupor. Irritated would get me nowhere.

"I didn't mean to upset you, Mom. I'm sorry. It's just—"

"You didn't upset me," she said quickly. "You're overwrought after all you've been through. I understand that. I think getting off that ridiculous boat and into a real house or at least an apartment might help you move on. But rambling on about your sister is certainly not going to accomplish anything."

I stayed silent, couldn't think of a word to say, really. Finally, when it was clear that in the stylized game of conversation with my mother I had the ball, I fumbled, lost all momentum. "I appreciate the call, Mom. I'm doing fine."

She finished with something like, "You call me if you need anything," and that was that.

I thought of her after she hung up, sitting at her desk in the kitchen, reinventing our conversation and editing the parts that caused her unease. For days after Elise jumped in that pool, I waited for her to fall apart. I wanted her to yell at me, punish me. I wanted her, Dad, one of them to ask what the hell I'd been thinking, socializing with my friends when I was supposed to be keeping an eye on Elise. Why wasn't I watching her? She couldn't swim all that well, for God's sake. Something between random flailing and an active dog paddle.

I wondered if anyone ever told them how she was calling to me. *Gina! Watch! Hey, Gina, look at this!* In my mind, I could see her calling to me, but that's just imagination. In reality, I'd never looked her way. I was at a table with my friends and we could all hear her. We rolled our eyes at my annoying little sister; then we'd gone back to our card game. Rummy. The umbrella at the table kept the sun at bay, and I remember the cool shade that fell over us, the bright sun that seemed to set everything outside our circle on fire.

But my parents never yelled. They barely noticed me, or each other. They stayed inside themselves, went back to a normal routine, as if Elise might be off at camp. And after that first afternoon, when my mother got to the pool and saw the paramedics trying to bring my sister back to life, I'm not sure I even heard her cry again.

But she did cry that day. She cried as she climbed into the ambulance. There was little to gain from the mad race to the hospital. They could have gone straight to the funeral home. But we didn't know the final truth then, and on the ride to the Emergency Room (a neighbor took me while Mom rode with Elise), I thought more about my mother's face than that of Elise. It didn't seem conceivable that anything truly permanent could happen to my sister. But my mother looking that way, sounding that way, was both thrilling and scary.

Then everything changed. Elise was gone, they said. The sounds I heard my mother make when they said that were unbearable; would bring souls back from heaven just to listen and recall the essence of pain. And, still, with all I was feeling that day, I was, on some level, mesmerized, enchanted that this person existed inside a woman I'd seen nearly every day of my life. It had to be avoidance on my part, to focus so intently on her, but I still recall it with the clarity of present time. My father hadn't arrived, never saw her that way, and I've since come to believe that something, someone, merely inhabited her for a brief moment. An angel, maybe, taking pity and becoming my mother in flesh so that no one would suspect the true coldness of her nature.

Standing with my phone still in my hand, I shook off the conversation with my mother. She was right about one thing. I'd become overwrought. Still, what was wrong with that? Anger. Insanity. Anything was better than the gnawed edges of numb regard.

I adjusted the towel around me. Water from my wet hair ran in crazy patterns down the sides of my arms, and I thought of Maxine, how horrified I'd been at her sustained, kinetic grief. The persistence of it wore me out. But she'd had it right then too. I wanted to be the kind of person who could throw something at a wall if it gave me an ounce of relief. I couldn't make my mother open up about Elise after nearly twenty years of silence. If a statute of limitations on emotion existed, I'd likely run out of chances on that one myself. But my pain over Ben hadn't yet become old and embedded. I could still make peace with his death, if I had the nerve. *Let yourself be happy if you can.* It was too soon to tell, but Maxine may have had the right answers all along.

19

∞

Reese

"Do you feel better?" Angel asked. She winced as Reese pulled the last of the old bandage off to look at her shoulder.

"That's what I'm supposed to be asking you," Reese said. They were sitting on the floor in Lane's den. The place had begun to feel like home in just a couple of days. Reese worried that it wasn't a good idea for that to happen.

"But yeah, I feel fine," Reese lied. She dabbed peroxide around the area of the wound. The scab looked clean, but the skin around it had gotten a little more red. "When was I not okay?" Angel seemed to always know when Reese was getting bad again, feeling that loss of herself.

"You needed to sleep yesterday, and when Lane asked if you wanted to go for a walk with us, you said you wanted to read, but I saw your hands shaking a little. You never want to go on walks or play outside when your hands are shaking."

"You're right," Reese said. "I got some pills that will make me better. They came this morning. It hasn't started working yet, but I'll feel like playing hopscotch pretty soon."

"Mom, I don't even play hopscotch anymore." Angel was smiling. At least her shoulder didn't hurt the way it had at first. She wasn't asking for the pain medication as much.

There was a physical therapy session coming up on Thursday. Reese made a mental note to ask about the redness. They told her at the hospital that the wound wasn't all that serious; only an infection could make it dangerous for the child.

"Mom?" Angel turned to face Reese as she finished putting ointment around the wound. "I gotta tell you something."

"What's that, baby?" Reese took a paper towel and wiped the goop off her fingers, then got out a clean bandage to put on the shoulder. When Angel didn't speak up right away, she moved to the couch and sat down, gave the girl her full attention. "Let's give that shoulder some open air for a minute. Go ahead. Tell me what's on your mind."

Angel sat down beside her. "I told," she said.

Reese went still. That could mean so many different things. She didn't want to upset Angel, make her feel responsible for anything bad. Reese felt guilty, imposing all the secrecy on such a young child.

"What did you tell?" She tried to keep her voice light, playful. She felt her fingers tingle, her hands shake in spite of her efforts to keep them steady. She hoped to God the pills kicked in soon. "I'm sure it's not a big deal, Angel. Just tell me what you said."

"I told Gina about my visits with Ben," she said. "About how he showed me puzzles."

Okay, okay. That was a big one. For Angel's sake, she had to stay calm. It simply complicated things. It didn't change anything. Not really. But she had hoped to have more time to sort out her options before she cracked that nut with Gina.

"Come here, baby." Reese pulled off the back of the large bandage, placed it gently on the wounded shoulder. "It's all right, Angel. It really is."

She tugged at Angel to come sit on her lap. The effort, the child's weight, made her feel weaker, but she took a breath, cleared her head, and willed herself to continue for Angel's sake. "I don't want you to worry about it. You didn't do anything bad."

"But you said not to talk about it, and I didn't mean to. It's just that I saw the grave and we started talking about Ben. She seemed nice to me when she talked about Ben and she hadn't been that nice before."

"When has she not been nice?" Reese asked the question mainly to stall, to figure out what to say to her daughter. But she knew more than she wanted to know when it came to Gina's feelings about children. At one point she'd hoped it would work to her advantage. She wasn't proud of that, but it was true.

"I don't know," Angel said. "She just never acted like she liked me much. But at the cemetery . . . well, she was different. It just came out about Ben when she started asking questions."

"Like I said." Reese rubbed the hair back off Angel's forehead. "Don't worry. No harm done. Is that why you wanted to go to church with Gina, because you heard her say Ben was buried there?"

Angel nodded.

"What's it like?" Reese asked. "Is it pretty where he is?" She felt tears, just around the rims of her eyes. She needed to change the subject. Turn on the television. Something.

"It's real pretty," Angel told her. "It's up on this hill and you can see over the trees at the church. The ocean is there."

Was it the ocean? Reese couldn't remember. A channel maybe, that fed into the Atlantic, not too far down. Ben had taken her sailing by the cottage. Out into the ocean too, where large broadside swells made her sick to her stomach. He'd taken Angel on their last trip down. Reese hadn't gone with them. She hadn't been invited.

"He doesn't have one of the big things on his grave yet," Angel told her.

"A tombstone?"

"Yeah, that."

The thought of Ben. The thought of Angel wanting to be close to him again. She would not have a full-blown cry. Not in front of Angel. Besides, her emotions had gotten close to the surface for a number of reasons. She had to keep a handle on herself.

"Want to go?" Angel asked.

"Go where?"

"To see Ben."

"Ben's not there, baby. I don't need to see his grave." The thought terrified her. Not so much the cemetery, the grave, but the church that went with it. She hadn't been in a church since that awful revival. The heel of the preacher's huge palm pressed against her forehead. Falling down in spite of herself. She'd told her friends that he'd pushed her, made it happen. They'd seen it happen, some of them, as their parents watched the preacher on television. They'd given her endless shit about it. But the frightening truth was, he hadn't pushed. He'd barely raised his hand to her before she fell.

"You got the gift," he'd whispered as he knelt over her. She lay paralyzed for seconds . . . minutes . . . ? "Don't turn your back on God's gifts. Good goes to bad when we deny the Lord."

Later, when the preacher made clear what gifts he thought she had, she'd turned her back on all of it—the church, her father, the whole fucking business of religion. All that remained was the memory, and she'd free herself of that too if she could.

"I just thought you might like it there." Angel spoke in a low mumble, refused to look at her mother. Then she stood up, walked across the room with no apparent destination in mind.

Reese knew the answer had come too fast. She hadn't considered why Angel was asking, what it meant to her daughter. Would it be so bad? If it meant something to Angel, she had to at least consider it. She wouldn't have to go in the church.

"Come to think of it," Reese said, "that cemetery is near the cottage we're moving into in a week or so. It wouldn't hurt to ride out and see the house, then stop by on the way back."

"Okay," Angel said, but she still kept her distance.

She had to be careful when it came to Angel's feelings about Ben. She'd wanted so much for them to have something special, a real relationship. Now it had backfired. She was left with bigger problems than before she'd brought Angel to visit him. She was left with not only her own grief, but Angel's as well.

She heard a car drive up. Probably Lane getting back from a dentist appointment she'd gone off to after breakfast. She stood up, tried to ignore the slight falter as her brain lingered behind her intended action. Just a hairbreadth of lag time. Nothing serious.

"Let's ride out to the cottage now," she said to Angel. "We can stop for lunch on the way."

"Can Lane go with us?" Angel looked out the window.

"Let's just make it a trip for the two of us." Reese didn't want to stay around Lane, around anyone, for too long, until she felt more normal again. If someone noticed, the questions would begin.

"Okay," Angel said, perking up.

They went out to greet Lane, whose bizarre speech pattern suggested a rough outing at the dentist.

"What happened?" Reese asked.

"Sick bastard," she managed, obviously forgetting her proximity to Angel. "I'm going to bed." She passed them with no greeting for Angel, which, more than her language, reflected the depth of her infirmity.

"Can I do anything for you?" Reese called back to her.

Best she could make out from the garbled reply, Lane had simply said, "Kill me." Reese laughed as she heard the screen door slam behind the older woman.

Glancing over toward the marina, Reese could make out Gina

standing outside in the cockpit of her boat, shading her eyes with her hand as she looked over toward Lane's house. Reese didn't want to run into her; she especially didn't want to get stuck with Ben's widow on her outing to the grave with Angel, not if that meant being grilled on Angel's revelations about her time with Ben. Best to keep things simple for the time being.

"Come on, baby," she said to Angel. "Let's get going."

As the two of them drove past the Ship's Store on the way out to the main road, she glanced in the rear mirror and saw Gina with that short-tempered dog of hers walking ahead on the leash. The two of them were on the path that led to Lane's house.

"Dodged that bullet," she mumbled.

"What?" Angel asked.

"Nothing, sweetheart," she said, making note of her daughter's arm in the sling. "Bad choice of words."

20

Gina

I could hear Lane coming to her door. When she opened it, she looked like the postoperative photo of a patient in a medical textbook. Her lower cheek and jaw had swelled on the left side; added to that was a face with no makeup and an expression chiseled from obvious abuse.

"What happened?" I stood in the doorway and stared while Georgie, oblivious to Lane's transformation, went in to find the bowl of food that stayed, waiting for her in the kitchen.

"Dentist," Lane said. Her temporary speech impediment added at least one *s* too many to the word. "I'm better." She spoke in fragments. "Medicine. Had to wait to take it. Driving. Okay now." She added the last part as if I'd protested.

"Can I get you anything?" I went to the kitchen and started in on the breakfast dishes that had been left in the sink. At the very least, Reese could clean up after herself and Angel.

"Don't need anything now," she managed. "Maybe a different dentist."

I looked over at her. She was already back on the couch, lying down. *Headline News* ran without sound on the television.

I liked working in Lane's kitchen with its full-sized appliances, ample sink and storage. No matter what I attempted with the boat's galley, it always felt like E-Z Bake cooking. After I finished up, I went in and sat down in the chair beside the couch. Lane stared at the TV. She looked pretty loopy.

"Is Reese around?" I asked, trying to sound casual. With all Lane had been through at the dentist, I didn't want to end up spilling out my miseries about Ben and the necklace. "I need to talk with her."

"She and Angel . . . off somewhere . . . don't know . . ." Her eyes were closing. Sleep could only do her good. I took the blue quilted throw from the back of the couch and put it over her.

It felt strange to be in Lane's house with her asleep on the couch. The talking heads on the television mouthed words that were certainly irrelevant when laid against the events in my life. That narrow perspective lacked vision, but I didn't care. I had to reclaim my own life before I worried about the world.

But how much of my life had been my own, even when Ben was alive? Loving him, it seemed, meant accepting his energy, the natural forces that moved with him. He wasn't to blame, never imposed his choices or his desires. But they were nearly impossible to deny. If Ben wanted us to sail, if he wanted us to volunteer at the burn ward of the hospital, or eat Italian food. Whatever he desired—regardless of how profound or trivial—carried the momentum of his enthusiasm.

The only thing I'd ever denied him was children, and he'd gone to work on that again, but with a greater intensity than ever before. It wasn't fair. Even now, months after his departure, I could still muster the indignation, the overwhelming frustration. He'd known the ground rules when we got married. It had been a deal-breaker at the time of the proposal.

"You don't want kids?" he'd asked when we began serious talks about our future. "Not ever?"

"No." I remember how my heart raced, how I'd fought to keep my voice steady as the discussion progressed. We'd gone out for seven months and I felt consumed by everything I felt for him. He'd mentioned marriage. The only barrier to cross before I agreed was "the talk."

"You're not even out of your twenties." He laughed. "How can you *know* that you don't want kids?"

So I'd told him. He knew that my younger sister had died, but he didn't know the story of how she lived. I remember we sat at a window seat, in the bar of a restaurant on the intracoastal waterway. The drawbridge lifted as a tall-masted sailboat motored through. And I watched it move, taking its time, unbothered by all the cars backed up on the road. The boat needed passage; all others could wait. I needed for him to understand that I wouldn't change my mind about children. So I took great care to be deliberate, to be clear.

"Elise used to hide in the basket of dirty laundry," I told him. "For some reason this made my mother angry. Normally, she might scold us about things, but she rarely raised her voice. But when Elise popped her head out of all those dirty towels and sheets and underwear, my mother would startle, and then she would yell. Not crazy yelling or anything, but for my mother, a remarkable display." I'd watch Elise drink it in, that rare spectacle of emotion from my mother. Even though it was all negative, Elise's eyes would look so excited, almost happy. "No matter how many times it happened, it played out the same. Elise lived for it. That sparking moment of attention."

Ben shook his head slightly as I explained this. I knew he didn't understand what that had to do with children, *our* children.

"I understood my mother's feelings," I told him. "My empathy went to *her*. And on some level, I knew I should step in and give Elise something, make up for that huge gap between what she wanted and what she got from my parents. But I couldn't. I couldn't give her that. And I hated that about myself, even as a kid. So it was this cycle that went around and around from the time I remember until the day Elise died."

"You were twelve years old, Gina," Ben said. "It wasn't your job."

"It could have been."

"You're not a cold person," he insisted. "You're not incapable of love. Just the opposite. Look at us."

"That's entirely different," I said. "You get to choose that the way I am is enough. You get to understand where the rest of it comes from. You already like yourself, Ben. You don't need my eyes on you to determine who you are. A child can't do any of those things. I can't guarantee that there is anything maternal inside me. My mother didn't have it. She still doesn't. It's a chance I can't take. Too much is at stake with a child involved."

"The idea that you understand what Elise needed means you aren't your mother. I love you, Gina," he said. "I think with time . . ."

"We can't go into it with that in mind. If we're wrong, it's too damaging. I've seen it. I'm telling you this now because I don't want you to feel in the future that I've deceived you about it in any way."

"With or without children, I'll accept whatever choices you need to make."

Part of it was my fault. Even I knew he didn't quite believe it. He didn't know how firmly my choice had been made. But I wanted to marry him. God, how I wanted to marry him. He'd given his word, and I knew without question that I would hold him to it. Both of us essentially looked the other way, away from the issue, so that we could have what we wanted at that moment: each other.

But my resolve was strong. I never wanted to feel the way I imagined my mother felt, bound to emotions she couldn't generate. I never wanted to make a child the victim of that nature. I took my mother's maternal restraint for granted when I was young, even began to empathize with it when my sister grew. I saw the damage as it occurred, and instead of bonding with her, the way siblings do, I gave Elise another obstacle to overcome: me.

As Elise's sister, I shared what I saw to be my mother's conflict, her guilt, at not having the resources to meet the younger girl's needs—although, as I got older, I was never sure how much my mother really struggled with these things. But even at twelve I understood that if you gave in to an enormous need like the one my sister had—the way some mothers do, the way a mother should—it can make you disappear.

"I'll accept this, if it is what you really need," Ben had said again, as if to convince himself. "I want to be with *you*. That's the only thing I know for sure."

From time to time Ben would bring it up, as if testing the waters to see if the temperature had changed. But he never pushed, never questioned my resolve, not until those last few months of our marriage. Over those weeks, his arguments to have children gained increasing, surprising momentum. An awful urgency. This remained the greatest strain on our time together.

Lane slept. Her swollen mouth and gums generated loud breathing noises that I found strangely comforting. I thought of Ben again, of how I'd gone to such lengths to be honest with him. How could he have kept so much from me?

I don't know when the idea occurred to me to go looking around in Reese's stuff. I don't know *if* it even occurred to me. But the door was open to the guest room just off the den, and from where I sat I could see Reese's duffel by the bed.

If Lane had opened her eyes, she could have seen what I was doing. I'd gone through Benjamin's things looking for answers, found almost more than I could accept. But I'd only ventured halfway. The rest of the answers lay with Reese—the ones she would tell me, and the ones I could find.

I had my arguments ready if Lane saw me. *She lied to me about Ben and the fact that he knew Angel. She somehow got Ben to lie to me too. I deserve to find some truth in all of this. I deserve to know.* But Lane didn't open her eyes. The dentist must have given her horse tranquilizers.

There, in Reese's duffel, I didn't find any answers about Ben. But I did find something else. The mysterious package. I assumed it was the one Charlie had mentioned. Inside the opened FedEx box were all manner of pills, at least four different bottles. I touched the flap of the package, searched the invoice slip for some indication of what I'd found. The pharmaceutical names meant nothing to me, looked like gibberish, in fact. But I did recognize one thing on the label of each bottle. My own name. A tremble went through me when I saw it, familiar and clear again, on the "Ship To" section of the invoice. GINA MELROSE. The package had been sent to me. The pills prescribed to *me*.

My cell phone began to ring and I felt caught, startled by some shrill alarm. I folded the invoice and put it in the pocket of my jeans. Hell, it had my fucking name on it. Let her explain that one if she noticed it was gone.

21

Reese

"Let me catch my breath." The incline slanted steadily up the hill. Nothing crazy, but Reese wasn't at her best in terms of stamina. Things would get better; she had to tell herself they would.

Angel waited. She must have been uncomfortable, her arm all trussed up in that heavy sling. But she didn't complain. Her patience never cracked, not for a moment. Reese felt proud of the way her daughter had handled everything over the last months, especially over the last days.

"You're terrific," Reese told her. "You know that?"

Angel offered a slight smile. She looked away, snapped a twig off a low branch, and twirled it between her fingers, the teardrop-shaped leaves spinning in the hot breeze. Reese could feel the salty moisture in the air. When she inhaled, she could taste it. A good place for Ben, she decided. A place where salt, sand, and tidal mud mingled without losing the essence of what they were.

"Let's go." Reese started up the hill again, enjoyed a small surge of strength, and felt almost grateful. "Where's Benjamin?" she asked when they reached the top, as if he might be sitting on a bench, waiting for them. But Angel had already moved ahead, showing her the way.

Before Reese reached the grave, Angel sat down beside the small, temporary marker that said MELROSE. At the foot of the plot, Ben's full name, his dates of birth and death, had been carved on a footstone that lay flat. Grass had already taken root around the edges, and she couldn't help but notice how quickly people's space on earth could be claimed once they were gone.

"He said he wanted me to visit, to stay with him some, as soon as he could find the right time to talk to Gina about it. He said I could have two special places, one with you and one at his house." Angel recounted Ben's promise with no apparent purpose but the simple telling. She didn't sound angry or sad. Reese wondered what her daughter really felt about Ben's presence in her life—and then his absence. Angel had seen him three times—total. But she'd taken him to her heart right away, trusted him. Then again, how could you know Ben and not fall for him?

"I don't think Gina would have let me come," she said in a voice that sounded older than God.

"Did Ben say that to you?" There it was again, Reese thought. The selfish, silly notion that Gina would have blown it, that she might have driven him away. What did it matter, after everything that had happened to Ben? And why did she want it to be that way, even now? Gina had been nothing but supportive since that awful first night.

"No," Angel answered, sitting on the ground, close to where Ben's head would lie beneath the soil. "Ben said that Gina was really nice. That I'd like her and he was sure she'd like me. But I don't think she does like me."

"Ben was really good at getting people to agree to his plans," Reese said. "If he'd had more time . . ."

"I don't think so," Angel said. Her lower lip had turned downward in a child's instinctive show of sadness. She didn't try to stop it, didn't seem self-conscious at all. Reese figured she could learn a lot from Angel's pure acceptance of her emotions. "I wanted him to be my daddy."

"I know, baby." Reese felt the need to hold her, but sensed that Angel needed space to let all her words out, into the open air. "It's what we all wanted."

Angel drew a star in a small patch of sandy dirt where grass had not taken root. She picked up a stick and skewered the middle of the star, leaving the stick planted upright in the dirt.

"He told me it could happen soon," Angel said. "But then we had to go to the mountains. I don't think he knew how to find us there."

The last sentence came out hard, firm—an accusation, of sorts. The questions were there—had been there for weeks—in Angel's eyes, but she didn't voice them. She had never second-guessed Reese's decisions about their lives. She might someday. Reese had thought of this, feared her choices wouldn't hold up in the long run.

She wondered how much Angel had guessed about their flight to the mountains. The truth was, she'd panicked, taken off with no plans in place. Ben had said he wanted to get help for her—that it had to be that way. She remembered all too well the "help" he'd gotten the first time when they were married. He was wrong. She didn't need that. People hovering, watching every move. Her problems didn't make her a child. *Help* meant one thing to Ben: taking charge. What if he'd decided she couldn't handle looking after Angel anymore? Then there was Gina to worry about on top of everything else.

He never let anything go once he'd made up his mind. So she'd left him again before it came to that, this time taking Angel with her on purpose. But Angel had already gotten so attached. Maybe if she'd explained more to him . . . But she couldn't go back and change anything. And she certainly couldn't take any responsibility for what happened to Ben. It simply happened. And if she hadn't left for those months, it's just as likely that Angel might have even been in the car with him when—

Reese's thoughts slammed to a halt. Not even in her meandering "what ifs" could she let her mind go there. A world without Ben was a terrible place, but a world without Angel . . . No. Not that.

"You know what?" Angel sounded like a kid again. She often went back and forth from her baby voice to an eerie maturity. Reese understood this, tried to keep up, to go with whatever the child offered.

"What, baby?"

"Even with Ben gone . . ." Tears came bright into her eyes. "Since I knew he wanted to be my daddy, it's like I have one, even though he's not exactly here."

Reese nodded; words thick in her throat wouldn't find their sound. She moved over beside Angel and held her. Long minutes passed. Through the trees beyond the church, Reese could see the water, and it calmed her somehow.

"That's exactly right," she said when she could finally speak. "You don't lose someone when they really love you. Ben would tell you that too."

Reese couldn't help but think of the irony. Ben was supposed to be her safety net for Angel. Now, it seemed, they were both flying high with nothing beneath them but a long drop to solid ground.

*   *   *

A man stood by the car when they got back down the hill. He wore blue jeans with a dress shirt open at the collar. He reminded Reese of an older version of the guys she'd known in college, guys who hit senior year and began to think about finding a job. Suddenly long hair was short. Ratty polo shirts gave way to dress shirts, the buttoned-down and laundered variety.

"Is this your car?" he asked. Something about him, his manner, seemed inviting, implied easy talk. His voice was Southern coastal, deep vowels with full round tones.

"Yes, it is. Is there a problem with parking here?" She glanced around the gravel lot beside the church. Hers was one of three cars in the lot, with nothing but open space around them.

"No." He smiled. "I just used to have an old Plymouth kind of like this. I was wondering who it belonged to, that's all. I'm Andrew Hanes, the preacher here at Mt. Sinai."

Okay. That was a surprise. She would have pegged him as anything but a country preacher.

"Reese Melrose." She extended her hand. "This is my daughter, Angel."

"Beautiful name." He looked at Angel. Reese liked the way his voice stayed the same when he talked to the child. He didn't address her like a simpleton, the way a lot of adults tended to do. "How'd you hurt your arm?"

"I had an accident." Angel mimicked Reese's response, didn't miss a beat.

"Well, I hope it heals up soon," he said. "That sling's got to be pretty uncomfortable in this heat."

"It's not that bad," Angel told him, polite but reserved. Angel's stock-in-trade. Angel could act a little warmer, Reese thought. She wasn't big on preachers, but this Reverend Hanes seemed okay.

"You know somebody up at the cemetery?" he asked, turning his attention to Reese.

"A relative. Died a couple of months ago, but I just found out."

"Oh, I remember. Benjamin Melrose."

He looked again at Angel, at her arm. Probably pieced it together, what had happened. The shooting had been all over the papers. But he didn't say anything.

"That's right," she told him, hoping the inquiry would end there.

"So then, you're related to Gina?" he asked. "Through Benjamin," he added. The question took her off guard, but when she thought about it, she remembered Gina saying she'd been coming on Sundays to the church. This guy would have preached at Ben's funeral.

"I guess that's right," Reese said. "Gina and I are just getting to know each other."

Preacher Hanes glanced up the hill, as if to acknowledge the dead relative. "Well, I'm sorry about everything that happened," he said. "I didn't know him, but from all I hear, he was a good man."

"Yes, he was." Reese nodded, felt oddly compelled to say more. The man's easy tone of conversation, his open face—these things made her feel better somehow. Better than she'd felt in days. The word "charisma" came to mind, but his manner seemed anything but contrived.

"So," she asked, "what do preachers do when they're not . . . preaching? Seems like a pretty cushy job except for having to get up early every Sunday."

Angel must have sensed a full-blown conversation coming on. She took off toward a playground set up behind the church.

"Oh, you'd be surprised at how busy we stay. Hospital visits, counseling, and that all-consuming prayer thing. Prayer. That alone is a full-time job." He smiled.

Irreverent. She liked that in a reverend. Well, as much as she liked anything in that breed of human. To her surprise, she felt strangely compelled to talk with this Preacher Hanes.

"What kind of counseling do you do?" She was biding time, trying to keep him in front of her. What the hell was she thinking?

"Marriage. Grief. Life. Everyone has a problem or two. For people who go to church, preachers are usually the first stop. After us, they go for the hired guns."

"Therapists."

"Yep."

God, he was cute. She glanced at Angel on the playground. Figured she had ten, fifteen minutes before her daughter got restless and started asking to go.

"So, are you any good at it? The counseling thing."

"I do my best. Most of the time it just helps for people to talk things through. Hearing it out loud, people find answers right there in front of them."

Two seagulls passed overhead, their high, arching call sounding even as they moved out of sight. Reese tried to think of what to say.

The preacher stood, gave her ample time to respond, to hold up her end of the chatter, but she couldn't seem to speak. Still, he didn't seem bothered by the silence. That was unusual for a man, for anyone, really. Reese found that most people couldn't abide quiet air. Finally, he glanced up the hill toward the cemetery. "Were you close to Mr. Melrose?"

"Yes," she answered him. "But we were closer a long time ago."

He probably thought she was a cousin, some relative who'd played with Ben when they were children together.

"Well, if you find that you need to talk, if there's anything troubling you—"

"No, I don't think so." She realized that she'd cut him off. "I wasn't asking for me. About what you do with people. I just don't know any preachers, and I was curious, that's all." The man was a stranger, regardless of how easy he was to talk to.

Part of her thought it would feel good. All the worries of the last few months pressed so tight inside her. What if she just opened up a little, let just enough out to ease the strain? Weren't preachers bound to some ethical code of secrecy? They couldn't go telling everything they heard or they'd get run out of town.

"How long have you been here?" she asked.

"A couple of years." His eyes, large and brown, kept a line of sight, directed toward her face, her eyes. "It's starting to feel like home."

Home. That concept had been a fluid one for most of her life, all of Angel's. She wondered what it would be like to claim a place as a real home.

"Are you okay?" Andrew Hanes was asking. She must have lost herself for a minute.

"I don't know. It's been a rough few months," she said. "I was just thinking that talking wouldn't be such a bad thing."

She thought of that last day in Boone. The frantic need to run, to get Angel someplace new and safe. Not to mention her own problems. The same things she'd been feeling for months and months before all that happened with Angel. Only afterward, when she'd gotten so frightened, she felt the volume turned up to full-blast. She had to keep Angel safe.

"I suppose I could use a sounding board," she said. "Someone to listen."

She looked over at Angel again. The girl used her legs to carry herself higher and higher, holding on to one side of the swing with her good hand, hooking her elbow tight around the other. It had to hurt, the pressure of the swing on those torn muscles. Watching her made Reese feel anxious. She knew she should call out, tell her to stop before she hurt herself again. But Angel looked so happy. The swing set seemed sturdy enough, a nice wooden construction. It looked new, with monkey bars attached, along with a small slide. Reese wondered if Preacher Charming had put it together himself. Shirt off. Sweating in the Charleston heat. That would have been something to watch.

"Do you have time now?" he asked. She tried to think of what he meant. "I've got an office in the back section of the church," he went on. " There's a window where we could watch your daughter play out here. The church secretary, Mary, is in today. She could keep an eye out for her too."

Reese felt her hands begin to tremble. Not so bad, but uncomfortable, distracting. The thought of that building, of going inside.

"I don't really do churches," she said. She glanced at him. He didn't seem surprised or offended by the remark. She let herself relax a little. "The buildings. I don't go in. And I should get back to a friend who's had a rough time at the dentist. But, maybe, sometime . . . I'm staying at the marina on Creekside Road, but I'll be moving into a cottage near here, over on Sullivan's Island, in a couple of weeks."

Angel walked up beside them, still breathing hard from her play. Her color was high, full of the excitement, the rise and free fall of a swing.

"Would you like me to meet you over at the marina? Maybe tomorrow? Are you free during the day?"

"Tomorrow I am," she said. "I have to work the rest of the week. That's a long way for you to come."

"It's okay," he said. "Tomorrow then. Maybe ten-thirty in the morning? At the coffee shop near the restaurant. No one will be there midmorning. It'll be a quiet place to talk."

"Great," she said. "I'll be there."

A woman walked up just as they finished their plans. Reese looked at her. Pretty, but thin. She seemed fragile and sad.

"This is my wife, Diane," the preacher said. "Diane, this is Reese Melrose. She and her daughter came out to the cemetery. She's related to Benjamin Melrose."

A wife. It wasn't a surprise, but it still seemed a shame. Reese realized that she'd hoped there was more to his offer than counseling and coffee.

"I'm sorry about Mr. Melrose," the wife said. "I didn't know him but I read about it when he was killed. It was a terrible accident."

Reese nodded. The woman regarded her with open suspicion. That preacher's wife thing didn't guarantee any smiles from this one. Reese had seen animals that had been mistreated. In Diane Hanes's eyes, Reese saw the look of some of those animals. Reese couldn't help believing that whatever had gone wrong in her life, it was her own damn fault. Her husband seemed nothing but solid and good.

"Are you just visiting?" the woman asked.

"Actually, we're moving near here." Reese laid her hand light on Angel's shoulder. "This is Angel, my daughter."

The woman's face softened. "Hi, Angel. I'm Mrs. Hanes." Reese noticed a little too much emphasis on the "Mrs." part, but maybe she had imagined it.

"We have to get back," Reese said, suddenly feeling the need to flee.

"Tomorrow at ten-thirty, then," Preacher Hanes said. His wife glanced over at him, but he didn't seem to notice.

"Ten-thirty." Reese opened the car door for Angel. As she came around to the other side, Andrew Hanes got there first, opened the driver's side door for her to get in.

Reese smiled. She didn't bother glancing to the side where his wife still stood. She knew the expression she would see if she bothered to turn her head. She'd seen that look before. And she felt ashamed admitting, even to herself, that it pleased her to think it could happen again.

22

Gina

"Where are you?" Derek sounded concerned when I answered the phone. He knew I'd gone to Lane's to confront Reese. A couple of hours had passed, I realized, but it seemed like minutes.

"I'm still at Lane's house," I told him. "I haven't seen Reese. She went off somewhere with Angel."

"Are you okay?" he asked. His concern shifted and he sounded vaguely irritated.

"Sort of. Yeah, I'm fine. What's up?"

"Well, those pancakes are wearing pretty thin. We'd talked about getting some lunch."

I didn't want to think about food. I wasn't even sure I could swallow anything. But I did want to be with Derek. In a matter of hours he'd become someone I longed to be near. A tiny part of me still felt wrong, wanting that. As if the desire for time with someone else meant a betrayal of Ben. And my fidelity or lack of it to Ben's memory led me to the biggest question that remained. *Did he cheat on me?*

"Gina . . . hello?"

"I'm here," I said. "Sorry I spaced out. I was just thinking that I better stay here. I don't want to miss Reese. I have to put this to rest."

"Okay. How 'bout I bring some sandwiches over there? The vendor brought a fresh batch in downstairs this morning. Is turkey all right?"

"That sounds good." The thought of him showing up at the door made everything else seem easier. "Lane's got some soda, so just bring sandwiches, maybe a bag of chips."

"Does Lane eat meat?"

I looked over at my sleeping friend, still out of it on the couch. I smiled in spite of myself.

"Not unless she can drink it through a straw," I said.

"What?"

"She went to the dentist this morning. Just bring stuff for you and me."

"Be there in a minute."

After I got off the phone, I sat on the couch and waited; didn't know what else to do, really. Lane slept. Even Georgie curled up for an afternoon siesta. But I stayed fully alert. My mind jumped from one thought to another, but none of them made much sense.

"Is she an addict?" I mumbled to myself, voicing the most likely explanation for what I'd found in Reese's bag, and there seemed to be no explanation for why she'd have them sent to me. I pulled the invoice out of my pocket. My name, care of the Ship's Store, and . . . my credit card. I was sure the last four numbers—the only ones to show up on the order—matched mine. I went to the kitchen and pulled out my wallet. My Visa was gone. Holy shit. People went to jail for doing that sort of thing. I put the invoice back in my pocket and tried to push the questions out of my head. I had to deal with one thing at a time, and while the stolen card presented a problem, my biggest concern remained Angel and Ben.

The need to sort out the necklace, the truth about their relationship, had to stay my first priority. Reese's problems, addiction or God knows what, would have to come second. Of course, it would become *my* problem if anyone tracked down illegal drugs that had been mailed to me.

I walked to the front window and looked outside. The loud hum of the air conditioner made the comings and goings of the marina a silent narrative, something like an old movie. I saw Derek come out of the deli beside the Ship's Store and I felt a strange sense of anticipation. I hadn't quickened at the thought of something, anything, in a full three months. Maybe even longer than that; it was hard to remember. The feeling came new, as if even the memory of happiness had been erased from my mind. Maybe it had been. Maybe I would experience life after Ben as a series of firsts. The same way life had finally begun again after Elise died. A different life entirely. I could see my existence laid out in segments. Two were completed, the third just beginning. And for a moment it seemed that all pure happiness occurred accidentally, without the opaque weight of expectation.

"Hey," Derek whispered as he came in the door. I motioned him to the kitchen. The last thing Lane would want was an audience as she slept.

"Any sign of Reese?" he asked.

"Nothing. I don't know where she would go for this long. She hasn't kept up with anybody around here, as far as I know."

I held off telling him about the package in Reese's things. Saying it out loud obligated me to deal with it in some way. I wasn't ready to deal with it, with whatever it meant.

"Maybe they went grocery shopping, something simple," he said.

"Maybe," I told him, "but I doubt it. Nothing Reese does is that ordinary."

We ate our sandwiches out of the wrappers, didn't bother with plates. I felt as if we were playing house, sitting at a real table, looking around at a full pantry, a fridge that held more than yogurt and beer without becoming crowded. I'd had all of it with Ben and it had never seemed remarkable then. But that had been somebody else's life; that had been a person who believed that Ben couldn't lie.

Sitting with Derek, pondering the miracle of adult domestic maturity, it was as if I'd regressed to a younger station in life since Ben had been gone. In other ways, I felt ancient since becoming a widow. No wonder I felt so messed up; the schizophrenic existence of widowhood had become difficult to negotiate.

"Gina?" He looked serious. "Do you want me here when you talk with her? I'll stay. I'll go. You make the call."

"It's got to be the two of us, just me and Reese. Maybe if you could take Angel for some ice cream. I don't think Lane is going to be up for babysitting this afternoon."

He nodded, took a bite of sandwich. I couldn't tell if being relegated to a service-oriented task disappointed him. He wanted to be part of my life, my inner life where it got messy and complicated. Most of those parts of me weren't so new. They existed before I became a widow. Ben hadn't wanted to be inside my head. He took the view that problems, funks, and all manner of downers could be overcome with a good game of tennis, a long afternoon sail. I never minded that approach. I wasn't much of a talker myself. But I felt strangely open to letting Derek in on the soft insides of my thoughts. This shift in my own perception startled me a little, made me nervous.

"We're going a little fast," I said, blurting it out without warning or context.

"What do you mean?" He looked appropriately bewildered.

"Us, whatever we are."

He smiled, looked sly and shy at the same time. "Darlin', *last week* was fast. I thought I was the soul of restraint last night."

He made me laugh, defused the neuroses before they became large and explosive.

"I mean emotionally," I explained. "I'm relying on you. I'm trusting where we are when I don't even know where we are. We've had one wild . . . not a date, I don't know what it was. And a really special night that ran into morning. Now I feel like—"

"Gina," he stopped me. "I'm here. I've wanted to be here for weeks. None of this is spontaneous for me. It's taken you a while to come around, to even see me that way. And," he added, "with good reason. You've been through a lot. I'm not blaming you. And I'm not pushing you. I'm here. I'm solid."

Solid. If he was so solid, why did I feel shaky? My perspective was shot, so I went with my gut. We sat catty-cornered at the edge of Lane's dinette and I leaned over the sandwiches and the soda. I kissed him, felt the surprise of his mouth, new again, even though I'd initiated the kiss, even though I'd been with him just hours before. His lips opened slightly; I could feel his breath going into my mouth. It seemed to travel warm through me, touching nerves that had long grown cold. Without analyzing why it felt good, I let it be what it was, and the yielding left me weak.

"Okay," he said, his face still close to mine. "I guess that's a yes on going out with me again."

Reese and Angel came through the door. Hot air from the afternoon followed them, cut through the air-conditioned room, effecting a brief change in the Freon-charged climate. Still, Reese looked cool in her loose blouse and skirt.

"Hey." I tried to sound casual as they made their way into the den.

Lane was awake, but still pretty groggy. Derek and I sat on the floor, as *Headline News* repeated itself through a second cycle of identical stories. The world should change a little faster. If nothing else, out of courtesy to cable news.

"What have you two been up to?" I asked.

"We went to see Ben." Angel kept her eyes on mine, a direct volley that I found impossible to return. She wanted me to react, but I stared at the child, rendered mute by the bold announcement. I felt my cheeks go warm, could see the two of them weeping over Benjamin's grave, and I registered a rush of irritation.

"That's nice," I finally managed.

"Angel wanted me to see how pretty it is at the cemetery," Reese said, shooting a harsh look in the girl's direction.

"It is beautiful, isn't it?" I forced the words from my mouth, refused to let an eight-year-old—not even eight yet—get the best of me. "It's the perfect spot, really."

An uncomfortable murmur of consensus followed, then silence.

"Listen," I said, after a several long seconds, "Maxine called me this morning. The family that had the place rented through Labor Day has had to cancel. The realty company has a cleaning crew coming through today, and Maxine's going out there this afternoon to pick up a few things she needs to take home."

"The good china?" Reese became her least likable self when Maxine's name entered a conversation. I wondered how Reese living in a cottage her former mother-in-law owned could possibly work.

"She said you could move in tomorrow, if you like," I said, ignoring her remark. "She's worked out terms, the rent, liability, and all that. She'll meet us in Mt. Pleasant at the realtor's office in the morning and sign everything."

"Us?" Reese asked.

"Yeah. Since I—"

"Right," she said. "I forgot. You're the grown-up in this arrangement, signing off on my credibility as a human being. Why is Maxine even coming? Can't they do this without her?"

"Maybe she wants to be there. Maybe she's trying to make an effort."

"That would be a first."

She sounded pissed. Far from the gratitude she'd displayed after her dicey conversation with Maxine. What the hell was I thinking, helping her?

"I can lay off if you want to work this out with her yourself." I'd had about enough.

"I'm sorry." Reese backed down. "This isn't easy for me to do."

I got up, took empty glasses of soda back to the kitchen without answering her.

"So," she said, finally, "she's really letting us do this, huh? What's the rent?"

"I don't know, but whatever it is, Maxine said the realtors were horrified, so it can't be that much." I came back in and sat down beside Derek on the floor. Reese leaned back on the couch. She looked uncomfortable, physically ill-at-ease, and Angel stayed near.

"Well, I'll need to pay her after my first paycheck," Reese said. "I'll get a little from the shifts I worked this week, but I'm cash-poor until I start working regularly. I hadn't counted on moving in this soon. It's going to be a hike, driving back and forth to work from there."

"It'll all work out," I said, for lack of anything better.

"That's what I keep telling myself."

Reese looked weary. I studied her eyes, her movements; tried to discern if she was high. The pills were way down on my list of issues, but I didn't want to deal with her if she seemed irrational. But she looked the same as always to me. Flaky, but she didn't need substance abuse to make her odd. I was angry with Reese, had been angry before she came in, and the field trip with Angel to the grave didn't make me feel more charitable. But I had to get a handle on myself. I couldn't go into my discussion with her on a hostile note, or she'd never open up, tell me the truth.

"Mom can't go in the morning," Angel announced as a delayed response to our conversation about the cottage.

I wondered what I was supposed to say in response. She was clearly addressing me. Derek stayed quiet, looked vaguely amused for some reason, which ticked me off even more. It wasn't a fucking game.

"Why's that, Angel?" Lane spoke up. Even she sounded terse. Her post-torture patience wasn't up to the usual standards.

" 'Cause she's got a date with the preacher."

I had to admit it was getting interesting.

"What preacher?" I couldn't help myself. The conversation was a train wreck, but a damned fascinating train wreck.

"The one out where Ben is buried."

Andrew Hanes? What was she up to with that?

"I don't have a *date*," Reese insisted. "I'm meeting him for coffee. Just to talk over some things."

"He's really, really married, Reese. Preachers tend to take that kind of thing seriously," I told her, just in case it mattered.

"I know that," she snapped back at me. Lane had closed her eyes again and Derek slipped into the kitchen to clean up our wrappers. "I met his wife. She's lovely. I needed some . . ." She stopped. "Well, people talk to preachers. You're not the only one having a hard time with all that's happened."

"I thought you didn't do the whole religion thing." I gave up on civility. The woman was predatory.

"Well, I break my own rules once in a while. It's not a crime." Her mouth was set. She looked off to the side.

Lane opened her eyes again and stood up, shook her head at both of us. "I'm going to take some more medicine, then lie down in my room. Just don't break any furniture." She shuffled off, left us to our stalemate.

"I can reschedule with the preacher," Reese said.

Angel stood beside her mother. I forced myself to remember that she was just a little girl, a child who had been dragged from town to town by a mother who couldn't tell fact from fiction to begin with. It wasn't the kid's fault, but she'd perfected her mother's look of smug indifference.

Still, part of me remembered the soft child who sat beside me at the cemetery. The delighted face when she completed her puzzle. In spite of myself, I felt a thaw go through me when I looked at the stone-set expression of her mouth, her eyes. It surprised me, the compassion I couldn't shake. How could I feel charity toward a child who offered nothing back, when I'd only mustered tolerance, at best, for a sister who openly begged for approval?

"I need to talk with you, Reese." I could sort out my feelings about Angel later. I'd put off the real issue of the day for too long. "Let's at least sit down."

This was Derek's cue. He came back into the room, all easy smiles.

"Hey, Angel," he said. "How 'bout some ice cream? We can see if the dolphins are feeding on the mud bank across from the marina."

Angel smiled and stood up, but before she took a step, Reese intervened.

"Where are you going?" She sounded near panic. Where the hell had that come from?

"Just to the Ship's Store." Derek's face was a question. "Then we'll hang out near the gazebo at the dock. You'll see us out the window."

"I'm sorry," Reese said. "I've been a little on edge today. I'd rather she stay close, that's all."

Reese didn't know Derek all that well. Her concern wasn't unreasonable when I thought about it. But how the hell could I talk with her if Angel stayed directly underfoot?

"I tell you what," Derek said. "Lane has some Rocky Road in the freezer and she gets Nickelodeon. How 'bout we stay right here and watch TV?"

Angel glanced over at Reese, saw her mother offer a slight nod.

"Okay," she said, going with Derek into the kitchen.

Reese looked at me. She looked as if she knew what was coming, and maybe she did.

"Can we sit out front on the porch?" I asked.

"It's hotter than hell out there," she said.

"I don't mind staying in here," I said, "but I don't know if you want Angel to listen in. To tell you the truth, I don't care. I'm not the one keeping secrets."

She stood up, walked toward the kitchen.

"Let me get a cold soda and I'll meet you out there." She looked so tired. But I had to get it over with, for everyone's sake.

"Do you want anything?" she called from the kitchen.

"Diet Sundrop if there's one in there."

"Got it," Reese answered.

I went out onto the porch and waited.

Reese walked out with the two soda cans in one hand. Her dark, curly hair looked damp, as if she'd splashed herself with water, then smoothed it back.

"Angel told you," she said before she'd even sat down.

I was sitting on the green porch glider. I'd watched Lane spray-paint it the week before. The chipped and dingy white of the metal had become lovely again in an instant. Reese sat opposite me in a matching chair. She handed the soda over, waited for me to respond.

"How long had she known him?" I asked.

"I told him about her just after the holidays. He drove to Richmond to meet her sometime in January. She saw him twice after that."

I'd gone to see my parents in January. A weekend visit that was a concession for having missed Christmas with them—again. Ben and I had started a tradition with Maxine. I told myself it had been that way because Maxine was alone. Truth was, I wanted to be with Maxine more than my own mother. So I'd gone off to my parents' house and he'd gone off to meet Angel. I wondered about the other times he'd been with her. Where was I?

I'd been thinking that confronting Reese would be the hard part, the axis of all the conflict. Turns out, I was wrong. All of the questions that had to follow seemed more difficult.

"Why didn't you say something before?" The question came out hard, an accusation. But it wasn't Reese I was accusing. Even I knew that.

"Everything happened so fast. I had no idea that Ben was gone when I got here, much less what he'd said to you. I felt like I should get the lay of the land, let you get used to the two of us before I filled you in on everything else. I thought he'd left you, Gina. That seemed like a logical explanation for you to be sleeping on a boat, for God's sake. And I know that there was—" She stopped, and I think my heart stopped too. "—tension between you," she finished.

The television sounded absurd inside the house. The manic orchestration of Looney Tunes provided the sound track for our conversation. I could feel my heart again, beating fast and unsure.

"Then why didn't he tell me?" Sweat formed at my hairline. Tears threatened to spill. The dampness came from all around. Even the inlet that met the edge of Lane's yard steamed the air with a salty haze. "Did you tell him not to say anything to me?" I hoped this was true. I wanted to blame Reese more than I wanted to breathe.

"No. Benjamin made his own decisions about what to say."

She must have seen the pain her words caused, because she

leaned toward me, rested her elbows on her knees. The timbre of her voice changed, softened as she spoke again.

"I know that he intended for you to know, Gina. We didn't have this secret pact or anything. But he thought he had time. I mean, who would have known he didn't have time?"

"Were you sleeping with him?" It sounded ridiculous as I asked it. I knew Ben better than that. But more than the child, more than anything, it was the question I wanted to hear her answer. The question that affirmed or negated my marriage.

Her face didn't register anything. No surprise, no confirmation. Her expression stayed passive, a formal portrait in living flesh.

"Did you?" I asked again.

"No." Her answer hung there. The small word I'd wanted to hear, but hardly believed.

"Then why did he lie?"

"What makes you think he lied, Gina?" She pulled her cigarettes out of the deep pocket of her skirt. Reached in again for matches. "Think about it." She lit up a menthol; the deep smell of tobacco covered the distance between us, brought her words closer than I wanted. My emotions gathered, began to have substance again. I wouldn't be the victim in this one. She wouldn't have that from me.

"He kept it from me," I said. "I know in your book that's not being dishonest, but we don't exactly agree on that one."

She reached over, let ashes drop in the hedges just over the porch rail. I thought maybe that was it, all she planned to offer me by way of explanation. I needed to keep her talking. I had to hear more so I could put my memory of Ben back together, keep it intact.

"Did you lie to him?" I asked. "Tell him that Angel was his? Did you skip the stories about your complicated sleeping arrangements at the time she was conceived?"

If I'd been closer to her, she might have struck me. Her mouth formed a rigid line of anger. Good. Let her get angry. Let her lose enough control to tell me the fucking truth for a change. "What did you tell him, Reese?"

"I told him the truth." With the cigarette loose between her fingers, she reached for her soda. But her hand shook as she picked it up from the wooden floor of the porch. The cold sweat off the can left a stain on the gray-painted planks. "I never lied to Ben—or to anyone, for that matter—about Angel."

"You think keeping her away from him for seven years wasn't lying?" I felt suddenly strong, and I wanted to cause injury. The pain could be someone else's for a change. "I don't know what that is if it's not a lie."

"I never spoke words to Benjamin that weren't true. Everything I said to him was right."

"I don't know, Reese. It's pretty fuzzy. The distinction between technically lying and simply withholding the truth. What else did you finally decide to open up about?"

She turned her head to look at me. "I told him that I still loved him." Not a twitch or a blink.

It stopped me, her admission. But then, she intended for it to. I took a breath and made myself move forward. "So that makes you a good citizen? After all those years?"

"I know that I kept things from him for a long time." She put down the drink. "But regardless of how you feel about it, lies by omission are a different animal. I won't apologize for anything I thought was necessary to give my daughter the life she needed."

"Okay. Well, just for fun, why don't you fill in the parts you left out? All the *omitted* scenes in your little drama."

The wind shifted her smoke into my nose. The cigarette bugged me all of a sudden. Everything about her bugged me. As if hearing my thoughts, she put her cigarette out on the top of her soda can, slipped the butt in the opening; I heard the sizzle as it hit the remains of her drink.

"I don't owe you any apologies for what I did to Ben," she said. "I loved him. He understood that."

She was right. It had always confused the hell out of me, but he did seem to understand her. And she loved him. I believed her on that one. But that didn't explain why she'd left him. Or why she'd come back with Angel in tow. But her love for him made perfect sense to me. The thought of it made me sick.

"What did he say when you told him about Angel? When you told him how you felt?"

I waited. From inside the house, Road Runner . . . the Coyote . . . Their endless chase continued. The frantic sounds brought Reese's silence into hard focus.

"Tell me."

She looked out across the inlet and I could see the line of her jaw, the edges of her profile, but not her eyes. I tried to figure out what she was focusing on, but there was nothing in that direction but still water and boats. She continued to look away as she spoke.

"He said that he was married to you. That he had a life with you. He wasn't interested in *playing family*—your words, not his—with me. He told me that you were the partner he needed."

A charter fishing boat motored by. The noise made us stop, wait for the sound to fade, and I took just a second to acknowledge the relief I felt at what she'd said.

"Then why didn't he tell me?" I started in again. I couldn't dwell on the small bit of ground I'd gained. I hadn't heard any real answers in all of her talk. "What kept him from talking with me about you? About Angel?"

"Oh, Jesus Christ, Gina!" She leaned back, dropped her head, and let out a dramatic breath. "He tried to tell you, for God's sake. Are you so fucking stupid that you don't see it?" She'd lost patience, was acting as if I'd missed something obvious. The hot air pushed close against my skin as I stared at her, unable to look away.

"He tried to tell you," she said again, as if repeating it would make it clear to me.

"A conversation about a child that might have been his kid? I don't think so. In fact, I'm pretty sure I'd remember having a talk like that with my husband."

"Children," she said, still trying to make her point. "He talked to you about children. What do you think he was getting at? Are you just plain simple or don't you want to know the truth?"

"You're offering *me* lessons on the truth?"

"There. You're changing the subject again. You don't want to hear it, do you? He talked with you about kids. Recently. Over and over, as a matter of fact, and you just couldn't listen. But he tried. God knows he tried."

Children? All those questions. All those arguments over some baby that didn't exist, would never exist. "He was talking about a baby," I said. "Having a baby. What does that—"

"Oh, stop!" She cut me off. "Just think for a second." Each syllable unfolded with a slow, deliberate cadence as spaces formed between the words. "He was talking about Angel."

Everything stopped. The boats. The birds. Even the television noises had gone away. In the still air, I could only hear blood rushing

inside my own head. Angel. Benjamin's desperation, the urgent peti-
tions. For Angel, a child he'd already claimed. All that was left was for
me to accept her.

"Gina?" she asked. "Did you hear what I said?" I nodded, but all I
could hear was Benjamin talking to me on the couch, in our bed, in
the car. Children. I had to rethink the idea of children. His voice
took on a pleading quality that I'd never heard before. The subject
had dominated the months before his death. I didn't understand.
For his sake, he said, I had to consider it.

For the first time, I did understand, but it was too late. In his
world, in the new world that had come to him, I *had* to listen. I had
to change my mind. Because if I didn't, it would have meant a choice.
A choice that he couldn't make.

"He wanted to work out an arrangement," she said. "Shared custody. He just needed some sign that you were softening, and he was
going to open up the idea to you."

That made sense, but at the same time, didn't. Some part of her
story rested off-kilter.

"Why would he do that without proof that she was his?" I tried to
find some way around it, some way to make her a liar. For an instant
I tried to think like Benjamin, to *be* Benjamin. Wouldn't he want to
know for sure before he ripped our life apart? "Why would he go
through all that without knowing for sure? It doesn't make any sense.
You must have let him think—"

"I told him the truth," Reese said again. She stood up, her bare
feet planted in a solid stance as if to bolster her point. "I told him I
didn't know. In fact, I told him I didn't want to know."

"Then why . . ." I began, but somehow got lost in my own question.

"Maybe . . ." Reese came and sat in the glider, but with a solid distance between us. "Maybe he thought it was his only chance at being
a father. Any kind of father."

"What do you mean?" But even as I asked, the logic of what she
said began to connect the pieces of my last months with Ben.

"You wouldn't have had a baby. You were so completely fucked
up about your little sister. He knew you'd never come around to that.
But a stepdaughter. You might accept that. It was his one shot. What
do you think, *Genes*? You think maybe he didn't want to lose that
chance by asking for *proof*? He didn't want to know for sure any more
than I did."

Genes. I heard the mocking tones when she said it, and I felt violated. Only when she used Ben's name for me did it occur to me all that he had confided in her. All about my sister. She knew about Elise. Tears came new and I stood up. I wanted to be away from her. I wanted to be in a place where she didn't exist. I never thought anything could be worse than losing Ben. But I'd been wrong about that. I'd been wrong about so many things.

"You must have thought you hit the jackpot," I said. "When he married someone who didn't want kids and you already had one, ready to serve up."

She gave me a bored look, said nothing, but the silence brought too many thoughts back to me, too many images of Ben and his efforts to persuade me.

"So if you had it all worked out, why did you disappear again, after he was already attached to Angel?" It was a throwaway question. Something to keep me from breaking down completely. But as I asked it, I saw her breathing change, a slight shift in her posture. I realized the power of what I'd said. "Why hadn't you tried to get in touch with him for all those months before he died?"

The rapid rise and fall of her chest inside her thin blouse belied her face, impassive and stonelike.

"Reese?"

She shook her head, such a subtle movement that I wondered if she'd responded at all.

"Ben was relentless," I answered for her, feeling suddenly bold. "Ben never gave up on an idea once he'd decided. That meant he wouldn't give up on Angel. But it also meant he wouldn't give up on me, on our marriage. And you really thought he would, didn't you? When you trotted out a kid and a story—some version of your *truth,* whatever it was—you thought he'd be so dazzled with the idea of a daughter that he'd shut down on me, and eventually leave. But that wasn't going to happen."

"No," she said without inflection, still without expression. "He wasn't going to do that." She planned to take whatever I threw at her. To let my anger run its course. Well, I didn't want to disappoint.

"So you packed up your toys and went home, took Angel away from him—again. Only this time he knew she existed. But he had no idea where you were, did he?"

She shook her head.

"When you told him about her, did you really think he would leave me?"

"I didn't know you," she said, with no effort at denying what I'd said. "I had no reason to think you'd be good to my daughter. Then when I found out you didn't even want children . . . I figured he'd eventually get fed up. Who knows? After all you put him through, maybe he was getting tired of it all. Maybe he realized what he lost and he was waiting for us to come back."

"But Ben never got fed up, and you know it." I kept my voice even. On some level, I'd won, if there was such a thing. And we both knew it. "He was the most optimistic person I ever met."

"I didn't know you, Gina," she said again, as if that justified everything. "And I sure as hell didn't know how you'd treat my daughter. And look how cold you've been to her. I was right, wasn't I?" It was her only defense. "I had no reason to believe—"

"It's okay, Reese." I stood up, motioned with my hand for her to stop, let it go. The last thing I wanted to sit through was some lame justification of her efforts to take my husband away. The fact was, in my heart of hearts, I didn't blame her.

After a minute, maybe two, she stood up. "I need to cool off." She looked a little unsteady on her feet, but it seemed to pass. "I forgot how hot this fucking place is in the summer."

I didn't mind the heat, and I didn't want to go inside. The thought of looking at Angel seemed too much to take. I walked to the edge of the porch, leaned against the house, and let the sun cover me full-on.

"I don't blame you for wanting him again," I said. "But what I can't figure out is why you ever left him in the first place. You had him, Reese. You had him and you left him. I'll never understand that." I didn't look at her, didn't expect any more answers.

"You're right. You wouldn't understand," she said.

I still didn't turn around, but when she opened the door to go inside, the cold rush of air from the house sent chills up my arms.

23

Reese

Derek sat on the floor opposite Angel, a deck of cards between them. "War!" Angel shouted.

"You can say that again," Reese mumbled.

Derek glanced up, looked beyond her to the front door.

"She's fine," Reese told him before he asked.

He nodded, went back to the game; but he seemed distracted, and after a few seconds said to Angel, "Let's leave the cards like they are and take a little break."

"Okay," Angel said, looking unbothered. She turned up the volume on a cartoon and settled on the couch to watch TV. Without looking Reese's way, Derek went out to the porch.

Reese picked up her pocketbook off the couch, took it to the kitchen where she'd seen Gina's purse on the table. Might as well get the credit card back where it belonged while Mr. Night Watchman kept her occupied. The confrontation had left Reese rattled, feeling foolish and nearly pathetic. Gina had been right. Part of her had thought Ben would drop everything and pick up where they'd left off. He'd always been there for her, before and after she left him. He'd always offered money and help when she got really stuck. But for the first time since she'd met Ben, she had to consider that maybe his efforts had nothing to do with love, and everything to do with pity.

"You're from Charleston." Those had been his first words to her as she had sat watching television in the lounge of the student center. Her sophomore year, his freshman.

"Are you psychic or just some everyday stalker?" She'd noticed him already, had asked a couple of friends from his dorm if they knew him.

"Stalker," he said. "With spies on the inside."

"Good. I'm a little freaked out by psychics."

He'd been younger by a year, but it never seemed that way. By the time she was a senior, they had an apartment together, and by the time she graduated, they were married. Mama Maxine hated her from the start, and his dad was pretty much a no show. Reese had no family she cared to involve in a wedding. So it made sense that they just slip off to Myrtle Beach to make everything official. Two nights at the Buccaneer Motel. That's what passed for a honeymoon, but she didn't care.

They'd kept it a secret until he started his senior year. Until his dad had put down the money for at least a semester's tuition. But the money didn't stop when his parents found out. It was odd, but she thought that always disappointed him a little—that his dad didn't get more upset, didn't seem to care one way or the other. His mother had an over-the-top fit, but she never held it against him. Reese, on the other hand, had been getting the blunt end of Maxine's anger ever since.

She opened Gina's wallet and slipped the credit card inside.

"Hi." Lane startled her, walked into the kitchen the very second Reese's hand left Gina's purse. If she saw anything, she didn't let on.

"You feeling better?" Reese asked.

"It's all relative, but yeah, I'm functional." Lane walked over to the cabinet and took out a mug. "I'm going to make some tea and then amuse myself by trying to drink it without dribbling. You can watch if you're bored. You want a cup of English Breakfast?"

"No, thanks. I can't drink hot stuff when it's ninety degrees out-side."

Reese sat down at the kitchen table, waited for Lane to put a kettle of water on the stove before she spoke up.

"I need to talk with you," she said to the older woman.

"Okay, hon," Lane said. "Can you give me a minute? I need to go grab my pills out of the bathroom. Will you listen for that water for a sec?"

"Sure."

Reese wondered if it was the right thing to do, to ask Lane. She didn't see any other choice. Gina wasn't a player, it seemed. Maybe the meds she got would make a huge difference in how she felt and it would never matter. But she couldn't count on it, not after what had happened in Boone. And she felt things getting worse. The woman she'd waited on at the restaurant, the one with the cane, had gotten her thinking. It seemed like some kind of sign, an omen that she needed to make a decision, to get things in order for Angel.

Reese had made up her mind. She would ask Lane to be Angel's legal guardian if something should happen to her. If she wasn't able to take care of her little girl, she couldn't think of anyone better than this woman she'd only known for a couple of days. Strange, the way life took you to the right places sometimes, all on its own.

The whistle started its slow build as the steam from the kettle grew more insistent. As she got up to move it off the burner, it occurred to her that the pressure inside the kettle seemed to match all the things going on inside her head. But the decision itself felt like most of the battle. She would talk with Lane. She would protect Angel, once and for all.

24

~

Gina

I sat on the porch rail, my back resting against the side of the house. I could feel the sweat inside my shirt, running between my breasts, down my sides. The small breeze off the inlet met slick skin, cooling me, providing unexpected relief.

"It's a sauna out here," Derek said. I hadn't heard him come out.

"Feels good to me. I'd like to sweat down to nothing, then start all over again."

"Well, don't." He smoothed the damp hair back, away from my face. His salty kiss reminded me of the kinship between humans and the sea. No wonder saltwater felt like home.

"What happened with you two?" he asked.

"Ben didn't sleep with Reese."

He waited for more, but I didn't know what else to say. So much of what Reese and I had said to each other made no sense without volumes of explanation to Derek. I realized how little he really knew about me. Strange, how it felt as if he should know everything.

"Is that all?" he finally asked. "You two were out here for a while. If that's all you settled, it was a long run for a short slide."

"We went around in circles about a lot of things," I explained. "But more than anything, I needed to know that Ben was faithful."

"Okay. But what about Angel?"

"Ben knew her, thought she might be his. I don't want to go into all the reasons he didn't tell me, but I'm not angry, not the way I was. I'm coming to terms with it. Can we talk about something else?"

He moved back, put some distance between us, and I realized how irritable I sounded.

"I'm sorry," I said. "You don't deserve to be snapped at." But it felt like too little too late. He offered a small nod, walked over to the glider, and sat down. He looked so young, and I felt so old.

"Listen Gina," he said, sounding tired. "I'm here when you need me. But that means I'm still around when the crisis is over. If that's not what you have in mind, then we don't have much to go on here."

"I know." I moved off the porch rail and into the shade. I settled in the chair. Reese's soda can sat empty on the ground beside me. A black smudge on top of the can marked the spot where she'd put out her cigarette.

"I'm not holding out on you," I said. "It's just that a lot of what Reese and I talked about involves ancient history. My history. She's not even out here anymore, and in my head, I keep arguing with her. Going back and forth. It's exhausting because I'm having to do her parts too."

He laughed. He wasn't angry. I couldn't stand the thought of him angry. Not on top of everything else. I worried that I was wanting— needing—too much from him too soon.

"I'm not even intending to keep anything from you. Anything in the past or the present. But I don't have the stomach to go through it now. One night soon, over beer and some more of those alligator fritters, or whatever the hell we ate last night, I'll talk about it. I promise."

"Fair enough." His body, his entire posture eased. I imagined a yielding, of sorts. I felt my own muscles, the ones in my arms, my neck, relax.

"And Derek?"

"Yeah?"

"Like I said, I don't feel angry with Ben anymore either."

"Okay," he said. Waited for me to make my point.

"Whether I agree with what he was doing or not, I think I understand why he did it. She gave me that much."

"Good," he said. "Understanding is a good thing." He shook his head slightly, as if to say, *And?*

"I want to be with you again."

"*Be* with me? Hang out and watch MTV, be with me? Or biblical sense, be with me?"

"Abraham. Moses." I felt myself smiling. It felt good.

"I always did like Sunday school."

I moved over beside him on the glider. For an instant I thought I could, should, let everything else go, once and for all. Let all my questions about Reese and Angel stay that way. But I had one more practical bit of information to sort out. The prescription receipts, with my name on them, were still folded in my pocket.

"So when do we begin this *being together* thing?" he asked.

"As soon as I get back from a quick errand."

"Not the answer I was looking for." He smiled. "But I'll take it."

"Listen, do you mind getting my pocketbook for me off the kitchen table?" I asked. "I don't want to see Reese again at the moment."

"Yes, ma'am." He stood up. "Men are like puppies. You dangle the notion of sex in front of us and we'll play 'go fetch' all day long."

"Well, as long as you're fetching, would you grab another soda for me while you're in there?"

"I'll be right back."

As I waited for Derek, I watched the boats coming and going through the inlet. It was a sight I'd seen with Benjamin dozens and dozens of times, and I'd looked at it every day for weeks since moving onto the boat. But for the first time since Ben died, I saw it from the vantage point of the present, not the past; a view less filtered by the fog of grief.

"Here you go." Derek came out and handed me my purse and a Diet Coke.

"And here I go," I said, leaving him standing, smiling on the porch.

Dr. Jenson's office was nearly empty. Minus flu season and the rash of early summer out-of-practice water sport injuries, I surmised that the good doctor had an August lull before the kids started passing around bugs after school started. Livie, his receptionist of a decade or more, raised her eyebrows at me when I came in.

"Oh my, you've had quite a week. Is everything okay?"

"You read the newspaper," I said.

"Everybody reads the newspaper. How about the little girl?"

"She's fine. I still feel like an idiot, though."

"Oh, honey." She shook her head. "Accidents happen. The best we can hope for is to live through them. You know that better than anybody."

Livie was a kind, blunt soul. What she lacked in tact, she made up for in heart. Plus she was damned efficient. Dr. Jenson said his practice would fall apart if she left, and I don't think he was exaggerating.

"I do know that," I told her. "Listen, do you think I could see Dr. Jenson for a couple of minutes? I've got some questions I need to ask him."

"He's in with somebody now, but he'll be done in a few minutes if you want to wait." The phone rang, and she put up her finger for me to hold on a second. After she'd made an appointment for someone, she put down the phone and gave me her attention. "Leigh Ann's free, if she can help you."

Leigh Ann was a nurse who'd only been around for about a year. I liked her well enough, but my questions involved more than I wanted to trust her with, so I said I'd wait for the doctor. Twenty minutes and two *People* magazines later, Livie told me to go on back.

I'd known Nile Jenson ever since I'd moved to Charleston, even before I met Ben. He was only about ten years older than I was, but he practiced medicine the old-fashioned way, with more common sense than highbrow science. It suited me just fine.

"You had some kind of scare the other night," he said, after I sat down in his office. "You and the kid both okay?"

"Okay is a relative term. But yeah, we've all recovered from that night, at least."

"So what's up?"

Another thing I liked about Nile Jenson. He had plenty of warmth, but he didn't waste a lot of time on chitchat.

"I need to get your opinion about something and I need to ask you not to come back with any questions."

"Is it something medical?"

"Yeah, but it may also be illegal." I needed to get that up front, let him know what he was getting into.

"That's tricky," he said. "I'll do my best, but I can't promise anything until I know what you're talking about."

It wasn't my ass on the line, so I didn't blame him for being cautious. I needed to find out what the hell was going on with Reese. I figured trusting the good Dr. Jenson was the least of my problems.

"What kind of drugs are these?" I handed the receipts to him. He looked them over, studied each one, and then looked up at me.

"You want to fill in the blanks for me here?" he asked. "Who is this Dr. Harris?"

"That would be a question, Doc."

"Come on, Gina," he said. "What's this about?"

"Can you tell me what they are first? Then I'll explain what I can. Are they worth something on the street, or do people get addicted to them?"

"No. Not these drugs. I don't know what you're getting at. Why would anyone prescribe these for you? Have you seen a specialist?" He seemed genuinely baffled, stared at me as if I'd sprouted a third ear.

"Someone *borrowed* my credit card without bothering to tell me about it. They used it to order these drugs. What are they?"

"Have you called the police?" He seemed focused on the practical aspects of the problem. I just wanted the information plain and simple.

"It's really complicated," I explained. "I don't want to turn anybody in. I just need to know if this person is addicted or something. I'd rather get them help than get them busted."

"These aren't drugs that anyone would normally abuse," he said, settling back in his chair. "The person who ordered these most likely has some neurological disorder. My guess would be MS."

"MS?" I inventoried my small knowledge of diseases, tried to remember exactly what that meant.

"Multiple sclerosis," he said. "But this is a pretty heavy cocktail. Is this person highly symptomatic?"

"Only if the symptoms include being crazy," I joked.

"I'm serious, Gina. Is she able to walk, lift things . . . you know, function normally?"

I thought about it. Certainly Reese didn't have the extreme problems he described, but there had been a general . . . clumsiness about her. I'd dismissed it as not being used to the boat, or other normal explanations.

"She has some problems with balance," I said. "But she's been on my boat a lot. Even coordinated people don't have good sea legs sometimes."

I thought of her on the boat with Maxine, unable to grasp the drink I was trying to hand her. That wasn't a balance problem. The bigger picture began to come into focus.

"If she wants to see me," he was saying, "I'll refer her to a good neurologist. Where did she get prescriptions for this stuff—and why did she put it in your name?"

"Those are both at the top of my list, Doc. I'll get back to you if I get any good answers. Are you planning to tell anybody about this?"

"I'll hold off for the moment," he said. "They're not narcotics, so I don't think we're talking about an abuse issue. But falsifying prescriptions—"

"I know," I interrupted him. "Just let me look into it first, okay?"

He nodded but appeared more uncomfortable than I would have liked.

"I'm sorry to put you in a bad position."

"We'll file it under patient confidentiality for the moment," he said. "But I'd feel better if you'd send her or him in, let me try to sort it out from a medical standpoint."

"I'll do my best."

I left him in his office, looking troubled. Seemed I spread good cheer everywhere I went.

I'd gotten information, or partial information, at least; but there were more questions than answers inside what I'd learned. Multiple sclerosis. Was it possible that Reese had that kind of problem? And Benjamin. Had he known about this one too? *How the hell did you ever get mixed up with this woman, Ben?* Even if he'd been standing in front of me, I doubt he could have answered that one.

25

∞

Reese

In the thin light of the Ship's Store storage room, Reese tried to memorize Charlie's features. She lay on top of a large, vinyl seat cushion that had long ago been discarded off someone's boat. Most likely Charlie, or somebody like him, had left it in the back room of the store for the purpose of such spontaneous encounters.

She wore the beaded chain belt that she'd had on with her skirt—that, and nothing more.

"Leave it on," he'd said when she reached to unfasten it, her blouse and skirt already in a heap on the floor. "I like that on you."

She'd felt the delicate, metal filigree rubbing between them as they came together. The very slight discomfort it caused brought her nerves to their finest edge. Afterward, she realized she'd never look at the belt again without thinking of Charlie.

"I need to get back out there," he said, sitting beside her, making no move to stand. "But damn! I can't leave you in here. Not looking like this."

She stayed on her back, the cool vinyl pressed against warm skin. She liked for him to look at her. She liked what she read in his face. She didn't want to think about what might come. A time when someone staring at her body would mean pity, rather than desire. But it hadn't come to that. Not yet. And with Angel off at the grocery store with Lane, she was free to deny everything else in her life. If only for a little while.

She thought of Lane with Angel, hoped their time together would help Lane make up her mind. Lane had seemed pleased at her request, said she'd have to think about it from all different angles before she could agree.

"You are some kind of pretty," Charlie said. "I could lose my job if I don't get back to work, though."

"That young guy helping you can hold everything down out there a little longer," she said. "He seems responsible. I think you've got a little more to finish here before we bother putting our clothes on."

"I told him I was getting a roll of paper for the cash register." He grinned. "I'm supposed to be in charge."

"Who says you're not in charge?" Just barely touching him, she ran her nails along the tender skin of his waist.

"Oh darlin'," he said, breathing hard. "I think we both know you're running this show. But what the fuck? I'm not complaining."

She looked at him, his tanned skin contradicting the light coloring of his hair. Even in the low light of a partially boarded up window, she could see the pale green of his eyes. As he bent toward her, giving in, she reached up. With light fingers, she touched his collarbone, his mouth. She vowed again to memorize him, to appreciate every second, every small moment of his body. She'd store up images that would outlast anything bad the future had to offer.

26

Gina

I passed the road to Mt. Sinai on my way to the rental cottage. I couldn't see the church, but I could make out part of the cemetery on the higher rise. I thought of Benjamin. He'd like to see me beginning to feel life again. For months I'd thought it impossible. I could see the world through a one-way mirror, but I couldn't reach it, and I couldn't be seen. I was almost afraid to trust that it was changing.

Georgie moved around, restless in the back of the car, looking for food that had been dropped and ignored. I'd swung by to get her after leaving Dr. Jenson's, had hauled her into the Volvo without a walk, and she'd sulked on the floorboard for half the ride.

But her pity party had ended and she jumped up on the backseat. Although the air conditioner running full-blast barely cooled the car, I left a back window partially open for her. She stuck her nose out to take in the smells. Even when the days went to 90 degrees or more, I couldn't bear to take this pleasure away.

I'd tried to call Maxine, but her cell wasn't on and the phone at the cottage was busy. I decided to take a chance and ride on out, see if she was still there.

Her car fit only halfway under the carport that sat underneath the house. Like most waterfront structures, the cottage had been built on stiltlike supports, to accommodate storm surges in the tide. Any normal car would have tucked neatly under, fully in the shade. But Maxine's extended outward, looked like an adult in a child's playhouse.

The cottage was fronted by deepwater shoreline. Prime real estate. The dock and the boathouse added property beyond the waterline, and a screened-in room on top of the boathouse had offered

Ben an option for make-out territory when he struck up summer romances. We'd made use of it ourselves a few times.

"I never got this lucky up here in high school," he told me late one night—after we'd slipped out of the cottage, where every move was audible from every other room in the house.

I looked out toward the side yard. The property line was defined by a marsh creek that emptied into the larger water. The place looked like a miniplantation existing on its own little peninsula.

"Come in!" Maxine called out when I employed the large brass door knocker.

"Hey," she said, after I found her in the largest bedroom, organizing towels in the closet used for linens. "I wasn't expecting to see you until the morning."

"I thought I'd ride out and lend a hand," I lied. "I tried to call, but the line here was busy."

"One of the cleaning girls was having it out with her boyfriend. I kept hearing her dial again after he apparently hung up on her. I just sent them off about twenty minutes ago." She looked around and made a face. "They were talking more than they were cleaning, anyway. I swear you'd never know they came at all."

The place looked fine to me, but I kept my mouth shut; didn't want to spoil her righteous indignation.

"So, did you tell her she could move in?" Maxine avoided saying Reese's name whenever possible.

"I did, and she seemed grateful." Again I lied. "She'll be at the real estate office in the morning."

As before, I was struck by Maxine's transformation. Even in everyday cleaning clothes she looked animated and young. She wore Capri pants with a man's button-down shirt. I wondered if the shirt belonged to her CPA friend. The pants looked new, and I guessed they would have to be. She was a couple of sizes smaller than she'd been at Ben's funeral.

"You look great," I said. Not a lie.

"It's having someone." She smiled. "It changes everything." She stopped folding for a moment. "But then, I'd say you know that first-hand. You're looking a lot better yourself."

"Want a soda?" I grinned, not taking the bait.

"Fine. You don't have to tell me . . . yet. But I want you to know I'm happy for you."

"Seriously. It's too early to say anything," I said, feeling a little guilty for trivializing my time with Derek. But it *was* early and I did want to be cautious. "But you're right," I added. "I do feel better than I have since . . ." I didn't need to finish. She knew.

She worked on putting stacks of blankets and sheets on the closet shelves. From the back, she was ageless . . . twenty . . . forty . . . fifty, younger than her actual age, for sure.

"Here, let me help," I said, watching her struggle to reach the highest shelf. I took the cotton blankets and put them away. "Wasn't the cleaning service supposed to do all this?"

"They just throw things in, any old way," she said, sitting on the edge of the bed. "I'd rather do it myself." She finished before I could reach her. On the floor, I saw a large department-store box. It looked like a shirt box, only bigger, with dates scrawled on the top in marker.

"What's that?" I asked.

"Old pictures. From when Ben was a kid."

We both stared at it, as if it might explode at the slightest touch.

"Why'd you leave them here?" I tried to sound casual, but my voice wasn't cooperating. It cracked on the last word, gave the question a manic quality.

"Don't worry, hon," she said. "I don't plan to go through them now. I don't think I could. But they are all the pictures from before Ben's father took off. He's either in them or took them. I didn't even want the box in my house. Just the thought of it—" She stopped, took a deep breath. "But I didn't want to throw it out either. I thought Ben might want them someday. And now . . . Well, now I don't quite know what to do with them."

We both looked at the box again. The sound of a passing boat measured the silence as it faded with growing distance. I thought of the pictures, loose and jumbled in a box; kept for someone who would never have them. And there was nothing I could say to make that thought easier for either of us. So I stayed quiet.

The air-conditioning hummed, hermetically sealed us off from the water and the marsh that existed just yards away. Early spring and late fall were the best times at the cottage, I recalled. With the windows and doors open to the screens, the coastal landscape permeated the pastel rooms, made them part of something large and unnamed.

"I have all that stuff of Ben's in storage," I said finally, hitting upon an idea. "Why don't I take the pictures there?"

"That would solve my problem," she said, sounding as relieved as I felt.

"Let me take them to the car now, so I don't forget." I picked up the box. Just before I got out the door, Maxine called out to me from the kitchen.

"As odd as it sounds," she said, "I'm going to make a pot of coffee. Want some?"

I needed to talk to her. Sitting in the kitchen with coffee might provide the best opportunity, I reasoned.

"Sure," I said.

"Regular or decaf?" she offered.

"I went to journalism school. I don't do decaf."

"That's my girl," she said. "In that case, would you like a little bourbon thrown in?"

"Even better." I took the box and put it in the back of my car.

The sun had gotten low; spread large over the property. But the house had fallen into the shadows. We sat at the table, booze and coffee sending mixed messages to my brain.

"Listen," I began. "I need to talk with you about something."

She tilted her head slightly by way of acknowledgment. Waited. I didn't know exactly how to begin. Every question seemed a larger opening to Pandora's box.

"Did you know anything about Reese having an illness?"

"Sure," she answered without hesitation, as if I should have known it too. "I didn't know the full extent of it until she was well gone—thank God—but it worried me to no end. I was sure she'd come back and play on his sympathy. That's the one thing I'll give her credit for. She stayed gone, finally. Let him get on with his life. He'd carried so much of that marriage to begin with that I was afraid . . . But that's old history now. She seems to be doing okay."

"Well," I said, trying to decide how much to tell her. "I'm not sure. I saw some pills, quite a lot of pills, really, that she had in her bag. My doctor said they would be used to treat MS."

Maxine sat back, took a sip of her coffee, seemed to be staring at something outside, but there was nothing to see. I wondered what vision might be in her head. Finally, she spoke. "That makes some sense. MS." She said it as if she'd missed something obvious.

"What did you think she had?"

"I didn't know, exactly. She'd been sent to a neurologist, so I knew it was something related to that. And I think she fell once or twice, fractured her shoulder the last time. The doctor suggested Ben get somebody out to the house. A physical therapist, or maybe a nurse trained to deal with whatever it was. The woman came every day during the week. I only found out about the nurse, or whatever she was, because she answered the phone when I called, and I asked Ben who she was. Apparently Reese wasn't too thrilled with her being there. I know Ben got frustrated that Reese wasn't even trying to co-operate with her.

"As far as the illness went, Ben said Reese didn't want him talking about it, so I let it be. I thought it had passed, though. I didn't think she was still sick when she left. But if it was MS, I guess that doesn't just up and go away."

"Do you think Ben knew everything?"

"I'm sure he did. I always figured that's why he went looking for her when she left, over and over. And why he kept helping her every time she called. You know he did that."

"Yeah," I said. "I know. But that was just Ben. You knew she went back and forth, leaving him?"

She nodded. "It went on for weeks. Ben was out of his mind."

"She told me about the times he went to bring her back. That he found her in Myrtle Beach, then in D.C., I think. Two or three places, he found her." I left out the story about the other men. Maxine already hated her, and she'd heard the confusion over Angel's paternity. No need to fuel any more of that anger.

"Well, he never talked too much about it—to me, at least. I caught the gist of it. But he knew how I felt about her. So, maybe he just didn't want me to weigh in. But at some point he just gave up. Sick or not sick, he couldn't be responsible for her forever. She was bad news for my son. When she divorced him, I was glad. When he married you, it was the happiest day of my life. I mean it, Gina. Even happier than the day he was born. So many worries went flying out the window that day. I knew that no matter what he felt he owed Reese, he'd never leave you to give it to her. He was safe the day he married you."

She made me sound larger than life. A mythical guardian. But maybe she was right. Ben needed protection from his own nature as much as anything else. He never believed in the existence of lost causes.

"Did he love me, Maxine?" It was a stupid question. Like asking your parents if you're smart, just to hear them say yes.

She looked over at me, smiled as if I was joking. Of course I knew the answer, but lately I hadn't felt it. Not the way I'd believed it every night listening to Ben sleep.

"Gina," she said, her words careful, deliberate. "I know you now, and I love you like a daughter. But I loved you before I even met you because of the way Ben felt. You were his partner. I think he loved you so much it surprised him."

"But he loved Reese too. I know he did. And that shouldn't bother me because it had nothing to do with me, but it does and—"

"I won't argue with you," she interrupted. "But it was a different kind of love. It was what you feel when you rescue an animal or volunteer at a hospital. Ben wanted to save the world, and the best place to start was Reese. He fell into rescuing Reese and it got to the point where I don't think he could tell the difference between that and love. He'd been so used to pairing love with worry, pity. With you, he felt free to be happy. Like I said, you were his partner. I never saw him happier."

His *partner*. Funny, I'd always felt a few paces behind him. For the first time, it occurred to me that with her illness, Reese must have felt she had miles to go before she even began to catch up.

"The only thing that kept your wedding day from total perfection was Ben's insistence on including his father."

Even on a reserved day, Maxine allowed herself to be more open, more unguarded, than most people. With late afternoon fatigue and a little alcohol settling in, she wasn't holding anything back.

"But the second he put that ring on your finger, he was free of her. He would never have left her. But when she left and he couldn't do anything about it, honest to God, I think he felt more relief than anything else. He'd never have said it, but I believe that's true. And even after it was over, if he'd known about Angel . . . Oh, I hate to think what would have happened."

I started to say it; it seemed that I should tell her about Ben and Angel. But at the moment, I knew it would be too much. My gut, every instinct I had, told me that. I'd have to tell her—and soon. But not on a night when she was living inside her memories at the cottage. She needed for everything she remembered about Ben to stay intact for a little while longer. I knew, firsthand, the consequences of having to rewrite history after someone has left you, gone out of your reach.

"Are you okay, hon?" Her hands were cupped around her mug, our coffee long grown cold.

"I'm fine."

The talk seemed to have played out. I had images of Ben struggling with Reese and some new illness that he may or may not have understood. I couldn't imagine why Reese would have left. Why she would have taken off with that hanging over her. God knows, Ben was good at taking care of things. Life had to have been easier for her with him.

My cell phone rang and I got up to get my purse. The bourbon had taken a toll on my coordination, but it also eased some of the demons that had been causing a stir inside me.

"Hey," Derek said after I answered.

I looked at the clock and realized it had been hours since I left him on the porch of Lane's house.

"Oh God, Derek. I'm sorry," I said. "I'm with Maxine, my mother-in-law, and I lost track of time."

"It's okay." He didn't sound exactly okay. But then, I wouldn't have been either. "I got Charlie to cover the security rounds for me tonight. I thought we were going to do something."

Irritation. Frustration. I didn't blame him for sounding ticked.

"Let me call you right back," I said.

Maxine was clearly planning to spend the night. There'd be no reason for her to drive home and then come back in the morning. I felt as if I ought to stay with her, but I wanted to be with Derek too.

"Go do something with him," she said before I could speak.

"We've already had cocktails," I said, raising my coffee. "What are you doing for dinner?"

"I'm going to ride out for a greasy hamburger, something I almost never do, and then watch *West Side Story*. It's on Bravo tonight. I have my plans, and you're not included, dear. Go, have fun. It's the best thing you can do for me."

"Maxine—"

"I'm glad you drove out this afternoon." She cut me off. "It's good to spend time with you that isn't so full of sadness. But you are dismissed. Go on out with this guy, Gina. Go out on a date. Ben's not coming back. It kills me to say it, and I know how much you wish it wasn't true. But he's not. And honestly, it's harder for me to see you waiting on him to come home than to know you're out having fun with someone who must be wonderful because your taste in men is flawless."

Her eyes were full of tears, but she was right. We were different than we'd been a month ago. The odd part of it was, I was different than I'd been three days before, although I wouldn't wish those days on anyone.

"Okay," I said. "Even if I argued longer, I'd lose. Ben had to get it from somewhere."

"You're damn right he did," she said, smiling. "One request."

"Shoot."

"Leave the critter with me. I'll be like a grandmother babysitting her while you're out."

We both stopped talking for a second when she said that. Thoughts of Angel, of her place in our strange domestic circumstances, remained present, but unspoken.

"Well, I love my dog, but thinking about her as a grandchild makes us both look pretty pathetic." I tried to joke our way past it, but my timing was off. "Come Christmas, don't go wrapping up a bunch of squeaky toys for her."

"Seriously, she'll keep me company," she said, having lost her banter. "And she'll let me know if someone's around. I'll buy some dog food when I go out."

"Okay. Deal. I'll get her from you tomorrow."

"Call him back," she said, eyes steady, serious as she looked at me.

"As soon as I get in the car. I promise."

She smiled again, and when I hugged her good-bye, she felt as small as a child.

27

Reese

$\mathcal{R}$ eese drove out to the highway, away from the marina. It was hot, but she turned off the air conditioner and rolled down all the windows. In her thin camisole with the barest of straps, she felt the late sun coming in sideways, touching her shoulders, her cheeks. She'd put her clothes back on at the Ship's Store, but had put on nothing underneath. Her bra and panties were tucked in her purse. She wanted to feel the soft cotton against her breasts, remind herself that she was still very much alive, and too young to think of her body as damaged and old.

Wind rushed in as she accelerated, skimmed her bare arms, making her aware of her skin, aware of the way her nerves had obeyed her for a change, offered pleasure she so badly needed. Charlie was a good kid. With a little instruction, he would be a terrific bed buddy. She wondered if she could let that happen. If she should. She didn't need life any more complicated than it already was.

"Where do you have to run off to?" he had asked as she left him. "I get off at five o'clock this week, remember? I'm taking over night rounds for Derek tonight, but that gives us a few hours."

"I'll see what time I get back," she said, glad to feel in control. "I have something to do first."

The teenager working the cash register looked up when they emerged from the storeroom. He got a goofy smile on his face and then looked away. Charlie had no roll of cash register paper with him. He didn't even pretend the situation wasn't as it seemed.

"I bet your errand could wait," Charlie said as she was heading for the door.

"I need to break a date." She smiled up at him.

"With who?"

"With a preacher," she told him, and left before he could find any more words.

She'd said it loud enough for the teenager to hear her too. The world had rarely delighted her in recent months. Sometimes it seemed as if it had been years. But at that moment she'd felt nearly giddy.

She took out a cigarette, rolled up the windows so she could light it, and decided air-conditioning would feel good after all. The first rush of nicotine went to her head, made the afternoon's pleasure complete. If Preacher Andrew had a beer stashed away at the rectory, the day would be all but perfect.

"He's still at the church." The wife stood at the door of her home. Reese knew enough about country churches to figure out the neat little house with the flower bed directly across the street from church property was free housing given to the preacher. She could have lived in a house like that, if all of the plans her bastard father had put in play for her had actually come to be.

"There but by the grace of God go I," she mumbled, staring into the neat little living room just inside the front door.

"What?" Diane Hanes looked puzzled, a little bit disturbed.

"Nothing," Reese said. "I was just thinking about going to church when I was a kid. So Preacher Andy's not home?" She threw in the nickname just to get a rise. From the look on the woman's face, it had done the trick. The humorless Mrs. Hanes made a point of glancing down at her rumpled clothes.

"He's still at the office, getting ready for the evening Bible study." Diane Hanes nodded toward the church, stepped back as if she was done with her part of the conversation.

"Could you call him for me?" Reese asked. "Tell him to come outside?"

The woman just stood there. Reese wondered if she'd heard the request.

"A quick ring?" She tried again. "Let him know somebody's here."

"It's right across the street." For a moment, confusion seemed to override the woman's irritation.

"I know," Reese said. "But I don't do churches. It's kind of a phobia."

"A phobia of churches?" Diane Hanes obviously planned to stand all day, sorting out the details of Reese's request. It wasn't that complicated.

"Just call him, please."

"All right." She stepped away from the door. From inside, the sound of laughter came from the television. A sitcom. This time of day, a rerun, Reese figured. She looked to see if there were children sprawled out, watching, but no one was in the room. Absent on-lookers, the TV played on in cheerful oblivion.

"He says to walk on over," the wife came back and told her. "He'll meet you outside."

Reese saw him come out of the side door before she reached the parking lot. She could feel the wife's eyes from across the street. That was okay with her. She'd never minded an audience.

"Preacher Andy? Where'd you come up with that?" He was smil-ing, obviously not bothered by whatever his wife told him.

"You seem more like an Andy to me," she said. "Andrew sounds like the guy who stays after school to finish his science project."

"What's Andy doing?"

"He's busy at football practice."

"You got me there," he said, walking out toward the playground. "I cared a lot more about football in high school than I did about sci-ence. So, what can I do for you?"

She followed him past a tetherball pole, sat down on a swing— the same one where, earlier in the day, she watched Angel manage to overcome the constraints of her injured arm. She wondered if a bet-ter, more cautious mother would have stopped the girl.

"I have a change of plans tomorrow," she explained. "The cottage Angel and I have arranged to move into has come available early. We meet with the realtors in the morning and then move in, I guess. I didn't want you showing up at the marina."

"Thanks for letting me know." He didn't say the obvious. That she could have called. She didn't even know what she hoped to accom-plish by driving all the way back out to the church. She only knew the idea of talking with him had seemed to make her feel better.

He sat down on the swing next to hers. She felt the entire struc-ture shimmy as he settled his weight. He had a solid quality about him that reassured her.

"Is there anything else on your mind?" He turned sideways to face her, straddled the seat, and leaned back on the rope. He looked and sounded casual, but his tone said that he took the conversation seriously.

"I'm not a good person," she said. "I want to be better for my daughter than I am. But I can't seem to be exactly who I want to be. I keep making all the wrong choices. Sometimes I even like the wrong choices."

She thought about Charlie. The smooth tan that covered the length of his torso.

"We aren't the ones to judge," he said. "God doesn't ask us to judge other people, or ourselves."

She winced at the platitude, felt dismissed by it. She expected something more, something better from him. Maybe he was like all the others.

"Yeah, well, I just spent the last hour before I came here screwing around with a guy—a kid, really—in the storage room of a marina store. He's almost a decade younger than I am. And I'm the one who suggested it. We did it twice." She kept her voice matter-of-fact, made direct contact with his dark, unblinking eyes. She tried to read his thoughts as she said it. "I think that's a no-brainer for bad behavior, don't you?"

"I've seen it all, Reese. At some point in my life, I've done most of it." He was shooting for world-weary, but he seemed a little hard-pressed to find his voice. "We all have our weaknesses. Our fallen moments." His breathing was off, coming with some effort. Good. The bastard was human, after all. "As much as you're trying to shock me, I doubt you will. You won't do much to rattle God either. He's seen more than I have, and has forgiven it."

The last part was pretty standard fare, but his effort had an honest quality.

"What has He forgiven you for, Preacher?"

"Things that I haven't managed to forgive in myself," he told her. "Why are you so mad at God?"

The question took her off guard. She thought about getting up to leave, going back to her car and forgetting about whatever it was she thought she could accomplish by driving out to see him. But he was right. She felt angry. And sitting one swing over was one of God's primary chess pieces in this neck of the woods. Part of her wanted to devastate the good preacher in order to satisfy that rage; another part of her wanted something from him, some kind of absolution.

"You've got a meeting tonight," she said, deciding to end the conversation after all.

"Not for an hour. Just talk if you want to. Whatever you've done, I've done worse. I'm in no position to judge, I promise you."

"You go first," she said. "What are you still paying for?"

He sat for a moment, looked across at his house, then over at the church. He took a deep breath, turned back to her.

"Infidelity," he said. "When I was still in the military. I haven't made a point of telling anyone except the pastor search committee about it. But I haven't ever tried to hush it up either. You asked, so I'll be honest."

She could see that. She could see him falling for somebody wrong. He may have thought it would surprise her, but she, of all people, knew that preachers could act as sorry as anybody else.

"Is that why your wife looks at me the way she does, why she's looking out the window at us right now?"

"Yes." He didn't miss a beat. "I'm sure it is. She has every right to doubt me. It was years ago, and we're working hard to get through it, still."

"Were you a preacher then?"

"Yes and no. I'd been to seminary, then thought I wanted to be career military, so I didn't have a church at the time." He stopped, as if waiting for her to say something. When she didn't, he said, "So that's it. My fallen moment. You seem to have something you need to get out. If that's the case, I'm here."

His confession didn't get to her, but his insight—it rattled her very soul. He seemed to know so much more than she'd told him.

"A question first," she said.

He nodded.

"Do you believe that when you reject something God has asked you to do, that He punishes you? That terrible things wouldn't happen if you'd gone along in the first place?"

He rocked slightly, back and forth, still facing her. She closed her eyes for a moment, felt the motion in the structure of the swing. She wondered if he was aware of her breasts, free inside her camisole; if he was afraid he would give in, make the mistake he'd made before. Then she stopped herself. She had other things to accomplish. Bringing him down wouldn't solve it, not in the long run—although the temptation remained.

"People have a lot of opinions about judgment," he said finally. "If you're asking what I believe, I think that it's the nature of this world for things to happen, good and bad. How we deal with the stuff that happens, good and bad, defines our relationship with God. I think sometimes things happen to influence our choices, but not to punish us."

She nodded. Wondered if it could be true. Bad things, good things, all random. One just as likely to happen as the other. Angel had happened, hadn't she? That outweighed any of the bad over the years.

"Why don't you tell me about it?"

"About what?" She felt her hands, her fingers, holding on to the swing. The tender part of her palms against the rough skin of the rope should have registered. But her hands had gone numb, and she planted her feet on the ground in case she lost her grip.

"Tell me what's on your mind," he said. "You're starting to find cracks in whatever's holding it in. I know the feeling, Reese. You'll be better once it's said."

She heard the call of a bird, the low, puffing baritone of an owl somewhere in the woods behind her. The sound coincided with her own voice as she began to tell him. That sound would remind her, she was sure, of the moment, both terrifying and free, when she began saying the words she'd never intended to say, to anyone, much less a near stranger. But there was an odd symmetry in telling this man—who was so similar to, and still so different from, the person who had caused it all.

And as she spoke, the scene lived in her head, came back new. She kept a tethering gaze on Andrew Hanes. If she let herself fully re-member with all the color and detail of reality, she would need a way back. He would have to be the way back.

"I was fourteen," she said. "Living with my father after my mom left us . . ."

The house smelled of collards. Her father had cooked them for lunch, seasoned with peppers and chunks of ham in the pot. To most, this was the side dish, something to go with a roast or a casse-role. But for her wild-eyed father, it was a meal, the only one he knew how to prepare from scratch. She always wondered who taught him—and why? His mother? Her mother? The lunch—Sunday din-ner, he called it—was long over, but the smell remained, and she was sure it would follow her to the evening's church revival where he'd insisted they go.

The service would be held at a large church in Columbia, more than an hour's drive away. It would be televised, the way most of this evangelist's red-faced rants were. Her dad knew the preacher, had driven miles to hear him, to talk with him, on several occasions, and gave money every time the man showed his face on TV. Her dad had never insisted that Reese go before, but that night he said she had no choice. She'd get in the car, he announced with an eerie calm, or he'd take that record player she couldn't seem to live without and toss it at the dump, along with every record he could find in her room. He was crazy enough to do it, so she put on her pale blue dress and waited for him to say it was time to go. Thank God, no one she knew would be there.

"Take off that necklace," he told her as they drove into the crowded parking lot outside the church.

"Why?" Her boyfriend had given it to her several months before. She never took it off.

"You need to shed all adornments before you go into the Lord's presence."

That sounded strange, even for her eccentric father. He spent his days high above others doing roof work, repairing gutters. Sometimes she thought she honestly believed he was higher than everybody else. Above all sin and temptation.

"And take that silver thing out of your hair," he said, again with no particular agitation. But it was far more than a request.

"It's just a clip. My hair will fall in my eyes if I don't pull it back."

He reached over, with methodical purpose, and pulled out the clip, along with a large section of hair. Her scalp stung and she felt too stunned to protest. He was odd, dismissive much of the time, but he'd never acted so strangely toward her before. The worst she'd seen of him consisted of hard, determined lectures about once a week or so.

Before she could sort out what had happened, he was out of the car, so she got out and followed him. Once inside, he took off for the front of the church, and she kept him in her peripheral vision as she scanned the crowds—something she always did at large gatherings—for her mother's face. Church was an unlikely place for her mom to show up, but she figured it never hurt to keep her eyes open. Although most of the seats had been taken, her father led them toward rows of folding chairs that had been added in the space between the pews and the pulpit to create extra seating. To Reese's surprise, her daddy led her to seats in the front row, the only empty seats in the entire front half of the sanctuary, best she could tell.

"Are you sure these don't belong to somebody already?" She didn't want to be so close. Besides the discomfort of such proximity to the evangelist himself, she was terrified that a camera, spanning close for an audience shot, would catch her, expose her to any friends or parents of friends who might be flipping channels.

"Just have a seat," he said. When she did, he left her there, went off toward a door that led into the back section of the church. She sat, aware of being alone and younger than anyone else around her. There were small children sitting on a parent's lap here and there, but no teenagers that she saw. A middle-age woman with a brown paper sack in her hand asked if she could have the empty seat.

"My daddy's coming back," Reese managed. The woman left, looking irritated.

By the time her father came back, the lights were being lowered and a bunch of white singers trying to do justice to black gospel had revved up in the choir loft behind the pulpit. The preacher came out and the energy pitched higher, to a near frenzy, in the large sanctuary. No wonder, Reese thought. The man carried half the wattage in the room by himself. She'd barely paid attention to him on TV, but sitting literally at his feet, she could see how people would be drawn in. How they would want to approach the source of such winning power.

She zoned out the content of what the evangelist said, focused instead on the singsong of his voice, the cadence that reminded her of a livestock auctioneer she'd heard once at the state fair. She felt odd, watching him. Compelled to take in his every movement. It wasn't so bad, couldn't go on for more than a couple of hours.

She stood for the hymns and sat for the prayers, figured they'd be leaving soon when the preacher asked for anyone seeking healing or cleansing of any sort to come forward. Lines formed in the aisles even before the organ music got into full swing. While she scanned the faces in the lines, out of habit still, she heard her father say, "Go on up there, child."

"What?" She hoped she'd misunderstood, that he was telling her they needed to leave. It was a long drive home.

"This is what we come for," he said. "Go on up."

"No, Daddy. I'm not going up there."

The music seemed everywhere. She heard one woman's voice, a shade off from the others, running parallel with those on key.

"Stand up, Reese," her daddy said, this time with a stern edge.

The preacher was suddenly there, right in front of her. She hadn't seen him come down to the sanctuary floor, but there he was. His presence startled her at the closer range. He was even younger than she had thought. Much younger than her father. But he had an ancient—no, not ancient—a timeless quality about him that seemed to make age and context irrelevant in his presence.

He reached out and took her hand, and because she didn't know what else to do, she let him. She let him lead her up, past other people who were standing in line, all the way up to the platform. And he positioned her, still standing, in a semicircle of worshipers who were swaying and calling out with no apparent concern for who might see them acting such a fool. "Let your soul cry out! Amen. Cry out for healing power! Amen." The minister shouted, and the random chorus of voices, some chanting, some singing, moved in a collective, urgent call. The sounds they made weren't even words, but she thought she understood them anyway.

And then she felt the preacher there again, in front of her. He was saying something, his words rhythmic and songlike, but not a song, and she wanted to sound out too, but she didn't seem to have a voice. She felt jostled from either side as the people around her moved and swayed. And then the preacher took hold of her wrist, raised her arm, placed the heel of his other hand on her forehead. The sweat of his palm mixed with the dampness of her brow. She smelled his robes, the harsh, laundered aroma tainted by new sweat and sweet tobacco. She'd smoked cigarettes once or twice with her boyfriend, usually in conjunction with fooling around, and the same smell on this man of God led her to greater confusion.

His hand offered light pressure on her forehead. The awareness of his touch took her focus. Only a soft, steady pressure. But then there was something else, something large, impossible to move through.

The next moment she could feel the carpet of the platform close against her arm, her cheek. She had fallen, but she didn't recall losing her balance, hitting the ground. Her blue dress had gathered high around her thighs and the preacher stood above her, watching.

She wanted to pull at her dress, to right herself, but she found she couldn't move. Embarrassed, she lay helpless, with no options that came to mind. Lights from the cameras told her she'd become the main attraction as he stood above her, smiling, reciting scripture she didn't recognize.

Then to her horror, he bent down and picked her up. His robes pressed against the back of her neck and knees and his warm breath fell on the exposed length of her neck. She felt nausea rise in her chest and fought it. The thought of vomiting seemed too much to consider. He carried her into a room. It must have been the dressing room for baptism candidates because all sizes of white, baptismal robes hung on a wooden rod at the back of the room.

"You've been chosen, child," he said, putting her down on a scratchy hand-me-down couch in the center of the room. "I had my notions. But I waited to see you tonight. God touched you tonight."

She sat up—suddenly, miraculously, able to move—and put her feet on the floor. "Chosen?"

"I've spoken to your father," he said. "Actually, *both* your fathers." He smiled, all white teeth and tanned skin. "Your earthly and your heavenly fathers. I've had a vision for some time, that a child bride would come to me, would fulfill this ministry."

"Bride?" She felt panic rise inside her chest. The thin cotton of her dress seemed slight protection from his eyes as he openly stared at her body.

"I'm alone," he said. "My wife passed over two years ago. I thought my ministry to be a solitary one after that. Until the visions told me otherwise. You have been my vision."

He reached and, without hurry, unbuttoned the front of her dress. One, two, three buttons. A certain terror seized her. "Stop," she barely managed to say with the small bit of voice she could muster. But he opened her dress to her waist. Laid his full hand on her bra, the first she'd ever bought, the only one she owned. All she could think was she'd have to buy more. At least one more. She'd never wear this one again. Never look at it . . .

"Stop," she said again, louder this time. "Please, stop." Her voice broke. But he hadn't stopped. In a way, it had never stopped. The nightmarish memory was almost worse than the reality, if that was possible. At least she'd assumed the reality would end. The memory returned over and over . . .

When he finally pulled away, he looked at her with sickly kindness.

"It's all right, child. When two were betrothed in God's scripture, they were as man and wife from the moment of promise. I realize there are laws of our time, so we won't speak of this. But our joining is clean in God's eyes. Your father understands and has agreed. In due time, you will legally come into my household, my ministry . . ."

She started to cry. She felt her own tears as they fell onto her exposed belly where the dress still gaped, like an open wound.

"It's a lot for you all at once. I understand. The responsibility must seem tremendous," he said, standing, adjusting his robe. He smiled with practiced benevolence. "I'll get your father, and the two of you can wait for me here. I need to join my assistants who continue to lay hands of healing. But I will return soon. In the meantime, your father can explain the arrangements."

He left, and the relief of knowing he was gone went through her, an involuntary tremble that traveled the length of her being. One door allowed for exit, and without bothering to gather her panties or button her dress, she slipped out before anyone could stop her. She went down a hall that she knew led away from the preacher. Away from the noise and song. Away from her father who, she realized, had most certainly decided to offer more to this man's ministry than money.

The telling of the story left Reese exhausted. A couple of cars had arrived in the parking lot and the mosquitoes were out, both signifying the Bible study would soon begin.

"I'm so sorry," Andrew said. He kept his eyes direct, refused any embarrassment that would have put the blame on her.

"You have to go," she said, looking toward the cars in the parking lot.

"Not just yet," Preacher Andrew said. "Those are the study leaders. No one else is here. You have time to finish. What did you do after you left all of them?"

She took a breath. The rest should be easy to tell, but it seemed such an effort nonetheless.

"For one thing, I never went back to my father's house again," she said, trying to put a casual note into her saga.

"I mean it," he said. "What did you do?"

"My uncle, one of my mother's twin brothers, he and his wife lived on an army base. He was career military. They were both nice, my uncles. I hadn't seen either one of them in a couple of years, but they used to come take me crabbing and fishing sometimes after my mom left. Anyway, I found my way to a gas station, got his number, and . . . He came and got me, let me come stay with them."

"So you just abandoned one life and started another. Just like that?"

"Sort of." Reese didn't want to talk anymore. Her head hurt from the memories, from the sound of her own voice. "My aunt drove me back to my old school every morning for a couple of weeks. Trying to keep things as normal as possible. But it was too much of a hassle, so I switched to the school at the base."

She didn't, couldn't, tell the rest of it. How some kids had seen the program and everyone knew about it. How, if they didn't make comments about it in front of her, which most did, she heard the laughter as soon as she passed by. Everyone, all her friends, deserted her—including her boyfriend, who couldn't even look her in the eye.

"It was okay," she said. "Switching schools."

"What did your father do about all of it?"

"I don't know. I never talked to the bastard again. My uncle Austin got some kind of court order that said he couldn't call me, couldn't come within a mile of me, something like that. It all worked out okay."

"Have you ever told anybody about this? Did you get any counseling?" Preacher Andrew seemed concerned, as if she was still that teenager.

"Not until now." She attempted to smile. "Aren't you the lucky one? Listen, it was a long time ago. And I wouldn't even be thinking about it but . . . so many things seem to be getting worse. Makes me wonder if I upset the natural order somehow by refusing, by running away. But that's really stupid. I know that much without hearing any advice from you. I don't know why I brought it up." She stood.

"Sit down, Reese," he said. "Please, just for a minute."

She sat back in the swing, oddly comfortable with this man who suddenly knew more about her than anyone else, with the exception of her uncles, who she hadn't seen in a good fifteen years.

"This is too much for you to have carried around by yourself."

"I've told you now," she said. "I just needed to tell somebody. Honestly. It's like, over the years, I'd let out a little bit here and there to people. Usually making jokes about TV preachers or whatever. Doing that seemed to ease some kind of pressure. But it has helped less and less as time goes on. You were right. I just needed to let it out, with somebody who wouldn't go talking about it all over the place. I mean, it's not the kind of thing you want everybody to hear. But now I feel better. Thanks, Preacher."

"There's more to it than just airing it out, Reese."

"What do you mean?"

"This whole notion of punishment. You do understand that you were a kid still, Reese. The asshole of a preacher, excuse my language—he was the one who needs forgiveness. And your dad doesn't win any prizes here either. You don't still think any of it is your fault, do you? What happened or anything that's happened since?"

She sat, let herself rock back and forth. It felt a little like being on the boat, she thought, being on a swing. The feeling could grow on you, feel more normal than solid earth if you let it.

"Years later," she told him. She stopped. It was time to stop all of this business of baring souls. But she'd gone so far with him already. And it felt all right. "I got sick. Something called multiple sclerosis. It's when—"

"I know what it is," he gently interrupted. "You think that had something to do with refusing to be some child bride to an evangelical minister? Reese, I can tell you right now, the two would have nothing to do with—"

"Wait," she said. "Just listen. The disease. It comes and goes, but when it's bad . . . Well, it starts to feel exactly the way I felt when that dirtbag preacher put his hand on my head. It's more isolated. A hand that won't pick something up, or my leg buckling, not letting me walk without grabbing something. When Angel was real little, sometimes, I couldn't even pick her up.

"Sometimes, it gets so bad I have to use a cane, and that makes it hard to find work. At least, any work that someone would hire me to do. And every time it gets bad, I remember being on that church platform. Losing myself and being carried off without a muscle I could move to stop it. And then I get scared. I'm afraid the day is coming when that happens again. When this disease takes more than a few fingers or leg muscles at a time. If it takes everything . . . Andrew, I've got a daughter. I guess I just wonder if there's something I could do . . . should do . . . to make things right."

He sat, watching her. He looked as helpless as she felt every time she thought of the worst that could happen.

"I went into the hospital, not too long ago," she continued when he didn't say anything. "And when I did, something terrible almost happened to Angel. That's why I came here, hoping that Ben could help. I'm working on the answers to everything, but I have to get so much settled. I feel like I'm running out of time."

More cars lined up in the parking lot. People holding their Bibles stepped out onto the dusty gravel, ruined their polished shoes before setting one foot inside the church. They looked over at Reese and Preacher Andrew. Reese realized that she didn't want to make him look bad anymore. She didn't want to punish him because he had joined the same club as that maniac evangelist all those years ago. In spite of his screwing around on his wife—which suddenly, Reese couldn't imagine—Andrew wasn't the same species as that horrible man. He was decent. Some things in the world you just had to believe, and everything about him told Reese that Andrew Hanes was a good man.

"I want to talk more about all this," he said, making note of the gathering crowd. "I'll be honest with you. I feel a little over my head. But I think I can help, and one thing I know for sure—and you *have* to understand this—what happened back then and whatever problems you're having now . . . They don't have anything to do with each other. If anyone's going to burn in hell, it's going to be that television fucker and not—" He stopped himself, took a breath. His face had become flushed. "I'm sorry. Sometimes the Marine in me gets the best of the preacher. But I'm working on it. It just makes me so mad. You're not to blame, Reese."

She wanted to believe that. Sometimes she did. *He* believed it. That seemed like enough peace of mind to last a little while. But eventually her doubts would return. The idea that some divine plan she had rejected years ago set off a terrible chain of events in the world, or at least in her world. The momentary paralysis at that awful revival had been a preview. Part of her even felt she deserved whatever she got.

"Thanks for listening," she said, standing up. As she stood, her balance faltered before she got her footing. She felt the weakness in her leg, the wild twitch of muscle over bone that she couldn't will away.

Andrew saw it. "Do your people here know, at least about the illness? Is there someone who can help? What about Gina? You've got to be able to call on family—"

"We're not really family," she said.

He shook his head, as if he didn't understand.

"I was married to Ben a long time ago. That's our only connection. I'm not exactly a beloved cousin—hers or his."

"I see." He had no more directives about family.

"Listen, I didn't mean to make this into your problem. Any of it. Don't worry. It helped just to talk about it," she said as she made her way toward her car. "It's been stuck in my head with nowhere to go for a long time."

"We should talk more," he called out.

Reese recognized the tone, the expression. He wanted to rescue her. It had been a long time since someone strong enough to do that had come along. Ben might have been the last one. Maybe she'd let him try. For the moment, just feeling a little bit better seemed to be enough.

"Enjoy your Kumbayah chanting, or whatever it is you do in there," she said as she reached her car. "And pray for me if you want to," she called over her shoulder. "It couldn't hurt."

The men and women going into the meeting stared as she got into her car. She glanced across the street and saw Diane Hanes standing in the doorway of her house. She had little intention, Reese surmised, of joining her husband.

She headed back toward the highway; as the Plymouth reached the stop sign for the main road, a familiar car went by. Gina, in her Volvo, didn't see Reese waiting to make the turn. Reese pulled out, trailing the car back toward the marina. She thought of what Andrew had said about Gina. Thinking they were related. If that was true at all, what an odd mixed-up family they'd become in just three days' time.

Reese turned on the radio, soft rock drivel that might help her relax. Then she lit her last cigarette of the day. She had let her story out, and the world hadn't cracked open underneath her. That was something, at least. The absence of the tightness, of the effort it took to hold the memory fast inside her brain, seemed to free her, leave space for optimism. She'd ride that small current of hope all the way back to her daughter; take it as a sign that maybe Lane had decided to say yes. Hearing that would put the greatest of her fears to rest.

28

Gina

I hung streamers up over the framed seascape on the wall in the den. As I decorated, I felt Angel watching me. She had lived in the cottage for over a week, but she still walked around and touched everything as if she wasn't quite sure it was real, if it would still be there when she got up every morning. With her birthday decorations nearly in place, Angel looked around as if the house had become Disneyland. She started toward the kitchen, then turned abruptly, ran back to her room.

"What are you doing?" Reese called out to her.

"I'm changing clothes."

It was her third change of outfit since I'd arrived less than an hour before. In spite of her injured arm, she'd gotten good at dressing herself, and doing just about anything else she wanted. She still wore the sling, but had perfect use of her hand. Reese said that by the time school started in a little less than a week, she'd have her shoulder taped but wouldn't need any other support.

"I'm almost done," Angel called out to no one in particular.

Even with the new things Lane had bought her, I wasn't sure she had many more fashion options to try.

She'd decided to have her party at the cottage, not to go to the pond as planned. A blessing all in all, since Reese was having more problems with her leg. The boat ride over would have been difficult, I suspected.

"Where should we put these?" Derek walked in with Charlie. Each of them had a couple of presents.

"Over on the coffee table," Lane directed.

I felt sorry for Reese. She'd missed one day of work already. Not a good thing to happen in your second week of employment. She sat on the couch and let Lane do her party thing. I assumed Lane had talked with her about all the arrangements.

"You want a drink or something?" I asked her.

"I'm fine," she said. She looked at me as if taking mental notes of some sort.

"You sure?" I felt uncomfortable, under scrutiny for no reason I could fathom. Maybe she was just wondering why I'd become so nice after our painful bout of honesty on Lane's porch the week before. She had to figure something was up, but when I looked at her, I couldn't see anything but her struggle. She appeared different to me in light of her illness.

"Well, I brought beer for the grown-ups. Bourbon if that won't do the trick," I said, "and about ten different kinds of soft drinks for Angel to pick from. She's going to be sugar-polluted for a week. Plus, I bought junk food with enough preservatives to kill small animals in a laboratory. We're talking Twinkies, Cheetos, the works."

"Really, I'm fine." She smiled, looked subdued, almost sad. "Thanks for bringing all that stuff. I can't believe I sprained my foot like that. Terrible timing."

That was her story. She turned her ankle. And she hadn't been lifting anything with her right hand, which she hadn't attempted to explain. I tried to call up some indignation about being kept in the dark, essentially lied to—again. But any anger I felt became dwarfed by sympathy. I'd kept my discovery of the credit card to myself, the fact that I knew what she'd done. The card had found its way back in my wallet, and it wasn't as if she'd gone out and bought new shoes or something. Jesus, the woman needed medicine, and without insurance . . . I'd seen my credit card bill. How did people live with those kinds of expenses?

"Well, if you change your mind, just speak up," I told her.

Charlie sat down beside her, and she gave him a more genuine grin. Apparently, they were together, or at least, according to marina gossip, had been *together* in enough unusual locations around the place to assume they were some sort of couple. She seemed happier with him beside her than she'd been since I got to the cottage.

"Gina," Lane called out from the kitchen. "Your cell phone is ringing."

"Okay." I got up, did the mad dash to get it out of my purse before the voice mail kicked in.

"Hello?"

Mom's voice greeted me on the other end. "Hope I'm not catching you in the middle of anything," she said.

She made the usual chitchat for a few minutes. Nothing was ever direct with my mother. But she eventually got around to the reason for the call.

"Your father has a meeting in Charleston next week, honey. I thought I might tag along. We'll have dinners on both nights—you're welcome to join us, of course—but I thought at the very least we could have a nice long lunch. I've been concerned about you."

"I'm fine, Mom," I said. "But sure, I'd love to have lunch."

She gave the details. She was staying at Charleston Place, had picked a four-star restaurant just down the street. Easy enough to remember. Fancy hotel. Ridiculously priced dining. Tuesday.

"That'll be great, Mom."

After I hung up, I stood in the kitchen, thinking about Lane, Derek, and Maxine, even Reese and Angel, in a strange, dysfunctional way. How did they come to feel like family—a few of them in little more than a week's time—when my own mother struck me as an acquaintance? At best, a family friend.

"Could you give me a quick hand here, Gina?" Lane was standing on a chair, attaching a piñata to a hook she had screwed into the popcorn composite ceiling. I hoped it wouldn't bother Maxine. Holes in the ceiling. I felt oddly accountable for the cottage. A gesture that I'd meant to be ceremonial had become, to my surprise, a genuine responsibility. "Hold the bat up and let's guess how low I need to make it for Angel to reach."

Birthday balloons filled with helium had been tied to every chair. Also Lane's idea. I looked at her, had never seen her so thrilled with herself before. She'd been called into service earlier in the morning when Reese had tried and failed to decorate the place herself.

"You need a grandchild, woman," I said. "I've never seen you like this before."

"Reese was just so upset, hurting herself like that. I told her not to worry. That she and Angel temporarily had a matched set of injuries. Truth is, I enjoy doing this."

Lane didn't know about Reese's condition. I didn't know how much to say. Reese had kept it to herself for a reason, I guessed. I'd only talked to Derek and Maxine, and even that seemed like trading in gossip. But Maxine had known something about it already, and Derek, well . . . Talking with Derek seemed more like thinking out loud. Strange, how naturally he had become part of my life—as if he'd been there all along and I hadn't quite noticed it. It was too early in our relationship to worry about the *issues,* my issues, that would eventually come up if we stayed together. I decided to enjoy the golden window, the time when talking about kids would have been premature. Absurd even.

"Angel doesn't know what to do with herself," I said to Lane as the girl yelled out to ask her mom where the pink scrunchie had gone.

"From the way she talks," Lane said, "I'm not sure she's ever had a real party. Even that thing with the clown she told us about was just her and her mom at a performance. She needs friends of her own, but that won't happen until school starts. In the meantime . . ." She put confetti in a large glass bowl, then mixed in Hershey's Kisses. "Well, it's up to us to make it festive for her." She put the bowl in the center of the table. Paper birthday place settings were already set up all around, and the cake—Cinderella Barbie complete with full-frosting couture—kept a place of honor on the counter.

I turned around, only to find Angel standing behind me. I wondered how much she overheard.

"Hi," I said.

She looked past me—through me, really—over toward Lane, and waited—eager but silent—for the older woman to notice her.

"You look nice," I said quietly, but she only put her finger to her lips for me to be quiet. This was Lane's moment, and if I wanted to be an extra in the scene, I'd have to keep my lips shut. Angel hadn't warmed back up to me. But after all she'd been through with her mother's problems, I'd become willing to offer her some slack.

With her good hand, the child pulled at the waistband of her knit skirt, straightened it. It had multicolor stripes that circled her little body. A bright pink T-shirt picked up the shade of one of the bands. On her shoulder a sticker, announcing the size of the matched set, had escaped her notice, so I reached over and pulled it off for her.

"Thanks," she said, still looking the other way.

The outfit must have been one of her new ensembles from Lane. They'd gone to Gap Kids in downtown Charleston a couple of days before, made a day of it with lunch and a horse-and-buggy ride.

"Look at it as an early present," Lane had explained when Reese protested the extravagance. "An outing and some clothes. Let me do this, okay?"

Reese had agreed. It occurred to me that the protest had only been for show in the first place, but I wasn't nearly as judgmental as I would have been a few days before.

Still trying to catch Lane's eye, Angel had lost her smile, had begun to look anxious. I coughed, an obvious, look-this-way fake sound, and Lane glanced over and grinned.

"Come here!" she said to the child. "Don't you look beautiful?"

Angel ran to her and hugged her.

"Were you saving this for the last minute?" Lane asked. "Trying to throw me off with all those other clothes?"

"No," Angel said. "I just couldn't decide. I thought I might ought to keep this one for sometime when I wouldn't spill on it. But I really wanted to wear it and—"

"It's your birthday, sweetheart." Lane gave her another squeeze. "There's nothing you can spill that I can't get out in the laundry, okay?"

"Okay." Angel became a different child when she smiled. I had to catch this on the fly because she rarely offered spontaneous cheer when I was around.

But I couldn't look at Angel anymore without thinking of Ben, of what he so desperately wanted from me. He wanted the green light to tell me about her. To share her with me. I'd never given it, and even if I wanted to share it with him now—something I'd yet to sort out—the opportunity had passed. Something had been lost between Ben and me in those weeks before his death. Something I couldn't name until Reese laid it all out for me. Even knowing didn't make the answers clear, and if there was blame for any of it, I didn't know where to pin it.

"Well, let's get this party started." Derek stood up, threw his hands up as if to say, *Anybody with me?*

"There's still someone else coming," Reese said.

"Who's that?" Lane asked.

"I invited Andrew Hanes and his wife," she said. "He's been a big help since we moved. Helping me figure out how everything works at the house. She brought over a casserole the other night."

A still, soundless moment took hold of the room. Derek was the first to speak. "Well, let me get some music on, at least." He flipped through a selection of CDs that had been collected at the cottage over the years. "How about Bob Marley? I've always liked whimsy with my revolution."

"Great," Reese answered, and in a moment Bob Marley's cheerful diatribes against oppression broke the awkward spell.

When Reese stood up from the couch, I saw her put her working hand on the back of a chair to steady herself. As she made her way to the kitchen, the effort that it took for her to walk became evident. I'd seen her two days before and there'd been no hint of such a decline. I took a step toward her, wondering how to offer help without making her feel pathetic, but Derek solved the problem, looping his arm around her waist, a gesture that appeared both flirtatious and natural.

"We're jammin'. . ." he sang, half carrying her in the pretense of a singsong walk.

He glanced over my way and I realized my eyes were tearing up. His look reminded me to be careful, his anthem of the past week. He remained wary when it came to Reese. He liked her well enough, but that was a far cry from trusting her. I blinked my eyes, felt the wetness on my lids, my lashes. Nothing a good deep breath couldn't keep in check. But I realized that Derek was right. My sympathy for Reese had completely clouded the fact that she had played me. Played Ben. I needed to stay careful, or at the very least, aware.

The anticipated Reverend Hanes was a no-show, so we gave up and went ahead with the cake. A doll confection, as promised, it looked too beautiful to taste like anything but cardboard; but Lane had made it from scratch, so there was hope. She'd gone out and bought a mold along with various how-to books.

"She's really pretty," Angel said, her eyes wide, staring at the creation as the candles burned down.

"Blow them out, Angel," Reese urged. Georgie had camped out underneath the table in anticipation of crumbs.

Within minutes Cinderella Barbie's voluminous ballgown looked more like the tattered rags of her pre–Fairy Godmother days. Halfway into second helpings, the good reverend made his appearance.

"Sorry I couldn't be here sooner," he said, the ordinary words elevated by his slow, sermon-rich voice. "Diane wasn't feeling well and I kept hoping she'd perk up, but . . ." He let the explanation trail off. He had a present in his hand, a book-sized package that looked suspiciously like a Bible. Nothing against the Good Book, but I'd gotten Bibles for presents occasionally when I was a kid and it had never ceased to inspire disappointment. Too bad she'd already opened the others. You always wanted the last one to be special, somehow.

"Have some cake, Preacher." Charlie sliced a piece of the doll's apparel, exposing her nonanatomically correct private area. "Whoops, I think Barbie's getting a little cold there." He served up the portion and grinned at the minister.

"I'll have another slice while you're at it," Derek said, raising his eyebrows.

"Barbie here ought to get tips," Charlie said, handing over a plate to Andrew. "Sorry, Preacher," he said. "I'll tone it down a little."

Preacher Andrew smiled, took the plate. "Don't worry. I was a Marine for almost ten years," he said. "It takes more than a naked doll to get me blushing."

The general laughter in the room died down quickly when Angel pushed through the adult bodies to reach the cake.

"Can I have her?" she asked, looking uncomfortable, pretty close to tears.

"Sure, baby," Reese said, pulling the doll from what was left of the cake dress. "You take her and wash her off. Nobody was trying to be mean."

Angel took the doll and ran off to the bathroom.

"I'm such an ass." Charlie stood, frosting-covered knife still in his hand, further incriminating himself. "A damn idiot."

Andrew and Derek looked at the floor too. They'd all become misbehaving boys.

We went back into the den. Wrapping paper littered the floor along with a new doll and various games. Angel had been delighted as she opened them, but her favorite gift, the one she wouldn't part with, was the pink digital watch Derek had given her. It played two songs, one from *Beauty and the Beast*, the other from *Aladdin*. The notes had the thin, metallic quality of computer chip sound, but the child couldn't get over it. A watch that told time and played music.

"Everybody set for drinks?" I asked before settling on the couch between Reese and Derek.

With Angel off tending to her doll, the party became an entirely adult gathering. The men, even the preacher, nursed bottles of beer, and the background reggae fed an atmosphere that evoked more smoky bar than a child's party. I'd moved on to bourbon myself, although the pull toward oblivion wasn't as strong as it had been in previous weeks. A good sign, I hoped. But looking around at the lot of us, I wondered if Angel had ever had a childhood.

"How're you feeling?" Andrew asked Reese.

She nodded, mouthed *okay,* and they exchanged something, a slightly prolonged glance, that implied things unspoken. Charlie noticed it too, looked more than a little ticked off that his girlfriend, or at the very least, his frequent date, seemed to have some undercurrent running with the preacher.

After a short while Angel came back. Cinderella Barbie had become Dishtowel Barbie. Safety pins secured her gingham strapless number in pinched-up gathers at the back.

"Beautiful," Reese said as Angel settled on the floor beside Georgie.

"She certainly looks more comfortable," Derek said, bending down to look at the doll. The way Angel looked up at him, I knew a crush had been established. She was safe with that one, I thought. *And so am I.* It came unbidden, that notion. But I didn't reject it. I didn't want to.

"Well, sweetheart," Lane said, standing up. "Happy birthday. I've got to get back home and it's a good drive back, but I'll see you tomorrow."

"Can't you stay here?" Angel asked. Lane must have seemed like a lifeline of stability to the child.

"No, but you get a good night's sleep and I'll be here before you know it." Then she turned to Reese. "Don't try to pick up. I'll come back in the morning and get everything in order. Are you working tomorrow?"

"I hope." Reese offered a weak smile, lifted her arm slightly, but, even so, it took obvious effort.

As I watched the exchange, I realized how often Lane had been looking after Angel, how much she'd taken on in just over a week's time. The odd part was, she seemed glad to have the two of them in her life. Even more peculiar was how much I'd come to rely on time at the cottage, if not exactly *with* them, at least in parallel with their lives. The drive to Sullivan's Island, hanging out around Reese and Angel, with Lane, Derek, and Charlie in frequent attendance, had become my nonworking routine.

"Okay, then," Lane said. "I'll check in on you and we'll sort the rest of the day then."

"You've done too much already," Reese said, then stopped. What alternative could she offer? She needed help, had no choice but to accept it. I suddenly felt guilty, the slovenly sibling.

"I've got the cleanup covered," I said. "Don't worry about that. Most of the dishes are paper and plastic, anyway."

"You sure?" Lane gathered her bag, checked for her keys.

"Yeah," I said. "It's a nice change. Puttering around in a place that's larger than a space module."

Lane left, but as it turned out, I didn't clean up. I sat on the couch with Reese, slightly buzzed from the bourbon, while Angel played with Georgie at our feet. And the boys—that's what the three of them seemed like together—made a game of it.

"It's the new millennium," Derek had announced after Lane took off. "Gender roles no longer apply. Let's get to it, boys."

"What?" Charlie cocked his head, stayed fast in his chair.

"Get off your ass," Derek shot back as he headed for the kitchen.

"What about Preacher here?" The edge of rivalry remained in Charlie's tone, but it sounded more like a game of touch football than serious jealousy over a woman. "Does *he* get to just lounge like a yard dog while we work."

"Depends." Derek turned around, one eyebrow went up. "If old Marines can learn new tricks."

Andrew shook his head, grinning, then stood up. The three of them bumbled their way through a passable cleanup, while Reese, Angel, and I watched—and laughed.

Derek had known that my efforts would have only pointed out what Reese couldn't do, but the three of them going at it became entertainment.

And I felt as if, without realizing it, I'd crossed over. I'd gone from existing back to almost living. I couldn't name the moment, but I knew for certain that it wasn't *before* Angel and Reese had landed on my boat that night. Strange, how terrible things can sometimes open doors as well as close them. I didn't know where I'd end up with my newfound optimism. But the final destination, for the evening, at least, would be Derek's bed, as it had been for several nights running. That would do for a short-term plan.

"Want me to help you with your pajamas?" I asked Angel, who barely qualified as awake from the look of her eyes.

"No, thank you," she said, polite but dismissive. Every time I spoke to the girl, I ended up feeling reprimanded.

"Well, don't stay up too much longer." I was improvising what a TV adult might say to a child. She looked at me as if I'd broken out in spots, a mixture of confusion and distaste.

She thanked everyone for her presents, took Fashion Disaster Barbie and the new pink watch and left the room, I assumed to put *herself* to bed. Fine with me.

Reese stood up. "I should get ready to turn in too," she told us. But she didn't try to move away from the chair. She had been sitting for most of the evening. I figured she had gotten a little stiff from staying in one position for so long. But when she tried to step forward, something happened. Her foot, her knee, something gave way and she landed in a heap on the floor.

"God, Reese!" I reached her before the guys, had a split second where our eyes met. The look of defeat told me more than anything else.

"Goddamn it!" she muttered.

"Here, let me help you get—"

"I'm fine," she cut me off. "My foot went to sleep." All three men knelt to help her. "I have a problem with circulation if I sit too long. It'll get better soon. I just have to work it out." Charlie tucked his head under her arm and lifted her to a standing position. She let him help her, seemed more at ease taking assistance from a man. "Thanks," she said, pushing him away once she had her footing. "I mean it, I'm fine." As she turned, a dark patch of color on the back of her pale skirt stood out like a bright flag against a flawless blue sky. Blood. On top of everything else, she'd started her period.

The men looked at me. One at a time, they all found excuses to go to the kitchen or the bathroom. I was on my own.

"Reese, " I began. "Your skirt . . ."

She looked down. "What?"

"In back."

She pulled the material around and looked behind. "Oh, shit." She sounded so tired.

"Let's get to your room," I said. "I'll rinse your skirt out and get you what you need."

She managed to stand. I tried to take her arm, but she pulled away, looked as if she might cry, but she didn't. Finally, she said, "Could you hand me that, please?"

I looked where she was pointing. A tall container, like an elongated bucket, sat by the door. It was full of umbrellas.

"You want an umbrella?"

She shook her head. "In there, with them."

I sorted through the handles until I found what she needed. A cane. I took it out and handed it to her. "Here you go." I tried to make my voice sound normal, like there was nothing unusual about handing a young woman an old man's walking cane.

I went with her, beside her, but not touching, not trying to give more than I was asked, and when we got into her room, she said, "The skirt. Could you . . . ? I don't want to sit down and stain the bed."

I unhooked it at the waist and helped her step out of it. Her underwear too. Without the full skirt—the only thing I'd seen her wear—her naked hips looked small, perfect, her legs tanned. I thought of her with Ben and then forced myself to shut the visions down before they could fully form. Ben was gone, and there was no competition between us.

"Thanks," she said, unbothered by her half-naked state. She made her way to the master bathroom, sat on the toilet, and put her cane within easy reach.

"What should I get for you?" I asked.

"Underwear in the bottom drawer," she said. "And pads in the cabinet over the sink."

I got them both and handed them to her. "Reese?" I wanted to tell her that I knew. She didn't have to make up stories about sprains and poor circulation. I wanted to tell her it was okay to let people help her. But after one look at her expression—the face of someone too defeated to care anymore—I let it go. There would be a better time to talk with her. Anytime would be a better time to talk with her.

"I'll put your skirt in the washing machine to soak. I can pretreat the stain."

"Thank you." Her voice had no life.

I picked her skirt and panties off the floor, and as I turned to leave the bedroom, I saw Angel in her room, still holding her doll, looking through the small crack left in the doorway.

"Your mom's okay," I said. I put down the soiled clothes and walked over to her, opened the door a little.

She nodded. Before I thought about it, I reached up and combed her hair with my fingers. Pulled the soft curls away from her eyes and tucked the hair behind her ear. Only after I'd done it did I realize how remarkable it was that she'd let me.

"Could you do these?" she asked, turning around. Two buttons on her pajamas flapped undone at the back on her neck. "I can't reach them," she explained.

I secured them for her, then picked up the clothes. "Want to help me put these in the laundry?" I asked.

She nodded.

"Come on."

She measured the soap, put it in with such a sense of purpose that I wanted to laugh and cry at the same time.

"I'll go to bed now," she said when we had finished.

I offered to tuck her in, but she didn't respond with a clear yeah or no. Simply shrugged her shoulders. I didn't want to push it too far, for either of us, so I just said good night to her in the hall.

Before I went across the hall to check on Reese, I heard Angel's voice, small but clear, coming from inside her room.

"Gina?" I couldn't recall her ever saying my name before. It sounded phonetic and strange coming from her.

"Yes?" I said quietly, not to sound too eager.

"Thanks for helping my mom."

I had trouble finding sufficient sound to answer her, but finally managed a chirpy "You bet." I listened closely for a few seconds to see if more would come from her. But it didn't, so I moved on.

When the crisis had passed, Reese came back out to the den, refused to go to bed. I thought of asking if she wanted me to stay, but she clearly needed to keep up a facade that nothing was really wrong, and I didn't have the energy to push her past it. And she did seem okay again; even appeared to be moving a little better.

The men were still on the porch, scared to come back in, I imagined. Derek wanted me to ride with him back to the marina, so I collected Georgie and went to his truck, a small red pickup he said he'd had since he was an undergrad. Georgie liked the back section behind the seat because he put towels down and an old fleece jacket for comfort.

Charlie agreed to drive my car back. I figured he planned to detour by Jesse's, a waterfront bar on the way. But I didn't care. The Volvo was worth more in insurance than resale, so unless he hurt himself or someone else, there wasn't much harm in letting him run loose with my keys.

Oddly enough, Andrew stayed around to close the party down. As we drove away, I saw Reese standing with him on the porch, the two of them already deep in some discussion before we cleared the driveway.

"I gotta say I can't help but like the guy," Derek said when I commented that Andrew and Reese seemed to have a lot to talk about. "But it's no wonder his wife isn't feeling all that well." He glanced back at the cottage in the rearview.

"Yeah. I don't know exactly what's going on there. I don't *think* he's sleeping with her. But he's not being very smart either. Small churches love gossip, and when it's the preacher . . ."

"Why don't you think he's sleeping with her?" Derek asked, eyes on the road ahead.

"He's a preacher. They don't do that sort of thing. At least they shouldn't."

"Well, of course they *shouldn't*. Didn't you read *The Thorn Birds*?" He caught himself, but it was too late.

"Well, Mr. Contemporary Lit major. So *you* read *The Thorn Birds*?" I leaned close to him, tried to see if he was blushing, but in the dim light of the car I couldn't tell.

"Only the sex scenes. My sister highlighted them for me. And let me tell you, there was no shortage of steam in that book."

"Okay." I smiled. "I'm reasonably convinced you're not gay."

"I don't know." He laughed. "I think you need to investigate, do a little more firsthand research to be sure."

"You think?" I leaned my head on his shoulder.

"Yes, I do. Why don't you go on up to my place and I'll run through my security rounds and meet you in a few?"

"Can you take Georgie?" I asked. "I don't feel like walking her." The dog heard her name, sat up behind us, as if to monitor any decisions made that concerned her.

"You have the leash?" he asked.

"It's at the apartment," I told him.

He shook his head, looked far more resigned than pleased.

Then I put my head back on his shoulder, rode the rest of the way without ever feeling the need to speak; when we got back to the marina, Georgie jumped out of the car and headed for Derek's apartment instead of the boat. It occurred to me that, when it came to emotions, dogs were probably smarter than people.

29

Reese

"I'm sorry about all that," Reese said. "I know that stuff makes guys uncomfortable."

"It's okay." Andrew leaned against the porch rail, looked out toward the water. "I'm married. And I have sisters."

She wondered why he was hanging around. Why she wanted so much for him to be there.

"Why don't you talk with your friends about everything that's going on with you? About your condition?" He offered the suggestion as if there were no consequences to declaring oneself a partial invalid.

"I'll tell them when I'm ready. I got to figure out a plan first. One that keeps me with Angel, but gives her some stability too. I'm working on it."

"Gina seems willing to help you."

Reese thought of Gina, felt the resentment begin to rise straight up through her chest. She was being too damn nice. Something was up. "I'm not sure about Gina, not yet." She kept her feelings out of her voice.

"Why?"

It couldn't be explained. Not all of it. "She blames me, I think, for things that went wrong with her and Ben before he died. I don't completely buy her generous act, that's all." She hadn't thought about it much, until the party. But Gina had been ready to spit fire about Angel and Ben on the porch at Lane's that day. Then suddenly she was all sweetness. Reese hadn't put it together until she saw Gina and Derek together, both of them moving around the cottage like it belonged to them.

"I don't think she has any real agenda, Reese," Andrew told her. He had a trusting nature. Reese liked that about him. But she knew there was always an agenda.

"I'm being careful. Let's leave it at that."

By the end of the evening, Reese thought, even Angel was buying Gina's act, warming up to her. Reese knew she'd wanted this at first, for Gina to take an interest in Angel. The child needed all the extended family available. But earlier in the night, it became clear to Reese that Gina wanted more. Derek, the cottage, and Angel thrown in the mix. Gina had blown it with Ben when he tried to bring Angel into her world. Maybe she didn't intend to make that mistake again. Angel already had a crush on Derek. Gina had to have noticed that. It made a nice picture, the three of them. She was the only thing that didn't fit in neatly. Her invalid status could be a legitimate excuse to push her out of the picture. *Stop it, Reese.*

"I'll talk with Lane before too long and see what she's decided," Reese said. "I think she'll agree pretty soon and then I'll tell her the whole story."

"Agree to what?" he asked.

"Being Angel's guardian, if something happens to me and I can't look after her."

"It's getting worse pretty fast, Reese. In just a week I've seen a decline."

"It gets worse. Then it gets better. I'm taking medicine." Reese felt irritated by his persistence.

"You need a doctor."

"Doctors need money. I don't happen to have any at the moment."

"You have a local address now," he said. "I'm pretty sure that qualifies you for care at the county hospital."

He was right, but Reese had to laugh.

"The story of my life," she said. "County health care. Indigent care. Pretty ironic, huh? I have a pricey waterfront address, but need freebies from the county hospital. Strange world, ain't it, Preacher?"

"You need to see a doctor," he said again, ignoring her dismissive tone. "Your medicine isn't working. Not the way it's supposed to."

"It takes time," she said. "It's only been a week. And besides that, when did you get to be an expert?"

"Since you told me, I've been reading. Looked it up on the Internet."

"And what did you figure out?" she asked.

"That they don't understand it. What makes it come and go . . . progress in some and not others."

"That about sums it up."

"But," he added, "they can do a lot to control symptoms."

"I know that. I told you, I'm on meds."

She made her way over to the porch swing, sat down. He stayed on the other side. Silence wasn't a problem for either of them. Minutes could pass without words and he never felt awkward. Just the opposite of Charlie, who'd read the phone book out loud before he'd endure a minute's lull in conversation. She wondered if Charlie would come around again, after seeing her so weak. She felt about a hundred years old, another species entirely from the woman on the vinyl mat in the storage room.

"I'll look into getting help," she said, trying to appease him. He seemed so troubled. Men always think there's a solution. But sometimes, she knew, there's nothing there but the problem. With her stronger leg, she began to push lightly back and forth. She liked the motion; it soothed her mind and her body.

"I could talk to my doctor," he said after a time. "See if he has any ideas. That would be a place to start."

"Let's don't talk about it right now," she said. "I'm too tired to make any plans tonight."

Another man might have taken it as a cue to leave, but Andrew seemed to understand that she wanted peaceful company. Not that they hadn't done their share of talking.

She'd opened up with him several times since that first long swing set confessional. Since then, seemed that no matter where she planned to go, she found her way to the church. She'd yet to set foot inside, but she would call him from the gas station at the main turnoff. He'd meet her outside when she arrived.

She'd told him about living with her uncle, until her aunt became so horrible. Then Reese decided it was better to leave. She'd been on her own since she was seventeen.

She'd told him about the nightmare with Angel. How'd she'd left the child with a friend when she had to go into the hospital in Boone, and the next thing she knew, she was listening to a terrified phone call from her daughter.

It was sketchy still, even to Reese. Angel didn't open up entirely, and Reese hadn't pushed it. But she thought back on all the things that Janet had told her in the past. She'd figured out that it involved Janet's boyfriend and an illegal deal gone bad. Drugs, most likely, although it didn't really matter. Angel never said what she saw going on, but whatever it was must have been enough to make someone want to come back for her. Janet had never returned, and Reese worried about what had happened to her. The first time the men came, Angel had been alone. She didn't answer the door, called Reese in her hospital room, frantic. By the time they came back, Reese was there to hear them calling out, asking for Angel to open the door. Reese was already packed and ready, and instead of going out the front of the building, they went down the fire escape.

Andrew had heard all of that. So many things no one else knew. He inspired her to tell the truth, to trust. She suspected that she was in love with him, and that it was mutual. But that was one thing they wouldn't talk about. She no longer had any desire to destroy him. And he'd made promises to his wife. But their meetings would have to end sometime. It was getting too difficult to be near him.

"What does your wife say about you being here?" she asked. Might as well get it out in the open.

"She thinks you're after me," he said, with no particular inflection in his voice. "She thinks I've just convinced myself that I'm only helping you, being a good pastor."

"So she's not assuming anything's happened between us?"

He glanced over her way, fixed his eyes on her without apology. Something did happen, she thought. Every time he looked at her like that. Part of her said, screw the wife and the church. Neither one of them had ever done anything for her. But it would bring him too far down. He'd hate her for it eventually. For making him weak. He'd already said he didn't want to make that mistake again. Neither his marriage nor his life's work could survive it.

"I don't know what she really believes," he said. "I hope she trusts what I tell her. As you know, she's had reason not to in the past."

A small breeze moved across the porch. Potted ferns responded with a swaying dance.

"Well, I won't come out to the church anymore." It wasn't like her, to be so generous. Unless it involved Angel, and then she'd move heaven and earth. Maybe Andrew's essential goodness had rubbed off on her. "And I don't think you should come here either. You've been great and I love you for it. I really do. But it's time to let it go. Before any real damage is done."

He stood watching her. The shadows made him look large and transparent, his shape shifting with the strange play of clouds and moonlight. The far bank of the opposite shore blended with the dark water, and the night appeared to be infinite.

"Can I help you with anything before I go?" he asked.

She'd wanted him to protest, at least a little. She didn't realize this until it became clear that he didn't intend to.

"No. I'm good."

He still didn't move. He stared out across the yard, down to the water.

"Will you call if you need me?" he asked finally.

"I'd like to say no," she told him, "but I'm too self-serving for that. So yes, I promise I'll call if I need you."

He turned without saying anything more and walked to his car. Watching him leave, she wondered if she could stick to it, if she could stay away from him entirely. She waited until he drove away to stand up. At least, she didn't want his parting image of her to be one of struggle. And when she was sure he'd driven well out of sight, she took her cane and made her way back inside.

30

∞

Gina

The restaurant was freezing. I preferred cozier bistros, places where ceiling fans and minimal AC output allowed the summer season to actually exist. But I had to admit, the food that arrived in front of me transcended the descriptions of ingredients described on the menu. With some alchemy of butter, onion, and fennel, a humble catfish became food of the gods. And in keeping with my mother's tastes, it was priced for the gods too. Still, she rarely missed when it came to dining out, and at least I wasn't paying.

"So who are all these people again?" she asked, sipping on her second glass of wine.

I'd tried to fill her in on Reese and Angel, on the preceding weeks—minus the shooting and the revelations about Ben and Angel. Angel was referred to as Reese's daughter, without further explanation. Reese was Ben's ex-wife. A surprise to Mom, but not a shock. Divorces weren't the stuff of polite conversation in my mother's circle. The less said, the better, so I'd never mentioned anything before.

"And I've been seeing someone." I decided it was time to tell her. "His name is Derek. He just finished a graduate program and he's working at the marina while he applies for writing jobs."

As I told her about him, I saw the rapid calculations she was making. After thirty-plus years of reading her, I could guess how it would come out. Graduate school canceled out the present, unfortunate blue-collar status. *And* the advanced degree, along with family still living in Savannah, all good. He was younger, but that could be overlooked.

"He sounds wonderful," she said. "I'm glad to see you getting on with your life. You've hardly been living at all these last months."

I made a mental note of suggesting the restaurant to Derek sometime when we wanted to go someplace nice. If I remembered to wear a turtleneck, it could make for a terrific evening.

"And this child," Mom said. "What's the story with her?"

"I don't know, exactly," I said truthfully. "I haven't gotten the whole story from Reese. She's raised her alone. I know that much."

Mom didn't dig any further. Why ask more than you care to know? But the thought of Angel stirred other, unfamiliar feelings in me. Sitting so close to the woman who shared my history with Elise, my shift in perspective seemed nothing short of remarkable.

"I've gotten kind of attached to her," I said, testing the waters. "Angel, I mean."

"She must be bright." Mom buttered her bread. Still skimmed the surface of serious inquiry. "Very engaging from the sound of it."

"Sometimes." I smiled, thinking of Angel in a mood. "But it's surprised me, actually." I wondered what it would take to crack my mother's social veneer.

"What has?" It was a casual inquiry.

"After all those years with Elise, never really . . ." Really what? Never wanting to be near her? "Feeling connected. Like a sister. I've never been around kids, let alone a single kid, for any length of time. Not since I was a kid myself. I like having her around sometimes."

Mom took a bite of her scallops, nodded as if I'd mentioned something I heard on the news.

Maybe if I climbed in a basket of dirty laundry, I thought; found the industrial-sized maintenance room at the hotel when we walked back, and borrowed a pile of soiled sheets and towels, maybe that would set her off. Maybe that would bring out the woman inside the well-groomed facade. But then again, maybe just talking about Elise would be enough. I'd come close on the phone when I opened up with my questions.

"Why is it," I said, treading carefully, "that I can get so fond of somebody's else's child, when I could barely pour a glass of milk for my sister without resenting it?"

She sat back in her chair, picked up her wine. The look on her face told me she didn't appreciate having a perfectly nice lunch botched up with my unpleasant, obsessive concern with a long-dead sibling.

"You were a child, Gina. Children see only their own concerns. I would hope that as an adult, you'd be capable of all kinds of feelings that weren't possible when you were twelve years old."

"It wasn't just me, Mom. I'm not trying to criticize. But you stayed as frustrated with Elise as I did."

She took a deep breath. I thought she might simply get up and leave. If we'd been on the phone, she would certainly have made her excuses—someone at the door, the oven timer going off—and said her good-byes. But I sat across from her. Unless she made a scene, there was no way around the conversation. I hadn't come to lunch planning it, but now I'd waded too deep to turn around.

"We weren't talking about me, Gina. Frankly, I don't care to discuss any shortcomings I might have had when it came to your sister. But as for you and your affection for this other child . . . Well, I doubt many children have the . . ." She paused, seemed to be looking for the right word. "Issues," she said finally. "The issues that your sister had."

"What do you mean?"

"Well, her problems, I mean. They're not that common." She looked genuinely perplexed, as if I had overlooked something completely obvious. "We were doing all that we could, but—"

"What problems?" I put down my fork, leaned forward so I could hear clearly. "What are you talking about?"

I saw something remarkable in my mother's eyes. Pain. I hadn't seen it in years. Not even at Elise's funeral.

"Mom?"

The waiter came and asked if we were doing all right. I nodded, waved him away, but didn't break eye contact with my mother. After an odd silence, she leaned slightly forward.

"Her developmental problems, Gina." She said it low, as if the other tables might hear and begin to judge her for having flawed offspring. "Academically, things were okay, of course. But in other areas, social and emotional areas, she had real problems. You knew all that."

"How was I supposed to know if you didn't tell me?"

"She didn't behave like other children. I thought you would . . ." She stopped, seemed to be searching for some outside help. "I suppose I thought you'd just figure it out. How could you not?"

"Well, I didn't. So please tell me now."

In spite of the substantial AC, I felt myself flushing hot. I waited for her. I would wait all day if I had to. I wanted her to finally tell me what I'd wanted to believe my entire life. That my sister's problems occurred *before* my feelings about her became obvious.

"Why do you think she followed you around all the time?" My mother still spoke in riddles; answered questions with more questions.

"It's what little sisters do."

"Not the way she did. You *had* to know that. She didn't have any friends. She didn't know how to have friends. She couldn't seem to understand what most kids know about getting along, about playing. She had developmental problems, Gina."

"But she did fine in school?"

"With the work, yes. I didn't say learning problems. She had emotional problems. We'd been to see a number of doctors, and finally, a child psychologist. Someone the school counselor recommended. He suggested we begin looking at special schools, and that's what we were doing when . . ." She stopped. I knew the rest all too well.

"Why didn't you tell me, Mom? About the psychologist. That you were thinking of another school."

"You were twelve years old, for goodness' sake. We thought we'd explain all of that to you when it happened, after we had it all worked out."

All the words had come so quickly. After twenty years of nothing. No explanations, no acknowledgment of the guilt my sister left with us. Suddenly, there were so many words. I felt anxious, as if she would turn again, take it all back, or worse, pretend it had never been said at all.

"But you loved her, didn't you?" It was a ridiculous question. Even I knew it. But I asked it anyway, and I let it stand, waited for an answer.

She looked at me, didn't look beyond me or to the side as I might have expected. The expression on her face looked something close to benevolent. I wanted to freeze-frame the moment. Keep her there just a little longer.

"Of course I loved her," she said finally. "The frustrating thing about Elise was that she needed so much, but she had no idea how to accept it. Even the doctors told us that, and it made me feel . . . I don't know, not *good*, but less *bad*, I suppose. She didn't have the wiring to understand the difference between one emotion and another. That's why anger and irritation registered as nothing but attention to her.

"I know I'm not the warmest person in the world, Gina. It's my nature and I won't apologize for that. But Elise had a disconnect that had nothing to do with me or your father. And it had nothing to do with you. I thought you understood. I'm sorry we let it go without sitting down with you."

She had cool water, if not ice, in her veins. I'd known that all my life. But if I really thought about it, when I was growing up, she'd given me most of what I asked for by way of attention, of parental concern. I'd judged her far more by what she withheld from Elise than what she did, or did not, give me. Even that was hypocritical. I could never fill the void of my sister's needs either. Here she was telling me that no one could. I felt as if I'd been underwater too long and had suddenly found the surface, found air.

"Your father's getting out of his meeting soon," she said, done with the discussion. I knew I would hear no more about Elise. But what more did I need? "Would you like to go back to the hotel, maybe have some coffee and visit with him for a bit?" she asked.

"Sure, Mom."

"Well, then," she said, picking up her purse. "Just let me give him my card and we can be on our way in a few minutes." She turned away from me, looking around for the waiter.

Within the dark-paneled existence of the restaurant, it could have been any time of day. But I could catch a glimpse of strong summer light through the windows across the room. The waiter took the card and came back, laid the leather folder on the table beside Mom.

"Let's go," she said.

She signed the check and stood up. I followed her out into the bright afternoon.

31

Reese

"Do they have my name on the roll?" Angel got out of the car, headed toward the school. Reese stayed slightly behind her.

"What do you mean, 'on the roll'?" Reese asked.

"Do they know I'm coming or do I have to tell them who I am when the teacher takes attendance?"

"You ask the strangest questions sometimes," Reese told her. "Yes, I came in last week and filled out all the papers. They know you're coming. That's when they told me Miss Reilly would be your teacher."

Angel's new backpack already had a broad grass stain smeared across one side, a soiled smudge of dirt near the bottom. Reese wondered how she could have gotten it dirty so fast.

"Did you fall down?" Reese watched Angel stop at the street crossing. The child did all the right things, waited for the car to motion her across before she stepped out into the street.

"No," Angel said. "I don't think so."

"Well, how did your new backpack get so dirty?"

"Same way my shoes did." Angel said. "I smushed them around in the yard. New stuff looks too . . . I don't know . . . new."

"Don't want to look like a rookie, huh?" Reese stopped for Angel to tie her shoe.

"What's a rookie?"

"On a sports team," she told her daughter, "it's the new player. Usually the youngest."

Angel nodded. Didn't comment one way or the other on the analogy. Ahead, at the school, several adults stood in the yard, greeting children. A circle drive full of school buses out front obscured the entrance.

"There's a second-grade hall, they told me," Reese explained.

"We'll ask as soon as we get inside. You've got a few minutes, so you won't be late. I talked with your teacher on the phone, but I'll introduce myself, meet her in person, and then I'll be gone pretty quick. Is that okay?"

Angel looked up at her, hesitated, her lips in a tight little line as if she had to work to keep her mouth closed.

"What?" Reese asked. Still, Angel didn't speak. "Do you want me to stay awhile? Are you nervous?"

The child shook her head no.

"Angel?"

"I kind of want to go in by myself," she said finally. "You can meet Miss Reilly soon if you want. But for the first day . . ."

"Why?" Reese didn't want to show hurt feelings. She wanted Angel to be happy and settled.

"I think that mostly first-grade moms go in," she explained. "Second-grade moms just drop off. At least that's what they did at my old school."

Unspoken rules of drop-off. Angel didn't want to look like a baby. Of course. Reese smiled, stopped at the corner well away from the school's front doors.

"Sure, hon," she said. "I forgot you're a whole year older now. How about I wait right here at the end of school for you to come out? We can meet and walk to the car."

Angel grinned, the first big smile Reese had seen all morning. She wondered how long the child had agonized over asking to go solo into her class.

As Angel walked away, her properly scuffed accessories lending a well-seasoned persona to her first day of school, Reese still felt afraid of all the uncertainty. She wanted Angel to have a long stint in a decent school. The neat, little elementary school fit the bill, but other parts of Reese's plans weren't going so well. Wait and see, she said to herself. Nothing had to be decided right away, and in the meantime Angel looked confident and happy.

She watched until Angel went into the building, then turned to walk back to the car. Letting down her guard, she allowed her left leg to give in to the lazy shuffle that she hadn't wanted Angel to see. Symptoms had gotten better since the day of the party, thank God. At least she could control her arm muscles enough to carry a tray of food, and she could walk well enough to get around the restaurant.

She could feel the weakness, but control it. Still, there were no guarantees that it would continue to improve, and fewer options than she had hoped to take up the slack if it didn't.

"Ma'am?" A driver, a middle-age man, rolled down the window of his SUV at the crosswalk. "Do you know where I can find the nearest gas station?"

"Two streets down and make a right. I forget the name of the street," she said. "The town's pretty small. You'll see it."

"Thanks," he said, and drove forward.

She could have roots in the place, if nothing else went wrong. Just a little luck and she could spend years giving strangers directions to places that would become more and more familiar as time went by. She watched the SUV turn and go toward the certainty of a town and a gas station that she knew would be there. "Please," she said to no one in particular. "Please, just let it work this time."

And as she cut across the street to make her way back to the car, the school bell rang, signaling the beginning of the first day of school.

32

∞

Gina

Derek pulled his pickup onto the dusty roadside beside the produce stand. A large black woman in a lavender shift sat on a stool behind the display of peaches, corn, and green beans. She greeted us with a nod, left us to our selections.

"Cucumbers," I said, pointing to a large bin. "I want a couple of those. And the tomatoes look good."

"Ever'thang's good." She fanned herself with an unopened piece of mail. "Just come in this morning, most of it."

Down the road, in the grassy median, a regal-looking woman walked beside a small boy. Her dark skin complemented the earth colors of her loose clothing. She balanced a large basket of produce on her head; only a slender brown arm reached up to touch it lightly as she made her way. Coming toward us, she moved with the assurance of absolute, physical ease.

"She somethin', ain't she?" The woman minding the stand saw us staring.

"Why does she do it that way?" I asked.

The large woman shrugged. "Tradition. Some keep to the old way. Not practical, but it do look pretty to see 'em. Not many left who'll fool with it."

The woman seemed to travel in slow motion. Heat off the asphalt bent the afternoon air, giving her a dreamlike quality. I craved her serenity, a feature often mistaken for wisdom. I wanted both; had neither. But when I looked over at Derek, I caught him watching *me*, not the elegant vision in the middle of the road, and I realized how different life had become for me.

"I want a watermelon," he said, walking to a huge bin sitting in the sun off to the side.

"It's messy and we'd need a big knife," I told him. We'd planned on an afternoon at the beach, decided an impromptu picnic would serve as a late lunch.

"Got the knife and a cutting board in the truck box," he told me.

"Well, unless they've been cleaned since you used them for gutting fish, no thanks. We can eat the watermelon at home."

"Don't worry," he said, which didn't answer my concerns one way or the other. He chose a large melon and brought it under the awning of the stand.

"Seven-fifty." The woman shooed a half-dozen black flies away from the register as she rang up our selections, and we waited for our change.

Low-country cadence occurred in the tempo of largo. Over time I'd learned to savor the pauses; so while we waited, I took in everything around us. Behind the stand, a man sat under a small tent, shucking corn. Two dogs shared his shade, looked as listless as the day itself. And farther out back, a small house—pale green clapboard—sat amid an eclectic collection of flowers thriving in makeshift planters. The bare brown yard framed the patchwork colors of the blooms.

" 'Preciate it," the woman said, making her way back to the stool.

Derek carried the oblong watermelon back to the truck and I picked up the worn-looking grocery bag holding the rest of our purchases. He laid the melon on the towels behind the seat, and I felt guilty that we'd left Georgie at the apartment.

"Where are we going?" I asked.

"Seabrook," he said without elaboration.

It was a private island, little more than a community with a beach club, golf course, and horse trails.

"It's gated. I don't think even your charm can get us in."

"No. But this will." He reached over into the glove compartment, pulled out a resident's pass for the island. "My aunt owns a creekside villa."

"Clever boy." I smiled as he pulled the truck back onto the highway in the direction of the island.

The boardwalk to the beach cut through an airless wooded patch, then over the dunes. Early mosquitoes and the larger dragonflies hovered, and I could smell the ocean, hear it. Even living on the water, the sound of waves and the feel of sand still pleased me.

"Did you bring a corkscrew?" I asked, looking at the overstuffed tote bag he carried at his side.

"Relax. I have everything." He walked slightly behind me, kept a hand on my waist. It felt good, his hand. I liked the notion of belonging with someone again.

Signs prohibiting straying onto the dunes dotted the path, as did posted reminders to close all blinds at night.

"Those signs really baffled me the first time I saw one," I told him, "telling everybody to close the blinds at night."

Residents within sight of the dunes had to shut out any light that might disorient the hatching sea turtles. After leaving their nests, they made their way to the ocean. In the daylight they were okay, but houselights at night somehow confused them, sent them off in the wrong direction.

"Have you ever seen them?" he asked. "Baby loggerheads?"

"Once, a few years ago on the beach at Kiawah. It was during the day and I saw a crowd of people circled around something. Three hatchlings had made it halfway to the surf, but one of them had gotten confused by a tidal pool."

"Anybody touch it?"

"They shooed the birds away to keep them from having a baby turtle entrée for lunch, but I don't know if they helped it or not."

We crested the walkway over the dune, saw the ocean. Strains of Warren Zevon drifted from someone's boom box down the beach. *"Never thought I'd pay so dearly, for what was already mine. For such a long, long time . . ."* I couldn't see where it came from, but approved of their tastes.

Only a half-dozen people or so made up the entire human element on the shore.

"Empty," I said.

"It's never crowded here. That's what I love about it. Even in the middle of the summer, there are more miles of beach than people to fill it."

"I guess gates and guards make a difference."

"Elitism at its best."

We looked at the huge stretches of sand in front of us, stepped off the wooden walkway to choose a spot. The heat of the sand burned my feet at the edges of my flip-flops, and I moved quickly toward the wet sand left behind by the low tide.

"I haven't been to the beach all summer," I said, suddenly realizing that my last outing to the ocean had been with Ben just days before he died. The thought brought instant, unexpected tears, and I turned away from Derek, into the wind, in hopes of getting it under control before he noticed. But it was too late.

"What's wrong?" he asked, taking my wrist as we continued to walk.

"Nothing," I said, fighting the feelings that had gripped me so suddenly.

He stopped, shook his head, and when he couldn't come up with the right words, he let go of my wrist and looked away.

"What?" I asked.

"If you won't talk to me about things, I can't . . ." He stopped again, let out a long breath. "He's dead, Gina. You're going to stumble over memories, and I'm going to know it. I'll feel lousy for a bit, but I'm not a complete jackass. The closer we get, it seems the less you tell me your feelings. That leaves me competing with a memory that I can't even talk about. I can handle *my* feelings. But not if you won't let me into that part of your head."

"It feels too weird. I don't know. I don't want to throw him in your face constantly. But he's in my head constantly, Derek. I can't do anything about that. I don't want to spoil our day."

"You can't spoil anything by talking with me," he said. "I'll get a little jealous sometimes. I'm human. But at least I won't feel shut out."

"Okay. I'll try to open up more. It was easier when you were just this . . . guy."

"Well, I'm not just a *guy* anymore. You've got to give me some credit. Come on, let's get a blanket down. Then you just say what's on your mind."

I told him everything. Sitting beside him with the late summer air coming off the water, I imagined the words as I said them, scattered and carried by the hefty breeze. It was an exorcism, of sorts. I told him about my life with Ben. The issue about children. I told him about Elise and my family. I had a new chapter to add in light of my recent conversation with my mother. I talked about Reese's changing behavior, her unexplained frostiness toward me, and the surprising new affection I'd developed for her daughter. Ben's daughter too, perhaps.

"I don't know what any of it means," I said.

"Maybe you should let your life happen more in the present," he said. "Without always thinking about how it relates to the past."

He was the present, and even I knew what would be best for us. But what I needed ran at odds with that sometimes. I hoped we could weather those times. I was a widow because of Ben. My present and my past had no clear boundaries. Not yet.

"Look at what you just found out about your sister," he was saying. "Your past just changed. You've lived with it for more than thirty years, and it just *changed*. After all this time. Even the past is a work-in-progress. Don't lay out so many absolute rules for yourself."

"It helped me a lot," I said. "To find out about Elise. To put that whole time in perspective. But I don't know if that makes a difference. I can't count on ever wanting . . . choosing, to have a child. I'm not making absolutes, Derek. Not like I would have even a month ago. But it's not fair to leave it unsaid either. We're not at a place where this is relevant, but—"

"You still don't understand." He stopped me, leaning his face close to mine. I waited for him to go on, but he didn't. Instead, he laid back, pulled me over beside him. The length of his thighs pressed in beside mine and I felt sand and skin against me.

Finally, he turned to face me. "You're relevant. That's all I know."

"I'm not sure I can live up to that," I said, barely able to speak through all of the emotion of the moment. "I just don't know if . . ."

I felt overwhelmed by his skin, his smell. So nearly undressed in our bathing suits, and lying together—but still in public on a beach, albeit a sparsely populated one. He had the flushed, fast breathing of a man unable to think beyond his libido. The heady lust phase of our relationship clouded any rational thought.

"Derek." I sat back, put a slight bit of distance between us.

"I'm sorry."

"God, don't apologize," I told him. "I'm the one who's confused. More confused than I've ever been."

He moved over, near me again. Relentless and beautiful. Like Ben, but different too. His face touched mine. He leaned into me, kissed me. Sand and sweat. "There's no one around anymore," he said, his voice hoarse, barely there.

"It's an open beach, Derek."

"And we have it to ourselves." I felt the movement of his lips against my hair when he spoke. "And we have an extra beach blanket for good measure."

He pulled out the light cover, put it over us, keeping the hot ocean breeze at bay. And in the dark, safe place he created for us under the cotton shelter, we took all that was now, and left the rest to another day. Afterward we swam and ate, drank our wine. Then we swam some more and slept until night fell over the beach around us. And as we covered ourselves again, for warmth as well as propriety, I saw the thinnest shards of light, the faint edges of the closed blinds on the houses beyond the dunes.

33

Reese

$\mathcal{S}$omeone had left a bottle of bourbon in the cottage. Most likely Gina, Reese figured, although the woman's appetite for alcohol seemed to be waning with the addition of a man and a reliable sex life to her routine. Reese poured herself a bourbon and Coke, then left it on the counter to go check on Angel. She'd looked in on the sleeping child six, maybe seven times, since the girl had gone to bed.

She couldn't put her finger on anything that was wrong. She felt edgy, more energy than purpose. Something worried her, and the response to all worry was to obsess over her daughter.

She felt a slight panic as she reached for the child's door, as if this time the bed might, indeed, be empty. It was ridiculous, she knew. Angel was safe, had been safe ever since they'd arrived. Well, except for crazy Gina's trigger-happy panic when they stepped onto the boat. But even that wasn't an ever-present danger. Only a freak accident. Then again, a freak accident had killed Benjamin, so there was always that to consider too. But no one had followed them from Boone. And no one here wanted to hurt Angel. She had to keep telling herself. She opened up the door, peeked in. Angel had kicked off her covers, so Reese went in and pulled the light blanket over her again.

Angel had enjoyed her first day at school. Miss Reilly had won her over right away and apparently Angel had made some friends. One girl walked down the sidewalk with her as Angel went to meet her mom. But before the two of them got to the corner, Angel stopped, said something to the girl, and the other child walked away.

"What was that about?" Reese asked.

"She wanted to come over, but I told her not right now."

"Why?" Reese sensed something she wasn't saying.

"I'm kind of tired."

Reese hadn't pushed. Angel had her own agenda most of the time, but Reese knew her well enough to trust her instincts on things, especially people.

She heard the phone ring in the kitchen, slipped out of Angel's room to answer it.

"Hey," Charlie said. Just the sound of his voice caused her to smile. Charlie was about as much fun as she'd ever had. No strings. Great sex.

"What's up?"

"I rented *The Big Lebowski*," he told her. "Thought you might like to watch something funny."

Ever since Charlie had discovered that a DVD player came with the cottage, he'd been bringing over movies every couple of nights. "This is great," he told her. "I was borrowing Derek's player all the time and he was starting to get pissed."

He always arrived after Angel had gone to sleep, and most of the time Reese liked the company. But on this particular evening, she didn't feel like a movie or the randy romp that followed.

"Why don't you hold on to it?" she told him. "We'll watch it to-morrow night."

She'd left Angel's door open, peeked in again for good measure, then closed it quietly. She couldn't shake the lingering worry. Maybe it was a by-product of the illness, a literal case of the nerves. The MS affected her mood sometimes. Who wouldn't get the jitters, knowing they could wake up the next morning unable to get out of bed? It had happened before. But the meds—which were beginning to run low—seemed to be keeping the worst of it at bay.

"Are you sure you're okay?" Joanna, one of the other waitresses had asked her, during the shift at lunch. She liked the woman, a fortyish bottle blonde who seemed to be lay-down-in-front-of-a-train loyal.

"Yeah, I'm fine." But she wasn't. Trouble was, fine wasn't in the cards, so she had to just deal.

She'd worked the lunch shift after she'd dropped off Angel, then got off in time to pick up her daughter. That schedule was great, but she couldn't pay the bills just working lunches. Even so, she begged off the dinner shift so she could be with Angel after her first day. Lane had been keeping Angel at her house most nights when Reese worked and Charlie helped out one night when Lane couldn't, but Angel didn't like him much, so that wasn't a good option. She had to get something figured out. Lane was willing, but she couldn't go on forever expecting the woman to give up her evenings, and Angel needed to be home at night since school had started.

Reese sat on the couch, flipped through a magazine, and tried to sort out her thoughts. Eventually, the nagging feeling and worried thoughts led her to the place she always ended up lately: Gina. She couldn't help but wonder what Ben's wife wanted. After the awful rant on the porch at Lane's that day, Gina had started acting like her best friend; or no, worse yet, like a somewhat patronizing older sister. At any rate, a total one eighty from the angry, suspicious woman, furious that Ben had seen Angel behind her back. She'd started showing up at the cottage all the time. Just checking in, she said. Then she launched into winning Angel's affection—something else she hadn't shown the slightest interest in before that day. And the maddening part was that it had worked. Angel lit up when she saw the Volvo come into the driveway.

"Why can't I stay on Gina's boat when you're at work sometimes?" Angel had asked more than once.

Reese couldn't say exactly what bothered her about Gina. She'd wanted her to come around, to accept Angel. But now she was convinced that Gina wanted something. She couldn't help but wonder what it would cost her if Ben's widow got whatever it was she was after.

34

∞

Gina

The cell phone rang, and I woke up, disoriented, feeling that the day had begun off-kilter. Derek was stirring on his side of the bed, and I looked at the clock: 12:45. Jesus! It was already afternoon.

By the time I came fully awake, voice mail had kicked in and I decided to get the message when I felt more functional.

"Hey," Derek said, barely opening his eyes. He glanced over at the clock and smiled. "Who'd be calling you this early?"

"I'll make the coffee," I said, shuffling toward the kitchen. "Then I'll check."

We'd stayed late on the beach the night before, watched the moon shift its angle over the water. Derek had called it a moon dial.

We'd packed up, sandy and satisfied, and driven back to an oyster shack on an inlet just off the island. I went on late rounds with Derek around the marina and then we stayed up talking until well after three. I felt as if we'd reentered the timeless existence of college where all-night studying—or occasionally, socializing—had cut into morning classes; made noon seem like the crack of dawn.

"We're grown-ups now," I said, handing him a cup of coffee. "We can't stay up all night just for the hell of it."

"I work as a night watchman, and you freelance. Not exactly conventional hours. Besides, let's wait till we're old to get boring."

It felt like a dig, somehow. The age reference. I decided I was being too sensitive.

I sat on the edge of the bed beside him and he put his coffee on the nightstand and pulled me down next to him.

"Stop it," he said.

"What?" I had no clue.

"Trying to analyze us. Save that for your stories."

He was right. I did run our relationship through my head over and over. Sometimes it seemed too easy with Derek, so void of effort. Could something that simple really be love? With Ben, there was always a feeling of challenge, of meeting his energy and his expectation. That was part of loving him. It wasn't a hurdle to be with Derek, and it had been going on for all of five minutes in the great scheme of things. I wondered if it would be harder to keep it than to let it happen in the first place.

"You're doing it," he said.

"Doing what?"

"Picking it apart. Why did he say that and do I feel the same way? Stop it."

"You're right." I sat up on top of him, straddled his waist with my legs like the conquering bully. Only he was laughing. He wasn't scared of me.

"Just let it be," he said. "For the near future, anyway. You've been handed a heavy life lately. Don't make me into more baggage."

"Okay, Mr. Metaphor. Does breakfast service come with all this advice?'

"Yes, ma'am." He pushed me to the side on the bed and got up. "It's called Denny's."

I watched him walk away toward the kitchen, registered a kind of happiness, and let it stand without further thought.

The voice mail was from Lane. I listened to it in the truck on our way to get food.

"Hi, Gina." She sounded funny, something off about her voice. "My crown's come off. Hurts like hell and I'm heading into Charleston to the dentist to get it fixed. I'm supposed to get Angel at school this afternoon and look after her through Reese's dinner shift.

"I hate to ask on short notice, but could you ride over there and get her for me and then stay at the cottage with her until I can pick her up? Call my cell and let me know. You'll want to get there a little early, meet her at the classroom so you can find her more easily. I've already left a note with your name at the school. They'll check your ID when you get there—even if the kid knows you they have all these rules—but there shouldn't be any problem. Please call me. Just leave a message if Mengele already has me in the chair."

I looked at my watch. One-fifteen. I'd have plenty of time to eat, but I had something I had to drop off at a leisure activities magazine in Charleston midafternoon. Artwork for my article had been sent to me by mistake. I wouldn't have enough time to turn it in before heading out to the school by three.

"I've got to pick Angel up this afternoon," I told Derek.

"Want me to come?"

"No, but I was wondering if you could drop some artwork by *Low-Country Leisure* this afternoon."

"No problem," he said. "I've got to pick up some marine parts in town anyway so I can make one trip."

We pulled into the parking lot of the restaurant. Several elderly couples were just coming out after finishing their meal.

"By the time we reach retirement age," Derek said, "we'll already be used to the elderly lifestyle. Sleeping in. Lunch at Denny's."

I had to admit, getting old was looking better every day.

"Ms. Melrose?" The woman at the front desk in the office repeated my name. I'd arrived early, as Lane suggested. "I'm sorry," she said, appearing somewhat suspicious. "I thought I met you when you signed Angel up, but you don't look familiar."

"I'm not Angel's mother. She's Melrose too, but—"

"Oh, here's the note," she said, looking relieved. "Yes. Gina. If you could just let me check your driver's license."

Schools were getting worse than airports. Then again, abductions weren't a joke, and if I were a parent, I imagined that I'd be reassured by the extensive gatekeeping.

"Good," she said, handing me back my license. "The bell's about to ring. It might be easiest if you went to her classroom and waited outside the door. It can get a little hectic finding a child when they're running helter-skelter after the bell. The second-grade hall is down there." She pointed toward nothing I could discern. "You'll see the sign."

After locating the hall, I matched up the room number, could see Angel's class through the porthole-sized window in the door. Angel sat in the middle of the room. With the rest of the M's, I imagined. Growing up with the last name Arthur not only made me the brunt of bad Camelot puns, but put me at the front right corner of every class, first through eighth grade. You'd think one teacher, just one, would have made seat assignments out in reverse alphabetical order.

The bell was located near the ceiling, just across the hall. I didn't realize this until the painful sound was searing into my eardrum.

"Jesus Christ!" I shouted, eliciting a nasty glance from the teacher positioned in the hall to monitor the mass exodus. "Sorry," I offered.

Angel came out near the end of the pack. She seemed to be in no hurry to leave. Miss Reilly, I guessed from the name on the door, came out just behind her. She was barely taller than Angel, with short hair to match her stature. She seemed young for a teacher, but then, the older I got, the younger people in their twenties looked.

"Where's Lane?" Angel said. She didn't appear to be disappointed, which cheered me some.

"The same tooth the dentist worked on the other week cracked or something. Fell out, I think. She's back at the dentist now." My explanation only underscored the horrors of age; not only to a clearly disturbed Angel, but, judging from her expression, the young Miss Reilly too. "She's fine. It's just a crown. They'll fix it up for her."

No one seemed terribly convinced.

"You want to see my me-apron?"

"Your *me-apron*?"

It sounded like an Irish possessive.

"The children made life-sized cutouts of themselves," Ms. Reilly explained. "We put an apron pocket on each 'child' and the kids drew pictures of things that would tell something about themselves to go in the apron. We have free time when the kids can go explore each other's pockets. Find out about each other."

Exploring each other's pockets. A dozen jokes ran through my mind, none appropriate for a grade-school visit. But I liked the concept. The boy students had aprons that looked like the canvas tool holders that builders wear. Girls had the kitchen variety. Guess gender-typing would never completely disappear, especially in the South. But the cutouts all had smiles drawn on the distorted little faces. Angel's looked particularly ragged. "That's great," I said.

"It's not very good," she said without any particular emotion. "But it was hard to do with my hurt arm."

I felt like hell thinking about her struggling to cut paper and draw pictures, but she didn't seem bothered at all.

"So what did you draw to put in your apron?" I asked.

She reached in. Her movements were awkward. No longer in a sling, her shoulder was wrapped in a large Ace bandage around her chest to keep it immobile. The night it happened seemed as if it had come from another lifetime. She pulled out a stack of small laminated pictures. A house, a watch, an attempt at drawing a doll of Barbie proportions . . . I knew the items, knew their history. It seemed, from her perspective, that life had begun the night she arrived on my boat.

"The cottage and my doll." She laid the pictures down on a desk as she went through them. "My watch." Then she came to a picture of people. Four people together, one clearly Angel herself, and another person kind of off to the side. "Here's me, Mom, Lane, and you," she said.

"And is that Ben over to that side?" The standoffish figure looked something like a man, although his hair was nearly as long as the others.

"No," she said. "That's Derek. Here's Ben." She handed me the last picture. I'm not sure most people would have recognized it, but I saw it clearly, green grass with the darker green mound of Ben's grave. Above the headstoneless plot hovered a figure. Short hair, but wearing some sort of dress.

"Is that Ben?" I asked, wondering why she envisioned him a cross-dresser.

"That's angel Ben," she said. "Not Angel, like my name, but a real one. Lane says he's watching over us, so that's what I meant."

I felt surprised by the tears that came to me so quickly, but even more surprised that they weren't the painful tears I'd become so accustomed to over the last months.

I looked at Angel and she seemed to be waiting for something. My approval maybe.

"He'd love that, Angel. Lane's right. He is looking out for us."

I made a mental note to tell Maxine. All of a sudden I realized there needed to be another woman in her family picture. Another grandmother. I'd have to work on that one.

Back at the cottage, I scrounged through kitchen cabinets and the fridge to find after-school snacks.

"What do you usually have?" I asked.

"Well, it depends." She put on her mock adult voice when she used this phrase but it was unsustainable, melted quickly back to kid. "Mom gives me peanut butter and jelly. Sometimes Fluffernutters. Lane wants me to eat fruit and stuff. She gave me tuna fish once, but I didn't eat it."

"I'm with your mom on this one," I said, joining in her scrunched-up tuna fish face. "I like tuna for dinner, but snacks ought to be . . ."

"Fun," she finished for me.

I found the whipped marshmallow and peanut butter, put them on bread, and gave the sandwich to her. Then I made one for myself. I hadn't been to the cottage in a few days, I realized. Only once since her birthday. Part of it was the time I was spending with Derek, part of it the weird vibe I'd started getting from Reese. But I had liked being there. With Maxine. With Angel. Something about the normalcy of it made me feel more like myself. Less widowed. It's what I'd tried to find for myself by moving to the boat, but more and more I realized that the boat was just another part of life with Ben. Derek's apartment, the cottage . . . they were places I could define for myself. And then there was Angel. I'd only just begun to figure out the tangle of feelings she brought to the table.

"You put more marshmallow on than Mom," she said, a white smear from her sandwich slashed across her cheek.

"Sorry."

"It's good." She grinned.

"Close your mouth," I said, looking away. "Half-chewed Fluffernutters ain't pretty."

We finished our sandwiches, watched the one cartoon she was allowed before homework. God, she was an honest child. Her boundaries seemed almost sacred to her.

Lane called several hours after we'd come in, offering to drive out and take over with Angel. But she sounded like hell, almost as bad as the time before, so I told her to stay put, I'd get dinner together for the two of us, and wait on Reese before I left. Within five minutes of mentioning dinner, the phone rang.

"How about hamburgers?" Derek asked.

"Lane called you," I said. "She couldn't stand shirking her responsibility, could she?"

"She couldn't stand subjecting Angel to your cooking, was the way I heard it."

"Fuck you," I said, then caught myself, looked around to see if Angel was in earshot. She was. I mouthed *sorry*, and she just shook her head as if the grown-up/child roles had been entirely switched like in one of those ubiquitous Disney movies.

"I'll be out in about half an hour," Derek was saying. "I know about you. How does Angel like her burgers?"

"Pickles and mayo," I said, remembering her preference from her birthday cookout.

"Gross." He sounded twelve.

"She's eight," I said. "Cut her some slack."

Angel had set the table with the seriousness of a State dinner. She even had water glasses and regular drink glasses. I had to stop her from putting out two forks.

"We're not having salad," I told her. "I'm not sure we'll even need one fork with hamburgers. Where did you learn all that stuff?"

"Mom worked for a caterer doing parties sometimes in the mountains where we lived. I'd go along to help."

I thought of Reese, struggling with her condition, trying to make enough money for the two of them. It couldn't have been easy. Ever. The miracle is that she didn't call on Ben to help out sooner. But then, she'd gotten money from time to time. He never kept it from me, but it was never up for discussion either. She hadn't asked for formal alimony and he felt like he'd owed her something. Looking back, anything formal would have brought Angel to light, so it made sense she'd want it the way it was.

"What about drinks?" Angel asked with enough force to make me realize it wasn't the first time she'd said it. She stood looking into the fridge. "Do you want beer, or that other bourbon stuff you drink?"

Even Angel had noticed my fondness for alcohol. It didn't surprise me, but it didn't make me feel good either. "I'll just have Diet Coke," I told her. "Or Sundrop if your mom has it."

After everything was set, I turned on the news, settled down to wait on the burgers.

"Dinner!" Derek called out, coming in the front door. Georgie followed at his heels. He cradled a white paper bag that smelled of griddle grease.

"Did you go to that diner in town?"

"You bet," he said. "I treat my girls right. Don't I, Angie?"

Angel just stood in front of him, grinning. I'd never seen her look more like a kid. I could just see her with Ben. Entirely smitten. Completely endearing. No wonder he'd loved her. Besides, she was his for the taking. She'd claimed him long before, beginning with Reese's stories, I was sure.

We portioned out the burgers and fries on place settings worthy of baked sole, and in the middle of feeling that so many things had gone right for a change, an unnamed wrong nagged at me. *Stop looking for something bad, Gina.* Pushing through grief to the other side was hard enough, but then feeling guilty for having done it was nothing short of perverse, as if being consumed with sadness equaled love. Losing someone conjured this particular Catch-22, but I wouldn't buy into it. I couldn't. Ben would want me happy, I told myself. Ben would want all of us happy.

"What are you doing here?" Reese came in the front door. From her tone, I gathered that finding Derek and me on her couch was not a happy surprise.

"Where's Lane?" she asked before either of us could answer.

Strands of loose, curly hair had escaped her ponytail, stuck to the dampness of her face. Low-country nights in September turned the outdoors into one large steambath.

"She had to go back to the dentist," I said. "Her crown came off."

"The one she just had worked on?" Reese walked by us, digging around in her purse. I hadn't expected a brass band greeting, but a small *Thanks for pitching in at the last minute* would have been nice.

"Yeah, that one. Listen, Angel's asleep already. She was exhausted for some reason. I picked her up at school today, and she had a lot of homework for a second-grade kid."

"They pile it on," she said, going into the kitchen to splash water on her face. She had a slightly manic quality about her and I wondered if something had gone wrong at work. I exchanged a glance with Derek and he raised his eyebrows, shrugged his shoulders. At least I wasn't crazy, imagining that something was really off with her.

"I met her teacher," I said when she came back into the room. "Young, but really nice. Do you feel like some kind of giant standing next to her, or what?" I laughed. She didn't. "I mean, I did. Just because she's so little. But she seems great. I looked at Angel's 'me-apron' stuff."

Reese didn't speak. She looked pale and her hands shook as she held a dish towel she'd used to dry them.

"Are you okay?" I asked. Derek had moved close to her, ready to catch her if she passed out, I imagined. She didn't look well. "Reese?"

"I'm fine," she said. "You both should go home now. I'm here."

I'd seen her become chilly to me over the last week or so. But this was dry ice compared to her other behavior.

"Reese, I don't know what's bothering you, but . . ."

Derek stood, mute. He wanted to get the hell out of Dodge, but he didn't want to leave me to deal with Reese by myself, I was sure.

"What is it that you want?" Reese said. It sounded resigned, as if the flood walls had crumbled and there was nothing to do but brace for the flood. "Lately you've been coming in here all cupcakes and cream. That, after you could barely look at me on the porch that day. You were spitting venom. What are you after? Do you want to play happy family in my house with my kid? Is that it?" She looked at Derek. Obviously, he was supposed to offer some insight into my ex-treme manipulation.

"Why don't you take the truck home?" I said. "Take Georgie with you, if you don't mind. I've got my car. I'll be back in a bit."

"Gina, I can wait outside if you just want to—"

"Go on home," I said again. "I'll meet you there."

He left, although I wasn't positive he would actually drive away. I wasn't so sure I wanted him to. I could see Reese working herself up to some kind of collapse. I didn't know enough about MS to know how it affected moods, but I didn't want to cause her to have an at-tack of some sort.

After he'd gone, I sat down on the couch. But I stayed taut, ready to respond if Reese gave any signal of breaking down.

"We only came . . . I came first, then Derek brought burgers. Lane called, and rather than bother you at work she figured she would get me to fill in. That's it. End of agenda. Honest."

She sat in the chair opposite me, looked to be coming down from her indignant rush of adrenaline.

"Let's talk this out, Reese. Something's been bothering you for a while now. What is it?"

"Just what I said," she answered, her fingers pulling lightly at her skirt. "I don't trust the change in you. You're practically phobic of children and now you can't get enough of Angel. You did everything but spit on me at Lane's, blaming me for Ben's lies. Now you're what? My best friend? Forgive me if I'm not sold. You have to have an agenda. I just don't know what it is."

"Reese, listen." I stopped. I'd hoped she would confide in me, but it had gone too far. And she was right. I had changed completely since I found out about her. It was time to talk. "I know, Reese. I know all about your . . . your condition, whatever you call it. I know you have MS."

If she looked white before, she looked ashen after I said that. I had somehow imagined she'd be relieved to hear me say it. Instead, she looked distraught.

"I understood a lot more after I found out," I tried to explain. "I understood why you needed to use my credit card. Why you needed to get help. I'd like to get you some help. It's what Ben would have done if he—"

"How did you find out so soon?"

"I went to my doctor, asked him about your meds . . ."

"No. About the Visa."

"I saw the receipts at Lane's house. I found them." I didn't elaborate. I didn't have to.

"You went through my stuff?" She sounded so righteous. How the hell could she get on any moral high horse about this one? "And then you waited this long to tell me? What, has this all been some kind of mind game to you?"

"Jesus Christ, Reese! You took my goddamn credit card. Ordered pills in *my name*! Don't even try to defend that, and don't try to make me sound like the guilty one here. That's fucking illegal, in case you hadn't noticed. I just said I want to get you help. Did you even hear me?"

"Get out," she said. Her voice was calm. Too calm.

"Reese, sit down. I want to talk about—"

"Get the fuck out of this house." Her voice went low and threatening. "You can have Maxine throw me out if you want to, but for tonight this is where I live and I want you to leave."

I wasn't making any progress with her. I wouldn't, not as long as she stayed in such a mood. I'd have Lane feel out the situation, then try to talk with her again tomorrow. I went to the kitchen to get my pocketbook, find my shoes. As I headed back toward the front door, I saw a crack in Angel's door, her small body just standing there, a visible sliver of pink pajamas.

"Reese." I kept my voice low, went close to her so the child wouldn't hear me. She kept a stonelike demeanor as I spoke. "Angel's at her door. She's awake. You'll need to talk with—"

"I know what I need to do for my daughter," she said, cutting me off.

I glanced back toward Angel, offered a little wave to let her know things were okay. Then I went out to my car, couldn't wait to escape to the real world. My new real world. A place where Derek would be waiting when I got back.

35

Reese

"No, no, no, no . . ." Angel kept saying it over and over, the word becoming a mantra. "I like it best here. Better than anyplace. I like Miss Reilly and our house. Please, Mommy. I don't want to go anywhere. No, no . . ."

Angel had on the pajamas Lane had bought for her in Charleston. She looked smaller, younger than when she wore Reese's old T-shirts for sleeping.

"I know, baby." Reese hugged the child, tried to get Angel calmed enough to listen. Finally the girl sat down beside her; spasmlike hiccups punctuated the new silence.

"I thought we were going to stay longer too," Reese told her. "I really did. That's why I came here in the first place, to find you a home. But Gina . . . I did something that was wrong. Not for bad reasons, but it was wrong. And Gina could tell someone. I might get in a lot of trouble."

"Gina won't tell anybody." Angel took on a no-nonsense tone. She let go of the pleading and began to reason with her mother. "I'll ask her not to and she won't. It'll be okay. Let's just stay a little while and see."

"It doesn't work that way, Angel. She's told other people now too. Her doctor, and I don't know how many others." Reese put her flat palm on Angel's cheek, smoothed back the tears. "I'm so sorry, Angel. I know you're happy here."

She'd toyed with the idea of leaving the child behind if it ever came to this. But that option didn't seem open to her now. Plus, selfishly, a life without Angel would be too empty for her to live. She'd always known that. That's why she'd run away from Ben that final time. She wished she could be a better person, a better mother. But she needed her daughter the way she needed air and food. And deep down, Angel needed her too. She had to believe that.

"It'll be like a vacation," she said. "You can catch up with school when we decide where to settle."

School. She thought of Angel's Miss Reilly, a woman she'd never met because Angel had asked her to stay away. But Gina had met her, liked her. Gina had seen Angel's projects, her classroom. She couldn't think too long on what this meant. An oversight, most likely. Gina hadn't known to wait at the corner. Reese would make a point of meeting the teacher at Angel's next school.

This part worried her the most. Where, with her increasing symptoms and decreasing ability to work, could she build a decent life for Angel in a good, safe neighborhood? This had been her best shot. Could Angel go back to living in dingy apartments and wearing thrift-store clothes?

"You'll see," Reese said, bending down to kiss Angel's head. "It'll be good."

Angel nodded. But she didn't move, just sat looking stunned and gutted. It broke Reese's heart, but what choice did she have? She could stay. Take whatever came to her and let Angel have, what? A motherless life with a community of strangers. Albeit well-meaning strangers. It was a crapshoot. It always had been. But Angel was better off staying with her.

"Go pack all your stuff," she told the girl. "We're not leaving in such a rush this time. Pack everything you want."

Angel stood up, her features deliberate and void of animation. "Okay," she said. She went off to her room to gather things, and Reese watched her go. One good thing came out of this attempt at a life. She found a safety net, at least. She went to her room, looked deep in the drawer, and found the manila folder, took out the documents she'd kept, papers that would protect Angel if something did happen to her.

What had that lawyer in Boone told her? What was his name again? A regular customer at the restaurant. Nice guy. He'd helped her draw up the papers.

"If she has a relative," he'd told her about Angel, "then she would go to her closest kin. If not, you'd need to appoint a legal guardian."

"What if there isn't anyone?" Reese asked, realizing there was only one answer.

"She'd go into custody of Child Services. They'd place her in a home."

Reese remembered the panic she'd felt when she realized all that was riding on her health. Foster care would be better than any relatives they could track down of hers. Even the uncle who took her in was old and divorced by now. And that was years ago. He could be dead for all she knew. But strangers, she could never let Angel go to strangers. She'd make a plan. That's when she got in touch with Ben.

That didn't matter now. None of the plans mattered except the one that she'd ended up with. The only one that would work. It wasn't perfect, and it was damned ironic, almost funny. But here it was. She'd get the papers notarized early tomorrow, then she and Angel would be on their way.

As she went to her room to pack up her belongings for yet another flight to another life, she wondered how many departures she and Angel would have to make before she finally got it right.

36

Gina

Ben and Derek were talking. Both dressed up. The music was good. Some live band playing Cajun music. On some level, I knew it was a dream, but it felt audible, tangible, almost livable. I'd come with Derek, but talked with Ben as if we'd been married all along. Everything seemed . . . okay.

When I woke up, I looked out the window, saw storm clouds, tight and hovering over the inlet. I loved the drama of storms in the summer. After days of heat, it always felt like nature's equivalent of hosing down the sidewalk.

"Hey," Derek said, coming out of the bathroom. "I went in there to keep quiet. Did I wake you, talking on the phone?"

"No, I didn't hear you at all. I had a dream. A weird one. I kind of woke up gradually out of it, I think."

"Did you tell Ben hello for me?" There was a slight edge to his tone, but I could tell he was fighting it. I worried that one day soon he'd decide that I was too damn much trouble.

"Was I talking?" I asked.

"Just a little, nothing detailed." He turned off the burner, poured hot water for tea.

"Well, I didn't have to tell him hello for you. You were both there. We all got along just great."

He nodded, sat down on the futon with his tea, didn't look directly at me.

"It feels strange," I said, getting out of bed and going to sit beside him. "I'm sorry if it's hard for you. Really, Derek, I—"

"The way I see it, it's something we can't help," he said. "We are who we are. You're a widow. You loved your husband. I've fallen in love with a widow who loved her husband."

He put his arm around me and I snuggled in close.

"You're different from Ben. A lot more mellow," I told him. "Easy."

"You're not the first person to call me easy." He grinned.

"I'm serious."

"Yeah? Is that okay?" He still smiled.

"Yeah, it is."

"What was Ben like? I mean, I saw him around, but I didn't know him." It seemed natural for him to ask. That was a good sign.

"He had to be acting on something. Always moving, thinking. Either planning or doing. That's why he loved sailing, I think. It demanded action and decision. I loved that about him, but it wore me out too. He was such a force of nature. Sometimes I wondered if I could keep up for years and years. I worried that I'd be a nervous wreck by our tenth anniversary."

That stopped me, thinking of anniversaries that would never come. I was walking on the edge of a cliff with my emotions, but so far I still had my footing. I looked at Derek. He was hanging in there too.

"But he was kind, like you. And fun. And he loved me. I never felt not loved. That's why it was so awful to think he kept things from me. Now I know he, at least, tried, wanted to talk about it."

Derek kissed my head. He would have listened more if I'd talked. But I had said enough.

"The call I got this morning," he said after a long moment. "It was from *Low-Country Leisure*."

"Oh yeah. I meant to tell you I gave them your name. They have a staff position open and I thought . . ."

He had an expression that didn't seem entirely happy.

"Was that okay?"

"Sure," he said. "When I dropped off your artwork I saw the notice posted there. I was thinking of applying. I just feel a little strange, going from being in bed with you to an interview with them."

"Derek, they asked me for names. I've read your stuff. No matter how good you are in the sack, I wouldn't have suggested you if you didn't have a good clip file. And they liked the fact that you'd been to graduate school, that you're serious and committed."

He raised his eyebrow, gave me a half smile.

"They'll either hire you or not after they see what you've done. That part won't have anything to do with me."

"All right." He settled back, brushed his hair away from his eyes. "I'm going in this morning to talk with them. It looks like a good place to get my foot in the door."

"I like working with them," I said. "It is a good place. Go. Shower. What time do you have to be there?"

"In about an hour. I better hurry."

Georgie was whining to go out, so I pulled my shorts on and looked around for her leash. When I opened the door to take her out, I saw Lane standing there, hand raised, getting ready to knock.

"Oh." She jumped. "Telepathy."

"Hey," I said. "Do you need Derek?"

"No, hon," she said, "I came to find you. You weren't answering your cell and—"

"Oh, right. We went to a movie last night and I turned the sound off. Sorry."

The uneasy pause that followed left us both looking at anything but each other.

"Guess it's not a big secret where I am most of the time these days," I said finally.

She put her hand on my arm. "Good for you, sweetheart. People around here don't give a damn how you spend your time, and me . . . Well, I'm just jealous." She laughed, broke the awkward spell.

"Come on in." I unhooked the dog's leash and the animal protested, camped out near the door for good measure.

"It's nice in here," Lane said, looking around the various sections of the room that made up Derek's studio. "I guess you've had a hand in that, huh?"

"God, no." I laughed. "He had it all fixed up before he met me. You never saw my house, did you? I have no taste at all."

She put her pocketbook on the island that separated the kitchen from the den/bedroom/dining room.

"So what's up?" I asked. I could still hear the shower running. I hoped Derek didn't come out wearing nothing.

"It's probably not a big deal. But the school called me. Angel hasn't been in class for a couple of days now. I'm listed as an emergency number, and they weren't able to get Reese on the phone to verify the absence so they called me."

"You think something's wrong?" I asked.

The shower stopped. I took preemptive action and went to the bathroom door. "Derek, Lane's out here with me."

"Okay," he called back. "Uh, could you pass me something, then?"

"What kind of something?"

"It's your call," he said. I found a flannel robe in the closet and handed it in to him.

"I feel like I should at least check on them. Reese hasn't asked me to help with Angel since I went to the dentist that day."

"I should have talked with you," I said, feeling bad that I hadn't filled her in on things with Reese. "She was upset for some reason that I was there. It didn't make much sense. There are other things you don't know about. Why don't I ride out to the cottage with you? I'll fill you in."

"You don't have to go. I would have just gone out there by my-self," Lane said, "but I don't have a key. So I thought—"

"No, I'm not doing anything now. I want to catch up with you anyway."

Derek came out, overdressed for the heat in flannel.

"Hey, Lane," he said. The studio suddenly became very small.

"Why don't you meet me at my place?" Lane said. "I'll drive."

She made a hasty exit.

"So what's that about?" Derek asked.

"Reese."

"Enough said." He shook his head. "You can fill me in later."

"Poor thing. Why didn't she just tell us?" Lane shook her head, kept one hand on the wheel while she fiddled with the air conditioner with the other. "So the sprained wrist and all those problems the other night . . . ?"

I'd told Lane all I knew, or at least suspected, about Reese.

"I've read some about it since I talked to my doctor. Symptoms can come and go, so it would make sense. But she didn't own up to anything when I talked to her about it, so I haven't heard it from her yet, but . . ." I settled deep into the comfort of Lane's Crown Victoria.

"Why are all these cars slowing down to let you pass?" I asked. Lane had a clear path on the highway.

"This is what most undercover police cars are," she smiled. "I get that all the time. Gives me a strange sense of power."

A snowy egret stood in the grassy median. In the time I'd lived near Charleston, the ubiquitous birds, regal though they were, had begun to seem like pigeons to me.

"Did you tell her we would all help her?" I could see the confusion on Lane's face. Reese didn't follow anyone's pattern of normal when it came to predicting a response.

"Yeah," I said. "Of course. That's when she really freaked out on me."

We didn't say much for the rest of the drive. I hoped we'd get to the cottage and find Reese happily playing hookey with Angel, both of them laughing at us for worrying. But I somehow doubted it. Things with Reese were never that easy.

37

∞

Reese

"What did you order?" Angel asked, taking a bite of the grilled cheese sandwich the waitress had just put in front of her.

"I'm not hungry," Reese lied. She smelled the melted cheese, could almost feel the texture of the bread in her mouth.

Half the place was smoking, so Reese broke her own rule about keeping her smoke away from Angel and lit up.

"Don't you ever start this," she said, taking in a long, satisfying drag. "It'll turn your lungs to black pitch."

"Why don't you stop?" Angel asked.

"Cancer's the least of my worries right now." That sounded harsh, too harsh for a child who'd been ripped from yet another town, another home. "I'm going to quit, baby doll. I need to get us settled someplace and I'll throw these things away. I promise."

Angel nodded, took a sip of her Dr Pepper.

After she finished eating, Angel went off to the bathroom. It was a single room that locked, and the door could be seen from the table, so Reese let her go off by herself.

"You want me to take this?" The waitress walked up, started to pick up Angel's plate.

"She might still be working on it." Reese reached out instinctively. Nearly half a grilled cheese and a handful of fries sat cold and abandoned. After the waitress left, she put out her cigarette, pulled the plate over in front of her, and started in on the leftovers.

If she was careful, that last paycheck, plus the little bit of money Andrew had given her when she went by the church before she left town, would get them food and another four or five nights in the motel. After that, she had to have some plan in mind.

At least her body seemed to be cooperating. But then, only so many things could go wrong before something had to go right.

38

∞

Gina

I'd walked through the cottage a half-dozen times before I saw the envelope on the kitchen counter. My name was on the front. I could hear Lane in the den on the cell phone. She was talking with the manager of Ollie's, trying to find out when Reese had last come into work. Best I could tell, she was getting an earful from the guy. Not a good sign.

The content of the document was clear enough. It made me medical power of attorney in case she couldn't make decisions for herself for any reason, gave me sole guardianship of Angel if Reese became unable to care for her. It didn't make much sense to me. Why me? My last interactions with her had been contentious, at best. She all but accused me of trying to make Angel part of my happy family fantasy while I schemed to cut her out of the picture altogether. Looking at the note, that's what she was handing me.

My name had been written in and initialed with blue ink, the change notarized. I studied the original name typed onto the document and my hands began to shake. Benjamin Melrose. What's more, on the last page I found his signature. He'd seen the same piece of paper I held. He'd read it, signed it. I started to feel the anger, the betrayal all over again. How could he have made such a decision without telling me? But then I thought of Angel. How could he not agree, under any circumstances?

"What's that?" Lane came into the kitchen.

I handed her the papers, sat down at the table. I felt disoriented, unable to move or function. The emotional equivalent of a concussion.

"Why me?" I asked as Lane sat down opposite me at the table. "You're the obvious choice. She doesn't even like me, much less trust me. I just don't—"

"I told her no," Lane said, still staring at the document.

"You what? She asked you about this?"

"She asked me about guardianship, in case something ever happened to her. She didn't mention she had a chronic condition, but she seemed so serious, insistent."

"And you turned her down?" I asked. I'd seen Lane with Angel, couldn't imagine the perfect grandmother saying no.

"I thought about it for a long time. I didn't imagine that it would ever be an issue, but I figured I should take it seriously. Maybe on some level I suspected more. She was . . . I don't know, really intense in her concern about it."

"But you and Angel are so close."

"I love that child," she said. "You know that. But I have my children to consider. If I agreed to something like that, I'd be parenting a teenager in my seventies, not to mention committing the bulk of what would be my estate to her care and education. I thought of going to the boys, but I knew they'd tell me to do it, to do whatever I thought was right. It didn't seem fair to them. I couldn't . . . Oh, that poor little kid."

"No, Lane. You're right. What did they say at Ollie's?"

Lane let out a long breath, laid the document on the table. "She was scheduled for lunch and dinner shifts yesterday and today. They haven't seen her."

I glanced over at the papers in front of Lane. The fold made the pages turn up slightly, and I saw scrawled writing in pencil on the back of the last page.

Dear Gina,

Don't think the irony of this is lost on me. We've never been friends. I doubt we ever will be. But as I think of the last weeks, you've been fair with me, and Ben trusted you. I'm hoping you will consider what I'm asking. That you will sign this and keep it someplace safe. I hope it never comes to this, but you know as well as I do that my condition is unpredictable. Angel needs a safety net. Much as I hate to admit it, if you can get over your bizarre weirdness about kids (and Ben was sure you would), you'd be good with Angel. As you know, I don't have many options, and if you're the best I can come up with, imagine how desperate I am. I don't mean to insult you. You've been more stand-up these last weeks

*than I could have expected. Some tension between us is inevitable,
but I don't want Angel to suffer because of it. Please sign this.
Otherwise, she'll face foster care and I don't think either of us want
that. This being said, I hope you never have to make good on the
commitment. We are off to make a new start (again). Your
information is with me and with Angel. If anything happens,
you'll be the person they call. Please consider this for Angel, and for
Ben.*

Reese

"She's gone," I told Lane.

"What do you mean, gone?"

"She's taken Angel to 'make a new start,' " I said.

"I thought that's what they were doing here."

"A *new* new start."

We sat looking at each other, wondering what to make of it, how
to respond. I wasn't sure we should do anything at all. Reese was an
adult. Angel was her daughter. And this had been the blueprint of
their lives. But all I could think about was Angel showing me the pictures in her me-apron. The cottage, the "family" she'd embraced that
included me, Lane, even Derek, along with her mom. And Ben looking on from above. I didn't know what the hell to do.

"Martha Mincey?" Lane was looking at the front page of the
document. "Isn't she the woman who works at the church?"

"Yeah, she is. Why?"

"She notarized this yesterday morning."

"Okay," I said. "That's a place to start, I guess. But Lane, I don't
even know if we should do anything. She's an adult."

"She's yanked that child out of school—again. Turned her life
upside down. I can't imagine why she'd want to leave, but it can't be
all that rational. For Angel's sake, I think we have to try and talk with
Reese. At least figure out what's going on. If she's sick, you'd think
she'd want a support system. And she got upset when you told her
we'd help her?"

"Yep."

"Well," Lane said. "I think we have to do something."

I still had my doubts but I couldn't pretend Reese's unexplained
flight made sense. I also couldn't say that it wasn't any of my business.
Angel had meant something to Ben, and could very well be his child.

At the same time, did I have any right to interfere in Reese's life with her daughter?

"Okay, let's at least go talk to Martha," I said.

There were no cars at the church. Usually on a weekday afternoon there were one or two, but as we walked to the side to get to the church office, the place appeared to be deserted.

"Maybe they take Thursdays off," I suggested.

The doors were locked, and knocking brought no one to answer. We turned to go back to the car when a voice called out from across the street.

"Do you need something?" Diane Hanes wore cutoffs and an oversized T-shirt. I'd never seen her casual before. It took me off guard.

"We were looking for Martha," I said. "She notarized something for Reese yesterday, and Reese and Angel have left town, we think. We're trying to sort out what's going on. Would Andrew have any idea?" I wondered if Reese might be a touchy subject with the reverend's wife. I thought of his solo arrival at the birthday party, his late-night tête-à-tête with Reese on the porch after we left.

"Andrew saw her yesterday morning when she came by." She seemed skittish, irritated. I didn't blame her. "They were mumbling about something—I have no idea what—and then he went with her across the street to get Martha to notarize whatever it was. To tell you the truth, if she's gone, it's not the end of the world." Then she seemed to catch herself, remember that she had to maintain some standards as a church wife. "I'm sorry. She's just caused some tension at our house. He's been counseling her on some problems."

"It's okay," I said, feeling for the first time that I could actually warm up to Diane Hanes. "Reese has driven us all crazy at one time or another over the last couple of weeks. She was married to my husband—before I ever met him." I wanted to make clear I hadn't acted as home wrecker in that particular breakup. "She's a tough one to deal with sometimes."

"Come on over if you want to." She took gardening gloves off her hands, slapped them against her leg to get the dirt off of them. "I'll wash up and get us some iced tea. We can try to reach Martha at

home. Andrew's at a pastor's retreat in Columbia, so the church office is closed for a couple of days."

As she said it, she nearly stopped midsentence before moving on.
I think all three of us made note of the coincidence. Pastor Hanes off
at a retreat. Reese off on another lark. *Dear God, don't let her have run
off with a preacher.*

Martha's phone rang and rang with, apparently, no answering
machine to intervene. Diane hung up the phone. Shook her head.

"When's Andrew due back?" I asked. "Do you think she might
have mentioned to him where she was going?"

The question hung for a second or two.

"Could be," she said. "He's due back by about dinner tonight. A
couple of hours, I guess. I could call and ask him, but he left the cell
phone with me."

"That's all right," I said. "I don't think it's urgent. I mean, it's not
unlike her to do this, and . . . well, Angel *is* her daughter."

Lane looked as if she might cry. She had worries that I hadn't
bought into completely.

"Listen," Diane said, "let me get you some tea."

We sat in her den and talked about everything but the obvious.
Andrew and Reese leaving on the same day made for odd coincidence, but voicing the concern would only make things worse. By the
time we reached the topic of potting soil—what kind works best in a
hot climate—we all realized it had reached a last-ditch effort at conversation. Lane and I made our excuses, told Diane to have Andrew
give us a ring when he got in.

Derek came to the cottage around eight-thirty. Lane and I had given
up on guessing at Reese's motives. Derek brought pizza that I ate
without tasting. A sitcom played on the television in the other room,
and the emptiness of the house struck me over and over again as I
listened to the canned laughter, then waited for Angel's full-bellied
giggle.

"It's almost nine o'clock." Lane looked at her watch. "I can't even
think of calling that poor woman to see if her husband has come
home, but you'd think he would have called us by now."

"Maybe she forgot to tell him."

Lane rolled her eyes over at me. "Do *you* really believe she's
thought of anything else since we left?"

Of course she hadn't.

Forty-five minutes later my cell phone rang.

"He's back." Diane Hanes's voice sounded thick, swollen no doubt from crying. "He came in a few minutes ago. His car broke down in a godawful stretch of road and he just hitched a ride back home. I'll let you talk to him." I could tell she'd spent her last bit of energy in relaying news, but the relief she felt spread through the phone line. I could feel it as it reached me.

"Hey, Gina." Andrew's low voice soothed the raw nerves of the evening. "Sorry I'm so late. Diane told me what's going on."

"Any ideas?" I asked.

"Not really. She said she needed to get back to a place where she could figure out all the options for some medical problems. A neurological condition she's had for some time."

"She told you about her MS?" I asked, surprised.

"A while ago, yeah."

"Would have been nice if she'd shared with the class," I half mumbled to myself.

"What?"

"Nothing. I'm sorry. So she didn't say anything specific to you?" I looked at Lane and Derek, shook my head.

"I was thinking she might mean the place in the mountains. You know, where she was before she came here."

"Boone?"

"That's it. I don't know. It's just a hunch. Sorry I can't help you more," he said.

Andrew Hanes *was* sorry he couldn't help. I believed him, and for the first time since I'd first seen them together, I think I believed he'd only been trying to help Reese. Nothing more.

"Let me know if you figure it out," he added.

"Will do."

He hung up the phone, most likely had to go pull his poor wife off the walls she'd been climbing for the past few hours.

"She only mentioned getting medical help. Nothing specific, but he thought she might have meant going back to Boone."

"So what do we do?" Lane sounded lost. She had a mother's worry.

"I don't have any deadlines for the next couple of days." I regretted it the moment I began to speak. "I can ride up to Boone. Just see if they're there and make sure everything is okay."

"Angel . . ." Lane said, without any apparent thought to finish beyond the girl's name. She just shook her head at me, wiped away some of the wetness in her eyes. "I can go with you," she finally offered. "Daniel's supposed to come in this weekend, but I can tell him to put it off for another couple of weeks."

Daniel, her son, made infrequent appearances because of his job. She looked forward to his visits for weeks.

"You stay, Lane," I said. "I'll be fine. It'll be a quick trip. Can you look after the dog for me?"

"Sure," Lane said.

"Listen," Derek offered. "I'll get Charlie to cover the security rounds for a couple of nights and I'll beg off at the marina. I'll probably be quitting pretty soon anyway." He smiled at me. "Why don't I go with you?"

I realized I hadn't even asked him about his interview at *Low Country Leisure.*

"So you got it? At the magazine?"

"I'll know in a day or two, but it looks good."

I hugged him. He felt solid, and real. For months I'd been embracing the idea of Ben. Something between longing and memory. Derek had bones and skin. I rested my face against his shirt. "That's great."

"So tomorrow morning," he said, "we'll go to the mountains."

"Tomorrow."

Just the thought of our departure eased some of the lines on Lane's face.

"Dr. Harris is in Blowing Rock for the day," the receptionist said.

I had the doctor's name and number on the invoices for Reese's medicine. I called when we got thirty miles or so outside of Boone, about the time it occurred to me that I couldn't just walk into his office unannounced and hope to see him before the beginning of the week. Doctors, unlike freelancers, had pretty tight schedules.

"We weren't planning on staying around too long," I told her. "We need to find out if a patient, Reese Melrose, has come in during the last couple of days. We're her relatives and—"

"Reese Melrose?" she asked, sounding more alarmed than the inquiry should have generated. "Let me put you on hold for a couple of minutes. Can you do that?"

"Sure."

Derek kept his eyes on the road and the scenery. We had our windows down and the sunny air had just enough chill for comfort. "You're on hold?" he asked.

I nodded, looked out my window at the low stone wall and the steep drop on the other side. Leaves hadn't begun to change, but the hazy blue mist that hung over the rolling mountains looked like every postcard I'd ever seen of Appalachia. I wondered why I'd never come before.

"Yes." The woman came back on the line. "Ms. . . ."

"Melrose," I said. "I'm Melrose too."

"Oh, a relative. Right." I could almost hear the relief in her voice. "Dr. Harris has to give a talk today at one o'clock. But he's free for about an hour after that. Do you mind meeting him in Blowing Rock? He's got an afternoon clinic there, so he won't be back here today."

"Is that a town?" I asked. It sounded vaguely obscene, but I kept my own sick thoughts to myself.

"Yes." She laughed. "I know it sounds odd. But it's a tourist attraction too. A large overhanging rock with a legend and everything. You should go see it. But listen, if you'll give me your number—I'm guessing this is a cell phone, right?"

"Right."

"I'll have Dr. Harris call you directly and you can figure out a place to meet and talk."

After I hung up, we rolled up the windows and I got out the map. Sure enough. *Blowing Rock.*

"Okay," I said to Derek. "A slight change of location." I sorted out the new route, told him what we should be looking for, and we continued on in silence, letting the scenery distract us from all the questions that Reese had left behind.

I met Dr. Harris at a local diner. The town—a village, really—looked like something out of Tom Sawyer. Shops on one side of the street, a park with a gazebo on the other. Dr. Harris was a large man, not overweight, but thick, imposing. By contrast, his demeanor was that of gentler size.

"I'm glad you're here," he said, sitting down to join me at the table. He made the chair look like something out of a preschool classroom. "I've been concerned since Reese left, but I had no way of following up on her."

The waitress came with menus.

"Coffee?" she asked.

We both smiled up at her. Nodded.

She turned our china coffee cups right side up on the saucers and poured.

"Did you drive up by yourself?" he asked. "My secretary said you came from Charleston. That's a long way."

"No, I came with a friend. He's off hiking around. We both thought I should probably talk with you by myself. This is all pretty confusing."

"I can imagine," he said, emptying a second sugar packet into his cup.

The waitress came back, pad in hand, and we ordered sandwiches. After she left, I launched into my questions. We both knew why I'd come. No need to pretend we'd met for a social visit.

"I'm guessing the answer is no from the sound of things," I said, "but has Reese been back here in the last few days? She left without letting any of us know."

"I haven't seen her since she took off from the hospital in exactly the same way."

"The hospital?" I had a mental picture of Reese running through the street with a hospital gown flying open as she made her getaway. "She was that bad?"

"She'd had a series of episodes, was apparently distraught over some disagreement with her ex-husband, thought he had an agenda with the daughter that upset her. Although it's hard to say what really happened. We had some new treatment options we thought would improve her situation dramatically, but . . ."

"She took off," I finished for him.

"She took off," he repeated.

The food arrived, but I felt too intent on conversation to waste time with a BLT. "She at least tried to continue treatment," I told him.

"How's that?"

"The prescriptions you gave her," I explained. "She filled them at some online pharmacy. Actually, she had them filled in my name because she'd taken my credit card, but that's another story. Anyway, she's been taking the meds for a couple of weeks, although she did have a kind of relapse or spell that lasted a few days about a week or so ago and—"

"What prescriptions?" he cut me off, looked genuinely confused.

"Three or four different kinds of pills."

He shook his head, took a sip of his coffee, and let out a long sigh.

"I didn't write anything for her," he said finally. "But I did misplace a prescription pad. I thought it must be lost in my car."

"That can't be good." I didn't know where to go with all of it. I didn't care to send Reese to jail. Partly for her sake, and partly for mine. I seemed to be the only option for guardianship in that event, and much as I had come to care for Angel, the idea of full-time responsibility scared the hell out of me. "That's not why I came here. I guess I should get to the real reason I'm trying to find her, Dr. Harris. I'm concerned about her, of course, but it's her daughter, Angel, who really takes the brunt of these disappearing acts."

"She's a lovely child, and it's a valid concern," he said.

"Is she in danger?"

"Well, the good news is that Reese has no aggressive tendencies, not that I've seen. It's possible that—"

"No." I stopped the analysis, determined to get to the point. "With her condition, is there a problem with her driving? Or is there a likelihood that she would become . . . I don't know, unable to keep Angel safe? I mean, she's looked after her all these years."

"Ms. Melrose," he said, looking suddenly concerned. "Have you spoken with anyone, any physicians about her problems?"

"Just my doctor. I showed him the invoices for the prescriptions. He explained the kind of medications they were. In his opinion."

"I thought you had more in-depth information about her problems. There are HIPAA regulations regarding patient information. I just thought that you were familiar . . . What kind of relation are you to her?"

"She was married to my late husband," I said, already fishing around in my pocketbook for the papers.

"I'm afraid I can't openly discuss her problems. If she confided in you or you sought treatment for her, it's one thing, but I can't discuss any additional information."

"Look at this," I said, laying the guardianship document on the table between us. "These papers ask me to look after Angel if something happens to Reese, but it also says something about being medical power of attorney."

He looked at the papers for a long time, flipped back and forth, reading the paragraphs in detail. One page in particular he read several times before he put it down. Then he looked up at me. "What would you like to know?"

"Well first, I guess, were you her neurologist? How well do you understand what was going on with her in terms of symptoms and the progression?"

"We had a neurologist who consulted on Reese." He still seemed to be weighing something in his mind, calculating how much to say. He glanced again at the papers, then back at me. "But she was admitted on my service."

"And you are . . . ?"

He leaned forward, rested on his elbows. "I am a psychiatrist."

I looked at him, waited. But he was waiting too. Waiting for me to catch on, I suppose. Waiting for me to sort something out. I had no trouble believing he was a psychiatrist. Getting an opinion out of him was like taking out a deep splinter. "Is that typical?" I asked. "With MS?"

"I wasn't seeing Reese for multiple sclerosis."

"Then what?" I asked point-blank.

He squeezed his eyes shut for a second, then opened them, as if trying to clear his vision before he went on.

"I see that your husband signed the papers. He's deceased?"

"He died about three months ago."

"But you haven't signed them. Did she make this change? To your name?"

"That's what the second, most recent notarization is," I told him.

"If you want me to speak frankly with you," he said, "I think you should sign that document."

I looked at him, wondered if I'd decided that's what I'd do. Would I agree to Reese's request? I thought about Angel, the last few times with her. If for no other reason, I had to do it for Ben. But I realized it wouldn't just be for Ben. The thought amazed me.

"Ms. Melrose?" The doctor was waiting.

"I'm going to sign it," I told him. "I need a notary. We left so quickly after I found out she was gone. I'm going to agree to this. Please take my word for it."

He looked at me for a few seconds. Sized me up, I suppose. Then he settled back in his chair. "All right," he said.

"So what were you treating Reese for?"

"Delusions," he said. "Auditory hallucinations, episodes of paranoia. And . . . she also had symptoms of a condition that did not exist in her."

"Oh, my God!" I could see Reese at the cottage, falling. The strained effort at getting up, then asking for her cane. Could someone make that up? Why would they want to? "Her MS was fake?"

"Not fake," he said. "Delusional. She believes that the disease is real, among other things. The medication we'd started her on helped her have a better grasp on reality for brief periods of time. I felt very excited for her. But as far as her MS went, for all that she went through with symptoms, she might as well have had it."

"But she doesn't."

"No," he said. "She doesn't."

"How did she know about all these?" I handed him the invoices for the prescriptions, and he glanced down at them briefly.

"Research," he said. "Libraries. Internet. She's convinced she has it, and she's smart. As I said, some of our breakthrough medications have had good results with delusional disorder. I had high hopes, but she left before we could see any results."

"Delusional disorder. Is that some kind of schizophrenia?" I struggled to process what he'd just told me.

"It's less intrusive. People who suffer with it are highly functional with behavior that falls into the range of normal most of the time." He sipped his coffee. "But they have persistent delusions that often involve being threatened in some way or having the symptoms of an illness, as Reese does. Nonbizarre things that could occur in reality. No space aliens or anything like that. Makes the illness harder to pin down until someone figures out that these things aren't real."

The place had cleared out entirely. We sat at a window table while all around us the waitstaff goofed off, began putting out settings for the dinner crowd.

"You said she had auditory hallucinations? She hears things that don't exist?"

"Yes, but the hallucinations aren't the prominent feature of the illness. They occur only as they feed into the delusions."

He pursed his lips, seemed defeated in a way, as if talking about

Reese reminded him of the one that, literally, got away. "What did she hear?"

"We've had a couple of examples, but the most worrisome involved Angel. Reese told us that she left her daughter with a friend when she was admitted to the hospital. She'd had a particularly bad day. She came to me with her arm all but paralyzed by what she called her condition. I said I wanted to admit her, and she went off to talk to someone, this friend. She said she asked her to meet Angel at home when the child walked back from her day camp at the school. They lived in apartments just across from the elementary building, so Angel walked back and forth. This *friend*, she said, would stay with little Angel.

"In retrospect, I should have seen a red flag. People with this problem can be very convincing. Well, just before she left the hospital—oh, about three days into her stay, the nurses said—Reese got a phone call from her little girl. I found out later that a neighbor suspected the child was alone and tried to get her to open the door. She wouldn't. So the neighbor called Child Services and they went over there. They thought they heard someone inside, but when they forced the door, there was no one there."

It was the most he'd spoken at a stretch. He looked exhausted, and I got the feeling he blamed himself a little for not seeing beyond Reese a little better. Protecting the child more.

"So Reese just left her there alone?"

"She honestly believed she wasn't alone. But the police investigated. No one named Janet lived in any of the apartments. No one Reese worked with had ever actually seen her. She didn't exist, Ms. Melrose. I know it's hard to grasp, but these things are as real in her mind as I am to you. After she left the hospital, went back to her daughter, well, who knows what Reese thought was happening? Who she thought had come to the door? And to answer your question from before, yes, I do believe the child is most likely in danger. I've spoken to the authorities here about it, in fact, but they haven't been able to come up with anything—speeding tickets, parking violations—that would give them a clue. I thought we were stuck until you called. That's why my office got in touch with me so quickly. Reese will never be a physical threat to the child, in my opinion; but her delusions, the things she believes and acts on, could very well be dangerous for the girl."

He talked some more about her paranoia, one in particular involving Ben, where it appeared that he'd been getting close to the truth about her illness, her real illness, and instead of seeing that he was right, she became fearful that he was making it up to shut her out of Angel's life. It made sense. She'd taken off that last time without telling him for a reason. No wonder she hadn't wanted to explain to me what those reasons were. It had to get confusing for her, keeping all the fantasies intact.

"Was she like this when she was married to Ben?" I asked, wondering how long Reese had managed to keep it hidden from people in her life.

"It's likely this is a long-standing problem," he said. "I can't say for sure. These tendencies are often inherited, and her family history is sketchy. There's some indication through medical records that her father was seen for problems, but it isn't well documented."

"Have you talked to her father?" I asked.

"He died several years back. But there was a restraining order on file from years ago, keeping him away from Reese from about the age of fourteen. An uncle took custody of her after she was apparently molested. I spoke to the uncle and he told me what little I know."

"Her father molested her?" I thought of her story about her father, the bizarre revival.

"No, but there were issues of negligence, child endangerment. Her father may have been party to it in some way. She didn't pursue charges once her father agreed to give up parental rights." He shifted in his seat and the wooden chair groaned under the stress of his movement.

"Oh, my God." So many demons. Had Ben known about any of it? "I had no idea."

Dr. Harris looked at his watch. "I'm sorry," he said, "but I've got clinic in a few minutes."

"That's fine. You've been really helpful."

Dr. Harris paid the check and I sat staring at the patterns in the grain of the wood floor. All I could think about was Angel. I could see her face every time a question was asked of her. She'd look over at Reese, try to sort out the puzzle, come up with the right response. She'd been covering for her mother for so long it must have been second nature to her. And exhausting. Dear God, it had to be exhausting.

"I don't know what else to say," I told Dr. Harris.

"See if you can find her, I suppose. Then get in touch with me and I can either continue my work with her or recommend someone close to Charleston." He pushed his chair back and got up, towered above me when he stood.

"But do let me know if you find her," he said.

As an afterthought, just as we walked out the door into the cool mountain afternoon, I asked, "How did she pay you?"

"In addition to my practice," he said, "I do work at the county hospital. As a county resident, she qualified for care. And I wanted to help her. It's not often, in a small area like this, that we see those kinds of cases."

I put out my hand. "Well, thank you again."

He shook my hand and we left each other, walked in opposite directions down the storybook village street.

I found Derek waiting in the gazebo across the street.

"Did you have a chance to hike around?" I asked. I was still reeling from the doctor's news about Reese. It sounded too bizarre to even repeat. But it was true.

"I went to *the* Blowing Rock, and there is, indeed, a rock."

"Did it blow?"

He smiled. "It was quite nice, actually. I hiked some trails around the park. It's gorgeous out there. I thought we might go back together this afternoon and . . . but, no. You're shaking your head. What's wrong? Okay, Gina, you look pretty freaked out. What happened?"

"Let's just sit down for a second," I said, realizing that I felt too shaky to stand. We sat on the steps of the gazebo, looked at the Disneyesque charm of the downtown street. The movie-set quality of the place only exaggerated the information all jumbled up in my brain.

"So, did he have any ideas about Reese?" Derek prompted.

"Oh, yeah," I said. "But not about where she might be."

"What, then?"

"This is really hard to believe, Derek. I mean if the guy wasn't a doctor, a real one with an office and everything, I just wouldn't believe it. But here goes . . ." I launched into the details of Reese. Of her real illness. And the few details I knew about her exodus from the hospital.

While I talked, I saw children begin walking through the park. School had let out, the essence of the space changing with their sounds. Angel had experienced a week, maybe two, of a normal existence like theirs. All the children in the park would wake up tomorrow and take the sameness for granted. I lamented so many things from my childhood, but even I had barely considered the notion of a home as anything extraordinary. Lunch money, ballet class, and spelling bees. The pictures Angel drew at school elevated normal childhood to a holy place.

"She made up all those problems with her leg?" Derek tried to make sense of what I told him. "The trouble with her hand?"

"She didn't make it up in the sense of a lie," I said. "Her mind invented it and then embraced it completely as the truth. She believes it, Derek."

"What about when this guy told her something different?"

"That's the strangest part. He thought he was getting her to come around with therapy, that he had new meds that he wanted to try. But she came back from a trip to Charleston all convinced that Ben had gotten to him, that there was some conspiracy to help Ben pass her off as crazy."

"Did Ben figure out what was really wrong with her?"

"I'm thinking he must have," I said. "And if he did, he wouldn't agree to let her go anywhere. So she took off again."

"Did you get any of this from Ben before he died?"

"Only how urgent he was getting, talking about kids and needing to change my mind."

Derek lay back on the cool floor of the gazebo. I followed him, stared up at the underside of the roof.

"Where to now?" he asked.

"I don't know. Andrew said she was going for medical help."

I pulled out my cell phone, scrolled down the numbers I'd dialed in the last few days. I got to the one that looked familiar and pushed the button.

"Hello, Mt. Sinai," Martha Mincey answered. I asked for the preacher. One last check with Andrew and then I had a hunch to follow.

"Hello." Andrew came on the phone.

"Listen, Andrew, did Reese say anything about how she was going to pay for the medical care she needed?"

"No, not when I saw her last," he said. "We'd talked about county medical services one time before; about how establishing residence made her eligible. But that's about it."

I thanked him and hung up.

"Car registry. A local address on your driver's license. Would that count for establishing residence in an area?" I asked.

"Some places would take that, I guess," Derek said. "Others might require a power bill or something. Why?"

"Reese has to be driving with a license issued somewhere. She's got South Carolina plates. Let's go to the local DMV before we take off, see if we can get somebody to look her up for us. They're bound to have a national database. If they won't help, I need to sweet-talk a state trooper."

39

∞

Reese

Reese remembered when arcade games at the beach pavilion only cost a dime. A dollar would buy ten games, even the ones that lasted a long time, like baseball. She'd loved the paperdoll-like figures that ran the bases on a curved track. The sound of the dense silver balls as they jumped the field and landed in the home-run section. She'd won a bear once on that game. Her uncle had brought her up from Charleston, gave her a stack of dimes the size of the Eiffel Tower.

"Did you ever bring me here before?" Angel asked.

"Yeah, do you remember? You were pretty young. Four or five."

"I remember, but not so much."

Reese had lived here for about a year with Angel, then just kept coming back to renew her tags and license. Her old landlord had let her switch her mailing address to the office, was nice enough to hang on to any mail that looked official. She'd gotten the upcoming year's registration from him the day before. That would be due soon. Something else to pay for. But it had to be done somewhere if she was going to keep a car, and she didn't stay in many places very long. Myrtle Beach was as good a place as any to technically call home.

Reese gave Angel five dollars to go buy tokens. That was a fortune, considering what she had ahead of her. But a kid ought to play arcade games at the beach. The anticipation of winning seemed to be a birthright, of sorts.

"Mom?" Angel's voice sounded small. "Is it okay if I buy two tickets on the roller coaster instead? We could go together."

Reese could hear the coaster, the Swamp Fox, outside the arcade pavilion. Rickety jerks followed by all-out squeals.

"You're kind of little," she told the child. "I don't know if they'll let you on or not."

"I'm just tall enough. I checked before."

Reese considered the ride, wondered if the hard shaking and rat-tling would be the best thing for her. She'd had more problems with her legs, particularly the left side. She'd paced back and forth in the motel room when she first got up, pushing through the spasms, and that had helped some. Thinking of the walk back to the motel, she suddenly wished she'd driven the short distance to the arcade. To-morrow she would check in with the doctors at the county clinic. But that could wait a day, and the ride looked like fun. What the hell.

"All right," she said. "Let's go."

They bought their tickets and climbed on, second from the front, so they would see the car tipping over the crest of the rise be-fore the fall. Below, Reese could see the hot dog stand that sat beside the coaster. Picnic tables offered a vantage point for watching the ups and downs that continued all day and through the night.

Traveling higher, Reese felt a fall of another kind would come soon. She'd felt it for several days. Her bones, her skin, every nerve told her something was close. She wondered if her body would betray her. Would she wake up unable to move, barely able to smile at her daughter? Or would it be someone like Gina to bring her down? Police at her door with talk of credit card fraud, passing off false pre-scriptions? Maybe something else, something she'd never antici-pated. But one thing she felt was certain—the fierce tumble, when it came, would be nothing like the safe thrill of an amusement ride. She put her arm tight around her daughter, held on as the world dropped out from beneath them both.

40
∞

Gina

We didn't reach Myrtle Beach until midmorning the following day. We'd planned to drive straight through, get there at some godawful part of the night, and crash at a cheesy motel. But after a few hours of driving, we realized that neither of us had the stamina.

"You're only twenty-six," I said to him the night before as we pulled off at an interstate Holiday Inn. I winced a little at the sound of his actual age. "You're supposed to be able to do weeklong road trips with no sleep at all."

"Old ladies bring you down," he said, grinning as he got out of the car.

We ate pizza in the room, then slept solid before getting up to hit the road again.

I hadn't been up to the Strand, the main strip at Myrtle Beach, in a few years. It looked cleaner, had a whitewashed sort of quality to it, like a grand old house with new shutters and paint.

"They've cleaned things up around here," I said. "It got really seedy for a while, but now it's all bright again."

"It's the Disney mafia," he said. "First Times Square. Next the world."

"That's weird. I was just thinking yesterday that Blowing Rock looked like the set of a Disney movie."

"Life is a Disney movie, darlin'. We're all extras," he said.

It was after season along the beachfront strip, which made for fewer cars and easier searching.

"Any idea where you want to check first?" Derek squinted, then pulled down the visor.

"Let's try cruising through motel parking lots. I've got to hope she'd pick someplace familiar, so that leaves out the newer hotels farther out."

"You really think she's here?"

"I don't know," I said. "She and Ben came here to get married, then she ran away here when she left Ben. She told me that. With her license and registration here too . . . I'm hoping. I need to call the county clinics again today, see if she's been in."

"Is it really called Horry County?" Derek chuckled. He could become twelve years old in an instant.

"Silent *H*," I told him.

"I can see why."

We'd gone to the address listed with the DMV for Reese. I wanted to cover all the bases, but I knew she wouldn't be there. At best, I thought some acquaintance might have taken over the place and maybe she would have gotten in touch with them. Too many maybes and no such luck. The old lady who talked to us through a crack in the door had "no recollection of a name such as Reese," and I wasn't sure she had much recollection in general. I thought of talking with the landlord, but he had dozens of rentals and lots of turnover. I didn't figure it was worth the time.

"This is the tip of one end of the main strip," I said. "Let's start here. We can cruise the beachfront motels first, then travel the opposite direction and try the places across the street."

"And that's your best idea?"

"That's it," I said.

He pulled into a motel lot and drove slowly, both of us looking for the maroon Plymouth with plates that read, "DOG-MAA."

"Why do you think she got those plates?" Derek asked.

"She told us once about some weirdness with a televangelist when she was a teenager. Maybe it has something to do with that. I mean, she's mentally ill. I'm not sure anything with Reese has to make sense anymore."

We finished the first parking lot, moved on to the next one down.

Nearly two hours later we saw the Plymouth, parked in front of a row of rooms at The Sandy Bucket, a motel with a neon sign in the shape of a child's beach pail. It occurred to me that Angel would have picked the place. It was the kind of decision Reese would indulge.

"I'll be damned." Derek shook his head. "We actually found her."

Only after I saw the car did I realize what a tremendous shot in the dark it had been. Thank God Reese was somewhat predictable within the context of her bizarre life.

I felt myself shaking. Scared? Relieved? I didn't know which. Maybe the confrontation alone was enough to give me the jitters. I thought of having Derek go in first, but that would have been just wrong. I had to do it.

"Ready?" Derek asked.

"God, no."

"I don't blame you."

"Listen," I said. "This is going to be really confusing for Angel. Maybe you should take her for a walk or something. You know, once I get to Reese."

"You're the boss on this one."

I got out, walked down to the office at the end of the building. A youngish guy, about Derek's age, sat smoking, watching a black-and-white TV.

"Need a room?" he asked when I got to the counter.

"No, I'm looking for my sister-in-law." That seemed a lot easier than explaining Reese in detail. "Reese Melrose."

"Funky lady with a kid? Wears hippie skirts and dangly jewelry?"

"That's the one," I told him.

"She ain't registered under Melrose, but I remember the first name. She says she's Reese . . . let me see here . . . Reese Hanes."

Nice. She'd married herself off to a preacher in her rich fantasy life.

"That's her," I said. "She's using her married name."

"Room 14."

I went back out into the afternoon. Wind off the ocean smelled of seaweed and salt. The postseason shore appeared nearly deserted. It went on forever out there. Looking at it, I remembered all the vacations my family had taken at Virginia Beach. Elise was terrified of the ocean, so she played in tidal pools, calm and warm as bathwater. Then I thought of her calling to me, jumping into the deep end of the pool. She must have been scared. Water higher than her head always terrified her.

"What'd he say?" Derek startled me.

"Room 14."

We walked back around to the row of rooms. They would be the cheaper options along that side. The rooms that looked out on the parking lot, where a view of the ocean meant a sideways glance out the window.

I knocked on the door to the room. After a while, I knocked again, but no one answered.

"We've got to stay someplace tonight anyway," Derek suggested. "Why don't we see if one of the rooms next door is open? We can hear them when they come in."

Sometimes the boy was sharp, I had to admit.

I don't know when Reese and Angel got back to the room. Derek and I had both fallen asleep. When I woke up, the day had moved into early evening, and opaque sky made it seem even later than that. But when I got next door, I could see Reese, asleep on top of the bed, through the open curtains. Angel lay beside her, lying on her back, eyes wide open, staring at the ceiling. Reese shifted, tugged at herself as if pulling a sweater or covers tighter around her. Angel got up, folded the bedspread over so it covered her mother; then she sat down in a chair opposite the bed and watched. Kept a vigil, of sorts.

It occurred to me how responsible the child felt for keeping her mother safe. It should be the other way around, but the way Angel sat guarding her mother . . . was like a parent standing watch over the sickbed of a baby. And I thought again of all the times Angel had looked over at her mom for cues, hints at what she should say, whether she should speak at all. Angel was the keeper of Reese's reality. Angel's confirmation made Reese more normal, more okay.

The AC unit had been turned off and the windows opened, so that only slight screens separated me from the two of them. I stood there, staring in, trying to decide whether to say something or to knock, when Angel turned her head. As she saw me her eyes opened wider, but she stayed absolutely still, didn't startle or make a noise. I put my finger to my lips and she slowly stood up, so as not to cause a lot of noise. She came over to the door and opened it carefully, and I motioned for her to follow me.

I hadn't thought of talking with Angel first, hadn't known I might have the chance, but it felt like the right thing to do. Once Reese saw me, the world could flip on its end pretty fast.

Angel and I walked over to my room. Our curtains were closed, so I told her to wait outside while I got Derek. He could stay with her mom while we had a talk.

We left Derek sitting in the lawn chair outside Reese's door. He could hear her calling for Angel if she woke up, and he could explain, then try to calm her. I didn't envy him. I walked with Angel out to the beach. We sat on the stone wall that separated the hotel property from the sand. Out on the water, a shrimp trawler rounded a sandy point at what looked to be the end of land. In reality, the jutting piece of beach was only a curve in the coastline, one of so many stretching along the South Carolina, Georgia, and Florida shores.

"Did you bring the police?" This was Angel's first question after we sat down. Poor kid, she was juggling all of Reese's heavy baggage; had been doing it, most likely, for as long as she could remember.

"No, Angel, I didn't bring any police," I said. "Did your mom think that's what I would do?"

She nodded, kept her eyes in direct contact with mine as if to detect the slightest hint of deception. "That's why we had to leave. She was scared you would tell them about something she did."

Reese had her problems, but, paranoid as it was, at least that particular fear held some logic—which I found somehow comforting.

Angel paused for a second, never taking her eyes from me, then said, "I told her you wouldn't."

"You were right." I reached out, took her hand. "I wouldn't. I don't want to get your mom in trouble. I'd like to help her, Angel."

"She says that when people tell you that, sometimes it's a trick."

"She's right, sometimes it is, but I promise I won't ever try to trick you. Do you believe that?"

She didn't answer, ignored the question, best I could tell. Instead she told me, "Mom says I'm supposed to go with you if something ever happens to her and she gets real sick and can't take care of me."

The wind blew her hair across her face, so I put my hand up and brushed the strands behind her ear. "That's right. But she'll be okay, your mom. It just might take a little while for her to get better."

"I know, sometimes she can't walk or pick up a bag of groceries and—"

"But she's not that kind of sick, honey." I had no idea how to explain mental illness, delusions, to a child who should still be playing pretend all the time. Her mother's make-believe had taken that option from Angel years ago.

"You know how sometimes your mom says things that you know aren't right?" I asked. "And then you go along with them just like what she said was true, but you know it wasn't?"

"I didn't want to be bad. I used to think it was our secret game," she said. "But now I don't."

"It isn't a game to your mom, Angel. And she's not trying to tell a lie either. It was okay to protect her."

Angel looked confused, and I realized how hard this was for an adult to understand, much less a child.

"The sickness makes her believe things that aren't right. But she really believes them, Angel. And I'm going to try to get her help so that she doesn't get so mixed up anymore. There's medicine that can help her."

I watched her. She dangled her feet off the wall, looked out at the water. I thought I almost saw her smile. Maybe hearing it made things easier for her. Maybe having an adult say it meant that she didn't have to work so hard to protect her mother.

"Medicine costs a lot of money," she said. "She doesn't have enough, I don't think."

Did I have *all* the answers? God knows, she knew all the questions. I couldn't believe she'd just turned eight. She had the worries of a senior citizen. Money, lies, illness . . . Being left alone. Being ripped from one life and deposited in another. Could I even begin to bring a childhood back for her? But at the cottage, with Lane and even Derek, she'd let herself be a kid. I'd seen it. She played with Barbie, got tickled over a Disney song coming out of a watch. She could do it if she had half a chance.

"There's money," I said, realizing what the words meant. Another check had come in the mail. I had two of them on the desk at Derek's apartment. I'd been trying to decide. "It's money from Ben." Her eyes all but begged me to be telling the truth.

"Ben?"

"Ben always helped your mom when she needed something. There's money he would want me to use to help her too. I can pay for doctors and medicine. We're going to make sure she gets okay."

"Are you sure?" It must have seemed like another cottage to Angel. Another school with a me-apron and a pretty teacher. It must have seemed like something she was scared to want again. To have and lose.

"I'm sure, Angel. The minute Ben laid eyes on you, he made a promise, I think, to look after you and your mom. How about I make good on that one for him, okay?"

"The money . . ." she began, and then stopped.

"Yeah?"

"You should use some of it too," she said.

"What do you mean?"

"Ben wanted to look after you too."

"Yeah, he did," I said. "He really did."

The scene with Reese was going to be worse than anything I could have dreamed up. Angel and I heard her just as we stood up to go back to the room. Screeching and ranting. *Fuck* this, and *goddamn* that, something breaking with a shattering sound. And all this at a volume that the shrimp trawler, now a tiny speck on the horizon, could probably hear carried out over the water. The handful of people walking on the beach all stopped and stared. Angel looked as if she would cry.

"Angel." I put my hands on her shoulders, could feel the bandages just under her shirt. Bandages that still taped the wounds I'd inflicted that first night. "Angel, listen. Do you trust me? Do you trust Derek?"

She stared past me at nothing, listened to her mother's sounds. Didn't respond.

"Angel," I said again, trying to add authority to my shaky tone. She turned and focused on my face. "I know that you've felt like it was your job to look after her. But now it can be my job. Ben knew she was sick. He would have helped make her better. He would want me to do it now. But you have to trust me because it's going to look like I'm fighting against her; doing something that she doesn't want. You have to trust me, Angel. I promise I'll do my best to help her." She turned away. "*Look at me!* Ben loved you, Angel. He did and so do I. That's the truth. But I can't help you, and I can't help her, if you don't trust me. Do you?"

Reese's sounds were escalating. I hated to think of what Derek was facing.

Angel nodded; tears streamed down her face.

"You'll let me help your mom?"

"Yes." Her sound came out small, just barely a word, then she reached up and grabbed me around the neck. She pulled with both arms, even her injured one showing surprising strength. It was a violent hold so tight that I thought we might both fall. She gripped my shirt, my skin, as if someone would try to pull her away. She held on the way Elise would have held on if I'd turned and gone to her when she called to me. If I'd tried, even for one second, to save her.

"Mommy," Angel sobbed as Reese screamed, "Get the fuck out!" at Derek.

I found my center of balance, reached around the child, and pulled her up. She wrapped her small legs around my waist, buried her face in my neck as I carried her back toward the sounds of her frantic mother. "I'm going to put you in my car, and then I'm going to help Derek, okay? Your mom's going to be fine."

Her response was in her body, pressed tight against my chest.

"It's going to be okay, Angel." I said it over and over, hoping to God I was telling her the truth. "Don't worry. It's going to be okay."

And as we moved toward the motel, I couldn't shake the feeling that the fierce little girl Ben had claimed was somehow saving me.

41

Reese

The room looked familiar. But then, maybe they all looked alike. Hospital clinics, like schools, seem to spring from one generic blueprint.

She remembered the roller coaster, then walking back from the Pavilion with Angel and arriving at the room exhausted. The rest wasn't that clear. Waking up. Angel gone. She saw Derek, but heard the rest of them too. Maybe the same ones from the mountains. The ones who came for Angel. Derek said something, talked as if the others weren't talking loudly and all at once. Was he with them? Maybe they weren't the same as the crowd from the mountains. The singsong voices sounded like something else. Like the gathering at the television preacher's revival. The chanting. Words that had syllables but didn't mean anything. Had they come back? Did they know about Angel?

"Reese?" A doctor stood in front of her. She'd seen him before. He'd talked to her, but she couldn't remember what he'd said. "We've been in touch with Dr. Harris in Boone," he told her. "We've started some preliminary treatment to make you feel better. The protocol of drugs he had you slated to follow up there can be picked up by your doctors in Charleston. In a day or so we'll be able to transfer you there with your family. Do you understand?"

"Where's Angel?"

"She's been here sitting with you. You've been pretty groggy from the sedation. She went to get some lunch with your friend who brought you in here."

She felt in pieces: That seemed to be the only way to describe it, as if parts of her brain had been scattered everywhere. Putting thoughts together seemed such a difficult task. But she didn't feel the overwhelming fear, the terror, that she'd felt before. Maybe that meant the danger had passed. A good sign.

"Where's Angel?" Before the doctor answered, she remembered he'd already told her. With Gina. She felt so tired. Too tired to do battle with the world anymore. Too tired to run away and reinvent her life with Angel yet another time. Maybe she'd give in. Maybe she had no choice but to give in.

"Hey there, sleepy."

Reese opened her eyes. How long had she been asleep? She was in a different room. It looked dark outside.

"How are you feeling?" Gina stood by her bed. Angel was with her on some kind of stool.

"Tired," Reese said.

"That's just the medicine," Gina told her. "It'll start to go away."

The medicine. That's why she had to leave Ben. That nurse and the others with her, the ones who stayed in the other room, they'd wanted to give her medicine too. Medicine that made her numb. Made her forget herself. Had Gina been there back then? One of them, maybe? She couldn't remember. She didn't think so. Sometimes she worried that Ben knew all about it. What they were doing. Other times, she was sure he didn't. But they wouldn't leave, so she had to. They wanted to use her illness, her weakness, to control her. She'd left and then she had Angel. She'd made a life with Angel.

"Don't want medicine," she managed.

"Reese." Gina spoke again. "You need medicine. We've got to get you back looking after Angel. You can't get better without help."

Help. Ben's words too. Needed to get her help. The hateful nurse had been help. Later, when she had taken Angel to Ben, all but given Angel to him, he started using that word again. Help. Only *that* time he said she needed help with her mind. She wasn't fucking crazy, she told him. She knew what that kind of help would do. It would take her out of the picture entirely, leave him free to let Angel forget her.

"Reese?"

So tired. So fucking tired. Maybe it was time to give up. She'd fought so long. It was time.

"Mommy?"

"Angel, baby." Reese lifted her arm. It weighed more than her entire body should weigh. Angel took her hand. "Just need to sleep, baby doll."

Gina might plot against her. But Ben's widow wouldn't hurt

Angel. Just like Ben, she'd look after Angel. It was time to be done with it. Time to let go.

"So sleepy . . ."

"You rest, Reese," Gina said. "Angel's fine. Everything's going to be okay."

Her eyes were closed, but she could feel Angel beside her on the bed. She could smell her soap and shampoo skin. Someone had made sure she took a bath.

"Love you, baby," she said, but she wasn't sure she'd actually spoken.

Angel pressed against her and she gave in, let sleep take her on toward easy rest.

42

∞

Gina

I sat on the bow of *River Rose*. Georgie barked from below, wanted to be out in the afternoon air. An early fall-like day, a preview, of sorts. The heat would return, but knowing that the season would change seemed vital. I'd been away from the boat, away from the marina, forever, it seemed, although it had only been a couple of weeks. I moved in with Angel at the cottage. Taking her to school, lounging around in the evenings with Derek. It felt okay, being the person taking care of her. But I wasn't a mother. And while I still wasn't sure I would ever want to be one, I also knew that my time spent with Angel improved me.

The wind had picked up, and I wished I had time to sail. My old life, the one with Ben and even the one after him, would have offered no resistance to such whims. For the first time in memory I couldn't choose my day without regard for anything else. Even work had been at my own discretion. And I realized that if Reese progressed the way they expected her to, part of me would miss plotting my days around school bells and homework projects.

"Hey, Gina." Charlie came out onto the fingerdock. "You heard from Reese?"

"I'm taking Angel over to see her this afternoon. We haven't been since she was admitted. They told us she needed isolated time for the early treatment."

"It's fucked up, huh? I mean, all that shit going on and she seemed so regular. I mean, regular in an *out there* kind of way. But a lot of people are out there."

I couldn't believe Charlie was the older cousin. He had a year on Derek, but seemed to be seventeen at best.

"Yeah," I said. "It's pretty freaky, all right."

He stood for a second looking out toward the mouth of the inlet, then looked back down at me.

"Good news?" he asked.

"What do you mean?"

He pointed to the envelopes in my hand, three of them.

I had to deal with all of them somehow. The original settlement check and a second one that had just arrived. Those would be easy. Reese and Angel would need the money. Truth be told, it wouldn't be so bad to ease my financial concerns for a while either. It wouldn't bring Ben back, but it couldn't make him any more *gone*.

The other envelope posed more of a problem. The DNA results. I'd forgotten about the hair samples, taking them to the lab the day I found out that Ben had met Angel. I knew what I wanted to do, but one other person would have to weigh in. That could come later. In the immediate future, I had to go by the bank, then pick up Angel at school and go to the hospital. For nearly two weeks the doctors had been treating Reese. They'd asked that all family and friends stay away, give the therapy and the meds a chance to begin healing her mind. I felt nervous, seeing her again. I wondered what a *healed* Reese would be like.

"Hey, Gina?" Charlie still stood there. I'd lost myself, forgotten about him.

"I'm sorry," I said. "I'm a little out of it."

"Well, you and Reese will have something in common, then." He grinned, but looked uneasy all the same.

"If Derek comes by after work," I said, "tell him to call my cell. He doesn't know I'm going to the hospital and he's not answering his cell."

"Okay," Charlie said, giving an awkward wave and taking off down the docks.

I sat for a minute more, enjoying the air, the predictable instability of a boat in water—the only place it truly belonged.

"Can Clara come over and spend the night?" Angel asked when I met her out in front of the school. "Her mom is right there. Can we ask her?"

Such a kid thing. Begging for a friend to come over. In the absence of Reese's problems, Angel had found an effortless path to childhood. She didn't have to learn; she simply had to *be*.

I walked over and introduced myself to the mother. She assumed

I was Angel's mother, and I let her. It wasn't right, but there'd be plenty of time to explain.

"I'll call you when we get back and you can bring her over," I said. "Probably around dinnertime. I'll get pizza for the girls."

It was settled. My night planned. A slumber party. I hoped Derek wouldn't mind.

On the drive to the hospital, Angel didn't say much. She fidgeted with the seat belt.

"This is all going to be okay," I told her. "This is the hardest part. But your mom's going to be pretty nervous too, so . . . cut her some slack, okay?"

She nodded, looked out the back window at the drawbridge rising behind us to let a tall-masted sloop through.

"Clara is a vegetarian," she said. "We can get veggie pizza, okay?"

The self-absorption was new and, I had to tell myself, okay. It was a trait that Elise had taken to extremes. But Angel wasn't Elise. Angel was simply trying to enjoy the freedom of being a child for the first time in her life.

"Veggie it is," I said.

They had a room where Angel could wait and watch television. I would go in and talk with Reese first, then they'd bring her daughter. I couldn't help but think that making it a large production—Angel's entrance—couldn't be the best for anyone. But I sent her off to watch *Princess Bride*, wished I could just go with her.

Reese sat on the floor, legs crossed Indian style. In front of her lay a large sketch pad. She hunched over, drawing something with a pencil. She wore Capri pants and a fitted white T-shirt, and it struck me as odd. I'd never seen her in clothes like that before.

"Hey," I said.

She looked up, her expression both pleasant and embarrassed. It would take some measure of *sanity* to feel embarrassed. I took it as a good sign.

"How's Angel?" She sounded anxious, eager.

"She's waiting in the TV room. She's good. This is weird for all of us."

She nodded, stood up, and dusted the back of her pants as if she'd been on the ground and not a spotless braided rug. I followed her to the window, to a small table with two chairs. Her bed sat in the corner, neatly made, covered with a quilt.

"This place is homey," I told her, making conversation.

She nodded, sat down in one of the chairs. "I'm sorry," she said before I had to fill in with something else trite and meaningless. "I put you through hell. You, Angel, everybody."

"It's an illness," I said. "You can't be blamed for it." I thought of Elise. I *had* blamed her. That was certainly something to live with. "How are you feeling?"

"Strange."

"Why?" Maybe the meds hadn't done all that we'd hoped. "The doctors say you're so much better."

"I am better. Don't worry. Crazy Reese is not putting on an act. Although," she paused, leaned forward, "how would you know?"

I felt my pulse click into higher gear, and I must have shown a certain concern because she leaned forward, put her hand on my arm. "No, no . . . for God's sake, lighten up. I just meant that it's strange to know, really *know,* that all those things were just in my head. It's pretty horrifying, really."

I wondered if they'd filled her in on what she'd done in the mountains. That she'd left Angel alone for all those days. If they were kind, they hadn't told her. Some things a mother should never know.

"Are they . . . ?" I couldn't think of the right word. What do imaginary people do? "Are the voices *gone*?"

"Not entirely," she said. "I still feel the tingling, the numbness in my fingers, my legs. When I wake up, just before I'm entirely conscious, I still hear things. Sometimes, when I'm fully awake even, it's still so clear. But it's not as bad, and I know—there's a part of me that *can* know, and understand—that they're not real. They were never good things," she added. "Not like that guy in the movie who missed his buddies, you know, the roommate and the kid?"

"*A Beautiful Mind.*"

"Yeah, that one. I don't miss anybody. Well, Janet maybe. But I'm glad to let the rest of them go to hell where they belong."

A maid came in, took the trash, and left some towels. Just like at a hotel. Outside the window, people took advantage of the cooler day to play Frisbee, sit and sun themselves. Reese looked pale. I wondered if she'd been outside, done anything that made her feel halfway normal. Or had all her time been spent sorting through her thoughts and memories and trying to catalog them into groups of what was real and what wasn't?

"This problem I have," she said. "It's pretty weird if what they say is true. But at least I'm not sick. Well, not sick like I thought I was." She smiled, but it came with effort. "It really is all true, isn't it?" She looked at me for independent confirmation, the permission to trust her doctors.

"Yeah," I said. "It is."

She wiped her eye with the back of her hand. Smudged the tears that were building across the side of her face.

"How did Angel stay so calm?" she asked. "With all that shit I was pulling? It kills me to think of everything I told her, all the times I dragged her away because—"

"Reese. Angel's okay. She's a great kid. You dragged her through a lot, but you also loved her. That counts for more than you realize. She's all right. I think she's relieved not to be sorting it all out anymore. That was pretty exhausting. But she's not damaged in ways that will hurt her forever. I really believe that."

"This problem," she said again, couldn't seem to call it anything else. "I didn't know."

"I know that," I said.

"I thought that—"

"It's okay, Reese. It's really okay. No one thinks it's your fault, and those papers you left . . ."

She looked up, waited.

"That was a hard thing for you to do," I said. "I know it was. But your mother instincts overrode the illness. I admire that, Reese, honest to God, I do."

"And what did you do with them? The papers."

"They're filed with a lawyer. I signed them. I'll look after Angel as long as you need me to."

She let out a long breath, looked away, out the window. "Thank you." She still didn't turn toward me.

"I'm not her mother, Reese. I won't try to be." I didn't know how to reassure her. "I think there's a muscle, a parenting muscle." She did look at me, finally. "I think it has to start developing when you're little. Playing dolls or looking after puppies. I don't know. But something that happens with the expectation of being a parent someday. I'm doing okay with Angel. I love Angel. But I don't have the parent muscle. I'm not sure I ever will. I'm just . . . What was it that you said in your note?"

"A safety net."

"Yeah, that's it. I can do that. But you've got the mom job in a lock. I'm not trying to take that place. I'll just be there, the safety net, in case I'm needed."

"Well, you caught her this time," Reese said. "And I'm grateful."

Reese showing gratitude. The moment embarrassed us both, so we fell silent, stared at the room around us. Finally, she spoke again.

"Gina?" Her voice went thin and very small. "I don't know how I'm going to pay for this." She looked around. "I've been in a lot of county clinics, and this isn't a no-insurance kind of place. The meals are too decent, for starters."

I'd never had a chance to tell her. To explain about the money.

"There was a settlement. After Ben died." Just thinking about those raw days in the lawyers' offices, sitting across from men who talked like it was a business deal. I guess to them, it was. "They settled for a bundle to keep it all out of court. I don't know if I could have gone through a trial or not. Hell, I could barely sit in on the meetings. But I've gotten a couple of really large checks and more will come."

"And?"

"There's enough for all of us. I can pay for your treatment and never even feel it, Reese."

"Gina, I—"

"Don't argue with me," I said. "I've sat down with the hospital and worked it out. It's all settled."

"I'm not arguing," she said. "I was going to say that I'm sorry you went through all that. I'm not sure it's worth any kind of money to have to sit through all that, especially after you've just buried somebody like Ben. But thank you. If I was a better person, I'd turn you down, but nobody's worried about too much moral fiber in my diet. Have you told Angel? She worries about money. Something an eight-year-old with a decent mother wouldn't be doing."

"I've told her. She just wants her mom back home."

"How do you know?"

I knew. But how did I know?

"The room beside hers at the cottage."

"What about it?" Reese asked.

"She tells me we have to keep that nice because it's your room."

She smiled at me, half bought it. So did I. So did Angel. Truth was, none of us knew when Reese would get out. The family thing—weird and dysfunctional by nature—was a work in progress.

"Angel is an amazing kid," I said. "She's taught me to feel things I didn't think were possible."

"So have you come to grips with all that stuff about your sister?" she asked.

"How much did Ben tell you about that?"

"Some," she said. "Some of it I figured out when he was talking with you on the phone."

I thought of Angel and Reese, in the room with Ben when he called me one of those times he saw them. It still stung, felt like a betrayal, but if I pulled back, saw the larger picture . . . If I saw Ben with Angel the way I'd been with her these last weeks, I had to forgive. I just had to.

"No." I answered her question. "I've made some progress. But I'm not sure coming to grips with it is in the cards entirely. I just have to accept the parts of it that helped me carve out, for better or worse, who I am, and then move forward, I guess."

"Is there a textbook where you go to get that crap?" Reese shook her head. "You sound just like the assholes who work in this place."

I laughed. Sane or not, Reese would stay herself. I didn't know if that was a good thing or not.

Someone knocked on the door. After Reese called for them to come in, I saw Angel look carefully around the door. She stepped into the room, followed by a guy, a nurse, I gathered. She and Reese just stared at each other. I envied the look on Reese's face, the unmistakable expression of a mother who'd just seen her child.

43

∞

Reese

"I'll let you two visit," Gina said.

Angel had just walked in the room. She stood near the door, far away, and Reese made no move to cross the room to her.

Gina kissed the girl on the head, whispered something to her. Angel nodded, then Gina left.

Reese felt shy around Angel for the first time in memory. How was she supposed to act now that she knew about all the make-believe she'd inflicted on her daughter? How could she change their relationship entirely when she still felt, even heard sometimes, so many of the things her rational self now knew were false?

"Hey," Reese said. Better to start small.

"Hey," Angel said, not crossing the room.

"I heard you're keeping my room at the cottage nice for me?"

The child nodded. Reese wanted to run over and hug her. She wanted to tell her she was sorry. But that would be too much. She had to stay calm.

"Listen, Angel," she began. "I want to talk with you. Can you come sit beside me? Let's sit on the bed."

Angel walked over to the bed, climbed on. Reese sat down, facing her daughter.

"I didn't know," Reese began.

Angel looked at her. Someone had pulled the girl's hair back into a ponytail. She looked more like a kid with it that way.

"I didn't know that all the stuff I said to you wasn't real."

"Gina told me," Angel said, looked like she wanted to say something else, but stopped.

"Go ahead, baby," Reese said. "I don't mind you asking anything you want to know."

"I just don't know," Angel said. "How you can hear something or feel something when it's not really there?"

Reese reached over, tied Angel's shoelace because it had come undone. "I don't know that either," she said. "I wish I understood too. But what I can do now that I couldn't before is listen to people who tell me what's real and what's not. The medicine helps me to do that. Gina will help both of us. And we'll stay here. No more running from place to place."

"Lane and Derek too?"

"Yeah," Reese said. "Lane and Derek too."

"Gina says I'll like Maxine a lot when I get to know her."

Reese shook her head. "And they say I'm the one who's delusional."

Angel's eyes were wide with questions, but Reese just moved over, took her daughter into a big full-arm hug. Then she turned on the small television in the corner of the room, found a station of afternoon cartoons.

"Come here," she said to Angel.

They sat side by side on the bed, their legs stretched out in front of them. After a while Angel crawled over into her mother's lap, and Reese realized that no matter where she was, Angel would always be her home.

Angel and Gina had been gone for about an hour when Reese heard another knock at the door. Andrew Hanes popped his head in. "Decent?" he asked.

"Are you kidding?" Reese smiled.

Reese suggested that they walk outside. The sun had gotten low, and the colors made the sky look like batik fabric.

They walked around the property, chatted the way they always had, easy and without trying. She felt more normal with Andrew Hanes than she ever had with anyone. Even in the middle of her delusions, her sanest self had prevailed with him.

"I brought you something," he said. "Against my better judgment. I figured you needed to deal with one thing at a time."

He pulled out a pack of menthols, matches stuck in the cellophane.

"God bless you, Preacher Andy." She grinned. "I only had a few stashed with my stuff when I got here, and I've been bumming ever since." She looked at the pack. "They're open."

"There're two gone." He smiled, looked at the ground. "Old cravings from my Marine days die hard. Although I'd never have been caught smoking that sissy menthol crap back then."

"So you'd sneak 'em while your wife wasn't looking," she said, sitting on an Adirondack chair. She held out the pack, offering him one. He shook his head no, sat opposite her, looked out across the lawn.

"She left." A statement, without emotion or elaboration.

"Come on," Reese said. "I'm not joking around."

"Neither am I." He turned to Reese, and she saw the sadness in his eyes that couldn't be found anywhere else in his demeanor.

"I'm sorry," she said. "Damn, I'm really sorry." She lit a menthol, inhaled deep, and felt her nerves loosen in an instant. Then she exhaled, watched the breeze take the smoke out over the grass. "Was it because of me?"

He squinted. The low sun came straight on across from them.

"Yes and no," he said. "She thought I'd run off with you."

"What!"

"She found out as soon as I got home that I didn't. But the problem for both of us was, she really thought it. The idea that she believed it, even for a couple of hours . . ." He stopped, took in deep pulls of air. "She said she couldn't live that way. Not trusting. She knows nothing happened with us, but . . ."

Chelsea, one of the student volunteers, came over and brought packets of caramels that some pharmaceutical rep had left for the patients. Andrew took one, thanked her, then looked back at Reese and shrugged his shoulders as if to say, *What can you do?*

"I'm laying waste all around, huh?" Reese wished she could feel a little worse about it than she did. She couldn't help but think that a sane person would feel like shit. But the woman had been a real bitch, best she could tell. "Are you okay?"

"Getting there," he said. He opened the bag, offered her a caramel.

"Me too," she told him, taking a piece of candy from the bag. "Me too."

44

∞

Gina

Angel and I didn't say much on the drive back to the cottage. "It's good for your mom to see you," I told her. "Did it feel okay, visiting with her?"

"Not at first," she said, "but then it did by the end."

"This was the hardest one, I bet. After this, you'll feel more at ease going there, until she feels like coming home."

She didn't offer any more thoughts, so I kept my attention on the road, occasionally glanced out the window at the old men who dotted the banks of the tidal creeks. Autumn fishing had moved into high season. With cane poles angled over the water, they watched us as we crossed over the foot-high bridges where the road cut across salt marsh.

"Here's my cell." I handed Angel my phone. "Do you know Clara's number?"

She smiled over at me, then concentrated on pushing the right numbers. By the time we reached home, we figured we had half an hour, tops, to get the place ready for Angel's sleepover.

"What should we do when Clara gets here?" Angel asked as we put clean sheets on the extra twin bed in her room.

"Well, let's think. What do you usually do at a sleepover?"

"I don't know," she said, not looking up from her work. "I never had one before."

I stopped, watched her secure a corner at the top of the bed. She didn't know how to complain, had never learned that kids her age griped and moaned all the time.

"You told her to bring her Barbie stuff, right?"

She nodded.

"That's probably good for an hour or so. Derek's going to make a cookout. He's got tofu burgers for Clara," I added. "And after dinner, if the mosquitoes aren't too bad, he can fish with the two of you off the dock."

We'd moved *River Rose* to the cottage dock. Derek was staying on her since he'd quit his job at the marina. *Low Country Leisure* had hired him right away. I could see the light on sometimes in the main cabin of the boat where, late at night, he worked on stories. I wanted to join him there, but until Reese was better, I would stay in the cottage with Angel. I'd learned to allow for life's fluid nature. Things changed every minute, but the current only headed one direction at a time. You had to make your best guess and then just ride it out.

"What do I do if we get stuck and can't figure out what to do?" Angel remained worried. She wanted her first slumber party to go well.

"Give me a signal," I said. "And I'll come suggest we make cookies or something. I can always get things moving again. What's our signal?"

Angel balled her fist, then tapped it onto her outstretched palm. An honest-to-God *signal*. I could work with that. I did it back to her. "Like that?" She nodded. "Okay," I said. "I'll watch for it."

After we'd gotten the room ready, Clara's mom called to say they were running a few minutes late. I decided that it was as good a time as any to do something I'd been thinking about for a few days.

"Come in my room, Angel," I said. "I've got something for you."

"What?" She smiled.

"It's a present. Kind of a late birthday present. Come on."

I had her sit on the bed while I got the jewelry box out of my drawer. Several days before, I'd found it in my pocket, left in there from that day at the storage facility. I'd been so upset that I hadn't even realized I'd taken it. It seemed different to me after all we'd been through, more comforting than painful.

"This is something I found," I said, sitting down beside her. "Ben bought it." I held out the box to her and she took it. "He bought it for you."

She sat with her hand in her lap, didn't try to open the box. "How do you know?" She looked up at me, her dark eyes serious. She looked afraid to believe.

"Open it and I'll tell you," I said.

She opened the box; the hinge creaked again, the way it had the last time I'd seen it. She stared at it for the longest time, and I could see the excitement as it began to fill her face. "Why is it for me?" She looked up at me again, this time smiling.

"What does it say inside the lid there?" I asked. "Can you read that?"

She looked. "Pe . . . peri . . ."

"Peridot," I told her.

"Peridot. August." At the last part she broke into a real grin.

"It's your birthstone," I said. "He got it for you after your last visit, I think, because it was in his office drawer at work. He never had a chance to give it to you."

I took it out of the box for her, and she turned her back to me, raised her hair, and made her neck long so I could clasp it on. Then she got up and went to the mirror over the bureau and stared at herself. She stood there looking until the doorbell rang, and even then, as excited as she was about her friend, she had trouble pulling herself away.

Later, as the two girls played in the den, Derek and I stayed in the kitchen slicing up tomatoes and lettuce, getting out plates for the cookout. I heard Clara stop in the middle of a pretend moment and tell Angel, "That's a pretty necklace."

Angel paused, then simply said, "My daddy bought it for me." Then they went on with their play.

While Derek worked on the charcoal, Lane arrived, bringing with her a mixed-berry pie and a surprise guest. Maxine got out on the passenger side of Lane's car. I saw her look at the cottage, questioning, no doubt, why she'd ever agreed. But, not one to go back on a decision, she followed Lane to the door.

"I called her yesterday," Lane said as they came inside, "badgered her until she agreed to come. She's staying at my house tonight, so we can make a good evening of it here."

"Well, Angel's got a friend over for a sleepover. Maxine, they found your stash of board games in the drawer, so they're having a game-a-thon in Angel's room."

"I forgot those old things were here," Maxine said, carrying a jug of sweet tea into the kitchen.

Lane went outside to help Derek, and I joined Maxine. I'd talked to her after the trip to Myrtle Beach, filled her in on all the news about Reese. I'd kept my distance since that time, wanted to give her the space she needed to work it out for herself.

"Have you been okay?" I asked. We sat down at the table. She ran her hand through her short hair.

"It's hard to undo a couple of decades of ill will," she said. "But it's wrong to hold something against a woman whose demons run that deep."

"I don't think she expects you to change your mind about her. But I hope you can try to get to know Angel. None of it is her fault. She's lived a life no kid should have to live—covering for her mother, keeping up with the stories, then constantly wondering how long they would be in any given place. It had to be exhausting."

Maxine didn't comment. Maybe she didn't know how to respond.

"What's on your mind?" I asked. I thought about the necklace, realized that I'd have to tell Maxine everything—sooner rather than later.

"I was thinking about Ben," she said, half reading my mind. "I was thinking that he probably knew more than I ever realized about Reese and her problems. He had to have some idea that things didn't add up."

"I think he'd started to figure it out," I told her. "There were other things he knew about too, Maxine."

She looked over, kept her gaze steady, waiting for me to tell her.

"He'd spent time with Angel." Her expression didn't change, but I saw the flush rising in her cheeks. I gave her a second or two, then I continued. I told her everything. All that I knew about Ben's visits with Angel—his plans and his appeals to me. I told her about Elise and all my problems. And I told her about the necklace.

"I gave it to her," I said. "Earlier today. She's wearing it."

When I finished, she leaned on her elbows on the table, rested her head in her hands. "He knew her," she said, more to herself than to me. I could see the tears on her face, but I tried not to start. I'd had enough of tears. Enough for this lifetime and the next.

"Are you okay?" I asked.

"I don't know," she answered. "I'm still breathing."

"Well, there's more," I said. "Let's get it all over with at once, huh?" She took a deep breath, stood up, and followed me. "There's something I've made a decision on," I said, "but you deserve to make up your mind for yourself."

I took her in my room, just as I'd led Angel in earlier that afternoon. It seemed to be a day for resolution. I'd taken the two envelopes to the bank, set up a series of accounts and investments that would allow for all of us to live, and Reese to get treatment, until the end of time, if that's what it took. But there was another envelope left.

"I had this done weeks ago," I began. "Right after I found out that Ben had spent time with Angel. I felt angry, and I wanted to go tearing up everybody else's world too."

I handed her the envelope. She looked at the address.

"They do genetic testing," I explained. "DNA. I had some of Angel's hair, and Ben's—just a few strands from one of his jackets."

Her tears had never completely stopped, but now began again in earnest, dripping onto the envelope in her hand.

"It's not opened," she said. "Do you know?"

I shook my head. The decision had been an easy one. The only one, really, that seemed like an option for me. But I couldn't, wouldn't, try to make the call for Maxine.

"Reese doesn't know," I said. "Of all her stories, that's one I believe. And Angel certainly believes that Ben was her dad. Maxine, Ben didn't even want to know. He accepted her, wanted her from the minute he knew she existed. Reese didn't lie to him, and he never asked her to find out for sure. So, I've decided that it would make no difference to me. I'm better off never looking at that piece of paper."

"But what if she doesn't belong to him?" she asked.

"I don't know. Define 'belong.' You're more of a mother to me than I've ever had before and we don't share an ounce of blood. But I'd do anything for you and you know it. She's a kid, Maxine. She belongs to whomever she loves. At least, that's the way I'm choosing to see it. I won't blame you if you have to know. If that's the case, I want you to take that home with you, and please never talk to me about it."

I could hear Derek rummaging in the kitchen. He'd be ready to put everything on the grill soon.

"I'm going to help Derek get the burgers on," I said. "Stay in here as long as you like. I know it's a lot to sort out."

I checked on the girls, asked them to help Lane get the condiments and drinks all ready. Then I got a couple of cold beers out of the fridge and took them outside where Derek was working.

"For the cook," I said, handing him a bottle. He took it, smiled, and kissed me.

A few minutes later, as I sat on top of the picnic table, doing little more than keeping him company, I saw Maxine coming out of the house. She paused for a second, glanced over my way, and then continued on down to the dock.

I watched her step onto my boat, Ben's boat. She moved forward, sat on the bow, and, as the breeze rattled the halyards against the steel mast, I watched her tear the envelope into little bits. She worked deliberately, without hurry. She tore until the envelope was gone, holding all of the paper full in her lap. Then she scooped up the entire pile, scattered the white pieces like ashes into the water below. The current moved quickly with the waning tide, and soon they were gone.

"Can I call my mom and tell her about my necklace?" Angel had come up beside me when I was looking the other way. Derek had gone inside and I was alone, watching the burgers for him. "Sure, honey, she'd like to hear about it. Where's Clara?"

"She got tired of playing, so she's watching *Stuart Little*. She asked me why I call you Gina. She thought you were my mom."

"What did you tell her?"

"I told her that you were married to my daddy. Is that all right?"

"That's perfect, sweetie."

She turned to go back in and call her mother, but after a few steps she turned. "Clara says that makes you my stepmom." She stood looking at me.

"Clara's right," I said. "I guess that's what I am."

"Good." She stood there smiling.

"Would you do me a favor?" I asked. "Before you call your mom?" She nodded.

"Maxine is walking back up from the dock. Would you show her your necklace?" She nodded, met Ben's mother halfway across the yard.

I saw her hold the necklace away from her neck for Maxine's inspection. Maxine didn't say anything for a second. I started to think

I'd made a mistake. But finally she managed a smile, told Angel how pretty it was. "Ben was good with jewelry. Picking it out, I mean." It seemed she had no idea what to say to Angel. It would take some time for the two of them.

As they walked back toward us, I heard Angel asking about Ben when he was growing up.

"Gina?" Maxine called out. "Did I see that box still sitting in your backseat?"

Box? I tried to think. "The pictures?"

"That's right. Are they there?" She and Angel came up beside me at the picnic table.

"Of course," I said. "Nothing ever leaves my car once it's been piled in. You know that."

"Later we'll get them," she said to Angel. It came out as a frail, tentative suggestion. "Sometime after dinner, I'll show you pictures of your daddy when he was your age."

As the two walked off together, I thought of what would happen as the evening moved on. We'd crowd around with our paper plates while Derek served burgers and Lane organized the side dishes. We'd done this before and we'd do it again, maybe with Reese home next time, and with a shifting cast of characters who would come and go.

And all at once I felt overwhelmed by the pleasure of gathered family—or what felt like a family to me. If accidents could take away the people we loved—the people we needed—then it only seemed right that the opposite could be true as well.

"Let's get ready to eat, people!" Derek called out as he came out of the cottage, spatula in hand.

I stood up to meet him, ready to help, as everyone came to answer his call.

Accidental Happiness

JEAN REYNOLDS PAGE

A Reader's Guide

A Conversation with Jean Reynolds Page

Diane Hammond is a writer and the author of two novels: Homesick Creek *and* Going to Bend. *She lives in Burbank, California.*

Diane Hammond: Your characters hold themselves and those around them to a very high moral standard. Is this a basic human obligation? If so, are we any good at it?

Jean Reynolds Page: I believe that it is the way we *like* to see ourselves. Whether we succeed or not, I think most people want to feel that it is possible to live within a code of deep humanity. For this reason, Gina must consider what responsibility she has toward a child her husband has embraced. It occurs to Gina much later in her relationship with Angel that the girl could actually offer something back to her.

DH: Much of your writing explores the need for family—families we are born to and those we assemble. Is this a universal human need, or one more common in women than in men?

JRP: Family is a universal need, I believe, but circumstances, more than gender, determine how family occurs. When I lived away from any of my relatives for the first time, I had moved to New York City after college. I made a lot of friends, but found only a small selection of people with whom I bonded on a much deeper level. This group included both women and men. We cared for each other when we got sick; celebrated promotions and birthdays together. They were my first line of defense against being overwhelmed by life. Our trust, our emotional commitment to each other, made us family—and when I see them now, we still respond to each other in those same familial terms.

After she was widowed, Gina didn't have a natural family to which she could turn, so she allowed Maxine and Lane inside that emotional circle. In a way, their "adoption" of her when she needed them opened her to the idea of an assembled, unconventional family—an idea that carried through after the arrival of Reese and Angel. The added bond of love for Ben gave further weight to this uncommon alliance.

DH: The story in *Accidental Happiness* peels back layer after layer of events, truths and emotions, and each layer informs the next. Did you know the entire story before you began to tell it, or did you discover some of it as you wrote?

JRP: That's the amazing thing I find about the writing process. Later events in the narrative relate to elements of the book that occurred before the book was fully formed. It's a kind of alchemy that I don't pretend to understand, but I'm so very grateful when it happens. When I speak at book clubs, I've said many times that the writing process, for me, is not remarkably different from the reading process. It's all about discovery. I do sketch out the narrative and I take notes. But once the characters become three dimensional, they take me through the story rather than the other way around.

DH: Some of your characters find redemption by looking at past events in new ways. This is especially true for Gina, but also for Reese. Do you think it took courage to reexamine history in these painful terms?

JRP: I think it always takes courage to accept changes in what we see as the historical certainties of our lives. Our past, for better or for worse, determines the very direction of our days and years. To admit that choices were made while relying on faulty information rocks the foundation of our existence. Gina's decision not to have children was based on her somewhat inaccurate perception of her sister. And it goes without saying that Reese's past was a minefield of delusion. To readjust for reality was to negate the choices that defined their lives, *and* to accept the losses that occurred because of those choices. It was brave, but I think it was also necessary. The acknowledgment of these errors begins the process of resolution for both characters.

DH: Reese's spiritual life was stunted by her father's abandonment and by the preacher's molestation. Did she reach out to Andrew Hanes in an effort to begin a spiritual healing process?

JRP: Yes, I think that's absolutely right. And perhaps as important as the spiritual healing was the emotional healing that came from facing her worst fears. For Reese, befriending Andrew Hanes was like stepping into the ocean again after nearly drowning. Each interaction with him made her feel stronger, bolder. So many aspects of her healing required intervention, but that was a step that she took all on her own; a decision that indicated on some level a willingness, a desire, even, to get better.

DH: As your title suggests, happiness is often elusive or accidental. Did your characters find it, by the book's end?

JRP: I don't believe they found an all-encompassing, forever happiness. I'm not sure that kind of stability is even compatible with the notion of happiness. But they did find the ability to feel joy again, to realize that it was part of their repertoire of emotions. I think for Reese, Gina, and Angel, that wasn't the case before their lives collided.

DH: What did you find most rewarding about writing *Accidental Happiness*?

JRP: I loved the process as a whole because, as I mentioned before, the characters took on a life that seemed beyond me. It's magical when that happens—and you're never quite sure it will, so there is an element of relief, also. On a deeper level, working through Gina's journey out of grief helped me to deal with the recent loss of my mother. As I look back, I'm sure this was the very reason I chose the subject of grief's aftermath.

DH: What are you working on now?

JRP: I'm just beginning to sort out another book. This one, like my first novel, *A Blessed Event*, is set in Texas and involves many of the themes and issues found in both of my books. Regardless of where I begin with a book, I seem to end with conflicted family histories paired with a current crisis. I don't know what I'm trying to teach myself, but I suppose I'll continue listening to my characters until I figure it out.

Reading Group Questions and Topics for Discussion

1. Jean Reynolds Page establishes an intense sense of place in the course of *Accidental Happiness*. Could the same story have been set in, for example, Minnesota? What might have been different, in that case?

2. Gina and Reese create multigenerational families. What do the older women (Lane, Maxine) provide for the younger ones? What does Angel, the youngest family member, give the adults?

3. The families in *Accidental Happiness* are matriarchal. How do the men (Derek, Charlie, Andrew) fit in, and how does their presence change the relationships among the women?

4. Death can also be life-giving. Lane, Maxine, Reese and Gina all have experienced catastrophic and recent losses. In what way do those losses help the characters begin new, richer lives?

5. Many of the characters live in temporary housing—Gina lives on *River Rose* when she's not at the storage facility; Reese and Angel live with Gina and Lane, and then in Maxine's cottage. Only Lane and Maxine are grounded in stable homes. How do the others' living arrangements affect their circumstances?

6. What role does dishonesty play in the relationships that develop between and among the women?

7. Was Reese a good mother?

8. Were there any clues before Gina met Dr. Harris in Blowing Rock that all was not well with Reese's mind as well as her body?

9. How does the dawning realization that Ben was hiding part of his life affect Gina's process of grieving?

10. Each character seeks shelter in the course of the book—physical shelter and psychic shelter. Where do they find it?

11. Much in this book is achieved with and over food: ice cream cones, birthday cake, a church potluck, burgers. What food encounters turn into pivotal moments in the unfolding story and what larger elements does food represent in the narrative?

12. For most of the book, Gina and Reese develop a relationship that is more familial than friendly. Do they ever begin to trust each other?

13. What does Gina accomplish when she gives Angel the necklace that Ben had bought for her?

14. By the end of the book, each woman has taken hold of her destiny. What might each one be doing six months after the book's end? With whom?

15. In the interview preceding these questions, Jean Reynolds Page discusses the title of the book, *Accidental Happiness,* and whether or not she believes happiness is accidental. Do you believe it is a deliberate choice or an accidental state? Did you feel the title was an apt one for this book?

JEAN REYNOLDS PAGE grew up in North Carolina and lived in Texas for ten years. She is also the author of *A Blessed Event*. She worked as an arts publicist in New York City and has written about dance for numerous publications. She lives in the Seattle area with her husband and three children.

Join the Reader's Circle
to enhance your book club or
personal reading experience.

Our FREE monthly e-newsletter gives you:

• Sneak-peek excerpts from our newest titles

• Exclusive interviews with your favorite authors

• Fun ideas to spice up your book club meetings:
creative activities, outings, and discussion topics

• Opportunities to invite an author to your next
book club meeting

• Anecdotes and pearls of wisdom from other book group
members . . . and the opportunity to share your own!

• Special offers and promotions giving you access to
advance copies of books, our Reader's Circle catalog,
and much more

To sign up, visit our website at
www.thereaderscircle.com
or send a blank e-mail to
sub_rc@info.randomhouse.com

 **When you see this seal on the outside,
there's a great book club read inside.**